A CELEBRATION OF LOVE

Saldanha Murphy Ridley

Llumina Press

Requests for permission to make copies of any part of this work should be mailed to Permissions Department, Llumina Press, PO Box 772246, Coral Springs, FL 33077-2246

ISBN: 1-59526-605-4

Printed in the United States of America by Llumina Press

Library of Congress Control Number: 2006907188

A CELEBRATION
OF LOVE

Thanks Cicely for
your support through out
the entire process. And
thanks for giving me the
inspiration to do a part II.
Love always
Saddaahn

ACKNOWLEDGEMENTS

Thanks Gail for always asking how things were going.
Thanks Shannon for saying you wanted to buy a copy.
Thanks Ridley for saying you regretted nearing the end of
it....Over the years, you've allowed me to enjoy my own
personal celebration.

Thanks Miss E. for instilling the dream in me that I could.

CHAPTER ONE

N ikki entered the convenience store, went to the refrigerated section, and studied it. She often craved orange juice after
exercising. There was one bottle left; happily, she grabbed it and
headed up the aisle towards the cash register.

As she got close to the register, a thirty-something, scroungy,
unkempt white man wearing a ball cap with a Confederate flag
emblem entered, almost hitting her with the door. He leered as he
passed.

A young black man wearing a navy blue cap and blue jeans in
the line said, "Hey! Watch the lady."

The man snarled at him, but kept walking.

Nikki got in line, a couple of people behind the man with the
navy blue cap. She noticed a display of Chick-O-Sticks, "These are
hard to find," she muttered, grabbing one. Blue Cap heard her and
peered over his shoulder.

Rebel Flag passed everyone and headed straight for the cashier.
"You don't have any orange juice?"

"What?" the cashier asked, irritated. "Get in the back of the
line."

"Look at my hands," said the man.

The cashier wasn't interested. "The truck's coming in later," he
said apathetically. "I believe you were next, ma'am."

Blue Cap watched the disheveled man pace back and forth.

"Look, I really need some orange juice," Rebel Flag said, wiping
his forehead.

"Look, you don't have to get excited, sir! I tell you what. Go
back there," he pointed towards the back of the line, "and when
you get up here, I'll look in the back and see if there's more."

Nikki studied the man. He was agitated, a little off balance, and
confused—things she had seen on a couple of occasions with her
grandmother. He started walking toward the back of the line, but

Nikki stopped him. It was a classic case of hypoglycemia. "You can have this one."

He half-smiled, surprising her. He took the jug of orange juice and went to the back of the line. He stumbled and sat on the floor. He opened the jug and took a gulp. Blue Cap came over and knelt beside him.

Nikki appeared, looking concerned. "I think you need to eat," she said, unrolling the plastic paper and holding the Chick-O-Stick up. He took a quick bite. The crunchy orange pieces fell into his mustache. The man's eyes rolled back, and he lapsed into seizures. Blue Cap cradled his head in his lap and laid him on the floor.

"I bet he's diabetic," he whispered to Nikki. "Either that, or he's had a stroke, but he seems a little young for that." He rolled up Rebel Flag's sleeve, but didn't see a bracelet. "He should be okay soon. Smart move—giving him that candy."

The cashier walked over to them. "Dang drunk!" He rubbed his chin and threw up his hands. "I'm calling an ambulance." He stormed over to the counter.

Suddenly, Rebel Flag snapped out of it and noticed all the people standing around, staring at him. "I'm okay!" he snapped and pushed them away as he tried to stand.

"Sir, you need to lie back down," Blue Cap said firmly.

"Yeah," the cashier grumped. "I can't have an accident in the store!" He dialed 911 and asked for help.

The man tried standing again. He pulled away from Blue Cap, and after a moment was able to stand by himself. His face flushed at the other customers' stares. He pulled himself together and stormed out the door.

"Hey! Where does he think he's going?" the cashier yelled. Then, to the phone, he said, "Never mind." He slammed it on the receiver. "Some people."

The cashier ran from behind the counter after the man, who got in the passenger side of an old vehicle. The driver pulled away as the cashier looked on.

"Hey, who's going to pay for this?" the cashier yelled, pointing to the open juice and candy left behind on the floor.

Blue Cap looked at Nikki. "Are you okay?" he asked, helping her stand.

"Yeah, I'm fine."

Yes, you are. Blue Cap smiled. She was a walking Coca-Cola bottle with a cute face. Her hair was pulled back into a ponytail. Her skin reminded him of creamy milk chocolate; it glistened with remnants of sweat. "Are you a medical student or something?" he asked. He couldn't imagine who else would have performed such a selfless act.

"No." She shook her head. He was very attractive, she noticed. She felt her face turning red. "Thanks for your help." She turned and headed for the door.

"What about your drink and Chick-O-Stick?" Blue Cap said, pointing to the opened jug and wrapper on the floor. "You want anything else? My treat?"

She thought about it for a second, and then she shook her head and pushed against the door rail.

Blue Cap laid his items on the counter top.

"Some people are crazy," the cashier said, ringing up his gas.

He watched the woman throw what appeared to be an old Maxima in reverse. "Yeah," he replied absently.

●●●

Kevin walked out of his apartment. It was a pretty morning, but very humid. He looked across the street and spotted someone jogging. As the woman got closer, he recognized her as the woman from the store a week prior.

"Good morning," he yelled to her, a hint of flirtatiousness in his voice.

Nikki heard, but plunged forward, pretending not to hear. She just wanted to get her exercise in without some man trying to pick her up.

"I said, 'good morning.'"

She looked. Usually, when she showed she wasn't interested, they left her alone. At first, she didn't recognize him because he had on business attire. Then she placed his face. It was the cute guy from the store. She smiled and waved cautiously.

Kevin waved back. He opened his car door, laid his jacket over the passenger seat, and sat in the vehicle. He started the car and pulled to the corner. The woman continued her jog. He thought to himself for a moment, and then he drove in the opposite direction.

● ● ●

The morning was quiet, and the sky was overcast. Kevin looked out the window. "Maybe I missed her," he thought to himself. After several minutes, her car pulled up. He jammed his favorite navy blue cap on and ran downstairs.

He watched her stretch as he drew closer. The chorus for Baby Face's "Soon as I Get Home" ran through his mind as he admired her beauty and grace.

His heart pounded, and his palms became sweaty, but he didn't let that faze him. He didn't know what it was about this girl, but he had to get to know her. Her head turned to see who was approaching. She smiled slightly, then turned and started out on the path.

Finally, he caught up to her and calmed his nerves enough to greet her. "You're late." He looked at his watch.

"Excuse me?" Her eyes rolled in her head playfully.

"I said you're late." He smiled brightly, pleased that she showed up at all.

The woman continued walking.

"Do you mind if I exercise with you?" he asked softly.

She shrugged.

They walked about halfway down the path.

"So," Kevin said, attempting to break the silence, "are you going to tell me your name?"

The woman shook her head quietly and smiled.

Okay, Kevin thought as his mind raced for another approach. "My name is Kevin. Kevin Maddox. I live over there in those condos," he said, pointing. The woman didn't reply. "You don't talk very much do you?"

"No. Not while I'm exercising. I guess I'm used to being alone."

"Ouch." He smiled, unaffected. "How long have you been exercising here?"

"A couple of weeks."

"Wow. A response!"

The woman began jogging, and he started along beside her. They jogged around the wall. Kevin tried to come up with the right words to say.

"Can I ask you another question?"

"I'm sure you'd ask even if I said no."

"See, we're getting to know each other already. What kind of food do you like?"

"What?" she dropped into a walk as they neared her car.

"What kind of food do you eat? You do eat, don't you?"

"Of course I eat. Look, if you're trying to ask me out—thanks, but I'm busy."

"Busy? With whom? Your boyfriend or something?"

Nikki eyed him. "I'm a student. That keeps me pretty busy."

"Everyone has to eat at some point. Right?"

"Look you seem like a nice guy—" *And you're really handsome,* she admitted to herself, "but I have a lot going on in my life right now."

"Do you like Italian?"

"What?"

"Do you like Italian? American? Greek?"

Nikki couldn't believe her ears. "Didn't you hear anything I just said?" she chuckled.

"Yeah. I heard you." They were back in front of his condo. He waited beside the wall as she walked to her car. "You said, 'I don't know you, so stop bothering me and leave me alone.'"

"I didn't say that," she giggled, then smiled softly.

"You're going to go out with me, then?"

The woman smiled and walked to her car.

Man, she's fine, Kevin thought to himself as he stood on the sidewalk watching her.

She smiled, as if considering his invitation, and then waved goodbye.

"See you next week," Kevin said softly. He watched her pull off and noticed a parking decal on her car for the first time. He wondered to himself briefly, and then climbed the stairs to the condominiums.

A couple of weeks later, the woman pulled up again at the same location. Kevin ran down the stairs to meet her. "Hello, stranger. Missed you last Saturday."

She smiled and began walking briskly.

"I was beginning to think I scared you off. Do you mind if I exercise with you again?"

"No."

They walked several yards together quietly.

"What are you studying in school?"

"Hmm?"

"Last week—excuse me, the week before last, you told me you were a student."

"I'm studying to be a social worker."

"Really?" he grinned. "DFACS, huh? House of Prayer?"

"Yeah." She smiled hesitantly. "Something like that. Where are you from?"

Kevin smiled to himself. "Dallas, Texas—not Georgia." He snickered. "Sometimes I forget I have to clarify that for people who are from around here."

"Who says I'm from around here?"

Kevin smiled. "Just a hunch."

"You're just a regular cowboy, huh?" she teased.

Kevin thought she sounded sexy calling him that.

"What do you do?" she asked softly.

"I'm a financial consultant."

"A financial consultant?" she repeated. "That sounds pretty important."

Kevin shrugged. "You never answered my question."

"Which one?"

"So we got jokes this morning?"

Nikki smiled, and he saw just how beautiful she was. "I asked if you were seeing anyone, but you never answered."

"No," she answered softly. Then she felt a snag. She looked down; a twig had torn her sleeve. "Ow."

Kevin walked over to assess the damage. "It's bleeding."

"What?"

"Your wrist is bleeding."

She examined the area again. Now she felt the burn.

Kevin placed his hand over the area. "If you apply pressure, it will help stop the bleeding."

"Thank you," she whispered, risking a brief look at his eyes. His eyes were the only reason she had allowed him to exercise with her in the first place. For the first time, she gazed openly at him, taking in his soft brownish-bronze complexion, full lips, and warm smile.

"I can clean it up for you, if you like. You don't want it to get infected," Kevin said.

"I'm sure it'll be fine." *Then again, I hate having blood on my clothes,* she thought to herself. "You're not going to try anything, are you?"

"Try anything? Besides, helping you to get better—no." *Come on; trust me.* He smiled warmly to reassure her he meant no harm.

They entered the building, and she began having second thoughts, but the bruise was starting to hurt, and the blood had already stained the cuff.

Kevin slid the key into the socket. "Ignore the mess."

She smiled back wearily.

"I'll be right back," he said, motioning her towards the sofa.

She sat down and watched him disappear down the hall. Besides a few dishes piled in the sink, the apartment was immaculate. She heard cabinets opening and closing in the bathroom. A few pictures of what she supposed were family members were scattered about the room.

Kevin came out of the bathroom with gloves on. "I thought I had some Neosporin, but I found something else that'll do the trick," he said, waving a bottle of alcohol.

"You're not going to pour that stuff on me!"

"Why not?"

"It stings!"

"Come on, give me your hand," he said, kneeling in front of her. She extended her wrist reluctantly.

"Turn your head."

"No."

"You're acting like a baby."

He turned her head slightly to the right. She blushed as his warm fingers touched the side of her face. He placed a trash bin under her arm and poured the solution over the cut.

"Ow," she flinched.

He held her hand firmly, but gently. "It'll only sting for a few seconds." His voice was calm and soothing. "Just relax." He patted the spot with gauze, put a Band-Aid on it, and threw the gauze, gloves, and Band-Aid wrapping in the trash. "You can look now."

She looked blankly at the area on her wrist.

Ooo, baby, do you want me to kiss it, too? Kevin stared at her.

"Where did you learn to do that?"

"My mom's a nurse. Well, she actually doesn't work as a nurse anymore," he corrected himself. "She went back to school and has her Master's in health administration."

"Is that your family?" She pointed to the bookcase.

"Yeah," he said, turning back around.

"Is that your sister?" She pointed out a photo of a woman in her twenties, dressed in a wedding gown, which rested on the mantle of the fireplace.

"No, that's my wife." He chuckled. "I'm just kiddin'. Yeah, that's her." He brought over another picture of the same woman posing with a man and a young child. "This is their most recent picture. That is her husband. He's a British African. That is my nephew, Pete."

"He's a cutie," she said, staring at the little boy. She felt Kevin staring at her.

"When did she get married?" She looked in his eyes. It worked; it broke his stare.

"About a year and a half ago."

She looked at him for a moment.

"Pete's her stepchild." He explained, then got up and washed his hands in the kitchen sink. "Would you like some water or something?" He opened the fridge. "I have a coup'la beers."

"No, thanks. I don't drink." She rose from the couch, obviously uncomfortable. "Well, thanks." She walked towards the door. "I really appreciate what you did. It feels better."

"No problem." Kevin walked to the door. "Maybe we can go out for breakfast next time. It'll be a lot more painless."

She blushed. "I better get going." She went to the stairwell and began walking down, then paused as if she had forgotten something. "Thanks."

"Can you at least tell me your name?"

"Nikki."

"See you soon," he said quietly as he watched her exit the building.

CHAPTER TWO

Kevin walked onto the campus. It was the last class he could go to search for Nikki. She hadn't shown up for her jog in two weeks, and he had begun to worry. He held a gift in his hands he hoped she would like. "This has got to be it—unless she lied to me, of course," he thought to himself, glancing down at the sheet of paper on which he had jotted down the building and room number the office had given him. He asked a couple of students on the sidewalk where the building was. They pointed him to it.

He walked into the building. The hallway was well lit, but empty. He climbed the stairs to the second floor, and looked at the room number again. He heard a voice as he approached and noticed the room had two entrances. He looked through the window of the door furthest from the front of the classroom. A stoic white man at the front of the class paced back and forth; there were PowerPoint slides on the screen. He looked around at the students for a second, and then spotted Nikki. The room was dark, but he was pretty sure it was she. He smiled to himself then ducked away from the door.

Minutes later, people began walking out. Kevin gripped the gift he had brought for her anxiously. Finally, Nikki emerged, walking with a white lady who appeared to be in her early thirties, away from Kevin.

"Nikki!" Kevin called, but she continued walking and chattering with her classmate. He moved closer and called again. Finally, she turned around, and their eyes met.

"See you later, Heather." She waved to her classmate, her eyes fixed on his.

Kevin smiled, trying to conceal his joy. With her hair done, wearing regular clothing, she was even prettier than he had imagined. She was almost angelic, standing under the cold fluorescent lights. Her dark, perfect skin glowed with a soft sheen. Her hair was drawn back with a clip, and it flowed delicately down her shoulders, giving her a sense of innocence, as well as refinement. Her face was flawless; if she was wearing makeup, he couldn't tell, except for the dark, berry-red, succulent lips that curved into a tantalizing smile as he drew near.

"These are for you," he said, handing her a fist full of Chick-O-Sticks wrapped in orange, pink, and white ribbons.

She took them, smiling, obviously flattered. "Thank you."

"I was beginning to wonder if your name was really 'Nikki.'" He smiled.

"It's not, really." She paused. "It's Veronica. Nikki's my nickname. But no one here knows me by that name."

"So you gave me an alias?" Kevin joked.

Nikki smiled, looking at the Chick-O-Sticks. She looked around. "How did you find me?"

"It wasn't easy," he admitted. "Can I walk you to your car?"

Nikki nodded.

"After you." Kevin gestured with his hand as he opened the door to the stairwell.

"So, I figure after all this, I could at least get your full name."

Kevin's speech was smooth. His eyes were bright, and he had a nice smile. She smiled shyly. "Veronica Jones."

"Veronica?" he teased. "No middle name?"

Nikki nodded her head. "Yeah, but I hate it."

"What is it?"

She looked at him.

"Come on," he grinned.

"Katrina," she said softly.

"Katrina." He repeated. *Sexy.* He smiled. "That's pretty. What's wrong with that?"

She shrugged. "I just don't like it."

They walked down the staircase and crossed a one-way street to the parking lot.

As they approached Nikki's car, she said, "Thanks," looking at the Chick-O-Sticks. "This was really sweet." Nikki smiled at him quietly.

"You're welcome." He smiled. "You know, there's a black heritage exhibit at the museum this weekend."

"Are you trying to ask me out?"

He grinned. "Is that a crime?" He slid his hands into his pockets and waited for her response.

He looked pathetic and cute, standing there, waiting for her to say something. *Maybe I will give him a chance*, she thought to herself. "Okay," she said softly. "But we'll just be hanging out as friends."

Kevin frowned slightly.

Nikki saw his reaction and giggled playfully. "I told you. I have a lot on my plate right now, and I'm not looking to start anything serious."

"Okay." He smiled back. *Whatever you want to call it*, he thought as she got in her car; he closed the door behind her.

She reached and took out a napkin from the glove compartment. She jotted something down, and then rolled down her window. "My address," she said, handing it to him. "The storm knocked out our phone line, and at the rate they're going, I'm not sure it'll be up by then."

Kevin looked at the paper, folded it, and leaned against the hood of the car. "See you Saturday, at ten AM?"

"Okay." Nikki smiled and turned the keys to her ignition.

Kevin watched her drive away, and then he unfolded the piece of paper and looked at the info again.

Kevin walked up to Nikki's apartment and tapped on the door several times. He couldn't wait to see her. He planned to take her to the museum, then to a matinee, and then dinner.

Finally, Nikki came to the door. She wore a sage cotton pajama short set. Kevin smiled warmly at seeing her thick and shapely legs for the first time.

"Kevin," Nikki gasped, remembering. "Kevin, I'm so sorry." She grabbed her head, as if she had completely forgotten. "I had to pick up my sister late last night. I'm sorry, but I won't be able to go with you."

"Your sister?" he tried to mask his surprise. "I didn't realize you had a sister."

"Yeah. She's here for the weekend." Nikki watched his lips curl, but could tell he was disappointed.

"So are you guys gonna go shopping or something?"

Nikki smiled to herself. "Yeah. Something like that." She giggled to offset her guilt; wondering how she had forgotten. "Come in, and I'll introduce you to her." She stepped back from the door.

Kevin walked into the modestly decorated apartment. As Nikki walked away, he looked around the living room. He could see the patio from where he stood. Besides the light coming through the patio door, the room was dark. He heard a door open, then a soft whisper.

After a few moments, Nikki came around the corner holding a little girl in her arms.

Kevin was taken aback, but he hoped he had concealed his surprise well.

The child was still in her pajamas and appeared to be three or four. Her arms were wrapped around Nikki's neck. "MiKayla, I want you to meet someone. This is Kevin, Kevin Maddox."

The little girl didn't say anything.

"She's still kind of asleep," Nikki whispered to Kevin. The little girl watched Kevin quietly. Nikki gave her a couple of quick taps on the butt. "Can you say hello?" she whispered in her sister's ear. MiKayla stared at Kevin blankly. Nikki tapped her again.

Finally, she rolled her head a little shyly. "Hello," she murmured. Her hair resembled Don King's.

"Hey, sunshine," he teased. "I didn't mean to wake you."

MiKayla moved closer to Nikki, who ran her fingers through her hair, looking at it hopelessly. The little girl and Kevin stared at each other.

"It's time for her to get up, anyway." Nikki looked down at her. "We got in late last night. My grandmother belongs to a group that goes on these trips, and at the last minute, she made up her mind to go."

"Your grandmother's got spunk," he said, hoping to steer the conversation another direction. He hoped his disappointment hadn't been too obvious. "I wish I could get my grandmother to do stuff like that."

Nikki laughed under her breath. "She's sixty-five going on forty, but I make her slow down sometimes."

"You said her name is MiKayla?"

"Yes, but we call her Kayla for short."

"How old is she?"

"She can tell you." She looked down. Kayla had her thumb in her mouth and rested her head against Nikki's collarbone. "Are you gonna tell him?"

Kayla shrugged quietly and shook her head.

"You're a big girl now. Go on — tell him."

After a few moments of contemplation, the little girl held her hand up and showed four fingers.

"She's a little shy, but she warms up once she gets to know you. Okay, baby." Nikki patted her sister's fanny a few times, and set her on her feet. "Why don't you go and watch cartoons? I think Clifford is on."

Kevin watched the little girl walk over to the couch and climb to the top of the cushion. She reached over and found the remote to turn on the TV. "She's really cute."

"Yeah," Nikki said softly as she watched Kayla.

Kevin had been planning to go out with Nikki for a long time. He didn't want to blow this opportunity. "You know—"

Nikki turned to look at him.

"I think the circus is in town. Maybe we could all go together."

"Oh, Kevin, I couldn't ask you to do something like that. You drove all the way over here once today and—"

"Don't worry about it." He smiled. "Come on, I've been looking forward to hanging out with you all week."

Nikki thought it over. "Well—"

"It'll be fun. Every kid likes the circus—even the big ones," he said, watching her reaction.

"Okay," she gave in, "but if you're gonna do all that, the least I can do is make lunch."

Oh, she can cook, too. Kevin smiled, grateful the offer had been extended. "Okay." He was excited about the afternoon. "I'll come by at two o'clock, and we'll take it from there."

"Okay," Nikki smiled.

Kevin began walking towards the door.

Nikki let him out. "I'll even make sure we're ready this time," she said, looking at MiKayla briefly.

Kevin smiled at her, and then turned to MiKayla. "Nice meeting you," he said, waving at MiKayla from the doorway.

MiKayla turned towards him, then back around, apparently bored.

"MiKayla?" Nikki called, annoyed by her sister's behavior, then she turned towards Kevin. "I'm sorry; she's a little grouch when she's sleepy."

"That's okay." Kevin smiled. "Two o'clock?"

Nikki nodded. "Two o'clock."

"Bye," he said, leaving for good this time.

"Bye." She smiled, and then moved to close the door.

After a few seconds lapsed, she cracked back open the door. She watched as he walked towards his car. She smiled to herself briefly, and then shut the door.

On his way to his car, Kevin stepped peppier, and he could no longer restrain his glee. Despite the unexpected occurrences, his day with Nikki had gone perfectly. First, the dinner she prepared was delicious; certainly the best pork chop and mashed potatoe combo he'd ever tasted east of the Mississippi.

At the circus, they'd had a great time. He enjoyed watching Nikki and Kayla's faces light up with wonder. If he hadn't known better, he'd have thought it was the first time Nikki had been to a circus, too. Afterwards, they hung out downtown and walked around the city, stopping for shakes at the Varsity. The conversation was easy and flowed freely, and the chemistry between them was electrifying.

Though he loved talking to her, since her sister was around, he would cut her some slack the remainder of the weekend. He grinned, stuck his key into his car, and looked back at her apartment. Next weekend was too far away.

"Nikki, you're coming over tonight, right?"

"Tonight? Is it time already?" Nikki had completely forgotten about the monthly card game with her cousin, Malcolm, and his wife, Anesa. "Sorry, 'Nesa, I can't come tonight."

"Nikki, this is twice in a row you've cancelled on us. School isn't that important, girl. Take a break!" Anesa fussed.

Nikki didn't know how Anesa would react, but decided she couldn't hold back any longer. "It's not really school."

"What do you mean?"

"I have a date." Her hands slid along her necklace chain.

"A date?" Anesa shouted. She couldn't believe her ears. She looked at her husband.

"Yeah."

"Wit' who?" Anesa transitioned into the Ebonics dialect whenever she got excited.

"Well," she paused, "his name is Kevin, and —"

Nikki's cousin got on the phone. "Nic-Nic, what's this about you having a date?"

"I met this guy about a month and a half ago, and we started going out."

"Does he have a job?"

"Yes," she said, rolling her eyes.

"What does he do?"

"He's a financial consultant."

"A financial consultant? I betcha he's the assistant manager at Micky Ds."

"He is not," Nikki laughed. Her cousin was like a big brother to her; he was going to want all the details.

"Does he live at home with his mom? He got his own place? What?"

"He has a condo," Nikki said.

"Have you seen it?"

"Yes."

"You didn't see a wife and kids up in there, did you?"

"No. He's single, and he's never been married."

"Did he tell you that?"

"No. I mean, he told me he was single; but from our conversation, I gathered he's never been married."

"How old is he?"

"Twenty-seven."

Malcolm was quiet for a moment, then, "He hasn't tried to make a move on you, or anything, has he?"

"No." Nikki smiled. "He's a Christian."

"Psh." Malcolm sucked his teeth and blew. "That's what they all say — until they try to sleep with you."

"Well, he hasn't tried to sleep with me. He's been a complete gentleman," Nikki assured him.

"All right, all right. Dude sounds like he's okay, but tell him that if he does something to you, he's gonna have to answer to me."

"Malcolm!" Nikki heard Anesa call in the background.

"Well I'm getting ready to go to work, but we'll see you next time?"

"Okay."

She heard a few giggles, a kiss, and then the wrestling of the phone. "So, Nikki, tell me more. Where does he work? What kind of job does he have? Is he cute, girl?"

"Very, but he's not my usual type," Nikki grinned. She wondered why she had waited so long to tell Anesa.

"I didn't know you had a type," Anesa joked. "What does he look like?"

"Well," Nikki paused, "he kind of has this golden-bronze complexion, and he's maybe three or four inches taller than me. He's not a pretty boy—I hate pretty boys—but he's cute. He's kind of like—" Nikki thought to herself. "Cuba Gooding Jr."

"So he has a nice body?"

"Yes," Nikki answered. "He used to compete, but since he travels a lot with his job, it's died down, but he still works out."

"Yeah? What kind of competitions?"

"Tae-kwon-do."

"Ummm. All right, girl. Tell me more. How old is he? Where does he work? What kind of car does he drive?"

"He's twenty-seven."

"Ummph. Twenty-seven. So this is an older man? All right."

"He works at HD Greene & Co. He drives a BMW."

"Color?"

"White."

"Umm. He does sound cute," Anesa laughed. "How much does he make?"

"'Nesa! I don't know," Nikki said quickly.

"Ballpark?"

"'Nesa!"

"Okay. Okay. Okay," she giggled. "Where have ya'll been out to?"

"We've gone to Sequoia's, and he took me to this black dance festival."

"Dance festival?"

"Yeah. It was really good, too. The group was called— Hold on a minute, I got the program right here." Nikki felt on top of the refrigerator for the program and pulled it down. "It was the Afro Kan Dance Gliders."

"Well, driving a BMW, he's definitely making more than minimum wage. Those things aren't cheap."

"I guess," Nikki said softly.

"Well, all right, little sis, I'm proud of you. You done gone and got yo'self a man!" Anesa laughed.

"We're just friends," Nikki corrected.

"'Friends'? Nic-Nic, I can see you smiling through this phone." Nikki chuckled.

"You must really like this guy."

"He's pretty nice. For our first date, he took Kayla and me to the circus, and I didn't even know Kayla was going to be with me that weekend."

"Now see, girl? That's good. A lot of men won't even date you if they know you got a child."

"He keeps calling me."

"And he knows Kayla's going to be staying with you beginning next summer?"

"Yes," she assured her. "He's different."

"'Different'?" Anesa smiled. "So you are bringing him to the next card game, right?"

There was silence on the phone.

"Actually, I was thinking tonight would be our last night seeing each other."

Anesa raised her eyebrows. "Why?"

"I just think he's looking for more than I can give him right now."

"Like what?" Anesa asked, instantly suspicious.

"No," Nikki corrected. "Not *that*. I told you, he's different. He hasn't even mentioned that."

Anesa breathed a sigh of relief. Her husband would have a fit if he thought someone was trying to get her in bed. "What's the problem, then? All jokes aside, he really sounds like a nice guy."

"I know, and he is, but I don't know if I'm ready for a—" she stuttered. "A—"

"The word is re-la-tion-ship, Nic-Nic," she said, emphasizing all the syllables. "And I don't know why you won't slow down and give yourself a chance to have one. Just go out and have fun. What's so wrong with that? If a relationship comes out of it—it comes."

Nikki breathed deeply. "Maybe you're right."

"I know I'm right. So, when are you going to bring him over?"

"Anesa?"

"What?"

She had never introduced any of the few guys she had dated to Malcolm. She knew how protective he was, and she wanted to make sure the relationship had potential before she put someone through that experience. "I told you—we're just friends."

"Good. Then bring him over."

"I'll think about it."

CHAPTER THREE

Nikki was relieved she had gotten out of the youth center early. The teens had had a special Friday evening gathering, and she'd had no choice but to cancel her date with Kevin. Now she wished she hadn't. Only half of the teens had shown up, and they were finished in no time flat. With Kevin traveling all week, being tied up with church on Sunday, and then catching up on her school work and carrying Kayla back to her grandma's, Fridays and Saturdays had become their date nights—the only days they could spend together.

Nikki pulled up to Kevin's condo. His car was parked in its usual spot beside the street. She looked at the second floor, and saw lamplight through the living room window. It had been a long week, and she was looking forward to relaxing with him. Perhaps they could catch a late movie.

Her palms got sweaty and her heart began to race as she walked toward his building. *I really like him,* she thought, as a grin swept across her face. The thought of seriously seeing someone half-excited and half-terrified her. Memories of the few guys she had dated in the past came to her mind. She was tired of the playa and thug wanna-bes. She wanted a real man, and that's what Kevin was. For now, she would give him a chance.

Kevin always treated her with respect, and though he was a little older, she was able to see the benefit of his age. He was smooth. She admired his wit and ambition, and though she knew he made good money, he didn't throw it in her face trying to prove anything. He was open and honest with her, and when she looked in his eyes, she saw genuineness. On their first date, they'd had a good time—and the next, and the next. There had been none of the usual games or awkwardness.

Kevin had taken her to a nice restaurant on their second date. When she was handed the menu, she opened it, and her jaw almost dropped to the floor at the prices. She calmly took a sip of water and peered at Kevin. If he had noticed her reaction, he hadn't let on. He was leaning back in his seat, contemplating his choice.

Later that evening, she had reflected on how gentlemanly he had been since they met, and wondered if it had all been building up to that point—the two of them alone, late at night, with a couple of good times under their belt—what she figured meant time for a good lay.

She remembered him bending over to kiss her, but she turned, whispering, "We're just friends."

He nodded, understanding, and gave her a big hug, instead.

She knew that would be the last night she saw him, but it wasn't. In fact, he called her when he got home, and they stayed on the phone until six o'clock the next morning. He picked her up around four, and they had breakfast together at IHOP. They had been hanging out every since.

Nikki was at Kevin's door now and rang the doorbell. She couldn't wait to see his face. He had been so disappointed that they couldn't meet. Yes, things seemed to be going well with them. Perhaps in time, things would go well with Kayla, too, but Nikki knew from her own experience that she was a hard nut to crack.

"Hi."

Nikki was flabbergasted. A light-skinned woman with long, black, wavy hair answered the door. She appeared to be in her mid twenties. She was shapely and her smile was infectious. She also appeared a little confused to see Nikki.

Nikki was furious. Kevin had been playing her all along, and here was the proof. If the woman were half as shocked as she was, it would explain the confusion. She smiled quickly to cover her hurt and surprise, and then suddenly, the woman brightened.

"Oh, you must be Nikki," she said, stepping back. "Come in. I've heard so much about you."

Nikki walked through the door. The woman wore a light, flirty fragrance that wafted into the air as she passed. Questions flooded her brain. *Who is she?*

The pleasant scent stirred again as she moved to close the door behind Nikki. "He was right." She studied Nikki's face. "You are very pretty."

Was that a compliment? Nikki smiled back cautiously.

"I'm sorry; I didn't introduce myself, did I? I'm Kacie, Kevin's sister—he's in the shower. I'll let him know you're here."

"Oh," Nikki smiled warmly, relieved. Kevin had shown her pictures of his sister before, but she had looked different in the photos.

Nikki sat down on the sofa. She watched Kacie disappear down the hallway and into Kevin's bedroom. She heard Kacie holler to Kevin in the shower, but after several attempts to get his attention, she gave up. It was hard to compete with Santana's "Oye Como Va" blaring from inside the bathroom.

Kacie sat across from Nikki on the couch. She explained that she'd had a long layover flight, so she called Kevin to pick her up from the airport. They talked for a while about Kevin. Kacie said she could tell her brother really liked Nikki.

Nikki grinned a little, but didn't want to let on that she really liked Kevin, too.

"So, are you in a sorority?" Kacie asked, switching subjects.

"No. At my school, black fraternities and sororities aren't that prominent."

"Yeah? Kevin went to a predominantly white school, too—nothing to join there but Geek Phi Geek."

They laughed.

"I just wouldn't have the time, anyway." She looked at Kacie. "What about you?"

"I'm a Delta," Kacie yawned. "Just like momma," she said, bringing her arms in from her stretch. "Oh, excuse me."

Kevin emerged from the bedroom.

Nikki's lips curved upwards instantly, but not so much to greet him. A towel was wrapped around his waist, and her eyes followed him closely as he stepped into the kitchen. His bronze, muscular body glistened with drops of water. His hairy chest, belly, and legs thrilled her, and his buttocks wrestled against the confines of the towel. She didn't mean to stare, but she couldn't tear her eyes away.

Kacie caught Nikki's gaze. "Boy, you have a guest! If you don't go and put some clothes on—"

Kevin blushed, finally noticing Nikki's presence. He was surprised to see her in his living room, sitting across from his sister—very pleasantly surprised.

After dinner, Kevin dropped Kacie at the airport. He pulled up to his building, behind Nikki's car.

"Is Kacie the oldest?"

"No, I am," Kevin responded. "She just thinks she is," he said, gripping the steering wheel as if he were still driving. "I love my sister, though, we're really close. She moved in with me for a few months after she graduated, but she didn't like Atlanta, and moved back home." In a way, he had his sister to thank for meeting Nikki. If she hadn't moved in and discovered his indiscretions, he probably would have never found the need to change his life and settle down.

"Hmm." Nikki started thinking. If she were to begin a serious relationship with Kevin, she needed to know if he planned to stick around. Dating was hard enough in big ole metro Atlanta; she couldn't imagine being in a long-distance relationship. "You ever thought about moving back?"

"Yeah," Kevin answered honestly. "But with the economy and all, and the war—now is just not the right time." That was almost the truth. In reality, Kevin was enjoying getting to know Nikki and their blossoming relationship; if she was everything he hoped, he wouldn't be leaving anytime soon.

Nikki breathed an inner sigh of relief. "What about your brother?" she continued, hoping he hadn't noticed her relief.

"Who—TJ?" Kevin smirked.

"Yeah. How do you get along?"

"TJ's cool. My parents are upset with him right now."

"Why?"

"He dropped out of school without telling them." Kevin smiled to himself, nodding.

"Dropped out?"

"Yeah. TJ—TJ's unique. I knew he wouldn't last. I love my parents, but they pushed him too hard to go to that school; he really didn't want to go."

"What was his major?"

"Math and physics."

Nikki was impressed.

"Yeah. He's like a genius. He can fix anything. He's been accepted to some school in California."

"So he hasn't really dropped out?"

"My parents don't see it that way."

"What will he be going to school for in California?"

"To learn how to make video games."

"What? That's a big difference."

Kevin put the car in neutral. "Are we still on for tomorrow?"

"Yes."

Kevin leaned towards her slowly.

Oh, no. You can't have my heart that easily, Nikki thought as she backed away.

"Come on, baby." He gazed at her and ran his fingers down the side of her face. "Don't be shy," he said, staring at her lips.

She wavered for a moment; but as much as she wanted to, she couldn't. "I'm not," she said, opening the door. "See you tomorrow." She closed the door behind her.

Kevin watched as she sat in her car. He was getting annoyed. This 'friends' junk was getting on his nerves.

If they were just friends, why did they talk to each other every day on the phone? Granted, sometimes it was just five or ten minutes, but more times than not, it was an hour, two hours, or even three—and if they were just friends, why had she agreed to go out with him every weekend for the past month? He wasn't going to waste his time with this girl, if this was all she wanted.

Then she smiled at him. The beauty of it melted his heart. *I am such a sucker,* he thought to himself. There had to be more there. He saw it in her eyes. Sometimes he caught her staring at him, but she would quickly turn her head, or pretend to be looking at something else.

He smiled back at her faintly, and waved as her car pulled ahead of him. Why couldn't he get through to her?

Kevin walked into his condo. He was exhausted, so he went straight to his bedroom and collapsed on the bed. Suddenly, the phone rang. "Hello?"

"Kevin?"

"Kacie?"

"I'm still in Atlanta. My flight got delayed."

"Really?"

"Yeah. But we're starting to board now. Anyway, I didn't want to call you back too late—with the time difference and all." She paused. "She's really nice. I like her."

Kevin smiled. "I'm glad I have your approval, but I'm not sure if she likes me like that. She's hard to read. I keep getting mixed signals."

"She likes you," Kacie said. "It's more than a friendship."

Kevin's heart thumped. "Did she say something?"

"No." She thought back to the cat-look Nikki had given her when she'd opened the door. For a minute, she'd thought she would have to set her straight, but Nikki had kept her cool. She liked that. "She didn't have to."

A voice over the airport's PA broke their conversation, calling her section to board. "I gotta go, but I'll catch you tomorrow. Okay?"

"Okay."

"Love you."

"Love you, too, sis." His heart was warmed by her words. "Bye."

●●●

Kevin looked at Nikki as they walked through Piedmont Botanical Gardens in the easy, fragrant breeze. She clung tenderly to his arm as they enjoyed the variety of flowers in the park.

"What?" Nikki asked shyly, noticing his gaze.

"I got some tickets this weekend for the Autumn Fest."

"Autumn Fest?" Nikki's eyes widened. "I thought those were sold out."

He smiled at her excitement. "They are, but I got my 'connections.'"

"Connections?" Nikki squeezed Kevin's arm.

Kevin chuckled to himself. No way was he going to let on that Randy, his mentor and like a second father in many ways, had given him the tickets after his daughter, son-in-law, and their friends couldn't make it.

Nikki couldn't believe she was going to the concert. Of all the concerts that came to town, this was *it*—the concert of concerts. She thought of the line up—LL Cool J, Doug E Fresh, Rob Base, MC Lyte, Big Daddy Kane, and Run DMC.

Kevin looked at Nikki. She was basking in thoughts of the concert. "So what does my eighties girl know about old school rap?" he smirked.

Nikki looked at him and rolled her eyes. "I know enough to know I wanna go. My cousin Malcolm used to listen to all of them."

"You wanna go?" Kevin teased.

"Yeah, I wanna go!" She jumped with excitement, and her breast brushed lightly against Kevin's arm.

Kevin turned to face her. Nikki's smile was bright and cheerful, and her eyes sparkled in the sunshine. Everything was perfect—a beautiful day, the walk, the garden and its scenery, the mood, the conversation.

He wanted to kiss her so bad. He leaned towards her slowly.

Nikki's heart raced.

Then he remembered what had happened only a few nights before. His head changed course from her lips to her ear. "I guess I'll take you," he whispered playfully, and then he turned quickly, trying to conceal his original motive.

She detached her arm from Kevin's, hoping he hadn't felt the race of her heart. She could have sworn he was about to kiss her. She restarted the conversation to mask her disappointment. "Who's your favorite artist?" she asked coolly, clapping her hands once. "Or group?"

Kevin thought to himself and shrugged. "My father used to be a DJ."

"Really?" she asked in surprise. She knew how religious his parents were and couldn't picture them in that setting.

"Yeah. I grew up listening to a lot of 60's and 70's stuff. Some of the new artists are good, but that was *real* music—Earth, Wind, and Fire, the Stylistics, The Isleys, Al Greene." He smiled, looking down at her again. "But my all-time favorite is Stevie Wonder."

"Stevie Wonder," Nikki echoed. "He's good."

Kevin reached over and tucked Nikki's arm back in his. "What about you?" he asked softly. "Who's your favorite?"

"Right now—" she grinned, "Justin Timberlake."

"Justin Timberlake," he scoffed.

"Hey," she chuckled. "That white boy can sing, and his music has good beats." She was disappointed that he hadn't kissed her, but relieved that the mood had lightened. "My all-time favorites are Sade and Maxwell."

"Sade." Kevin nodded, as if she hadn't made a bad selection.

"So," Nikki squeezed Kevin's arm. "Is that how your parents met? Your father was DJ-ing, and your mother saw him?"

Kevin smiled. "That's what my father says, but my mother denies it. She swears she was just in the club to help a friend."

"Help her friend do what?"

Kevin shrugged. "That's what we always ask."

Nikki chuckled. "Sounds like a Malcolm and Anesa story. It's amazing how two people in the same place can come up with totally different versions of a story."

Speaking of which — Kevin needed her to know that he was interested in her, that he wasn't someone who just showed up occasionally. He really liked Nikki, and he was ready to take their relationship to the next level. "I'd like you to invite Malcolm and Anesa to come."

Nikki almost snapped her neck looking up at him. "Are you sure? Are you sure that you're ready to meet my cousin?"

"Yes, I'm sure, baby," he answered softly.

Nikki felt herself growing warm. She loved when he called her that. "Okay." Her hand slipped down from his arm into his hand. "I'll call and ask them tonight."

● ● ●

"Can you believe what happened to Jam Master J?" Anesa looked across the table at Nikki.

Nikki shook her head. "I can't believe someone would kill him in the studio like that."

Anesa shook her head. "That was nice, though — what they did at the concert on his behalf."

"Yeah." Nikki smiled hesitantly, looking towards the counter where Malcolm and Kevin were talking.

Anesa knew Run DMC was one of Nikki's favorite old school rap groups, but she was more concerned with what was going on with Malcolm and Kevin. Anesa grabbed Nikki's hands and drew them across the table. "He's really nice, girl."

"Yeah." She smiled, and lifted an Oreo shake to her lips.

"And Malcolm — don't worry about him. I can tell he likes him, too."

Nikki's face glowed. The worst was over.

"Look, man, thanks again for the concert."

"No problem," Kevin smiled.

"Look'a here, man," Malcolm looked down, then scratched behind his ear. "My cousin really likes you."

Kevin looked over at the table. "I really like her, too."

"Yeah," Malcolm said, rubbing the back of his head. "Look, man, you don't seem the type, and I know that this is you and Nic-Nic's thing, but she's my youngest cousin." He laughed. "She's practically my sister." He got serious. "I love that girl, and she's been through a lot. If you're the kind of brother that likes to run games—just walk away. Otherwise, I just ask that you respect her."

Kevin looked at him. "I won't treat her any differently than I would expect someone to treat my own sister."

"All right," Malcolm smiled. They patted each other's shoulder. "So, who do you think is going to win the Super Bowl this year?"

"What's taking those two so long?" asked Nikki.

"I don't know," Anesa said. "Hey." She reached across the table and felt Nikki's hand. "I missed my period last month—and the month before."

"What?" Nikki spun her head back to face her friend.

Anesa grinned.

"Are you saying—?"

Anesa nodded her head. "After seeing you with Kayla this past summer," she wiped a tear from her eyes, "we decided it was time to try again."

"'Nesa!" Nikki jumped up and ran around the table. Anesa met her halfway, and they hugged. Kevin looked over, startled.

"I'm going to be a father soon," Malcolm said at Kevin's puzzled glance.

CHAPTER FOUR

Nikki turned the ignition to her 1987 Toyota Cressida, but the car didn't budge.

Kayla stirred sleepily in the back seat.

Nikki tried again, but it wouldn't start.

Kevin came over after several attempts. "Car problems?"

"Yeah."

"Pop the hood." He walked to the front of the car and looked under the hood. Then he walked back to Nikki, sitting in the driver's seat. "I'm not even gonna front; I don't know anything about cars. I think it needs to be taken in. How are you going to get Kayla back to your grandmother?"

"She'll just have to stay with me overnight. I'll take her back after the car is fixed tomorrow."

"You'll miss class."

Nikki didn't respond.

"Come on. I'll take her back tonight."

"I couldn't ask you to do that!"

"You didn't."

Nikki struggled with the door. The knob to her grandmother's house was notorious for its stubbornness. She leaned against it a bit and tried again. Kayla yawned.

Nikki sighed, annoyed. "Can you hold her for me, please?"

He reached for Kayla and held her. Kayla and Kevin studied each other quietly. Kevin smiled, but her expression went unchanged.

Nikki sighed as the door swung open. "Thanks." She smiled at Kevin, taking Kayla. He picked up the car seat and carried it into the house. Nikki felt against the wall, and the kitchen light came on. Nikki glanced over her shoulder. "I'm going to put her to bed."

Kevin watched them disappear down the hall. He took a seat on the old sofa in the living room.

"Grandma?" Nikki called. She tapped on her grandmother's door.

"I'll be right out," she heard a muffled voice reply.

She was probably in the bathroom, Nikki thought. She went to the bedroom opposite her grandmother's, placed Kayla on the bed, sat beside the child, and began undressing her.

"Nikki?" her grandmother called, seeing the light in the living room. "If you're going to be late, I wish you would— Oh!" She broke off when she saw Kevin sitting on the couch and smiled quickly.

Kevin rose to introduce himself.

Nikki ran into the living room for a quick intro. "Grandma, this is my friend Kevin."

"Hey."

"This is my grandmother, Odessa."

Kevin tipped his head, and they shook hands. Odessa stared at him for a moment. "It's a pleasure to meet you. Nikki didn't tell me she was bringing a friend," she said, as if Nikki had left the room.

"I'm going to finish tucking in Kayla," Nikki said, though she knew her grandmother hadn't heard a word. She didn't repeat herself. Odessa was on a mission—she wouldn't hear her, anyway.

Nikki went back to Kayla's room. Kayla had already taken off her shirt and put on her pajama top, but needed help getting her pants on. Kayla often got thirsty in the middle of the night, so Nikki got up to fetch some water for her. "Go use the bathroom; I'll be in to help you in a second." She watched her scurry off to the restroom, and walked to the kitchen.

"What's your name again?"

Kevin smiled. "Kevin." Odessa stared at him. "Kevin Maddox," he added.

Her eyes twinkled. "It has a nice ring to it." She glanced in Nikki's direction. "I haven't meet too many of Nikki's friends. Actually, you're the first." She looked back at Nikki.

Nikki cut the faucet on and returned the stare.

Kevin said nothing, but smiled and nodded.

"Would you like anything?" Odessa clapped her hand to her chest and gave Nikki an indignant look. "You didn't offer the man anything to drink?"

Nikki frowned at Odessa.

"I'm fine," Kevin assured her.

Odessa dropped her hand into her lap. "So tell me about your-self — what do you do?"

Nikki walked back down the hallway. She helped Kayla in the restroom then followed her back to her bedroom. She set the water on top of the nightstand, helped Kayla into bed, and pulled the covers over her. Kayla didn't demand she read her a book, so Nikki sat on the bed beside her. Something was troubling her. "What are you thinking about?" she asked, adjusting the covers.

"When will I live with you?"

Nikki leaned on one arm. She hadn't expected that question. She smiled. "Next summer."

Kayla's face contorted. "That's a long way away."

Nikki played with the covers. "Not really," she assured her. Kayla looked as if something else was on her mind. "What else 'ya thinking 'bout?"

"Grandma's going to Beulah's Place tomorrow," Kayla frowned. She looked at the door as if she expected Odessa to enter the room. "There's nothing but old people there." Her face snarled with disapproval. "I hate it," she whispered confidentially. "You're more fun."

Nikki sat up a little. "There's a big age difference between you and Grandma. Some people her age like to do stuff like that."

"Well, I hate it!" Kayla folded her arms.

Nikki kissed her on the forehead. "Just remember — she may be old, but she's still your grandmother, and she loves you." She kissed her on the lips. "And so do I."

Kayla's mood shifted. "I love you, too." She smiled, settling under the comforter.

"Goodnight, baby. I'll see you in a couple of weeks. Okay?" Nikki saw Kayla's little nod as she closed the door behind her. She heard Kevin and her grandmother in the living room.

"Do you have any kids?" came her grandmother's voice.

She strode into the room, breaking up the "interview."

"Grandma, we have to go," she said, pulling Kevin's hand.

Odessa watched them closely; their hands fell apart once he rose.

"It was nice meeting you. Mrs. Jones," he said, and took her hand in a gentle, but formal shake.

"Odessa," she smiled. "Call me Odessa."

Kevin nodded and walked out the door.

Nikki hugged her and kissed her cheek, but her grandmother held her motionless for a moment. "Are you seeing him?" she whispered.

Nikki said nothing and shrugged.

"What does that mean?"

Nikki repeated the gesture.

"Answer me, child," she demanded.

Nikki didn't say a word.

"Nikki?" she tried to whisper, but her voice was too loud.

Once, again, Nikki refused to answer.

"You know, the 'Lawd don't like ugly," Odessa mumbled as Nikki walked out the door and strode towards the car.

Nikki looked back at her. She shivered and rubbed her hands over her shoulders. Then she smiled as Kevin opened the door for her. Her grandmother stood in the doorway of her house, watching them.

Kevin went around the car and climbed into the driver's seat. He noticed her hands running up and down her arms. "You're cold?" He reached into his back seat, grabbed his jacket, and draped it over her shoulders. They backed away and drove off.

Kevin pulled up outside Nikki's apartment complex. A thunderstorm had settled over the city, and the temperature had dropped considerably as the weather set in. Nikki and Kevin decided to wait in the car until the rain eased up.

"It's freezing!" Nikki shivered inside Kevin's jacket. She rested her head against the window.

"You're still cold?"

"You're still not?" she joked. "I really appreciate you taking Kayla back for me."

"I don't mind, Nikki." He replied softly, adjusting the temperature dial.

"I know, but I wanted to thank you anyway," she whispered. "I'm sorry about earlier."

"What do you mean?" He couldn't remember anything that had happened for her to be apologizing.

"My grandmother." She paused. "I know she asked you a hundred and fifty million questions." They laughed. "She's been trying to marry me off ever since I agreed to take in Kayla. Trying to set me up on 'blind dates', and stuff." Her voice trailed remembering some of the supposedly impromptu introductions. Though some of her grandmother's choices were just plain suspect, admittedly others were nice. But nonetheless Nikki knew finding a man was a task that she had to complete on her on, and she was in no particular rush to do it. "Anyway, I hope you weren't offended."

"Why would I be?" Kevin smiled. He could tell she was uncomfortable with the topic, so he thought of another one. "I've wanted to ask you something." Kevin had his elbow propped on the door; he brushed his hand over his head, and then leaned his head into it. "I know your father died, and that he used to drink, but how did Kayla end up with your grandmother?"

Nikki hugged herself. "I actually didn't find out about Kayla until a couple of years ago, when my father died," she said, recalling the event.

●●●

Nikki struggled to hold the grocery bags and open the door, hearing the phone ringing inside the apartment. Finally, she rushed in and managed to set the items down in time to answer the phone.

"Hello?"

There was a long silence.

"Hello?" Nikki was about to hang up when she heard, "Veronica?"

She froze. She couldn't believe her ears. It was her father. "How did you get this number?"

"Mama gave it to me."

"I don't want to talk to you."

"Veronica, please—"

She shook her head violently. "Don't ever call here again," she said, slamming the phone down.

A few days later, Nikki was preparing to go to class. She packed her lunch as she watched the TV from the kitchen. She caught the news every morning for the traffic and weather report. The telephone rang.

"Hello?"

"Nikki?"

"Grandma," she smiled. "I'm surprised to hear from you so early this morning."

"Nikki. I have to tell you something. Are you sitting down?"

Nikki sat down on one of the kitchen stools. "Okay."

"Your father died last night."

Nikki gasped and held her hand to her chest. Tears streamed down her face. She hated her father; she didn't understand why she was crying.

"His funeral's Friday. I know you're in school and all, so... When do you think you can come?"

Memories flashed through Nikki's head "I'm not coming," she whispered.

"What do you mean? Nikki, I know your father wasn't perfect, but he was still your father."

Nikki could hardly get the words out. She wiped a tear from her eyes. "I'm not coming." She shook her head.

Her grandmother was silent for a moment. "That's a shame; your sister was looking forward to meeting you."

Nikki perked up. "Sister?"

"Yes. MiKayla." Her grandmother paused. Her voice dropped. "He didn't tell you about her, did he? He promised he would."

Nikki was shocked.

"Yeah," Odessa continued. "It's not Jackie's child, though."

"How old is she? Where does she live?"

"She's eighteen months. She'll be two in June. But anyway—"

"I'll be there," Nikki stated firmly.

● ● ●

Nikki was deliberately late to the funeral home. She wanted to meet her sister, but she didn't want her grandmother to hassle her. A small group of people was gathered towards the front, but they were all adults. She looked around, but saw no one else. She sat in the back. Her grandmother glanced towards the door, saw her, and started making her way over. She stood.

"Nikki."

She hugged her grandmother, who looked surprisingly good.

"Don't you want to sit up here with the rest of us?"

"No, Grandma," she smiled. "I'm fine back here."

A woman walked in, carrying a child on her shoulder. Nikki looked over quickly. She could see the child's back, but not its head or face.

"Melissa," called Nikki's grandmother.

The child turned around. It was a little boy.

"I'm so glad you could make it," said Odessa. She took Melissa's hand and squeezed it. "This is Jim's oldest daughter, Veronica."

"Nice to meet you." said Melissa. The little boy rested his head again on her shoulder.

"You too," Nikki said, nodding. They were quiet for a moment, and then her grandmother motioned the woman towards the body and she continued to the front.

"You're not gonna even go up to see him?"

Nikki pulled her grandmother into the hallway. Jim was her only child; it would kill her if she found out his secret. "Grandma, I don't think I should be here anymore."

"You just got here." Her grandmother gave her a hard stare. "Veronica, I know your father wasn't perfect, but sugar, he loved you. He wasn't the same after you left, and the time that you almost—" She looked down. "Well, it almost killed him. Your father loved you, Veronica." She shook her head. "I know he was an alcoholic, but after you left Jackie divorced him, and it was like he didn't have a reason to live anymore. He almost drank himself to death."

"So this is my fault?" Nikki asked, agitated and gesturing wildly.

"No, Nikki. That's not what I'm saying. That's not what I'm saying at all. Your father regretted not being there for you. When Kayla was born, it was as if he had a new beginning—as if he was trying to make up for everything he had done wrong with you through her, but by then, it was too late. He had destroyed his liver." Her grandmother took her hand and held it. "Please, do it for me."

Nikki shook her head. "I can't do it, Grandma. I shouldn't have come." She began to walk away.

"Nikki, it's a disease," her grandmother shouted.

Nikki stopped and walked back.

"Alcohol destroys many black families. He couldn't help it."

"He couldn't help it?" Nikki stared at her grandmother. She wanted to tell her so badly, but couldn't. "Grandma, do you actually believe that?"

Odessa didn't say anything.

Nikki backed away and threw her hands up. "I can't." She grabbed her purse, and exited the building. Tears streamed from her eyes; she could hardly see. She sat on a bench outside to pull herself together.

A car pulled up and parked. A black woman in her early thirties got out, opened the rear door, pulled a toddler out of the car, and began walking towards the funeral home. Nikki could tell that the child was a girl, but couldn't get a good look at her.

Nikki wiped her face and followed them. The woman stopped in front of her grandmother. They talked for a few minutes, and her grandmother took the child and bounced her gently in her arms, talking to her sweetly. Without a backwards glance, the strange woman turned and walked away.

Nikki wanted to move closer, but sat where she had before, watching as her grandmother took the child to the coffin. The child looked quietly at the body then turned her head and laid it on her grandmother's shoulder.

Nikki and her grandmother's eyes met. Odessa seemed surprised to see her. She started over, bringing the little girl. Nikki rose from the bench. "MiKayla," her grandmother whispered. "This is your sister."

The little girl had her thumb in her mouth. She lifted her head briefly, waved, then laid it back down. Nikki opened her arms, and her grandmother passed Kayla to her. She took her thumb out of her mouth and studied Nikki's face.

"Why don't I give you two some time alone?" Odessa said. She turned around and returned to the gathering of mourners.

Later that evening, Nikki followed her grandmother home. They parked, and she helped her grandmother get Kayla out of her car seat. Inside the house, children's toys were scattered everywhere. Kayla ran to one of her toys, plopped down on the floor, and began playing with it.

"Who was that woman who dropped MiKayla off?"

"That was her foster parent. Mrs. Lynch."

"Foster parent?"

Nikki's grandmother pulled a pitcher out of the refrigerator and placed it on the counter. "MiKayla's mother abandoned her." She shook her head. "Strung out on dope and booze." She poured juice into three cups. "Kayla's going to be staying with me."

Nikki frowned. "You?" She didn't know her grandmother's exact age, but she was at least in her early sixties. With her blood pressure problems and diabetes, Nikki didn't see how she would manage.

"Yes, me! No grandchild of mine is staying in no foster home." Odessa motioned for Kayla, seconds later she came running in. She held a cup out to her, but the child shook her head. "You're not thirsty?"

Kayla shook her head again.

"Okay." Odessa placed the cup on the counter, put the jug into the refrigerator, and then went to use the restroom.

Nikki wandered into the living room and sat down. She handed Kayla a toy.

Kayla smiled at her, took it out of her hand, and resumed playing.

Nikki stared at her quietly.

"Where are your things?" asked Odessa as she walked down the hall towards her.

Nikki looked away from Kayla. "I didn't plan to stay."

"You know you're welcome."

Nikki looked at Kayla, then at her grandmother. "I know, but I think I should be heading back."

"Okay. You've always had a mind of your own."

Nikki walked over to Kayla. "Bye." She wiggled her fingers back and forth.

Kayla looked at her and waved.

Nikki hugged her grandmother and left.

● ● ●

Nikki turned to Kevin. "A few days later, I called and told her I wanted to keep Kayla. At first, she said no. I was too young, I'd never had kids of my own; I wasn't married; I was in school." She rattled off all the excuses. "But a few days later, she said I could, as long as I finished school first. So for now, I pick her up every other weekend, and in the spring, since my load will be lighter, I'll get her more."

Kevin nodded his head.

"This past summer she stayed with me. I was scared at first, but we really bonded. And now that I'm in a bigger apartment," she said proudly, "things are working out."

Kevin looked at her and smiled admiringly. "It must have taken a lot for you to offer to do that."

"She's my sister," Nikki declared.

They sat quietly for a moment, watching the raindrops fall on the window. "I better get going. You have to go to work early in the morning."

Kevin looked at her. "I like spending time with you, Nikki," he whispered. "I don't care if I don't get any sleep." He played with her hair for a moment, his warm hand caressing her cheek.

His eyes were innocent, big, and brown. They frightened her. "I better get going."

Kevin came around the car to meet her with his umbrella. They made a dash for her apartment as the rain picked up even more, coming down so hard that their clothes were soaked.

Inside the dark apartment, only the lightning's glare penetrated her patio blinds. After a few seconds fumbling around in the dark, Nikki found the knob to turn on the light.

Kevin was waiting next to the door. She liked that he always saw her into her apartment. "Thanks, Kevin—for everything."

"It was my pleasure," he said. "Goodnight." He kissed her on the cheek in the same place he had caressed earlier.

Nikki's heart seemed to beat a thousand times faster. She could feel his warm breath on her cheek. "Goodnight."

Kevin wanted to kiss her badly, but he reached for the doorknob.

"Oh!" Nikki exclaimed. "You may need this." She gestured to the jacket, pulling frantically on the zipper, but it was stuck.

Kevin examined it. "I think your shirt's caught. I don't want to tear it."

Nikki held her shirt down as Kevin gently tugged at the zipper. She could feel his body heat. He stopped suddenly, studying it from another angle, and began tugging at it again.

Kevin inhaled the sweet scent of her skin. He liked the way she watched him.

Finally, blouse was freed. They stared at each other, their lips only inches apart.

Kevin couldn't resist any longer. They had been dating for almost two months without even kissing. It had been torture. He pulled on the ends of the jacket, dragging her towards him. He watched to see if she pulled back, but to his surprise and satisfaction, she didn't resist. Her eyes were drawn to his lips, just as his were to hers. Kevin wrapped his arms around Nikki's waist and tilted his head a little.

Their lips touched—softly, curiously. Kevin's were even juicer than she had imagined. They were soft and warm, and his tongue was tangy and moist.

He felt a little guilty, but he couldn't take his eyes off her. He watched until her eyes rolled back in her head.

They were finally kissing. He closed his eyes and concentrated on it. He felt her knees give a little, and her body slumped in his arms. He smirked, tickled with her reaction. He wrapped her arms around his neck and held her securely. She was finally in his arms, and he was not about to let her go.

CHAPTER FIVE

Kevin had been inviting Nikki to church for months. She woke up that morning and decided to go. She scurried to get Kayla ready.

She walked towards the building and saw Kevin standing at the door. "Good morning," he said, smiling at them, holding the door open. Kayla looked around the foyer curiously, and then out of the corner of her eye, she saw Kevin kiss Nikki on the cheek.

"Is this okay?" Nikki whispered to Kevin, motioning towards her pants.

He looked her up and down. "Baby, I always think you look beautiful."

Just when she was about to explain what she really meant, Kevin wrapped his arm around her waist and gently pushed her forward. They entered the auditorium, where Nikki spotted several other women in pantsuits. She sighed, relieved.

Almost immediately, a man stopped them. From his manner, Nikki assumed he was one of the church's leaders.

"Kevin, I didn't know you had a girlfriend," he grinned.

Kevin and Nikki looked at each other.

Finally, Nikki spoke. "We're actually just—"

"She's a mighty pretty thing, too," the man cut her off.

"Thank you," Nikki muttered.

He looked down at Kayla, who clung to Nikki shyly. "And what's your name?"

"Her name is MiKayla."

"A pretty name for a pretty girl."

"What do you say, Kayla?"

"Thank you," she said softly.

"What are you thanking me for? I didn't create you. God created you."

MiKayla smiled back.

"You know, I have a grandchild about your age. Would you like to meet her?"

She nodded.

The man was about to take MiKayla's hand when Nikki stopped him. "Thanks, but I'd prefer she stay with me."

The man nodded. "Okay. Well, she'll be up here in a little bit." He looked at MiKayla. "You can meet her then, okay?"

She nodded.

Nikki looked around for a moment. Something was different about the church, but she didn't know what.

"Come on." Kevin smiled and took her hand. They walked toward the middle aisle and sat down. "You okay?"

Nikki looked at him and nodded. "I've gone to church with Jackie, Malcolm, Anesa, or Aunt Becca, but not often. This is all really new to me."

"You've visited me," he said.

Nikki looked at him, confused.

He pointed at the ceiling. "A building isn't the church. The people make the church."

Nikki smiled at him. "Oh—you know what I mean."

They listened to the invocation, and then the song leader rose. Nikki stared at him blankly, daydreaming. Kevin nudged her a little. She looked and saw that he had the songbook turned to a hymn. He began singing. Nikki stared at the words. She had no idea how to read music.

"Just listen to the tune," Kevin whispered.

After services, they ran into the older gentleman again, who informed everyone that walked by that they were 'an item.' Normally, she would've been annoyed by the attention, but for some reason, it didn't bother her.

Finally, they were able to leave the auditorium. Then—

"Kevin!"

It was a female voice. A woman who appeared to be in her early thirties approached. "I didn't realize you were coming to this service. I would have met you—"

Kevin quickly put his arm around Nikki's shoulder. "Natalie, this is my girlfriend, Veronica." He squeezed Nikki's shoulder.

Nikki grimaced, and then smiled quickly.

"Oh?" It was the woman's turn to make a face. "Veronica? Nice to meet you," she said politely, trying to conceal her surprise. Her disappointment was evident. They shook hands briefly. "I'm sorry; I have to run, but it was nice meeting you." She dashed off.

"Umm-hmm." Nikki mumbled, suddenly understanding the real reason she had agreed to come to the service. Call it intuition, but she knew that not only was Kevin good looking, he was a good man, and she hoped that once the women in church saw that he was seriously dating someone, they would lose interest.

"Who was that?" she asked as they continued into the parking lot, Kayla trailing closely behind.

Kevin grinned. "Just one of the sisters from the singles' ministry."

"Looks like she wants to be more than a sister," Nikki said sassily.

"Well, she's too late."

"So I heard. I'm your 'girlfriend,' now?"

Kevin hugged Nikki, grinning. "You heard the man."

They went to Golden Corral for dinner. Nikki looked at Kevin. "You never told me you could sing."

Kevin blushed. "Can I?"

"You sounded good to me." Nikki looked at Kayla and back at Kevin. "That's it."

"What?"

"Where were the instruments? I've never seen a church without instruments."

Kevin smiled. "They were there."

Nikki looked at him, confused.

"You didn't see them?"

She shook her head.

"I didn't see them, either," Kayla announced.

Kevin took his index finger and rode it up and down Kayla's neck. She giggled.

"There it is."

Nikki smiled. Kayla was starting to loosen up around him.

He did it again.

Kayla giggled more.

"Excuse me, sir?" an Asian waitress interrupted them. "More tea?"

"Yeah. Thanks."

She looked at his glass, trying to remember. "Sweet, or unsweet?"

"Sweet."

"One moment."

Kevin watched her until she disappeared behind a wall.

He cleared his throat and changed his pitch to a higher one. "Waaaaw," he exaggerated, making a karate sound. "I make it sweet for you, sir."

Kayla roared with laughter; she could hardly control herself.

"Kevin!"

"What?" he grinned, watching Nikki shake her head disapprovingly, but he could tell that she wanted to laugh, too.

"Grandma." Nikki sat Kayla down on the couch and tied her shoelaces. "I told you I can't stay the weekend. I have to catch up on some studying."

"Mmm-hmmm." Odessa looked at her, smiling. She hoped her granddaughter didn't think she was that big a fool. "It's that Kevin fellow—isn't it?" She sat back in her seat, lit a cigarette, and took a drag.

"Grandma, don't smoke around Kayla, please."

"Don't smoke around Kayla," Odessa mocked as she pounded the butt into the ashtray. "I smoked around you, and you all right."

Nikki ignored her. She grabbed the car seat and lifted Kayla.

Odessa threw her hands up, remembering something. "Wait. There's something I need to give you."

Nikki heard the phone ring. She sat Kayla back down and placed the car seat next to the couch.

Odessa ran to her bedroom.

"Hello," she heard her grandmother answer.

Nikki looked at her watch and sighed. Kayla hadn't been ready when she got there, and they were supposed to be meeting Kevin in a couple of hours. Kayla had just awakened from her afternoon nap. "Ready to spend some time with me?" She rubbed her hand over Kayla's forehead.

Kayla looked up at her, dazed.

"No," came Odessa's voice from the other room. "I'm going to be by myself this weekend. Nikki's not staying, and she's taking Kayla with her. Yeah." Her grandmother paused. "Girl, let me tell you about my oldest grandbaby. Yeah. Nikki. Girl, she done gone and got ha'self a boyfriend, dragged him up in the house, and didn't even let me know nothin'. Yeah." Odessa came out of the room with the cordless phone still planted to the side of her face. "I haven't seen much of Miss Nikki, lately," she said.

"He wasn't my boyfriend at the time," Nikki interjected.

"Hold on. Hold on," Odessa said into the phone. Then she turned to Nikki. "You won't believe who was here the other day."

Nikki shrugged, clueless.

"Jackie." Odessa grinned.

Jackie? Nikki thought. Her heart hit the floor.

"Yeah." Odessa read her face. "And she looked good, too. Said she has a home in Charlotte now. Said she went back to school to get her degree in interior design. Now she's working on another bachelor's degree in business." She dropped a sheet of paper in her hand. "She told me to give this to you. Huh! Maybe I'll go back to school." She paused then shifted the phone back to her ear. "No, I ain't too old, neither."

What was Jackie doing in Penetra? Nikki opened the sheet of paper. A phone number was printed on it.

Odessa lifted from the phone briefly. "She told me to tell you to call her," she whispered, patting Nikki on the shoulder. Then she sat down at the kitchen table. "Anyway," she continued to the phone, "what you doing this weekend?"

Nikki stared at the number again. It had been six years since she had seen Jackie. She bent over and kissed Odessa on the cheek. "Thanks," she whispered. She turned to Kayla and grabbed her hand. "Come on, Kayla," she said, helping her off the couch.

Nikki and Kevin were about to walk off. Kayla rushed to Nikki and tugged at her hand. "I want to go with you."

Nikki looked into her sister's puppy-dog eyes. As payback for Kevin's generosity, her cousins had gotten them tickets to Six Flags. The five of them had spent all day together; she hadn't had a moment alone with Kevin. "Baby, I know you want to, but you're not big enough to go on this ride, yet." She stood. "You'd have nightmares and not be able to sleep tonight. Stay with Malcolm and 'Nesa. I'll only be gone a few minutes. Okay?"

Kayla didn't respond. Nikki stared into her sister's fearful eyes. She didn't understand. She was behaving as if she was leaving her with complete strangers.

"Come on, baby," Kevin said, pulling Nikki away.

"Don't worry. She'll be back." Anesa scooted Kayla against her leg.

Kayla watched Nikki and Kevin climb into a cart and buckle up. Nikki rested her head against Kevin's shoulder. They chatted carelessly. Her sister hadn't given her a second thought.

The ride jerked, and the carts pulled slowly into the haunted house. Her sister smiled at her and waved, but Kayla turned her head, as if something had caught her attention.

Kevin squeezed Nikki as they entered into the house. He was glad they had gotten the last seat. The exterior's bright lights grew dim as they entered the dark mouth of the cave. Nikki's forehead brushed his chin, and she nestled her head into his chest.

"I never thought I'd get you alone," he teased into her ear. Then he lifted her chin and kissed her.

In the mist of the blood curling screams and spooky props, they kissed and held each other tight.

Kayla watched as the first cart emerged from the darkness. Finally, she spotted her sister and Kevin, and the cars slowly came to a stop. Kevin put his hands on Nikki's waist and helped her out of the cart.

They walked away from the ride holding hands, laughing giddily.

Anesa bent down to Kayla. "Your sister is falling in love," she explained.

Kayla glared hatefully at Nikki and Kevin as they approached.

"Let's go." Nikki smiled warmly, and moved to take Kayla's hand.

Kayla stared at her blankly.

"Kayla?" Nikki frowned. "I said let's go."

Finally, Kayla took her hand. She kept her head low and kicked the dirt as she walked.

"Pick the book you want. I'll be back in a second." Nikki cracked the door to Kayla's bedroom and headed towards the living room. Kevin stood by the door, waiting for her devotedly.

"I really had a good time tonight," Nikki announced, staring into his big, brown eyes.

"I did, too," he said, pulling her close.

"Kevin." Nikki's head jerked towards the hallway. Her sister had a way of creeping up when she least expected.

Kevin opened the door, and before she knew it, he had whisked her into the dark corridors of her apartment complex.

Kayla sat up in bed. She couldn't hear anything. She tiptoed past her sister's bedroom, down the hallway, and into the living room, but to her surprise, it was empty.

The front door was ajar. She eased up to it and tried to look through the crack, but the opening was too small. She perched on the loveseat and carefully teased open the blinds.

Kevin was kissing her sister. His back was against the wall, and he held Nikki in his arms. Kayla stared quietly for a moment, wondering how they could breathe and do that at the same time. She slouched down into the sofa, sulking.

"Goodnight, sweet baby." Kevin kissed Nikki a last time. He watched her wave, and then she disappeared into the apartment and closed the door.

Nikki leaned against the door and caught her breath. No one had ever kissed her like Kevin, and it usually took her a few seconds to recuperate.

"Did you find a book, baby?" Nikki smiled, walking towards Kayla's bed. Kayla didn't say anything. Her head was turned away, but Nikki could see she was still awake. "Kayla, did you hear me talking to you?" Nikki was tired of her attitude. She had been acting funny all night. "Kayla." Nikki pulled her face towards her so she could look at her.

"Leave me alone!" Kayla snatched her head back.

Nikki froze. She was used to the tears that came from whippings and threats, but not this. "Kayla, what's wrong, baby?" She rubbed her sister's stomach; it always made her feel good. "Kayla? Kayla, turn around and talk to me, baby."

Finally, the child rolled over. "How long is he going to be around?" she sniffled.

Nikki blinked, caught off guard. "Why do you ask?"

Kayla shrugged. "I liked it better when he wasn't with us. Now he's always around."

Nikki shook her head and smiled. She understood. "Come here, baby," she said, easing Kayla in her lap. "Kevin and I, we—we enjoy spending time together. That doesn't mean I don't enjoy my time with you." She squeezed her. "It's just—now you have to share me. Kind of like the way your grandmother and I share you." She squeezed her again. "That way, you get the best of both worlds, 'cause you have two people who love you and want to spend time with you. Neither of us can always have you when we want, but that's okay, as long as we still spend time together. That's all that matters."

"What's going to happen to me when he takes you away?"

Nikki stared at her, puzzled. "Takes me away? What do you mean? I'm not going anywhere."

"Grandma said my mother met someone, and he took her away."

"Your grandmother told you that?"

Kayla nodded her head.

It was a lot easier than explaining that her mother had been on drugs, but it wasn't the truth. "The truth is, Kayla, no one took your mother away; she chose to go. One day, when you're old enough, I'll explain why. Right now, you need to understand that whatever I do, or whomever I'm with, you'll always be with me. Understand?"

Kayla nodded her head.

"We're flesh and blood. Nothing will ever change that." She rubbed her head. "As for Kevin—I don't know what the future holds for us, but we like each other, and he wants to spend time with me because he cares for me. Will you be happy for your big sister—that I found someone who cares about me and makes me happy?"

Kayla nodded.

"Thank you." Nikki kissed her sister on the temple and rocked her in her arms.

CHAPTER SIX

"So," Kevin put two glasses in the sink and walked over to join Nikki in the living room, "you think we should cut back on seeing each other on the weekends you have her?"

Nikki frowned, settling onto the couch. "No. She just has to get used to you being around, that's all."

Kevin plopped down beside her, smiling. "Do you realize that's the first time you've assigned any longevity to our relationship?"

"I'm your girlfriend, aren't I? I at least give it a couple of months," she joked.

Kevin wished he could break down the walls of this mystifying woman. He thought he knew just how to do it. "Come here," he said, pulling her legs into his lap. He began massaging her feet.

"You said your mom taught you how to cook?" she asked, resting her head on the shoulder of the sofa, enjoying the pampering.

"Yeah."

"That's funny. I figured most boys got off without learning that."

"My mom always told me I needed to learn to cook for myself. She always said, 'Even if you get married, your wife isn't going to have the time, energy, or desire to cook all the time.'"

"I like your mom," Nikki smiled. Kevin's fingers kneaded the sole of her foot. "Umm. That feels good."

"Did you learn to cook from your mom?"

"No." Nikki sat up a little.

"You taught yourself?"

"My stepmother taught me." Nikki laid her head back on the sofa pillow.

"Step mom?"

"Yeah. It's funny; I never called her that when my father was alive."

"I didn't realize your father remarried."

"Yeah. Her name is Jackie. One Saturday, I was watching Soul Train. I had gotten up at seven in the morning to watch cartoons. After a while, she said either I could help her clean the house, or come in the kitchen and help her cook, but I couldn't watch TV. She didn't like me watching more than a certain number of hours a day. She tried to get me to read, or find something else to do. What do you think I chose?"

Kevin smiled. "Did you get along with her?"

"Yeah," Nikki mumbled softly.

"Have you seen her recently?"

"No." Nikki's face saddened. "I haven't seen her since I left."

They sat quietly for several minutes as Kevin rubbed her feet and lower legs. He watched her face, enjoying her reaction as he massaged her deeply. Her lips puckered slightly and how she let out a soft moan whenever she really liked a spot, and though her eyes were closed, they seemed to sink further into her head the deeper he kneaded. He wondered at the expression that she would wear if they made love.

Kevin glided his hands over her thighs, stopping just below the hem of her skirt, and reversed direction, heading back down her leg.

"Oh," Nikki moaned. With each stroke, another block of tension was released. "That feels so good."

Kevin stopped, and just when Nikki thought he was finished, he patted the area in front of him. Nikki moved over eagerly, happy to be in submission to his fingers. She sat on the couch between his legs.

Kevin began rubbing her shoulders. He needed to show her how gentle, yet firm, he could be.

"You are so good with your hands," Nikki whispered, enjoying it. Then she turned to look at Kevin, thinking of the romantic, candlelit dinner he had just prepared. "I should be doing this to you."

Kevin turned her head back around and resumed. He traced the line of her shoulder blades. Nikki sat up a little, and he worked his fingers down the length of her back, then folded her hair into his hands and pulled it away from her neck. *Oh, baby, you're about to find out what else I'm good at*, he thought as he wrapped his arms around her and kissed her lightly at the nape of her neck. His tongue roamed down her neck, tracing the path his lips had touched.

Nikki got nervous. This needed to end. She fell back into his arms, looking for a distraction. "I really like you," she whispered, trailing her fingers across his hands.

"I really like you, too," he said, kissing her on the cheek and squeezing her a little. "What is it, exactly, that you like about me?"

Nikki turned towards him and thought for a moment.

Kevin could tell she wanted to say something, but had decided against it. "What?" he whispered.

She looked at him shyly. "I like your smile," she said, kissing him. "When you get really happy, it's kind of—" she paused, wrinkling her nose. "Goofy." She giggled. Then she tried to mimic him. She started to laugh hysterically and couldn't stop. "I can't do it." She fanned herself with her hand. "Something about the way you turn up your nose." She smiled, kissing him on that part of his anatomy. "But you just do it when you get really excited."

"Goofy?" Kevin blushed. Had he known it gave her such joy he'd have wrinkled his nose for her at every glance.

"Yeah," she grinned, rubbing his hand with hers.

"But you like it, right?"

"Yes," she whispered. She rubbed her hand over and around his face. "You have such a sweet face." She turned and kissed him on the lips.

"What else?"

She leaned back in his arms, and looked up at the ceiling. "Let's see. I think you're a nice person. I know that sounds general, but I do. There just aren't enough nice, good people in the world." She looked at him and smiled. "Especially men."

He snuggled close. Though he could have, he decided not to comment on the tail end of her statement.

"I like your voice. I like your sense of humor." She giggled. "I like your kisses."

He planted one on her lips.

"I like your maturity." She thought hard. "You seem pretty mellow—like it would take a lot to upset you." She paused. "I don't know—you're just different." Then she smiled mischievously.

"What?" Kevin egged, sensing she wanted to say something else.

"And I like your buns," she finally said shyly.

"You like my buns, huh?" Kevin flirted, nuzzling her with his face.

"Okay, I'm done." She faced him. "What do you like about me?"

Kevin shrugged. "Everything."

"Come on, be more specific. You can't like 'everything' about someone."

Kevin squeezed her. He knew one thing he liked, and that was being with her. All his problems seemed to vanish in a puff. Being with her was like heaven itself. She made him forget his past and think about his future. The only thing that mattered was this snapshot in time. He couldn't think how to make the evening more perfect. A beautiful woman in his arms telling him what she liked about him—where did he get so lucky?

"I like your maturity, and that you're a go-getter." He kissed her. "You're caring." He kissed her again. "And smart. And," he grinned, "just in case you couldn't tell—I like your kisses, too. I think you're sophisticated. Like I said—" He shrugged. "Everything."

Nikki turned towards him and smiled.

"When I first met you," he continued, "I thought you were so fine." He ran his fingers down her arm. "Your beautiful black skin, your smile, and your eyes—I wanted to ask you out then, but I was too afraid. So I waited, and watched, and did everything I could to get your attention."

"Like follow me?" she chuckled. "What made you finally decide to ask me out?" she whispered.

"I don't know." He moved closer. "I think it was the look you gave me."

"What kind of look?" Nikki whispered.

He twined his fingers into her hair and drew her closer. "Curiosity."

Their lips touched gently. Electrical impulses shot up her spine at the taste of Kevin's lips. She pulled away.

"Hey," she said. She moved his arm from around her shoulder. "Why don't you show me some of your karate moves?"

Kevin shook his head. He stood and walked into the kitchen. Nikki followed. "Come on. What? You afraid I'll beat you up?"

Kevin laughed under his breath and shook his head firmly.

"Well, come on, then." Nikki slapped his face playfully.

Kevin ignored her. He leaned his glass against the refrigerator's water dispenser lever and got a drink.

Nikki gave up and turned to walk back to the couch.

"Got 'ya." Kevin wrapped his arms around her, laughing. He picked her up in his arms and twirled her around, then laid her on the carpet. They kissed.

Suddenly, Nikki flipped over, dumping Kevin onto his back.

Kevin felt her start to turn, but didn't give her a fight. He'd much rather it this way, anyway. He enjoyed watching her hover over him, looking triumphant. She looked so sexy with her booty poking up in the air and her voluptuous breasts dangling dangerously close to his face. He grinned. "You got me."

Nikki's eyes dropped, and she noticed the thin line of a scar on his right side, underneath his arm, close to his heart. "Oh, baby, what's this?" she asked, sliding her finger over it tenderly, wondering why she hadn't noticed it before.

Kevin wondered how he had been so careless. He never let it show. "It's nothing," he said quickly, pulling his shirt down. "It's from a scuffle I got in, in high school."

Nikki looked at him, surprised. "A fight? I never imagined *you* as the rowdy type." She joked. "What happened?"

Kevin wanted to get off the subject. "I don't remember much. I kinda blacked out."

"Blacked out?"

"Yeah," Kevin whispered softly, gazing lustfully into her eyes, hoping that it would divert her.

"What?" Nikki asked naively.

Kevin didn't respond. He was tired of talk. He pulled her body close. He needed to be inside her.

Their lips touched, and they enjoyed the sensation.

Kevin rolled Nikki gently to her back. He knew she was inexperienced, and he was prepared for it; he would take things slow. He moved towards her and kissed her tenderly. She stared into his eyes, blank. Kevin moved his hand and gently closed her eyes. They kissed deeply, escaping into sweet rapture. He rose and walked the short distance to turn off the standing lamp beside the sofa. He wanted things as comfortable as possible for her. He wondered if he should pick her up and take her to his bed, but when he looked in her eyes, he knew she wanted to proceed immediately.

She looked scrumptious; and he was ready to dine. His heart raced with anticipation as he returned to her on the floor. He reached over to the couch and propped a pillow under her, then settled his body on top of hers. It had been a long time since Kevin had "made love," but that was exactly what he wanted to do now. He kissed her, and their tongues collided. His hands caressed her body, and he touched her in areas previously confined to his dreams.

Nikki closed her eyes. She had never let anyone go this far, but with Kevin, she didn't mind. Her body was a prisoner to his touch, his hands delivering thrills that vibrated throughout her body and made her melt.

Then Nikki felt a bulge pressing firmly through his pants, against her leg. She gulped. A memory flashed through her mind — one she had tried to forget. "Wait!"

"Don't worry. I have a condom," he whispered discreetly in her ear, continuing to kiss her.

Nikki was paralyzed. She couldn't breathe.

Kevin noticed her stiffness. He looked in her eyes, but she wasn't looking at him. She was gazing at something far distant. He drew back. "You okay?"

Nikki jumped up, and Kevin's body was unceremoniously dumped to the floor. She clasped her blouse shut and looked around — searching for something only she could see.

"Nikki, baby — what's wrong?" He stood, walked towards her, reached to touch her, but she stepped away.

She touched her forehead and motioned him to stop. "I need to leave," she said desperately. She found her shoes and put them on.

Kevin kicked himself. "Nikki —" He watched as she fumbled around looking for her things. "Nikki, baby, please don't leave. I'm sorry. I just thought that — that —" he stuttered. "You know — that you wanted this."

"I just need to leave," Nikki repeated, searching for her purse.

"Nikki, please don't leave, baby. I promise I won't try. I'm sorry."

Nikki found her purse and held it against her chest. "I have to leave now."

"Nikki —" Kevin followed her as she marched towards the door. "Baby, wait."

She opened the door.

Kevin's heart accelerated. "Nikki!" he called after her, but he knew he couldn't stop her.

She walked out the door and closed it. Her feet pounded as she ran down the stairs.

Kevin formed a partial fist and raised it over his head, a feeling of guilt overtaking him. He ran after her, through the front entrance of the apartment, down the stairs, and outside, to find Nikki already in her car.

"Nikki!" he shouted from the front entrance of his condo, but his shout went unnoticed. She pulled off into the darkness.

Kevin stared into the distance in disbelief. The evening had been so wonderful. He couldn't understand what had caused everything to go wrong. He looked around to see if any of his neighbors were looking on, then he climbed back up the stairs to his unit.

CHAPTER SEVEN

F ive days later.

Kevin stared at the phone. He hadn't slept well all week. He hadn't meant for things to get out of hand the last time he saw Nikki. Though he had asked God to forgive him, he still beat himself up for not being able to control himself. What if she had wanted to do it, he wondered. Would he have been able to stop?

Why hadn't he stopped himself from buying the condoms? He had preplanned sin, and he hated himself for that. It would have been different if he had had to pause and tell her he had to make a run to the store, but no, that wasn't the way it happened. He had gone to the store days earlier, sifted through the selection of condoms carefully, and purchased them, hoping for a chance to need them.

He wondered if he should call her again. He understood why she hadn't returned his phone calls. He was supposed to be a Christian—an example for her. His actions saddened him. Maybe it was better she hadn't responded.

Fantasies about them strolling through a park and holding hands were not at the top of his list. His desire for Nikki had grown stronger and stronger. He had found it difficult, extremely difficult, to keep thoughts of her pure. His prayers seemed to fail, because every time he saw her, he was weaker.

Was he too weak to date a non-Christian? Then he thought of Laura.

He needed to talk to Nikki. Apologize and explain himself. Showing up at her doorstep may frighten her, be too pushy, and he didn't want to further damage their relationship. An email was too impersonal; besides, with one click his message could be deleted.

He needed to talk to someone. He thought about the brothers at church, but he feared that they would criticize him. "Things like that happen when you date a non-Christian." Finally, he decided to speak to his sister; she would know what to do.

He remembered her wedding reception, watching her light up and dance with Joe.

Emptiness set in. He recalled thinking that surely God would have not been so selfish to only supply a sprinkling of good women on the earth. He needed to get serious and change his ways if he wanted to find one of them. His days of casual sexual encounters had to end.

He began dialing the numbers, and he hung up. He thought for a moment. He picked up the phone again. Even though she would fuss at him, at least she was family.

"Hello?"

"What 'cha doing?" Kevin tried to sound happy.

"Kevin? I'm surprised you're not out with Nikki." Kacie looked at the clock on the wall; it was about six PM her time. "Early date?"

Kevin didn't know what to say.

"Oh," Kacie said, as if she'd figured it out. "Nikki stayed with her grandmother this weekend."

Kevin sighed. "I think we broke up."

"Broke up? Ya'll just started dating! Kevin, what did you do?"

"Why did I have to do something?"

"Because!"

"Because what?"

"You 'think' you broke up? Either you did or you didn't."

Kevin got tired of the chatter. "Kacie," he breathed. "Okay, I messed up."

Kacie went silent. Kevin thought about what to say. It was difficult talking to his sister. "The last time I saw her was on Monday, and things kind of — you know — went too far."

He heard silence.

"We kissed, and I ended up fondling her a little bit."

Kacie sighed, relieved.

"Anyway, I want to talk to her, to apologize, but she won't return my calls."

"Have you tried going to see her?"

"No." He paused. "I've been out of town all week, and she usually picks up Kayla on Friday. Showing up at her doorstep, the way things left off — I didn't think it was appropriate."

"You think she's mad at you, or doesn't want to see you again?"

Kevin shrugged. "I don't know. From a woman's perspective, what do I do, Kacie? She won't call me back."

"If you really want to talk to her, and you think she's avoiding you, try meeting her on campus. Mail her a letter—but you don't know if she'll read it."

"Exactly."

Kacie shrugged. "Try to call her again. She's got to answer the phone at some point."

A little while later, Kacie hung up the phone. She was happy her brother had confided in her. He had certainly changed a lot. When she had moved in with him and discovered the sort of life he led, she had confronted him and told him she was afraid for his soul. Unapologetically, he told him his life wasn't an "after school special," and that he had needs. Sadly, his needs involved sex, and not much in the way of affection or commitment, and there always seemed to be women, one in particular, who were willing to satisfy those needs, letting themselves be used like whores.

Weekend after weekend, his 'stray,' as she had endearingly named her, came over—and week after week, he missed worship services. He had not attempted to change, even after what she said, and that had saddened her as much as it enraged her knowing that her own brother, of all people, was participating in the degradation of women—sleeping with them, then sending them on their way.

Fed up, she threatened to move—pointing out that he was blaming every woman for Toni's sins. They had a huge argument, and Kevin told her that maybe moving back to Texas was the best thing. Kacie had been so hurt. He had no feelings for the girl, but he had chosen her over his own blood. Shortly after, she moved, but not before giving him a piece of her mind, and cursing him out. He had never spoken an unkind word to her, not in all their disputes, and for her outburst, she paid dearly. Months passed. Kevin wouldn't speak to her. Only when he found out about Joe did he begin behaving like a big brother again.

She hated that she had let so much time pass without speaking. Though at the time, two years had passed, the wounds Toni had left were just as new. Kevin had been hurting, but she failed miserably at being compassionate. This time, she planned to get it right.

Kevin lay in bed. A ray of sun penetrated his blinds, drifted across the walls, and settled on his face. Saturday morning. He used to look forward to Saturdays, but not today. After talking to his sister, the answer was still not clear. He wondered again if things were for the best this way. He thought of his own mother and father. His mom had grown up in the church, but his dad hadn't. His mother had been integral in bringing his father to Christ.

Though he had talked about the Lord in spurts, Nikki seemed to have little interest. He often wondered if she was going to church for him or Kayla, since Kayla really seemed to like it. Deep inside, he knew the real reason he hadn't minded that Nikki hadn't called. He was sinking quickly for her, and once he plummeted, it wouldn't be so easy for him to break away. The fear of getting hurt again paralyzed him.

He had finally done it. Underneath the rigidity and the 'friend-ship' masquerade, he had unveiled an absolute princess. She was fun without being silly, a characteristic that had frequently turned him off younger women. Nikki was mature and intelligent.

He admired her tenacity, that she was working to put herself through school, and that she was taking on the responsibility of her four-year-old half-sister — especially since he knew she hadn't cared much for her father. She took good care of her sister. She was loving and patient, though sometimes pushy. She wouldn't be a lazy parent, like so many.

Parent, he caught himself. *Whoa.*

He fussed at himself for having such thoughts. He couldn't let things stand the way they were. He would at least apologize to her, though she may well refuse to see him again. He would try again, and if she didn't call back, he would pay her a visit during the week.

He picked up the phone. Perhaps he could catch her early, before she and Kayla did their bi-weekly library run. He dialed the numbers anxiously.

Nikki ran to answer the phone. Anesa had rescheduled the card game earlier in the week; it was probably her calling to remind her. Only Anesa called so early on Saturday morning. "'Nesa, I—"

"Nikki?"

She could see Kayla coloring in the living room.

"I'm sorry for calling so early. Did I wake you?"

"No, no." She felt her heart race. *Darn it.* Why hadn't she let the voice mail catch it? "I'm sorry I've been so busy," she mustered. "I haven't had the chance to call you back."

Kevin knew why she hadn't called. Then, to his surprise, he said, "Would you like to go out later today?"

Nikki thought for a moment.

Kevin felt his throat turn dry. The silence was torture.

"Sure."

"Okay." Kevin breathed a sigh of relief.

"Kayla's with me."

"Okay." He looked at his watch.

Kevin walked Nikki and Kayla to the door. Kayla danced frantically as Nikki unlocked the door. She bolted inside as soon as it opened, heading straight to the bathroom. Kevin followed Nikki into the living room. He smiled when he saw her exercise machine. He remembered thinking she was trying to avoid him when she didn't show up to jog.

Nikki took her jacket off. She folded it over her arm and turned to hang it, but Kevin gently grabbed her hand. "Look, Nikki, about the other night—" He looked down and brushed the sleeve of her jacket. "I just wanted to apologize."

"Kevin, you don't have to apologize." Nikki said before he could finish. Christian or not, Kevin was a man; he had needs. She had figured it was only a matter of time before he needed those needs fulfilled.

"Yes, yes, I do." He listened for Kayla. He heard her leave the bathroom and walk into her bedroom. He motioned for Nikki to sit on the couch. "Look," he said. "I really like you."

"And I really like you, too," Nikki replied.

Kevin blushed. He took her hands, placed them in his lap, and rubbed them. Nikki seemed to relax a little, and that relaxed him. "I've had to struggle with this for a long time."

He paused. He didn't know how Nikki would react to what he was about to say. "I can't lie to you, baby, I've been in a lot of relationships, but none were what you and I have.

"Before I met you, I had decided to get my life together. I started going to church—there was a sister. She got me to come to her apartment." He looked at Nikki, and her face told him to spare her the details. "Anyway, when I showed up for service that Sunday, she acted like nothing had happened. I couldn't live my life like that anymore. There was something better out there for me. Something deeper. I think that something better is you."

Nikki blushed.

He squeezed her hand. "Look, Nikki, you're special to me, and I don't wanna mess things up between us. I shouldn't have touched you like that. I'm sorry. Will you forgive me?"

She planted a kiss on his cheek. "Yes," she whispered. Though she was impressed that he was trying to stick to his Christian morals, she wondered how long it would last.

He closed his eyes and hugged her. "You're still my baby?"

"Of course," Nikki whispered.

He kissed her, relieved he hadn't screwed things up.

Nikki rested her head on his shoulder, relieved, too. She had strong feelings for Kevin, but she didn't think she was ready for sex. She was relieved she had more time.

"I better get going." He kissed her forehead.

Nikki didn't want him to leave, but she had to help her sister undress and get her into bed.

"See you at church tomorrow?" he asked, still feeling guilty.

Nikki smiled and nodded.

"Oh." He stepped back from the door. "I've been meaning to ask you—" He stalled. "I'd like you to come home with me—for Christmas."

Nikki's face brightened, but then reality set in. "The past couple of years, I've spent Christmas at my grandma's with Kayla. I wouldn't want to be without her."

"I assumed that," he answered matter-of-factly. "I want her to come along, too."

"I can't afford—" Nikki resisted.

Kevin cut her off. "I wouldn't ask you to do something with me if I wasn't willing to foot the bill."

Though Nikki couldn't think of any more excuses, she hadn't made up her mind. "I don't know. I'll have to get back to you."

"Okay." Kevin's mood dipped. "I'll understand either way," he said, kissing her cheek. "Just think about it."

He walked through the front door, and Nikki closed it behind him, collapsing against the wood. She didn't know what to do.

"Kevin asked me to go home with him for Christmas," she said softly. She sat on her bed and propped the cordless phone on her left shoulder. She bent over and began painting her toenails.

"What? That's great!" Anesa twirled the telephone cord in her hand. "When are ya'll leaving?"

Nikki hesitated. "I don't know if I'm going."

"Why not? I thought you liked Kevin."

"I do," she exclaimed. "I just—I don't know."

Anesa was annoyed. In her mind, Nikki was making excuses. "What? Girl, the man wants you to meet his family! Meet his family." A thought popped into her head. "Does he want you to leave Kayla behind or something?"

"No. No, he actually told me to bring her."

"Well, see? What's the problem?"

Nikki hesitated. She brushed a coat of polish on her big toe. "I don't know. His family seems so different from mine. What if they don't like me? What if his mother doesn't think I'm good enough for her son?"

"Veronica, listen—the man wants you to meet his family! He really likes you. I don't think he cares about the past. And his family—if they don't like you—screw them!"

Nikki chuckled. Anesa had a way with words.

"Nic-Nic, you're a wonderful person; if they can't see that, that's their problem, because obviously, Kevin sees it. Plus, I thought you said you met his sister?"

"I did."

"Well?"

"She's nice. We got along." She finished one foot and began working on the other.

"See?"

"I guess you're right. I'm just nervous."

"He's met us. Don't you think he got nervous?"

"I suppose, but it's different."

"How so?"

"You all live here. He can meet ya'll anytime," she explained. "But when you're paying for three plane tickets, food, and lodging, it sheds a different light on the matter."

Anesa smiled. "My girl Nikki—in a real relationship."

Nikki blushed. "You know, when I told Kevin what happened during your first pregnancy, we prayed for you."

"Really?" Anesa said softly.

"Well, it was mostly him, but we did it together. He's just sweet like that."

Anesa chuckled. A tear came to her eye. "Well, thank him for me." She heard Malcolm enter. "Okay?"

"Okay."

"Don't forget."

"'Nesa?"

"Look, girl, I gotta go. Yo' cousin is here, and he looks hungry."

"Okay. Tell him I said hello."

"Okay, girl."

"Thanks, Anesa."

"You're welcome."

"Bye."

CHAPTER EIGHT

Nikki looked at the Mercedes and the Audi parked in the driveway. Kevin touched her hand. "Don't worry, baby, they'll love you. Trust me."

Nikki got out of the rental car, stretched, and let MiKayla out while Kevin unloaded the trunk. *Nice house,* she thought as she picked Kayla up and looked around blankly. It was a two-story, all-brick home in a well-to-do neighborhood. As they trailed up the driveway, she saw a curtain move, but didn't catch the face.

"Hello," Priscilla said moments later, standing in the doorway, grinning.

Nikki recognized Kevin's mother from pictures. She was dark-skinned with a slim frame—a truly gorgeous woman.

"Hi." Nikki hoped her nervousness wasn't evident.

"Mom, this is my girlfriend, Veronica. This is my mom, Priscilla."

Priscilla took Nikki's hand in hers, and they shook.

"Nice to meet you, Mrs. Maddox."

She waved her hand dismissively. "Priscilla," she corrected. She stepped back from the door to let them in. "You must be Kayla," she said before Kevin could introduce them.

Nikki set her down.

Kayla studied Priscilla cautiously.

Meanwhile, Kevin continued the introductions. "This is my grandmother, Nettie."

Nikki tried to shake hands, but Nettie swept her into a hug.

"Nice to meet you, baby."

Nikki smiled shyly.

Nettie faced Kevin. "Mmm. Not bad."

Kevin blushed. "And this is my father, Philip."

Nikki nodded her head once. His father was a big, tall man.

Philip took his hands out of his pockets and shook hers warmly. "Welcome, Veronica."

Nettie looked at Kayla. "My, you have such a cute little girl."

"She is a doll, isn't she?" Priscilla smiled at Kayla, and then turned to Philip.

"She's not my mommy. She's my sister." Kayla finally said, looking up at Nettie.

"Oh?" Nettie eyed Nikki and Kayla, confused.

"Mom," Priscilla smiled. "Why don't you go into the kitchen while I help them get settled?"

Kayla looked at Philip shyly.

Philip nodded and smiled.

Priscilla turned to Nikki and Kayla. "Let me show you where you will be sleeping." She took Nikki by the shoulder. "Kevin, you can put your stuff in the guest room." She said, motioning him down the hall.

Kayla trailed behind Nikki and Priscilla. She looked up at Philip and waved.

He waved back at her playfully.

"Come on, Kayla." Nikki said, taking her hand as they climbed up the stairs.

"Well, this is it."

Nikki looked around the room. There were two twin beds separated by a window. "Thanks." Though Kevin had told her he hadn't lived at home since he started school, she could tell that the things in the room were his.

"You can put your things in that closet."

Nikki opened the closet door. There was a Run DMC poster still hanging in it. She picked up a trophy. It was an award for the best high school wrestler for the year 1992-1993.

"Kayla, why don't you take that one—" Nikki pointed to the bed farthest from the door. "And I'll take this one." She plopped her purse down. They heard a noise and felt a vibration.

"Oh, that must be Kacie," said Priscilla. "I sent her to get some ice. Sorry about the noise. The garage is under you."

They went downstairs to the kitchen. "Hey, girl," Kacie said, hugging Nikki.

"Hey." Nikki looked over and saw Pete propped up on the counter.

"This is my stepson, Pete. Pete, this is Ms. Nikki and Kayla."

Nikki spoke to him, but his eyes were fixed on Kayla.

Philip entered the room. "So, that's what we're planning to do next with the house," he was saying.

Kevin followed behind him then spotted Nikki. Kayla was hanging onto Nikki arms and swinging around in them loosely. He smiled and winked at Nikki.

Kacie looked around. "Everyone's here. Let's eat."

"Philip, will you say grace?" Priscilla said, taking a roast from the oven. The smell was intoxicating, and Kayla's eyes brightened.

"Wait. What about TJ, Angela, and Joe?" Kevin asked.

Priscilla looked uneasy. "They'll be here later."

"And Joe won't be here until tomorrow," Kacie said, taking Pete off the counter. "He's on call until late tonight."

After they finished the dinner, they sat around the table talking for a long time. It was still early afternoon, but after a surprisingly hefty portion of Priscilla's food, Nikki felt the shadows of sleep creeping over her.

Kevin sensed her sudden fatigue and smirked. His mom's cooking always had that effect. He leaned over. "Baby, why don't you go lay down?" he instructed, more than asked.

"I'm okay," Nikki whispered back. The last thing she wanted was to offend his family. With everyone sitting around talking, getting up and leaving was just not good manners.

"Where's TJ?" asked Kacie. "I thought he would've been here by now."

"I don't know," Priscilla said, looking at Philip.

"I know why he isn't here." Nettie sat up in her seat. "That sorry nigga owes me money."

"Momma." Priscilla looked at her disapprovingly. Her eyes darted towards Nikki. *We have a guest.*

Nettie rolled her eyes. "I ain't seen that sorry grandson of mine since he came by asking me for money." She rose stoutly in her seat. "Huh. Sorry nigga promised he would fix my leaky faucet. That was last week. Ain't seen 'im since."

"Momma, don't call your own grandson *that*."

"I'll call him anything I please."

"It's your fault, Granny," Kacie cut in. "You spoiled him."

"Spoiled is one thing—deluded is another. Where does he get off running around town with that white chick, anyway?"

The table fell silent.

Kevin sat in his seat soberly. As much as he respected his grandmother, he didn't agree with her on this one. Kevin watched his father. He knew he was annoyed. Every year, his grandmother made it her personal mission to address 'state of our race' matters. This year, she had ammunition. TJ was dating a white girl.

"Why can't he get a pretty little black girl, like Nikki?" Nettie said, reaching over and squeezing Nikki's hand.

Oh, here we go. Kevin read his father's face and watched him roll his eyes.

Nikki blushed. Everyone's eyes were on her.

"Going around dating some white girl. Ugh! They ain't got no butts, no rhythm, no—"

"Where you been, Granny? *In Living Color* changed all that."

"Pff. She don't want him." She looked at them cleverly. "I know what she wants."

"Mama!" Priscilla gasped, embarrassed. Her eyes darted to Kayla and Pete.

"I tell you the truth." She leaned back in the seat. "After while, at the pace America's going, there won't be no races. That's what's wrong with black men. As soon as they can, they go and get themselves a—" she paused. Her face lit up as if she was saying something magical. "White woman. A beautiful black girl passes by—and nothing. A barely 'okay' white woman passes by, and they're almost foaming at the mouth. What's gonna happen to young, black, single women? No white man gonna want them, that's for sure."

"Granny, please. That's not true." Kacie looked at her. "You don't know how many times I get hit on by white men."

She snapped back. "Sugar, you just a white girl with a tan."

"What about the rest of us?" Priscilla challenged, as if she were pleading a case before a jury.

"It doesn't matter, anyway, because God loves us all," Kacie butted in. "Everyone on Earth came from one couple." She held up her index finger to illustrate. "One." She shrugged. "Besides, most black people living in America are mixed anyway, whether we want to admit it or not."

Nettie rolled her eyes at Priscilla, then Philip. "Not on our side of the family."

"Mama!" Priscilla snapped, fed up.

Philip's light-skinned face was red.

"Don't start." Priscilla widened her eyes. *Behave.*

Nettie smirked and rocked herself in her chair, feeling proud and accomplished. Someone in the family had to speak against her grandson's wanton, foolish behavior, and since his father wouldn't take matters into his own hands, as the matriarch, it was her God-given duty.

Philip rose. As much as he enjoyed the conversation and personal insults, he had to get busy. "Honey, I'm going to work on my lesson for tonight."

Priscilla nodded, and he walked out.

They heard loud music approaching outside. The vibrations reverberated through the walls. "Here he comes," Priscilla said. She sipped her coffee, thinking about Nikki and all the wonderful things Kevin had said about her. She admired that Nikki had a steady job to finance her way through school, maintained her own apartment, and was helping to raise her sister. She was a respectable citizen, something she wasn't sure her son could claim. Though they were approximately the same age, they were like night and day. She wished TJ were half as mature and responsible as Nikki.

"Who?" Nikki arched her eyebrow, looking at Kevin, confused.

Before he could answer, Priscilla did. "TJ. He always comes over playing that racket."

Finally, the music quieted.

Kevin flipped the curtain and peered outside. "Oh, he got it."

Everyone went to look out the window. Nikki squeezed a peek between Kacie and Nettie. *That's TJ?* Nikki was taken aback. He looked nothing like the photo she had seen at Kevin's house. He was tall and athletic looking, with dark brown skin, shoulder-length dreads, and an earring in his ear.

"I don't know why he turns down the music. Everybody in the neighborhood has heard it by the time he pulls up," Priscilla muttered.

TJ's girlfriend climbed out of the blue 1972 Chevrolet Chevelle.

Priscilla sat back down at the table.

Kevin met them at the door. "Man, you just keep growing and growing." They embraced. "But I'm still your big brother." He motioned towards Nikki. "This is my lady, Veronica." He crossed the room, wrapped his arms around her, and kissed her cheek.

"Nice to meet you," Nikki smiled warmly.

"You too," TJ smiled.

"Her little sister, MiKayla, is running around here somewhere with Pete." He turned to TJ's girlfriend. "This is Angela."

Nikki and Angela shook hands.

"By the way, nice ride, man," said Kevin.

"Thank you," TJ grinned.

Nikki heard a faint voice from the kitchen.

"Xavier, I think someone's calling you," Angela said, pointing towards the kitchen.

Xavier? Nikki thought.

Kevin saw the expression on Nikki's face. "Xavier is his real name. We just call him TJ."

They walked into the kitchen where Priscilla, Kevin's grandmother, and Kacie sat.

"I'll be back," Kevin said, leaning over and kissing Nikki on the lips.

"Okay" Nikki whispered softly, kissing him back.

Kacie leaned over to Priscilla. "Those two sure seem to do a lot of kissing."

Priscilla nodded and took another sip of coffee.

"Hey, Grandma," TJ said, walking over to Nettie. He moved to kiss her, but she turned her cheek. "Granny?" He looked at her hard. "You ain't gon' kiss me?"

She shook her head.

"So it's like that?"

"TJ?" Philip's voice rang from the other room.

"We'll catch ya'll in a few minutes," TJ said. He held the door for Angela then looked back at Nettie.

"Come see me later," Nettie finally said. "I didn't want to say nothing in front of your little girlfriend."

"What?"

"You know what," Nettie said, easing back into her chair.

He looked at her, puzzled, and then walked out the door.

Kacie turned to Nettie. "She got a big butt, Granny."

"Humph!" Her grandma tipped her head to the side.

Priscilla and Kacie giggled.

Kayla ran into the room, a look of disgust on her face. She ran up to Nikki and wrapped her arms around her waist.

Nikki picked her up and set her in her lap.

Kayla cupped her mouth and tried to whisper in Nikki's ear, but her voice carried across the room. "He keeps trying to kiss me." She frowned and wiped the side of her cheek.

Kacie overheard.

Pete ran into the kitchen with a big smile on his face and came up behind Kayla.

"Hold up! Hold up! Hold up! Hold up!" Kacie said, thrusting her hand against his chest. "Leave her alone."

Pete didn't look at her.

"Do you understand me?"

Pete stood silent.

"Pete?"

He didn't say a word. He poked his lips out. "When will my daddy be here?"

"Tomorrow." Kacie rose. "Say you're sorry."

Pete turned and marched out of the room.

"Hmmph." Nettie watched the door swing. "You know what that boy needs? A good butt-whipping."

"I know, Grandma," Kacie said, frustrated. "Trust me, I know. His mother doesn't want me to spank him."

Nettie laughed. "Humph. What's Joe's excuse? The boy is spoiled rotten."

"He's good most of the time," said Kacie, "but when he doesn't get his way, it's all over." She sighed. "How do you get Kayla to be so well-mannered?"

Nikki looked down at Kayla. She had rested her head against her chest and was sucking on her thumb, but her eyes were closed. Nikki plucked the thumb out of her mouth. Kayla nestled her head further into Nikki's chest. "She's pretty mellow. I haven't had to spank her very much at all. I think because she stays with my grandmother." She paused, purposely directing her conversation towards Kacie instead of Nettie. "She doesn't act as wild as other kids, though she certainly has her moments."

"How old is she again?"

"She's four and a half."

"She's a small four." Priscilla briefly rubbed Kayla's head.

They nodded in agreement.

"So, how is it that you and your grandmother are raising her?" asked Nettie.

"Mom," Priscilla said, exasperated.

"What happened to your mother and father?"

"I'm sorry. You'll have to excuse my mother," Priscilla interjected. "She's nosy."

"That's okay," Nikki said softly. She rocked Kayla back and forth as the child drifted off to sleep. "My—our—father passed away a couple of years ago, and *her* mother—" She paused, looking at Kayla, "is on d-r-u-g-s. My own mother passed away in a car accident when I was eight."

"So tragic." Nettie shook her head. "Kayla's mother—she's never tried to get her?"

"No," Nikki shook her head, "and after May, she won't be able to." She planted a kiss on Kayla's forehead. "Legally, she'll be mine."

"I don't understand it." Nettie sat back. "Never tried to see about her own daughter?"

Nikki shook her head. "No. And my grandma's been in the same place for at least the last twenty-two years."

Nettie perked up. "Is that how old you are?"

Priscilla waved her hand. "Baby, don't try to answer every question that woman asks you. If you do, you'll be exhausted."

"Mmm-hmm." Kacie nodded. "I know Joe was."

Nikki was feeling awkward. Kevin wasn't in the room, and all eyes were on her. She looked at Kayla. "I'm going to take her upstairs."

"Take your time, honey," Kacie said, watching.

"What?" Nettie shrugged. She knew she was being a little nosy, but she didn't care. Kevin was her grandson, and she needed to find out as much as she could about the new lady in his life.

"Come on, Kayla. Let's go upstairs." Nikki sat Kayla down, and the girl walked alongside her, sleepily holding her hand. They walked out of the kitchen when Nikki noticed Kayla's teddy was missing. "Where's Mr. Huggs?"

Kayla looked up at her. She placed her finger to her lips, as if she was thinking, and walked sleepily down the hall.

Kevin entered the living room and saw Kayla walking around the corner. "Having a good time so far?" He wrapped his arms around her and kissed her.

"Yes." Then Nikki chuckled. "Our grandmothers are a lot alike."

"I'm sorry," he said, kissing her again.

Nikki shook her head, signifying she didn't mind. Suddenly she heard a scream, laughter, and then footsteps.

Kayla bolted into the living room.

Pete ran in, close behind her.

Kayla darted behind Kevin, clutching Mr. Huggs tightly.

"Whoa!" Kevin threw his hands up, stopping his nephew dead in his tracks. "What's going on here?"

Nikki turned to Kevin. "Pete's been trying to kiss Kayla."

Kayla moved to stand beside Nikki, and Kevin knelt down in front of Pete, who was still giggling.

"Pete, she doesn't want you to kiss her."

Pete smiled. It was obvious to Kevin that what he had said hadn't sunk in, so he decided to try a different approach. "No means no, man. Listen, ten, thirteen years from now, if you try a stunt like this—do you know what will happen?"

Pete shook his head.

"You'll end up in jail."

Pete's eyes got big.

"Yeah," he continued. "Women don't like it when you come on too strong." He stiffened his chin. "That's right—ten—fifteen years from now, they'd have you locked up for sexual harassment."

Pete's eyes got even bigger, and his jaw dropped open.

He said sex! Kayla gasped and covered her mouth.

"If you don't stop, when Uncle Bennie comes over—you ever meet Uncle Bennie?"

Pete shook his head.

"He's a police officer, and if you don't stop..."

Nikki covered her face; she wanted to laugh so badly.

Kevin continued, "I'm going to tell him, and he's going to take his police cuffs and wrap them around your wrists—just like this." He tugged, demonstrating. "You don't want that, do you?"

"But I'm too young to go to jail!"

Kevin looked at him. "They're always trying to make examples of us." He paused. "You'll be the youngest convict in the world! No more girls, man. No more kisses—even if they want you to. You want a nice ride when you get big, don't you?"

Pete nodded.

"None of that. No good job, no good money—that means no nice ride and no pretty girls."

"Kevin." Nikki slapped him on the shoulder.

Kevin shrugged then continued. "At least you'll be in the *Guinness Book of World Records*." Kevin rose. "Now go play."

Pete sped off.

"And don't try to kiss her anymore."

"Kevin," Nikki grinned at him. "You ought to be ashamed of yourself. Scaring that boy like that."

Kevin shrugged.

Kayla looked at him adoringly.

"Come on, baby. It's time for your nap," Nikki said, taking Kayla by the hand.

Kayla followed obediently, but she stared at Kevin as she walked away.

Kevin watched Nikki and Kayla until they reached the top of the stairs and the door to his bedroom closed. He headed towards the kitchen and overheard the women talking.

"What kind of mother abandons her own child?" asked his grandmother.

"I don't know," replied his mother testily, "and frankly, it's none of our business. I told you not to go asking that girl a lot questions, Momma."

He smiled mischievously and walked into the kitchen. "Nikki just ran upstairs, distraught. What did you all do to my girlfriend?"

"It was Granny," Kacie tattled. "She ran the girl off—all up in the girl's personal business, asking her ten million questions."

Nettie smiled. "Nice," she said, nodding, giving her seal of approval. Priscilla smiled softly and sipped on her coffee.

"You better stick with her from now on when Granny's around. You know how she is," warned Kacie.

Nettie waved at her. "Come on over here, baby," she motioned to Kevin. "How long you been dating that girl? She sure is young."

"Only in age, Grandma," he said bending over and kissing her on the cheek. Then he turned to Kacie. "You ready?"

"Ready?" Kacie eyed him. "I know you're trying to get there before rush hour, but we can't leave for the mall right now. Nikki'll be back down any minute."

Kevin remembered the look in Nikki's eyes. "Trust me. No, she won't. She's taking a nap with her sister."

Nettie cleared her throat. "You know this girl awfully well."

"We've been dating for four months," he said, answering her unspoken question. Yes, this relationship was legit.

"I see," Nettie said playfully.

Kayla peered through the cracked door, watching silently as Philip worked on his message for the evening. She pushed through the door, walked into the office, and stood in the middle of the room. "Hello."

Philip turned around, surprised. He rested his eyeglasses on his belly. "Hey," he said. "Last I heard you were taking a nap."

Kayla shrugged nonchalantly. "I was."

Philip rose and picked her up in his arms. She felt more special to him than Pete, who they hardly ever saw. His mother was so strict—and funny when it came to letting him spend the holiday with members of her ex-husband's family. They never got to pick him up or vacation with him. Philip was already almost fifty years old, and he wondered how long it would be until they had real grandchildren.

Philip propped Kayla in his arms and showed her pictures of their family. He pointed to a picture of himself as a little boy, then to a picture of Kevin at about her age.

Kayla stared at the picture; Kevin had sported an Afro. She glanced at Philip from the corner of her eye. She had liked him instantly. She leaned in and kissed his cheek.

"Why, thank you," he said, surprised. "Aren't you sweet?"

"MiKayla?" Nikki called, interrupting them. She had seen the kiss as she came down the hall. "I'm so sorry, Mr. Maddox," she said, taking Kayla out of his arms.

"That's okay, I needed the break."

Nikki set her on the floor to walk.

"Philip, Nikki. You can call me Philip."

"Okay," she said softly and nodded.

They began walking away. She had never seen Kayla cuddle up to a complete stranger before, yet alone kiss them. Nikki was relieved it was a member of Kevin's family.

Kayla looked back and waved at Philip.

He waved back pleasantly.

CHAPTER NINE

N ikki walked down the long corridor, Kayla in tow. She made a sharp turn and peered down the hall. There was a room on the left, just as Kacie had described.

Kacie had suggested Nikki take Kayla to the age-appropriate Bible class. Normally, Nikki would have been reluctant, but as soon as she entered the building, she got a good feeling about the place. After they arrived, Kevin's parents had gone their own direction, and Kevin was tied up talking to older members who, judging from their reactions, likely hadn't seen him since he'd left Texas five years ago.

Nikki entered the classroom, hoping it was the right one. She spotted a woman hanging pictures on a bulletin board. She appeared a little older than Nikki, but not much.

Nikki tapped on the door, and the woman turned around. "Hey," she said, greeting her warmly.

"Where are Nikki and MiKayla?" Priscilla asked, walking towards Kevin and Kacie as they chatted in the hallway.

"She took MiKayla downstairs to class," Kacie answered.

Priscilla's face turned grim. She looked at Kevin. "There's something I've been meaning to tell you." She paused. "Antonia is back."

Kevin stared at her, hard. He didn't believe it.

"She's teaching Kayla's age group." Kevin's face went from brown to bright red. "I'm sorry. I wanted to tell you earlier, but—"

Kevin lowered his head and took a step back. He was fuming. "I don't want Kayla in her classroom," he whispered.

"She's changed, Kevin," she said softly.

"Priscilla?" A woman wearing a bright red dress and a mistletoe pin approached. "Can you help us for a moment?"

Priscilla sighed. "Okay." She smiled back, hiding the family crisis. "I'll be there in a sec." The woman walked away, and Priscilla turned her full attention back to Kevin and his sister.

"I'll go get them," Kacie said, grinning mischievously.

"No." Priscilla looked at her sternly. "Don't you go down there."

"Priscilla?"

"Coming!" she called, smiling at the woman. Then she turned and looked at Kevin. He knew what he had to do.

"My boyfriend's father wanted to get here early. Hope I'm not disturbing anything." Nikki smiled.

"Oh, no, honey. Come right in," said the woman, walking towards them.

"I'm Veronica," Nikki announced, then looked down. "And this is MiKayla."

"Nice to meet you," she said, shaking her hand. "I'm Antonia Tyler."

"Kayla," Nikki said as the girl wiggled out of her coat, "this is your teacher, Ms. Tyler."

The woman waved her hand. "She can just call me Toni. I'm not that old—yet," she laughed.

Nikki hung Kayla's coat on a wooden coat hanger.

Toni walked over to a file cabinet and took out a piece of paper and box of crayons. "Where are you all visiting from?"

Kayla took the sheet and began scribbling on it right away.

"Atlanta."

"Oh, the ATL?"

Nikki took her coat off.

"How long did it take you to get here?"

"A couple of hours," she answered, then frowned. "We flew in. I thought for sure I would die. It was my first flight," Nikki explained, "and it was really turbulent."

"Really?"

"Yeah."

"Did you get scared, too?" Antonia asked, looking down at Kayla.

Kayla shook her head.

"She's flown before. Plus, she was asleep the whole time. It amazed me. I couldn't sleep at all. If it wasn't for my boyfriend, I would have gone insane."

"I'm sorry. Sounds like you had a rough first flight."

"Yeah." Nikki joked.

Toni looked at Kayla. "She's so pretty. She looks just like you."

Nikki smiled. She was used to it and didn't feel the need to explain. "Thank you."

Toni looked over Nikki's shoulder. "Your tag's sticking out." She moved behind her. She tucked it in. "Are you here visiting family?"

"No. I'm here with my boyfriend."

"Oh, that's right. You told me, didn't you?" The woman smiled. She smoothed her hands over Nikki's shoulder pads as if making everything perfect. "So—"

Nikki turned to thank her, but saw Kevin coming in the room. He snatched Kayla's jacket from the coat hanger, then picked her up out of the chair.

"Who's your boyfriend?"

"Kevin?" Nikki frowned at him, confused.

"Let's go upstairs, baby." Kevin gestured with his head to Nikki as he stood in the entrance. He avoided looking at Toni.

Toni stared at Kevin as if she had seen a ghost.

Nikki walked towards him. Kacie had said taking MiKayla to the class was okay, and Kevin had always tried to get her to take Kayla to the classes at the church in Atlanta. She couldn't understand his apparent urgency to leave. She moved to take her coat, which she had draped over the back of a chair.

Kevin turned his attention to Kayla. "You want to sit upstairs with me?"

Kayla nodded her head excitedly.

Nikki followed them through the door. "It was nice meeting you," she said, looking back at Toni. Nikki was embarrassed at Kevin's behavior. He hadn't even spoken to the woman.

"Kevin," Nikki gasped. "What's the rush?"

"Nothing. I just didn't want Kayla there by herself, that's all." He jogged up the stairs, toting Kayla on his hip. "My father's speaking tonight, and she should be upstairs with the rest of the family."

The rest of the family? Nikki caught her breath, though not from the exertion of the stairs.

"Anyway, she just told me she'd rather sit with me. Isn't that right?"

Kayla nodded.

"Is that okay?" Kevin said, finally pausing at the top of the stairs.

Nikki fumbled up behind him and stopped. She was humbled. Kevin really cared about her, and he was probably trying to show them off to his friends and family. She liked that. "Okay."

"Thank you," he said, leaning over and kissing her on the cheek. "It means a lot to me."

Kacie looked at Kevin and Nikki. They sat opposite her, nestled together on the couch. "Shoot, I'm tired. How long are ya'll planning to stay up?"

"Umm." Nikki raised her head and peered at the grandfather clock across the room. "Probably another thirty minutes or so for me."

Kevin looked at Kacie, then down at Nikki.

What? She looked at him, wondering if she had missed something. Kevin kissed her on the forehead and squeezed her. She smiled up at him.

Kacie formed a quick smile as Nikki turned to face her. She stood and stretched, smiling. "Well, I guess I'll be going to bed now." She grabbed her glass and took it in the kitchen. "I'll see you two lovebirds in the morning," she said, walking past them. "Goodnight." She eyeballed Kevin, but smiled at Nikki.

"Goodnight," Kevin and Nikki said, almost simultaneously.

Nikki turned and watched Kacie walk to the top of the stairs until she disappeared into the hallway. She turned back to Kevin. "No offense, but I thought your sister was never going to leave." She smiled and kissed him.

Nikki rested her head on Kevin's chest, and he wrapped his arms around her. They sat there, quietly enjoying each other's company.

"I'm really glad you and Kayla came."

Nikki turned her face up. "I'm glad we came too." She smiled, thinking. "So do you think I started dating you because you have a nice car?"

Kevin's brow furrowed, and then he remembered what he had said to Pete earlier and grinned. "No."

Nikki lay back into in his arms, but faced him this time.

Kevin smiled at her quietly and twined his fingers with hers. "Nikki, there's something I need to tell you." He became serious.

"What is it?"

"I—" he stuttered. "I was engaged—about five years ago."

Nikki sat up.

"But it was brief."

"Engaged?" she repeated. "To whom?"

"Toni." He scratched his eyebrow with his thumbnail. "Mi-Kayla's teacher."

Nikki was speechless. "How come you never mentioned this before?" she asked, wondering what other secrets he had.

"It was a long time ago, baby."

Now she understood. She had seen Toni after services. She and Kayla were waiting in the car for Kevin when she saw her pass. She had smiled and waved because she was looking her way, but Toni never smiled back. Nikki realized that Toni's eyes weren't on her at all, but staring past her, to where Kevin stood.

Nikki squeezed Kevin's hands. Though he said it was a long time ago, judging from his actions, whatever she had done, he hadn't forgotten. "What happened?"

Kevin rubbed his hand over hers. "It's a long story."

"I have time, Kevin."

Kevin sat back on the couch and stared at the fireplace. "Basically—"

"I want to hear the whole story," Nikki interrupted.

"I met Antonia in high school. She was a friend of my sister's. We dated from my junior year through my senior year. When I went to college, she broke it off; she said I would find some college girl and forget about her.

"My senior year in college, I ran into her on campus. She told me she was living and going to school here because her tuition upstate was too high."

Kevin looked at Nikki. She was getting annoyed with the minor details.

He clutched her hand. "She told me she was pregnant." He sighed. "And I, wanting to do the right thing, asked her to marry me." He could tell Nikki hadn't fully bought the explanation. "I thought I was in love. I thought she was a good person, but—" he shook his head. "Things just collapsed. I guess my first clue should have been her reaction when I told my family we were expecting." He chuckled and rubbed the back of his neck. "I'll never forget it. We were here," he looked around the room, "for Thanksgiving dinner, and I announced her pregnancy and our impending marriage." He shrugged. "I figured it was time; she kept trying to put it off, but I figured the whole family was here, and —" He shrugged. "What better time could there be?"

"You have a child you never told me about?" Nikki's voice trembled. She wanted to cry. Her Mister Perfect was not so perfect, after all.

"No," Kevin answered, firmly squeezing her hand. "I don't." He squeezed her hand. "It was a lie." He paused. "She was never pregnant. In her mind, we were never engaged. It was all a big lie." He played with her hand, reminiscing. "I went to her apartment one day, and she told me she didn't want to get married." He smirked. "I hadn't talked to her in several days." He shook his head. "I thought she was just mad at me for telling my family, but that wasn't it.

"I later found out that she had been with her boyfriend — some guy she dated upstate — that weekend. She had never been pregnant; she had just played me the whole time to get back with him."

Nikki rubbed Kevin's back.

"My mother was furious that I was having a baby out of wedlock. Once I told her what had happened, I thought she would tell me I shouldn't have gotten myself in that situation in the first place." He had thought she would be furious, but she wasn't. She was quite calm.

"What did she say?" Nikki scooted closer.

Priscilla had stared at him, almost as she felt sorry for him, as if she had known what Toni meant to him. "She didn't say anything." He shrugged. "She was disappointed, though. A week before Toni's disappearance, she had gone out and bought all these clothes and books for her." He chuckled. "Even a couple of outfits for the baby. My mom may get angry, but she doesn't hold onto things like Kacie and me. When Kacie found out that Toni had lied, she exploded." He shook his head. "She went over there and beat her up." Kevin remembered walking into the hallway and seeing Kacie on top of Toni — "My brother loved you, stupid."

"What?" Nikki's mouth dropped open. "Sweet old Kacie beat somebody up?"

"My sister was — can be — very mean, if you get on her bad side." He paused. "Anyway, I almost did something I had promised myself I would never do. When she told me she didn't want to get married, that was one thing, but when she told me she'd had an abortion and taken my child from me—" He shook his head. "I slammed my fist into the wall next to her head."

"After we broke up, my grades started slipping. So my parents contacted Randy. He helped get me into a grad school in Atlanta."

Nikki listened carefully. She thought back to her meeting with Toni; she had measured her up subconsciously. Nikki knew that guys often dated girls with similar features, but she and Toni shared none. The girl was light-skinned, and slightly taller, and though, they were about the same weight, Nikki considered herself much more shapely. Nikki's hair was long and thick; Toni's was short to medium-length. Other than seeming to have nice mannerisms, nothing extraordinary stood out.

Suddenly, a fit of jealously came over Nikki. Average or not, Kevin loved this girl deeply—enough to ask her to be his wife, and that meant a lot. Nikki secretly wondered if she measured up to her, or to the standard that he initially had.

Kevin noticed Nikki's sudden reflection. He felt bad not letting her know about Toni sooner and wanted to assure her that it was completely in the past. He caressed her face. "But everything happens for a reason," he said, kissing her forehead. "Everything."

Nikki smiled. She fell into his arms and nestled her head into his chest. The flames from the fireplace leapt. Kevin's heart beat beneath his sweater. She felt cherished.

CHAPTER TEN

"How did you guys meet?" Angela asked, looking at Nikki and Kevin.

There was a small gathering at Kevin's parent's house on Christmas day. The family sat around in the living room talking, laughing, and drinking apple cider.

"Well," Nikki began. She sat up a little on Kevin's lap. They were on one of the chairs that had been pulled from the dining room. She was perched on his knee, and he had his arms wrapped around her waist. "I was exercising one day, at this park on Ponce De Leon, and he came running up behind me."

They started to laugh.

"He ran up behind you?" His mother frowned.

Kevin tugged at her waist playfully. "Tell the whole story."

They were captivated as she told them how she and Kevin had met at the convenience store; then Kevin had seen her jogging one day and made a special effort to greet her. "After he gave me the Chick-O-Sticks," she paused. "I couldn't say no."

"Aw," Kevin's family sighed romantically.

Joseph held up his fist and gave Kevin dap. "That was smooth, brother. Smooth."

TJ could no longer refrain himself. "What a wuss!" he shouted, laughing.

Angela elbowed him.

Kevin puffed his chest out proudly. "Hey, I got what I wanted." He squeezed Nikki. "Didn't I?"

Nikki and Kevin smiled and gave each other a peck on the lips.

Priscilla and Kacie looked at each other, corroborating their suspicions.

"So how did you two meet?" Joe asked Angela.

"Yeah," Nikki seconded.

Priscilla and Philip looked away. Kacie bowed her head.

Angela paused. "We meet at Good Fellas," she said, looking at
TJ, who had lowered his head, too.

Joe and Nikki nodded.

Priscilla broke in. "Who's up for some games?"

"What you got?" The doctor asked, trying to break the uncomfortable silence.

Nikki looked at Kevin, confused. She didn't know what Good
Fellas was, or understand the sudden quietness.

"We got board games and cards!"

"Cards!" Philip exclaimed.

"Daddy, you gonna be my partner, right?"

"Yeah, baby." Philip cleared a space to his side for Kacie.

"Oh, no!" Priscilla waved her hands. "Not you two together."

"Don't get mad because Daddy and I whipped up on you and
TJ the last time."

"That was the last time." Priscilla said firmly.

Priscilla put on some R&B Christmas music, and they sat
around the table, ate popcorn and cookies, and drank apple cider
and punch. The night began to grow long, and Nikki didn't win
many games.

Kacie slammed her cards on the table.

Philip looked at her, wide-eyed.

"You got me!" Joe said, shaking his head and laying down his
spread.

"That's right, baby!" Philip gave Kacie a high-five.

Nikki watched quietly. Even through all the trash-talk, this family sincerely loved each other.

"I hate you." Priscilla gritted her teeth at Kacie and Philip.

"Who's up for another round?" Philip slapped his hand on the
table and laughed hysterically to rub it in.

"I'll play you again," Angela smiled.

"Well, come on then." Kacie looked at Angela daringly. "We got
plen-tay of butt-whipping to go around."

Kacie and Philip whispered to each other.

"Hey, cut that out!" Kevin looked at them, leaning his head
against Nikki's leg.

"The game hasn't started yet." Kacie looked at him and rolled
her eyes, then began to deal the cards again. "You up, Nikki?"

"No. I better quit while I'm ahead," she said, stretching. She
watched Kevin, who took on another hand. She examined it as he

tried to explain how to play more effectively, but from time to time, she watched Kacie and Philip. Her mind wandered, and she thought of her own father and their relationship. Suddenly, the room was too warm, and the music made it hard to think. She popped off the couch.

Kevin's head jerked back. "Where are you going?" he mouthed.

"To check on MiKayla," Nikki mouthed back. She walked down the hall to the guest bedroom, peeped inside, and saw Nettie dozing off in the Lazy Boy and Kayla and Pete chattering back and forth in front of the TV.

"Nikki!" Kayla exclaimed, rising to hug her.

"Having a good time?"

Kayla nodded.

Pete walked up to her. "Is my dad still playing?"

"Yes, he is."

Pete moped, and then sat back down.

She looked down at her watch; it was almost nine o'clock. "You ready for bed, yet?"

Kayla shook her head.

"Okay," Nikki mumbled.

"We're going to watch *The Lion King* next!"

"Yeah!" Pete exclaimed.

"Okay," Nikki breathed, "but you can't stay up too late."

"Okay."

Nikki walked back down the hall. She wanted to be alone for a while. She opened the doors to the balcony and walked outside. The night was crisp, and she wondered if she should go back inside to get her coat, but decided against it.

She walked to the edge of the balcony and looked over. Philip had turned one of the trees in the backyard into a Christmas tree. The lights glimmered softly in the evergreen's branches. The smell of the pine brought back memories.

"What are you doing out here?" Kevin closed the doors behind him.

Nikki turned around. Her arms were folded, and she held them close to her body. "I just wanted some fresh air," she said, turning back towards the tree.

Kevin wrapped his arms around her. "You okay?" He kissed her cheek. "It's not like you to be out in the cold like this."

"I really like your family," she said quietly, still staring into the yard.

"They really like you, too," he murmured softly in her ear, starting to rock her.

"How do you know?" Nikki tried to look up at him, but her head was trapped under his chin.

He kissed her cheek. "You know what I want to do?"

"What?" Nikki smiled, turning towards him.

"Dance with you."

"What? The church boy who never takes me dancing? I thought you didn't like dancing."

"Just not the dirty kind—with all the bumping and grinding and teasing. I'd rather just have sex."

"Sex? Is that why you won't take me dancing? What does that have to do with anything?"

Kevin looked at her. "I'm a man, baby. It has a lot to do with everything, and that's why I don't go. And why I'm certainly not taking you," he grumbled. The mere thought sickened him.

"That's it? That's so childish," Nikki teased. "I always suspected you were the jealous type."

"Whatever. I do know one thing. No man's putting his paws on you 'cept me." Suddenly, he got serious. "Come on." He rocked her to the side. "Next song."

Nikki peered over his shoulder; the card game was still going on inside. "Okay." She leaned her forehead against Kevin's chin, and they stared at the Christmas tree and talked for several more minutes. She felt better and began to forget her earlier grim thoughts. "When did your grandfather pass?"

Kevin looked into the distance. "About five years ago."

"How long were they married?"

"Almost fifty years."

"That's incredible. You don't hear of people staying together that long these days. Were they happy?"

"Very." Kevin looked down at her. "They were the cutest couple." He laughed. "My grandmother fussed at him a lot, though, always telling him to watch his diet and stuff."

"You think people can stay married for a long time like that today?"

"Absolutely," Kevin answered. He looked at her for a moment. His voice became more serious. "My father and mother have been married for almost thirty years. I mean—they've had their share of problems, but they worked through them. What? You don't think so?"

"So much has changed. The world is different." She nestled her head into his chest. "I'm not saying it can't happen. But why take the risk?"

"Risk? You speak of marriage as if you were investing in short-term stock."

Nikki shrugged. "All I'm saying is that life offers no guarantees. Most people go in with all these expectations and dreams, only to find out a few years down the road that it was all in vain."

"You think being in love, getting married, and having a family is in vain?" Kevin couldn't believe his ears. "Come on, baby; you can't be that cynical."

The song on the radio changed. "Come on," he said, twirling Nikki in his arms, relieved to change the subject. "Let's dance."

"What?"

"You thought I'd forgotten?"

Nikki sulked, but smiled as she settled into Kevin's embrace. He took her in his arms, and they began to dance slowly.

Nikki listened to the music, and remembered the song. It was Charlie Brown's "Please Come Home for Christmas."

"I don't want to dance to this song."

Kevin looked at her. "Why not?"

"Because," she said, her voice dropping, "it's not very befitting."

"What do you mean?" Kevin was perplexed.

"It's bad luck."

"Why do you say that?" he asked softly.

She'd had a few flings here and there, and many infatuations, but she had never truly been in love before. "Because I could," she hedged, "possibly, see myself falling in love with you."

Kevin held her gaze. *I'm already there, baby.*

She continued, not reading his expression—maybe because she wasn't ready to know. "I wouldn't want anything to jinx it." She kissed him on the lips. "See, I'm not so cynical after all, huh?"

Kevin nodded. *However long it takes,* he told himself. He would show Nikki what it was like to be in love.

They kissed, and Kevin squeezed her tightly. He didn't want the night to end.

Priscilla walked to the balcony door and was about to open it when she noticed her son and Nikki kissing.

She was happy he had found someone. She knew that once he met the right person, his life would turn around. Though Toni had come to Phillip and her to apologize, she had never apologized to Kevin. Part of that was Priscilla's fault. Toni had given her number to Priscilla to give to Kevin, but now, seeing this pair together, she was glad she had ripped the sheet to shreds. Kevin had been so in love with Toni, she had been afraid he would forgive her and take her back.

His love for Veronica was deeper and more mature. Her prayers had been answered about him returning to the Lord; perhaps her prayers were being answered in this regard, too. She turned and walked back to the living room.

Several minutes later, Kevin and Nikki were dancing slowly to the music.

"It's cold out here!" said Kacie, interrupting their rendezvous. She closed the door behind her and walked towards them, shivering and rubbing her arms. "Ya'll can't find a place to snuggle in the heat?"

"Give us a moment, Kacie." Kevin said.

"Okay." She rubbed her hands together, blew in them, and walked back towards the house. "Momma's looking for you," she said, then closed the door behind her.

Nikki's eyes found Kevin's, and they pressed their foreheads together. "I better get back inside. Kayla's probably asleep by now."

He stared at her mouth. Their lips were inches apart and moving closer.

"Nikki," said Kayla from the door. "I'm sleepy."

Nikki instinctively pulled away from Kevin. "I thought you were going to watch *The Lion King*," she teased.

"We started. Pete fell asleep." Kayla yawned. "I'm beat."

Kevin and Nikki laughed. Kayla's eyes sank. Nikki picked her up.

"I have her." Kevin took Kayla from her arms. Kayla's head flopped to his shoulder, her arms hanging loosely around his neck. They walked into the house and headed down the hallway. Because of the interruption, Kevin didn't get a chance to do what he had planned. Knowing that they would be headed back the next day, tonight was it. "Why don't you meet me back down here in a few minutes?"

Nikki nodded her head. "Okay."

"Kevin," Priscilla called, seeing him in the hall.

Immediately, he knew something was wrong.

Priscilla sighed. "Can you take your grandmother home?"

He arched his brow. "I thought she was staying here tonight."

"I tried to talk to her. She wants to go home." She threw up her hands and walked off.

"My grandfather died this time of the year," he told Nikki, and sighed. "My grandmother tends to get depressed and want to be alone."

Nikki had been looking forward to meeting back up with him, but she nodded her head in understanding and took Kayla from him. "I'm sorry." She brushed her hand against his arm. "I guess I'll see you in the morning."

He kissed her on the lips and said goodnight. She waved at TJ, who was coming towards them, and walked towards the steps.

"Yo, man, Angie and I are about to roll out," said TJ to Kevin.

They shook hands and briefly hugged.

"All right." TJ turned to walk away.

Kevin stopped him. "So what do you think?" he said quietly, looking towards the stairwell. Nikki had put Kayla down and was walking alongside her up the stairwell.

TJ looked at them. "She's nice." He grinned and licked his lips. "Real nice."

"Hey!" Kevin said, and elbowed him in the stomach.

TJ bent over, holding his stomach, laughing. "Hey, just kidding, man." He straightened. "She's nice, man. For real."

Kevin smiled. He looked around to make sure no one was near. "I think she's the one."

"For real?" TJ asked casually.

Kevin sensed ambiguity in his brother's voice. "What?"

TJ looked towards the stairwell. The door to Nikki and Kayla's room was closing. "It's just that—you know—"

"What?"

"You know—" TJ looked at the stairwell again. "She got a kid and all."

"Kayla's her sister."

"Yeah, I know, but you know—" He shrugged. "You ready for all that?"

Maybe TJ was right. His relationship with Kayla was only so-so, and seeing her once every two weeks was one thing, but soon she would be living with Nikki, and he hadn't spent too much time with her.

TJ saw Nettie walking around the corner, her coat on, and her purse in hand. "Uh-oh. Here she comes." He looked down and scratched his head.

Kevin turned to look at Nettie.

TJ hit him in the chest. "Yo, man, I better check you later." They hugged again. "Love you, man."

"Love you, too."

TJ looked at Nettie. He puckered his lips and made kissing noises at her. "Love you, Granny."

She looked at him, waved her hand, and turned to Kevin. "I'm ready to go."

"I know, Granny. I just need to grab my jacket. Meet me at the front door."

Nettie huffed, looked at TJ and rolled her eyes, then walked away.

"When are you gonna pay Grandma back, man?"

"I am, man. I just really forgot." He looked at him. "And don't worry; I hooked her up for Christmas."

Nikki gazed around the bedroom, taking a break from her reading. She couldn't believe she had actually made this trip with Kevin. She smiled to herself as she took it all in, then she looked at Kayla, asleep in the bed across from her.

Suddenly, she heard a soft whisking noise. She looked at Kayla, but her sister was still asleep. She rose slowly off the bed and headed towards the door, where she thought she had heard the noise.

A small white sheet of paper lay on the floor.

Kevin.

She bent down and picked up the paper. She looked at Kayla again and unfolded the sheet to read it:

I really enjoyed tonight. I hope my family hasn't scared you too much. Dancing with you was magical.

PS – If you're not too sleepy, I want to show you something. Meet me downstairs. It'll only take a second.

Nikki smiled. She turned off the lamp and closed the door behind her. She walked softly across the hardwood floors, and down the stairs, trying not to disturb anyone.

It was dark, but there was enough illumination from the Christmas lights blinking outside that she could see the couch. There was a blanket on it, and a drink on the side table. Nikki walked through the kitchen, but no one was in there, either. Down the hall, she looked through the sliding doors to see if Kevin was waiting for her on the balcony, but he wasn't there.

Then, out of the darkness, Kevin grabbed her. Nikki jumped, gasping. "Shhh," he hushed her playfully. He placed his hands on her face and brought it close to his. "I want to show you something," he whispered.

"What?" she whispered back.

He led her to the bathroom and cut the light on.

The sudden glare made Nikki's eyes ache.

"I'm sorry," he said, "but stay like that." He covered her eyes with his hand.

"Okay," Nikki whispered. He moved his hand away, and she kept her eyes closed.

He draped something cold around her neck, and her skin twitched.

"Ok," he whispered into her ear.

Nikki opened her eyes. She looked at the necklace that adorned her neck then drew closer to the mirror to inspect it. Her eyes flicked over to Kevin then back to the mirror, and she smiled. "This is for me?" she asked. The jewels glimmered in the soft light.

"Yes," Kevin grinned, pleased at her delighted expression.

Nikki traced the contours of the pendant. It was Kevin's birthstone, cut into a heart shape, and bordered with diamonds. She was speechless. "This is so pretty. Thank you."

"You're welcome." He kissed her softly. "Wait, there's more."

"More?" Nikki asked, puzzled.

He dug into his pocket and handed her a key.

She looked at it and turned it over a few times. "What is this? The key to your heart?" she joked.

"Something like that." He brushed her cheek with his finger then kissed her. "It's the key to my place. I want you to know that we can share things." He lifted his finger and traced the necklace around her neck. "Hopefully this is just the beginning of many things that we'll share."

Nikki blushed. The way his hand caressed her clavicle, she had a feeling he was talking about more than his condo.

Kevin bent over and kissed her gently. "I don't want any more secrets between us. Okay?" He pressed his forehead against Nikki's. "Whenever you think you feel—" He paused, wrinkling his forehead for emphasis, "even a slight headache coming on—I wanna know."

Nikki smiled.

"When you drive down the road and experience déjà vu, I wanna know. When you go to rub your eye, and an eyelash falls in the sink—I want to know.

Nikki stared at him. He claimed he was no good at writing it, but she thought he was pretty poetic.

"I wanna know everything there is to know about you, girl, and then some."

Nikki braced herself, swept away. It was the sweetest thing anyone had ever said to her. She fell into his arms, and they kissed passionately.

"I can't believe how fast the time has gone." Kacie smiled brightly as they stood in the foyer saying their goodbyes. The thought of the family parting again saddened her.

"I can't, either. It feels like we just got here yesterday," Nikki agreed. She looked at Kayla, who stared back at her emotionlessly.

Priscilla looked at Kayla. Her head was down, and she seemed sad. "I'm sorry Philip wasn't here to tell you goodbye," she said, eyeing her. "He had an early meeting with a client this morning, but I'll make sure he calls Kevin when he gets a break."

Kayla perked up hearing Philip's name.

Nikki draped Kayla's black and pink zip-up jacket over her shoulders, and Kayla pulled her arms through the sleeves.

"Oh, I almost forgot!" Priscilla exclaimed. She turned towards the kitchen, motioning for Kevin to follow.

"So," Kacie grinned. "You ready for the flight back?"

Priscilla headed towards the fridge. She opened it and sifted through the shelves for a moment.

Kevin swallowed hard, anticipating what his mother might say.

"Here it is." She plopped the zucchini loaf into his hand, and turned to face him.

"Thanks," he said. "Nikki loves it."

There was a long moment of silence.

Finally, she motioned him to come to her, and they embraced. She squeezed him and looked in his eyes. Her son was in love. It was very sweet. "I guess there goes any chance of you moving back home?"

Kevin dropped his head, blushing. It was pointless trying to hide anything from her. She could read him like a book.

Priscilla knew she was right on.

He was a grown man, but she still felt the need to shelter him. Seeing how crushed he was after things fell apart with Toni had taken a toll on her, too; she didn't want to see him hurt again. Though she felt Nikki was quite mature, it didn't make up for the fact that she was very young.

Priscilla had Kevin when she was only twenty-two years old, and had gotten married the same year. But that had been the norm, and things were different then. People nowadays got married in their late twenties and early thirties, and she sensed that Nikki wasn't completely ready to settle down.

She patted him on the hand. "Just take your time, okay?"

Kevin nodded.

Nikki hugged Kacie. From the foyer, she saw Kevin and his mother in the kitchen. His back was turned towards her. She saw him lean over and kiss his mother affectionately on the cheek.

"Kevin," Kacie called. "Nikki and Kayla are about to leave you."

Kevin walked towards Nikki. He seemed quieter than usual. He handed her the zucchini loaf.

"Thanks, Priscilla. It's delicious."

"You're welcome." They embraced.

When Nikki pulled back, she caught a look in Priscilla's eyes that she hadn't noticed before and wondered what they had discussed.

CHAPTER ELEVEN

I t had been a long day, and all Kevin wanted to do was talk to Nikki for a bit, and then turn in. He had tried to call her at home, but hadn't gotten an answer. He finally concluded that she must have stayed late at the library studying again. He hated that. Downtown Atlanta was not the safest place for a young woman to be alone late at night.

He wished she had a cell phone, but Nikki scoffed whenever he mentioned getting one for her, saying she didn't need one and hated being tracked. He wish he could convince her that he wasn't trying to track her—she was his woman, and he wanted to make sure she was safe. Though exhausted, his nerves wouldn't allow him to rest not knowing if she had made it home for the night. He would call again once he arrived home and if he didn't reach her by then he would be hitting the campus.

He entered his condo, and immediately noticed the dull light coming from his bedroom. His heart relaxed. He stood at the doorway and saw that Nikki had fallen asleep under the covers. Her books and papers were scattered all over the bed, and though the TV was on, the volume had been turned so low it was barely audible. He smiled, wondering how long she had been there. He wanted to make his home hers, as much as he could. He quietly closed the door, went into the living room, and lay on the sofa.

Nikki awakened, confused. She couldn't remember when she had drifted off. She wondered if Kevin had gotten there yet. She hadn't heard him come in. She looked at the clock. *Eleven o'clock?* She moved into the living room and saw Kevin asleep on the couch. She moved closer, studying his face, then sat down beside him. "Kevin," she whispered, shaking him. He didn't budge. "Kevin," she said, shaking him harder. Finally, his eyes opened. He smiled when he saw her face. "I didn't mean to displace you."

"That's okay." He began to rise.

Nikki pushed on his chest to stop him. "You don't have to get up."

He rose a little and stretched. "I'm okay, baby. You didn't come out here to tell me you were leaving, did you? You haven't been here long enough for your scent to get embedded in the sheets yet."

Nikki blushed.

"Why don't you go lay back down? I'll be fine here."

"I didn't plan to stay this long. Besides, I want you to get some sleep in your bed."

"What? You can have my bed. Stay the night."

"Okay," Nikki said, finally giving in. She watched Kevin lay back down; he seemed appeased now that she had told him she would stay. She leaned back on her elbow. "I like being here with you. I feel safe here."

"Safe?" He rose off the shoulder a little. "You should. I'm not going to let anything happen to you."

"There's something I wanted to talk to you about." She hesitated. "Remember the other night, when we were doing that book?"

Kevin smiled. "*365 Questions for Couples*?"

She grinned quickly. "I still can't believe you have never been interested in a three-some. Even if it weren't a *sin*." She used her fingers to imply sarcastic quote marks.

He nodded and smiled. "I told you; I'm a one-woman man, and that would be too distracting."

"You say it like you've done it."

He lowered his eyes and sat up a bit more. "What's really on your mind, baby?" he asked softly.

Nikki looked at him shyly. Her fingers were suddenly fascinating, and she couldn't stop playing with them.

"Nikki?" Kevin lifted her chin.

"Yeah," she finally answered. "Remember the question you asked me?"

"Which one?"

"If I had ever been in a hospital before?"

"Yeah. You said you had been—with your grandmother." He shrugged. "Most people have."

Nikki lowered her head.

"Nikki?" Kevin gently raised her chin again.

"I've been in the hospital," she said softly. "Not visiting. As a patient." She paused. "When I was fifteen, I tried to commit suicide."

Kevin was speechless. He looked at Nikki, but her eyes eluded his, and he could tell she was uncomfortable. "Why?" he asked softly.

She shrugged. "I didn't know what else to do at the time."

"You didn't know what else to do about what?"

"It's a long story. Forget it."

Kevin looked into her face; it was contorted with shame. He wrapped his arms around her and held her close. He wasn't letting her get off that easily. "I have time." He put his hand on her shoulder and rubbed gently. "Nikki, baby, I can't be there for you if you don't open up."

"Okay." She pulled away and took a deep breath. She swallowed. "Kevin, I know you think I'm a virgin."

Kevin frowned. This was going in a direction he hadn't expected.

"I'm not."

Kevin's heart relaxed. "Baby, that doesn't matter," he tried assuring her, but Nikki lifted her hand to silence him.

"Please. Let me finish." Her hands traced and retraced the pattern in the fabric of Kevin's sofa. "My father started molesting me when I was seven."

"What?" he asked in disbelief.

"My father mo—"

"I heard you. I just can't believe it," Kevin said, shaking his head. He didn't understand how people could sexually abuse children, especially their own.

"I'm sorry. I wanted to tell you before, but I've never told anyone. I thought you might, you know, look at me funny or think differently about me."

Kevin extended his hand and pulled her body close. "Nikki, I'm your man. I'd never look at you funny for something like that."

"My mother died several years ago. I think I was about eight. My dad remarried a few months after her death. I remember him promising my aunt that he would stay in contact with her and let me spend summers with her and Malcolm, but after the funeral—I never saw them.

"He married Jackie. The first couple of years were good, but by the time I was nine, there was constant friction between them. My father was always traveling, and even when he *was* in town, he was never at home. "

"Was she nice to you?"

"Jackie? Yeah. Jackie cared for me as if I were her own. I don't know why. After a while, he didn't go to their bedroom anymore, but straight to the couch. I would hear him come in—doors slamming, loud exchanges—he'd finally just sit on the couch and blast the TV. One night, he came into my room. I was on the bed, crying. He sat next to me and said, 'It's okay. Sometimes grown people talk this way to each other.'"

Nikki paused and hung her head. "That's when it happened," she whispered. "The second time."

"What do you mean?" Kevin asked. His heart pained for her.

"There had been a lapse since the first time it happened, years earlier; I told myself I had had a bad dream. The first time he did it, my mom was still alive. He picked me up for the weekend... But I never told my mother; I didn't know how. I remember coming home crying, and she must have thought I was just upset about being with him, because I distinctly remember her telling me to give him a chance. She had no idea what had happened." She felt tears coming on, but held them back. "He didn't do it all the time. Just occasionally." She laughed at the way it sounded in her own ears. "But as I got older, it happened more and more, until I couldn't stand it any longer."

There was a long silence. Kevin didn't know how to respond. Finally, he wrapped his arms around her. "I'm sorry, baby. I'm sorry you had to go through that." He paused. "You ever considered counseling?"

"Counseling?" She lifted her head. "It's behind me now. I'm fine."

"Nikki, you just don't get over something like this. I don't think it would hurt you to see someone. You were a little girl. Your father had no right to do that to you. Something like this could affect you the rest of your life."

"I—" Nikki resisted.

Kevin lifted her chin and gazed into her eyes. "I'll go with you."

"Ms. Jones."

The receptionist stood in the doorway. She turned and looked at Kevin. His hand rode gently up and down her backside. Finally, she stood, and he stood with her. She looked around the empty waiting area nervously, wishing she could walk back out the door, but it was far too late now.

"Right this way." The woman gestured down the hall.

Nikki's head spun. Though she had told Kevin about her past, she didn't think she was ready for him to hear every detail. She stopped in the doorway and turned towards him. She shook her head. "I think this is something I need to do alone right now," she said apologetically. "I'm sorry."

Kevin smiled warmly. "That's okay. I'll be here waiting for you. Okay?"

"Okay," she nodded.

He bent over and kissed her forehead.

Nikki and the receptionist started down the hall. Kevin watched as the door closed behind them, then walked to the corner and eased back into the seat.

Kevin closed the passenger door, popped in on his side, and started the ignition. He peered at Nikki, who stared out of her window quietly. He didn't know what they had discussed, but it had taken a physical toll on her. Her eyes were darker than he had ever known, and she was solemn and mournful.

Kevin's grip tightened on the stirring wheel. His beautiful, bright girlfriend had been zombified at his suggestion. Anxiety overtook him, and he had to break the silence. "You hungry?" he asked softly.

Nikki nodded her head, but never turned around.

"If you ever want to talk about it, I'm here," he said, in the strongest voice he could muster. Seeing Nikki like this was tearing him apart.

"I know," Nikki whispered. She stared out the window at the brick homes that lined the street. As she passed each one, she marveled at how similar, yet distinctive, each was. The neighborhood looked ordinary, like a typical American street, and from the outside, it looked like the people inside lived happy, prosperous lives.

Then she found herself staring through the windows of each house they passed, hoping to get a glimpse of the people within. She knew that the outside was not necessarily a reflection of the inside.

It was all too familiar. For years, she had thought that segment of life was behind her. The truth was that it wasn't. Every facet of her new life reflected the hurt and pain of the old.

Finally, she could hold back the tears no longer. She felt her shoulders give, and the tears rushed down her face.

"Nikki?" Kevin looked at her. Her shoulders were slumped, and her hands hid her face. He spotted the parking lot of an empty store and immediately pulled into it. He turned the ignition off. "Baby," he whispered, reaching for her. He lifted her chin to face her, and her eyes were full of tears.

She shook her head, not wanting to remember some of the things she told the psychologist.

He pulled her towards him and held her tightly. "It's gonna be okay."

Nikki hugged him back intensely, partly because she didn't want him to see her cry, but also because it felt so good. For years, she had carried the burden alone. Now, she had Kevin. She no longer had to carry it by herself. Finally, she pulled back and looked at him.

His big brown eyes stared back into hers, full of concern and compassion.

She breathed deeply as he stroked her face. Though she had told him about the molestation and suicide attempt, she hadn't told him the worst of it. She closed her eyes, feeling the soft caress of Kevin's fingers. "There's something else I need to tell you."

"I'm listening," he said.

"I never really planned to commit suicide." She looked out the window.

"Of course. No one really plans suicide."

"No," Nikki sniffled. "That's not what I mean. That day, I came home from school. My father's car was parked in the driveway, and I knew something was up. He never came home that early. As I walked towards the house, I heard him and Jackie arguing. She had found out he was cheating on her, and she wanted a divorce, but she wanted to take me with her." Nikki laughed, remembering. "I couldn't believe she had asked such a thing." She nodded, still amazed. "I was not even her daughter, but she cared for me more than my own father."

She shook her head. "Of course, my father told her she was crazy. I was his daughter, and he would never let her take me." Nikki paused for a long time, staring out the window. "So I decided to kill him." She took a deep breath and closed her eyes.

Kevin's hands got sweaty, and he felt awkward, but he continued listening.

"That night, while my father slept, I walked into the living room. I stood over him with a knife in my hand." She shook her head. "I stood over him for God knows how long—but I couldn't do it." She sobbed. "I just couldn't do it."

Kevin stroked the back of her neck.

"So, instead, I went to the bathroom, got a bottle of Jackie's sleeping pills, and swallowed them all. Then I went back to my room, locked the door, got under the covers, and waited." She hugged herself, remembering. "And for the first time in a long time, I *knew* I was safe."

There was a long silence. Finally, Kevin squeezed her hand.

"I can't go back," Nikki blurted, shaking her head. "Kayla can't see me like this." She shook her head in despair. "She can't ever know."

"It's going to be okay, baby," Kevin said, embracing her. Relief swept over him. He was beginning to think she was about to have a nervous breakdown, so her decision not to go back was music to his ears. He kissed her and rocked her in his arms.

Kevin tucked Nikki in bed. The three-hour session had taken a toll on her, physically and mentally, and he wanted her to rest, but just as he was about to walk out of the bedroom, Nikki called him.

"Are you leaving?" she asked rising.

"I don't have to," he whispered. "If you need me, I'll stay."

"Please," she said, hoping to convince him. "For the night."

"Okay." Kevin nodded, glad she had asked. Recalling the past had been a traumatic experience for her, and he really didn't want to leave her alone.

"Okay," Nikki whispered, easing back under the covers. She watched until Kevin cut the light to her bedroom and cracked the door, then rolled to her side and closed her eyes.

Nikki slept for a couple of hours, but now found herself tossing and turning relentlessly. Something in her subconscious was bothering her, and she hadn't quite sorted out what it was. She finally gave up the notion of sleeping and sat up. She could hear the TV in the living room.

The TV's glare illuminated her path as she walked towards the living room. She found Kevin asleep on the couch, just as he said he would be.

She found the remote control and turned the television off. She rubbed her shoulders. January was the coldest month of the season, and on several consecutive days, the temperature had dropped below freezing. Since she never made a habit of falling asleep on the sofa near bedtime, she hadn't realized how drafty it could get in the front room. She went to the thermometer and turned it up, then went to the linen closet, pulled out a blanket, walked back to the sofa, and draped it over Kevin.

She sat on the edge of the sofa and watched as he slept. A sense of unease had settled in her. She knew morning would come, and Kevin would eventually have to leave. She only hoped not for good…

"Kevin," she whispered. His face twitched slightly; otherwise, he didn't budge.

She took her hand, pressed it under his shirt, and felt his belly. Soft, curly hair crinkled under her hand as she shook him.

"Nikki," he said groggily, opening his eyes. "What's wrong?"

"I wanted to ask you something." Her eyes shifted.

Kevin hoisted himself up.

She looked at him shyly. "It's about what I told you earlier."

He pulled his legs against his chest and wrapped his arms around them, giving her his full attention.

"Do you think—" She paused. "Do you think I'm crazy because I almost killed my father?"

"Come here, baby," Kevin said, extending his hands.

Nikki scooted towards him and laid her head on his shoulder.

"I don't think you're crazy, baby." He kissed her forehead gently. "Not at all." He smirked. "Of course, I know not to piss you off, now."

Nikki giggled, and her lips curled.

He kissed her. "That's what I've been waiting to see all day."

Silence grasped the room again, and Kevin knew something was still bothering her. "Was that what you wanted to say?"

Nikki had never dreamt she could get a good man, but Kevin's persistence had proven her wrong—or so she hoped. "If you want to stop seeing me—" She faltered. "I'll understand."

Kevin frowned, and he shook his head, thinking he had missed something. "And why would I want to stop seeing you?"

"I feel like the 'Bag Lady.'" Nikki answered, referring to one of Erykah Badu's hits.

"No." Kevin shook his head. "Far from it. Nikki, you're very special to me. I care a lot about you. And nothing you've said has changed my opinion of you." He still wasn't ready to tell her, but he lifted her chin and let his eyes speak for him. *I love you.*

"Thank you," Nikki whispered. Then she noticed a troubled look on Kevin's face. "What?"

Kevin scratched his head a little, wondering how to phrase his next question.

Nikki's heart jumped. "Just say it, Kevin."

"Did—" he started, "Did Jackie know about any of it?"

Her heart relaxed. "She pieced it together once I went to the hospital. She was planning to kick him out, but by then..." Her voice drifted.

Kevin lay back down on the sofa. He reached out his hand and drew Nikki to him. She lay on top of him and nestled her head into his chest. Kevin fluffed the blanket and wrapped it around her. Finally, they drifted off to sleep together, each enjoying the heat of the other's body and relishing the protection of each other's arms.

CHAPTER TWELVE

N ikki rose from Kevin's arms. "Come on; it's your bedtime," she said to Kayla, who had fallen asleep on her side. They had spent Friday evening at home with popcorn and movies.

Kayla rose sluggishly.

Nikki stood. "I'll be right back."

"Okay," Kevin grinned, taking in her sexy smile. He eased back into the couch. He watched until Nikki and Kayla disappeared into Kayla's bedroom.

After dressing Kayla in her nightclothes, Nikki tucked her in bed. "No story for you tonight, kiddo," she announced, looking at the heaviness in her baby sister's eyes.

Kevin heard them down the hall.

"Night-night," Nikki, said leaning over and kissing her forehead.

"Goodnight," Kayla whispered, covering herself more securely in the comforter.

Nikki reached over and cut off the lamp on her nightstand. A night-light switched on automatically. Nikki walked down the hallway. A few moments alone with Kevin were just what she needed to top off the night.

She set down on the couch and snuggled her chin next to his.

Kevin flipped through a few channels, then he couldn't resist any longer. He scooted up a little, breaking Nikki's embrace and looked down at her.

"What?" Nikki asked puzzled.

Nikki turned the light on in Kayla's room. Kayla squinted and held her arm over her eyes. Kevin walked into the room. He turned her lamp on, and Nikki cut the main light off. Kevin hunched down beside MiKayla. "I want you to get up for a second, sunshine."

Kayla looked at him. "But I just got in."

"I know, I know." He pulled back the covers and lifted her out the bed. He kneeled to the side of her bed and motioned for her to do the same.

"We're going to pray." Kevin clasped his hands together. "You know what that means, right?"

MiKayla nodded her head excitedly. She put her hands together, mimicking him.

Nikki looked at them and smiled. The two of them were a sight. Kevin was so good with MiKayla.

"Okay. You go first, and then I'll go."

MiKayla was quiet for a moment, and then she closed her eyes tightly. "Thank you, God, for this beautiful day. Thank you for Nikki, my grandma, and Kevin." She grinned and looked at Kevin.

"Amen?" Kevin asked.

"Oh," she smiled. She closed her eyes again. "Amen."

"Okay, your turn," she whispered to Kevin, keeping her eyes shut.

Kevin closed his eyes. "Thank you, God, for—" he paused, "MiKayla, and the heart that she has to seek and understand you."

MiKayla smiled.

"Thank you for Nikki, my beautiful girlfriend, who keeps a smile on my face every moment of the day. I pray that you will bless her life, because she's been a tremendous blessing in mine. Thank you, Father, for my family. I pray for the elders and leadership of the church and the church—that your kingdom will continue to grow." He paused. "Amen." He opened his eyes and looked at MiKayla.

"What are elders?"

"They are the men who lead the church."

"Oh." A light bulb went off in MiKayla's head. "Like your daddy?"

He picked her up and put her back into the bed. "Actually, my father's not an elder."

"He's not?"

"No. He's a minister—an evangelism minister." He tucked the covers back over her. "That means he spreads the good news."

"Like a reporter? Like Monica Kaufman?"

"Mmm. Not quite. She gives good and bad news. But my father just tells the good news—about Jesus."

"Jesus?"

"Yes."

MiKayla looked at him for a moment. "Oh, okay."

"Goodnight, sunshine. I want you to do that every night. Okay?"

"Okay," Kayla nodded excitedly.

He kissed her forehead, reached for the lamp on her nightstand, and turned out the light.

Nikki moved away from the doorway. Kevin walked out, and she cracked the door. "You were so cute together."

He took her hand and kissed it.

As they were walking down the hall, Nikki thought about what Kevin said. He had said she was a "blessing," and she remembered, quite vividly, from going to service with him that a blessing was a gift that God specifically designed for a person. He orchestrated its delivery, to enhance another's life.

A few people in her life had told her they loved her. Some people had told her she was special, and sometimes complete strangers told her she had a good heart and should stay "blessed." But no one had ever just flat out told her that she *was* a blessing. That was different. "Did you mean what you said back there?" she asked, stopping in the middle of the hallway.

"What?"

"You know —" she half stuttered, feeling uneasy saying it. "The part about me being a 'blessing'?"

Kevin looked at her. Here she was, almost a quarter of a century old, and no one had ever said those words to her. "I wouldn't joke about something like that, baby."

She seemed surprised.

"You want me to tuck you in and pray with you, too?" he asked mischievously.

Nikki waved her hand and stepped into the kitchen.

"What's wrong?" Kevin followed behind her.

Nikki put her glass under the faucet and cut the filter on, then ran the water. "I don't see how you get all into that."

"What do mean?"

Nikki shrugged. She rested her back against the kitchen counter. "I believe in God, but I've never had faith like you."

Kevin burst out laughing.

"What's so funny?" Nikki asked.

"I'm sorry — I guess it's not funny. I just never imagined anyone categorizing me like that."

"Why not?" Nikki sat down at the table.

"Well you know about my past, Nikki."

"Oh, yeah—your playa' years," Nikki mumbled.

"No," he corrected. "I was never a player. There was just always this understanding."

Understanding, Nikki frowned looking at him. "Maybe for you," she said, imagining all the hearts he must have broken. She couldn't understand how people could do something so intimate and not have any feelings for the person.

Kevin continued. "Anyway, I'm surprised my parents never disowned me." He smiled. "Thanks, though; I'm trying."

Nikki laid her hand on his shoulder and patted it. "I'd say you're doing more than trying."

"What about you, Nikki? How do you see yourself? You know—your relationship with God?"

Nikki shook her head and took a sip of water.

Though she had given him the I-don't-want-to-go-there look, he had to bring the topic up some way. He thought about some of the things she had said before. He put his hand over hers. "I've been mad at God before."

Nikki took another sip and set her glass down in front of her. Though she didn't know much by way of religion, Kevin's alluding that she held anger towards God seemed sacrilegious, and made her feel very uneasy. "I'm not mad. I've felt abandoned at times, but anger—"

"Maybe you should come with me sometimes on Sunday nights?"

Nikki frowned. "Nah, that's all right. Besides, a lot of times, I have to drop MiKayla off on Sunday nights, and—"

"There are churches over here, too," he interrupted.

"Baby, I'm just not like you, okay?" Nikki blurted.

Kevin backed off. "I'm sorry. I wasn't trying to pressure you. It was just a suggestion."

They retreated to the couch. Nikki sank her head into Kevin's chest. She moaned with delight as his fingers gently pianoed the rigid spots on her neck.

"What are you thinking about?" Kevin looked down at Nikki.

"Jackie." She boosted herself up more and laid against his side. "Sometimes I wonder if she stayed married to my father for me. I remember my prom. This senior, Mike, asked me to go out with him. Jackie and I went and picked out a dress. It wasn't hard to find; I already had in mind what I wanted to wear, so when I saw it, I knew." She sighed. "Then my father found out, and he told me I couldn't go. I was so mad. It was one thing I really wanted to do, and there my father was, telling me no." She smiled. "I don't know how, but she convinced him."

"Have you ever considered getting in contact with her?"

"Yeah, but—" Nikki shrugged the question off.

"Yeah, but what?"

"I guess," she hesitated, thinking heavily. "I guess, deep down inside, a part of me feels like—like I'd be betraying my mother."

"Why do you think you'd be betraying your mother?"

"I don't know. I guess it's silly."

Kevin held her close, teasing her hair with his fingers. "You don't have to be blood to be family."

She looked at him, puzzled. He wasn't making sense.

"Family is more than blood. It's common beliefs, values. Family is people who know who you truly are and love you anyway. That's what family's about, baby. You shouldn't shut people out of your life just because they aren't blood. Look at you and Kayla. Even though she's not your whole sister, do you love her any less?"

"Of course not," Nikki quickly answered, reflecting on what he said.

"I think you should contact her."

"Contact her?" Nikki laughed. "She doesn't want to talk to me. Not after what I said."

"Didn't she give your grandmother her number to give to you?"

"Yeah, but—" She shrugged. She couldn't explain why she didn't believe it. She had thought Jackie hated her after the way she left, not calling for so long, and being cold when she finally did.

Then there was Kayla. Though she knew Jackie wasn't a vindictive woman, the thought of those two together didn't set well with her. She was sure Jackie would have had to meet her when she stopped by her grandmother's house, and if they were to ever meet, she would have to bring her baby sister up. It just seemed too weird.

Her head was spinning. Exhausted, she sank into Kevin's stomach for relief. She closed her eyes as his hands gently stroked her back.

Several minutes of silence elapsed, but Nikki didn't mind. When they first started dating, there had been an unspoken pressure to fill every second with conversation, but now she didn't feel the need. Just being in Kevin's presence calmed her, and she wouldn't trade snuggling next to his warm, hard body for anything.

She was becoming dependent on him—like the air that she breathed. She thought back to the conversation they'd had before. "Kevin." Her voice broke the silence.

"What is it, baby?" His voice was soft and tender.

"I was just thinking about what you told me before—about your past—the women." She looked at him. "I have a hard time imagining you being so cold."

Kevin chuckled.

"You'll never be cold like that with me, will you?"

Kevin saw the apprehension in Nikki's eyes. "No, baby."

CHAPTER THIRTEEN

"Tell me the last sentence you read."

Nikki smiled. Though her eyes had been covered, she knew that voice. It was sensuous and low, soothing. "Kevin!" she shouted. She swung around, and Kevin's fingers fell from her eyes. She jumped from her seat and rushed into his arms.

Kevin's heart warmed. The bright, cheery smile on Nikki's face was just what he needed. He squeezed her tightly and rocked her in his arms. He loved the feel of her. Whenever he went away, he craved the moment they were together again. He hoped today would be the end of that.

Nikki pulled back to look at him.

"I'm surprised you haven't asked what I'm doing here."

"Right now, I could care less." They kissed lightly. Nikki laid her head on his collarbone. "Mmm, baby, I missed you. So much."

Kevin looked around the library. It was crowded and noisy. Though he had given her the key to his home, it was here in the library that he could find her when he wasn't there. He didn't understand it. "Baby, why don't you just go to my place and study?"

She looked into his eyes. "I hate being there when you're not. It makes me miss you more."

He reached over, grabbed Nikki's backpack, and draped it over his shoulder. Then he grabbed the textbook she had been reading and closed it, tucking it away under his right arm. "Come on," he said, taking Nikki's hand.

Nikki loved it when he showed up and waltzed her away. It made her feel special. She grabbed her purse, and they left. "Kayla told me you called," she said as they walked towards the parking lot.

Kevin remembered their conversation. "Yeah. Since I wasn't able to see her last weekend, I didn't want her to forget about me."

"She won't." Nikki swung his hand playfully. "She adores you."

Kevin blushed. He opened the car door for Nikki then closed it. He took a deep breath. He had been rehearsing what to say and playing out in his mind how things would go. He opened the driver's side, placed her things in the back seat, and sat beside her. "Baby, I came back early because I have a job interview. Tomorrow."

"An interview?" Nikki's voice rang high. Her heart skipped a beat. She remembered all the times he had told her he could easily find a job back home. The only reason he hadn't moved before was that he wanted to build more equity in his condo.

Kevin didn't want to tell her just yet that she had been his sole motivation, or that he had been toiling over the decision for well over a month.

"I didn't even know you were looking." She knew how much he wanted to be back with his family — but what about her? "I knew you didn't like your current job, but — with the war and the economy, I thought you said trying to get another one right now was too risky."

Kevin tilted his head. He remembered, too, but now things were different. "Well—" He ran his finger down her face. "This position has come up, and I thought it over. The man said all I have to do is show up tomorrow, fill out the paperwork, and the job is mine. It'll give me an opportunity to work more with my degree." He shrugged. "The benefits and holidays are excellent—"

Nikki turned her head and stared out the window, tuning Kevin's words out. *So this was why he had come back so early — to break things off.* She would have never made a decision to leave without consulting him. How could he make a decision like that without even thinking of her? She wanted to cry.

"And working with Randy—"

She heard him. *Randy?* Her heart lifted. Randy was local.

"Yeah," Kevin said, low.

He reached over and touched her hand, pulled it up to his lips, and kissed it. He had saved the best for last. "Plus, it'll give us a chance to spend more time together. That is—if you want." He thought of her classes. "If we can."

Suddenly, she understood. Kevin looked up to Randy. She knew he felt a sense of obligation since he had helped him get into grad school and settled in when he moved, but he had still taken the time to think of her and of how the new job would affect their relationship. She was flattered.

She was relieved he had brought up the subject, because she had been too afraid. Though they often spent all weekend together, it was still just the weekend, and Nikki felt herself needing to see him more. "I'd like that," Nikki said, gazing into his eyes. She scooted even closer and pressed her lips against Kevin's.

Wow, Kevin thought as he pulled away, dazed.

Shivers went through her body. She ran her fingers alongside his face. "What?"

Kevin stared at her. Times like this, he wanted to make love to her so badly.

"Kevin, what is it?" He looked so serious it scared her.

He ran his thumb over her lips. They were soft and moist. Finally, he shook his head. He closed his eyes, tracing his hand along the length of her arm until he reached her hand against his face. He turned it towards his mouth and kissed her palm, then bent and kissed her once more on the lips. It was true love. One day, their time would come.

He turned the ignition on his Beamer. They buckled up and pulled off.

●●●

Kevin bowed. His instructor bowed, too. Nikki smiled, watching them. They walked off the mat towards her. Kevin looked adorable in his white karate suite.

The instructor huffed. "See you kept in shape," he said, wiping sweat from his face.

"I tried," Kevin said, wiping sweat from his face, too.

"So I'm going to see you around here now?" The instructor said, sipping bottled water and passing one to Kevin. "From now on?"

"Three times a week," Kevin asserted wiping sweat from his neck and pecs.

"And no more traveling on the weekends when I need you the most?"

"No more," Kevin said. He put his arm around Nikki. "A lot has changed."

The instructor looked at Nikki. His lips curled. "I see."

●●●

"Are you sure you're up to this?" Kevin hugged Nikki. They had entered the Church of Christ, located only miles from her apartment. This was a big step for her—trying to find a church that she could attend in her own neighborhood. He wanted to make sure that she wasn't just going just for him. He prayed that she would establish her own relationship with God, be baptized, and become a Christian.

Nikki looked around the sanctuary and took a deep breath. "I'm sure," she answered.

Returning to worship on Sunday evenings was the single most religious act of devotion she'd ever committed. Although the idea of church scared her, experiencing it now didn't scare her at all; she actually felt calm.

Nikki peered at Kevin as they sat in one of the pews. He squeezed her leg; she could tell he was excited. She was excited, too.

CHAPTER FOURTEEN

Jackie relaxed in her bathtub. She loved the feel of the warm, sudsy water against her skin. King, her feline companion, walked into the bathroom. She looked at him and mentally warned him not to bother her.

The phone's ring startled her, but she decided not to answer it. It had been a long day—a long week. She didn't have the energy to talk to anyone. She settled back into the water and closed her eyes.

King rubbed his head under her hand, then looked up and purred.

Jackie opened her eyes and looked at him, "Not even you will destroy my quiet time," she said, rolling her eyes. She dipped her hand in the tub and flung water on him.

He jumped back and looked at her, indignant. She lifted her hand and waved as if she was going to flick more water at him, but he dashed out the door.

Nikki heard the front door open. She pressed the receiver and shoved the sheet of paper with Jackie's number on it into her pocket. "Hey," she said, slipping out of the bedroom.

"Hey, baby. Did I wake you?"

"No." She smiled. "I didn't expect you so early. I didn't get the chance to cook yet."

He cut off her march to the kitchen. "I missed you," he said, wrapping his arms around her.

Nikki smiled up at him and wrapped her arms around his neck. "I missed you, too."

They kissed, but Kevin sensed something was wrong. "You okay, baby?"

"Yeah. Just tired, I guess."

"Long week?" He felt Nikki nod her head. "Well, I have the perfect solution." He pulled some movies from his briefcase. "We don't have to go anywhere. I figured you'd be tired. I hate my baby to be all tired. Go back and relax. I'll cook. Okay?"

Nikki smiled and kissed him. "Thanks, sweetie."

Jackie examined the number on the caller ID. Her clients called her from the oddest places; whenever they had an idea, they wanted to call her and discuss it with her immediately. She picked up the phone and dialed the numbers to access her voice mail.

"Hello."

Her heart froze.

"This is Nikki."

Jackie covered her mouth, recognizing her voice.

"It's been a while since my grandmother gave me your number; I apologize for not calling sooner. I'm still living in Atlanta. I'm doing good... There have been some new developments in my life. Anyway, I just wanted to let you know that my grandmother did give me your number." There was a long pause. "And—if you'd like to—to—" The line went blank.

Jackie replayed the message and listened. She played it repeatedly, but each time it was the same thing—silence and an abrupt ending. She'd had no problems with her voice mail before, so why would it malfunction on such an important phone call?

Jackie wondered if she could call Nikki at the number on the caller ID. Her fingers seemed to get in the way as she dialed. The phone rang. Her heart raced.

"Hello?"

She smiled, hearing the male voice. This must be one of the 'new developments.' "Hi." She paused. "May I speak to Nikki?"

Kevin arched his eyebrow in surprise. Anesa had called Nikki a few times at his house, but never this late at night. "She's not here," he answered, suddenly realizing it wasn't she.

"Oh? Okay." Jackie said, about to hang up.

"Would you like to leave a message?"

Jackie was quiet for a moment. The curiosity was killing her. "Are you her husband?"

"Me?" Kevin asked, chuckling. "No. I'm her boyfriend. I can't conceive her letting me get too far beyond that."

"Can you let her know that—that Jackie called?"

"Jackie?" Kevin found himself short of words.

"Yeah," she breathed.

"You missed her by a few minutes. She went home like fifteen minutes ago."

Jackie nodded, clinging to the phone tightly.

"I'll let her know you called." Kevin thought to himself. "I know she'll be happy to hear it."

"Really?" Tears began to stream down her cheeks.

Kevin didn't know what to say. "Let me give you her home number so you can reach her directly."

"No." Jackie wiped her face. "That's okay. I actually got this one from my caller ID. She didn't leave me her number. I wouldn't want to impose."

Kevin knew he needed to get those two together. "She'll be back on Sunday, if you want to try back then."

Jackie nodded. A cloud of guilt swept over her. "That's okay," she sighed. "Just let her know I called."

Nikki grabbed Kevin's hand. "Thanks, baby."

"You're welcome."

She dropped his hand and stepped onto the escalator. They gazed at each other for a few moments then Nikki turned away. The last time she was at the airport, she hadn't tried to familiarize herself with it. She looked around blankly, and then began to walk down the hallway. It veered left, and her eyes searched each new face she passed. She had arrived early, just in case. They didn't have long, and she didn't want to risk missing her.

"Nikki."

She turned in the direction of the voice, but didn't see anyone familiar. Her eyes searched desperately before spotting a waving hand.

"Jackie?" Nikki walked towards her cautiously. She couldn't believe her eyes. She'd never known her age, but figured she was probably in her upper thirties now. She looked more beautiful than she remembered.

"It's me, Nikki." Jackie's face shone with joy. They stopped before they got too close to each other. "I hardly recognized you." Her eyes searched her. "Turn around."

Nikki turned around, slowly, deliberately, as if she were posing for cameramen on a runway.

"You look so mature." She mused studying her breasts and face. "And womanly." She giggled. "You always did have a big butt."

They laughed.

"You look good yourself," Nikki beamed.

"Well, come on." Jackie motioned her into a gourmet coffee shop. "Have a cappuccino with me."

"Okay." Nikki's heart raced as she followed her inside. They ordered drinks and found a table, sitting across from each other.

"So where did you fly in from, again?"

"New Orleans." She slurped her drink. "I have my own business."

"My grandmother told me. What was it, interior design?"

"Yeah, and I'm getting a degree in business. I work out of my home. No traveling to an office. I choose my own hours. I love it. What are you in school for?"

"Social work," Nikki mumbled, lowering her head and sipping.

"Really?" Suddenly, Jackie felt uncomfortable. She took another sip.

Nikki twisted the straw wrapper. Jackie and her father had never had children. Only weeks before she left, she found out it wasn't by choice. Jackie couldn't have kids.

Nikki wasn't sure if Jackie knew about MiKayla, but it was something she couldn't hide. She had to be told. She sat up a little, rested her arms on the table, and clasped her hands together. "Jackie, I have a sister." She breathed. "A younger sister."

Jackie gulped, setting the drink down. "Yes, your grandmother told me."

Nikki's heart relaxed. She didn't have to be the one to tell her.

"What's her name?" Jackie smiled. "Kaye, Kaylan?"

"MiKayla." Nikki's lips curled proudly.

"Yes." She leaned forward. "She wasn't there at the time, but your grandmother showed me the picture of her on the bookcase."

"That old thing?" Without thinking, she grabbed her purse and pulled out her billfold. "That was when she was two." She extended her arm across the table. "This is a picture of us two summers ago."

In the picture, Kayla set in Nikki's lap.

Nikki flipped to the next. "This is the most recent picture of her—from last Christmas."

Jackie studied Kayla's photo. A strange silence ensued. Nikki found herself on the brink of becoming fidgety, when Jackie finally handed her back the billfold.

"She looks just like you," Jackie said. It was if they had made a pact not to bring up her father. "And sweet, too, I bet?"

"She is. Thank you." She reached across the table to take the pictures when Jackie blocked her hand.

"Who is this good-looking fellow?"

Nikki looked down; she was pointing to a picture of Kevin. She had been so nervous about disclosing Kayla that she had completely forgotten him. Her face glowed. "Kevin."

"Your boyfriend? The guy I spoke to on the phone?" She had seen him and Nikki in front of the escalator, but hadn't realized it was Nikki.

Nikki nodded. "That's him."

"How long have you been seeing each other?" Jackie asked, happy to switch subjects.

Nikki grinned. "For a few months."

Jackie began licking the froth off the straw. "Mmm. Anything serious?"

"Maybe." Nikki shrugged.

"Maybe?" Jackie studied her face. "Come on," she teased. "I sense that he's more than just a maybe." She probed. "Something permanent, perhaps?"

Nikki shrugged again. She thought to herself quietly for a moment. "We'll see," she said in a low voice, surprising herself. She threaded her fingers through the necklace.

"Did he give you that?"

Nikki looked down. "Yeah."

"Oh." She motioned to her to move close. "Let me see it."

Nikki scooted towards her and held the necklace up while Jackie inspected it.

"Nice," Jackie nodded approvingly, leaning back in her seat.

"He gave it to me for Christmas," Nikki said, reminiscing.

"Tell me about him. What's he like? If you had to describe him in two words, what would they be?"

As easy as it sounded, trying to wrap Kevin up in two words was impossible. Her face muscles tightened as she blushed. "How 'bout one?"

Jackie listened.

Nikki propped her elbows on the table. "Incredible."

"Mmm?" Jackie smiled. "Incredible?"

Nikki bobbed her head. "I've never met a man who'll wash and fold my clothes when I take 'em to his place. Kiss and massage my feet," she said, wiggling them, "and paint my toes."

"Paint your toes!" Jackie shouted.

"Shh," Nikki giggled, motioning Jackie to speak low. "You can never tell him I told you."

"Mmm. He really spoils you." She watched Nikki's face. "Sounds like love," she insinuated, though the answer was more than evident.

"Maybe."

Jackie watched her closely. Nikki gazed into space.

"Most of the guys I dated in the past didn't last for more than a month or two, but Kevin—he's so genuine, compassionate, and kind." She shrugged. "I've never met anyone like him. He even has me going to church."

"I thought you hated church."

Nikki smiled. "I never hated it. Just never understood."

Jackie choked. "Wow. That's deep. Taking on the faith of another?" Jackie arched her eyebrow. "You sure it's just a maybe?"

"Excuse me, sista'." A black man in his late thirties or early forties approached their table. He was smooth, like Denzel, and had a smile that almost melted even Nikki's heart. "If you," he faced Jackie, then Nikki, "or your sister want another one," he motioned toward the drinks, "I'll be more than happy to buy."

Jackie blushed.

Nikki saw the chemistry. She smiled. Jackie had always been her father's wife, so she never looked at her that way, but with her smooth caramel skin, pretty white teeth, and sandy brown hair styled into spirals, she could see how any man would want her.

Jackie looked at her empty drink. There was nothing left but malt and air. She imagined how she must have looked, sipping on an empty straw. "No," she said. "We," she gestured at Nikki, "were just about to leave, unfortunately, but thank you."

"You're welcome." He nodded. "Good day, ladies." He walked away.

"No tellin' what was going through his mind." Jackie laughed.

"Yeah," Nikki said. "I guess you better head out. You don't want to miss your flight." Nikki's heart sank. They were just getting started. There was so much more she wanted to say.

"You're right." Jackie pulled on her tote and stood.

Nikki stood, too. They walked out of the café together, and Nikki walked Jackie as far she could before they encountered a security gate.

"I guess this is good-bye." Jackie smiled hesitantly.

"For now." Nikki touched her hand. "I'll be in touch."

"You do that." Jackie turned and scanned the airport. She wanted to hug Nikki, but decided not to push it. "Goodbye." She turned and walked down the aisle.

"Goodbye," Nikki said lowly, then turned and walked to the other side of the airport. Kevin was sitting in the lobby, reading a magazine. She walked up and stood over him.

"Has it been thirty minutes already?"

"Yeah," Nikki said softly.

"Hey." He felt her cheek. "You'll see her again." He kissed her forehead.

"I know." She took his hand, and they walked out of the airport.

"So what did you talk about?"

"You." Nikki grinned mischievously.

"Me?"

"Yeah," she said, walking sassily towards his car.

"You talked about me the whole time?"

"No." Nikki shook her head. "But a good bit of it."

He was grinning now, too. "What did you discuss, specifically?"

"I'm not telling."

"Yes, you are."

"No, I'm not."

"Yes, you are." He wrapped his arms around her and tickled the side of her belly.

"Aaah!" Nikki gasped, giggling. She hit him playfully on the chest as she wiggled out of his grip. "Don't do that."

"I know your spots," Kevin warned.

Nikki rolled her eyes at him.

CHAPTER FIFTEEN

"Hello?"

Nikki's heart dropped. Kevin sounded stuffy and gravelly, as if a dump truck had run over him. "Kevin, what's wrong? You sound horrible."

"I don't know. Something just came over me."

"Why didn't you call?"

"I didn't want to bother you with your test and all."

"Kevin, you're sick!"

"I'm okay. I just need to rest."

"I'm coming over!"

Kevin heard someone wrestling with the door. He rose as quickly as he could, but Nikki stepped in before he managed to open it. She saw Kevin's stumbling, and was immediately disturbed. He looked exactly the way he sounded on the phone.

"I don't want you here!" Kevin fussed. "You don't need to get sick and miss class."

"I'll be fine," she said, guiding him back to his spot on the sofa. The kitchen was spotless except for a bottle of Nyquil on the countertop. From his dazed stupor and the smell of alcohol on his breath, she knew he had already had some. "How much of that stuff did you take?"

Kevin rested his head on the back of the sofa. "The regular amount."

Nikki's temperature spiked. How could he be sick and not think she would be concerned? "You haven't eaten anything, you sound horrible, and you didn't call to let me know you were sick!"

"I'm sorry, baby. I'm sorry." Kevin's voice rang high. Nikki's nurturing spirit was what had attracted him; it was one of the reasons he loved her so much. He realized now that he hadn't been doing her a favor by not exposing her to his illness.

Nikki's manner softened. "Come on," she said, pulling him to stand. She threw his arm around her neck, buckling as her 125 lb frame struggled to support him. "Here we go," she announced, trying to ease him onto the bed, but then she tipped and fell over him.

"I'm sorry, baby," Kevin muttered.

Nikki pulled herself up and felt his skin. "Kevin, you're burning up!" He had on a heavy cotton sweater and a pair of matching corduroy pants. "Let's get this off of you." He babbled something as she pulled his sweater over his head. "Baby, stay with me." She slapped him in the face lightly. "Where're your shorts?"

"Top drawer."

She tugged at his buckle. "I'm going to get them," she said. "You need to take these off."

Nikki heard him mumble something else, and then he rose and dangled his legs over the edge of the bed. She walked to the drawer and found a pair of shorts. She heard a thump, turned around, and saw Kevin laid out flat on the bed. His pants were halfway down, just over his knees. She stood there startled. She had fully intended on leaving the room first, how did he mistake her for thinking she meant for him to undress now?

She walked towards the bed slowly. "Kevin," she said, tilting her head as she approached. "Wake up, baby. Put these on." She dangled the shorts in his face. "Kevin?" she called again, but he was out cold. She didn't know what to do. She ruminated a moment, deciding that since he was already stripped down to his drawers it'd be best to just finish up the task. She sighed inwardly, and then proceeded.

Nikki lifted his legs and threw them back on the bed. She pulled at his pants and slid the legs off one at a time. She picked up the shorts and clutched them hesitantly, then maneuvered his legs and slid the shorts up. Though previously her eyes purposely darted over that section of his body, when she reached his waist, she noticed that he was more than adequately compensated. She paused, sitting over him, overwhelmed with curiosity. His breathing resembled snoring because of the nasal congestion. Kevin lay in her presence, half-naked, so drunk she could do to him whatever she pleased, and he would never know.

She convinced herself to respect his privacy; that was off-limits to her—at least for now. She pulled the covers over him and kissed him on the cheek.

Back in the kitchen, she unloaded the groceries she had brought. After a few servings of her homemade chicken soup, Kevin would be himself in no time.

"Hello, Kevin."

Kevin turned, hearing his name. It was Shantelle. "Shantelle?" he gulped.

"Kevin, I—" Coming out of the mall bathroom, Kayla stopped dead at the sight of the woman.

Kevin cleared his throat. "This is my girlfriend's sister, Kayla. Kayla, this is Shantelle."

Girlfriend? The word echoed in Shantelle's head. Time after time, she had slept with him and he hadn't given her the time of day. At first, it had been a sexual thing, but by the time his sister moved in, she had fallen in love with him. His sister made no attempt to conceal her disdain, and she had tried suppressing her feelings. She had thought the feelings might be mutual, but they were not.

Kevin never looked in her eyes when they made love, and though he had let her sleep over once, she found him nestled under the covers on the couch in the morning. He was a heartless, self-centered jerk, and she'd sworn that if she saw him again, she would let him have it.

Her lips curled slightly as she extended her hand. He had better be glad this little girl was here. "Hey there."

Kayla looked at her hand blankly, and then turned away. She didn't know if it was the strange silence between Shantelle and Kevin, or the guilty way he looked at her, but she didn't like this woman one bit.

"Kayla?"

She heard the disapproval in Kevin's voice, but didn't care.

"Figures." Shantelle began to walk off, heading back into the crush of weekend shoppers.

"Shantelle." Kevin started after her, and then remembered Kayla. "Stay here," he instructed.

Kayla watched as Kevin caught up to the woman a few feet away. Though she couldn't hear them talking, she thought she saw Kevin mouth, "I'm sorry." Anger burned within her. She liked Kevin, but not if he was two-timing her sister.

Moments later, Kevin stared at Shantelle's back. His apology had fallen on deaf ears. Admittedly, he had never cared for Shantelle the way she had cared for him, but the last thing he wanted was for her to think she had been used. They had come together for one thing. Not until the morning that she stepped into the living room fighting mad had he realized her feelings had changed.

He couldn't have given her more at that time, anyway. Not until he met Nikki did he realize he still had the capacity to love. "Let's go, sunshine." Kevin said, pulling Kayla toward him.

Kevin pulled up to a park and looked back at Kayla as she stared towards the playground. It was odd being alone with her, but necessary for their relationship to grow.

He had wanted to do something to repay Nikki for taking care of him all week while he was sick, so he had made an appointment for her at Spa Sydell and a local salon to get her hair done. While Nikki spent a day alone, being pampered, he was watching Kayla.

As they approached the merry-go-round, Kayla held Kevin's hand tightly. Bigger kids were already playing on it—probably eleven and twelve year olds—swinging the younger kids.

Kevin felt Kayla's body jerk away from him. The little kids yelled and screamed so loudly that he couldn't tell whether they were screams of horror or glee. He pulled Kayla towards an empty swing set. "Why don't we try over here first?"

She sat on the wide black belt, and Kevin pushed her gently. Kayla loved the crisp breeze rushing through her hair as she swung higher and higher. She had needed Kevin's pushes at first, but now her athletic little legs took over.

She swung for a long time happily, but boredom overcame her as none of the other kids gave up their spaces on the merry-go-round. She dragged her feet in the sand, and the swing slowed to a stop.

Kevin was seated across from her on a bench, watching. "You okay, sunshine?"

Kayla looked at him. An hour ago, they had been at the mall having the time of their lives. They had purchased shakes and gone to a music and video store, but now they were here, and she wasn't having fun anymore.

Kevin pulled on the chain. "You okay?" he asked maneuvering into the empty swing beside hers. He tugged the chain. "I know you want to say something. Come on. I'm listening."

"Who was that woman?"

Kevin sat back in his seat. It wasn't the question he had expected. He guessed his body language had spoken louder than he knew when they ran into Shantelle at the mall. Kayla stared at him.

"Someone I dated in the past—long before your sister."

"Thought so," Kayla sulked.

Kevin reached over and stroked her face. "But it's over—and has been for a long time. Your sister and I don't date other people behind each other's backs."

"How do you feel about my sister?"

Kevin was speechless, especially since she had showed little interest in their relationship for the longest time. He wondered at the motive behind all the questions. "I really like your sister, MiKayla."

"Oh." Her head tipped down.

He stopped swinging. "What's wrong?"

"You said you liked her." She frowned. "You don't love her?"

Kevin blushed. "I never said *that*."

Kayla's face brightened. "So you do love her?"

Kevin rose, stood behind Kayla, and began pushing her again. "Yes, sunshine. Yes, I do love her."

"Yes!" Kayla squealed, pumping her arm with glee. "Now all you have to do is ask her to marry you."

"Whoa. Whoa. Whoa." He stopped. "Things aren't always so simple."

"What do you mean?"

"I mean—" he paused. "Wait a minute. You sure do ask a lot of questions. Why do you want to know all this, anyway?"

Kayla shrugged. "Because she loves you. And I thought when people loved—"

"She told you she loved me?"

"No. 'Isn't it obvious?' That's what Aunt 'Nesa says."

Kevin's shoulders sank.

Kayla began swinging herself again. "As I was saying, I thought once people fall in love, they marry."

"Not necessarily, sunshine. Anyway, you're too little to be worried about all of this."

"I'm not worried," Kayla corrected. "Just curious."

"Curious?"

"Yeah."

"Okay, baby." He sat back down in the swing next to her. "So what do you think?"

Kayla slowed her pace, and then looked at him, confused.

"You think she'd say yes?" he asked conversationally.

Kayla nodded her head, giggling.

After several minutes, the other kids left the merry-go-round for the monkey bars. Kayla wanted to go on the merry-go-round, so he stopped the swing, but just before she dashed off, he called her back.

"Let's keep this conversation between us. Okay?"

Kayla nodded.

"Ugh," Nikki exclaimed.

"What?" Kevin blushed, covering his mouth.

Nikki turned his face, viewing it from the side.

Kevin looked at her, confused. He had, not too long ago, popped a mint in his mouth.

"I'll be back," she said, disappearing into the bathroom. She came back with Q-tips and toilet tissue. "Come on. Lay down," she said, patting her lap. One of her pet peeves was seeing wax in people's ears.

Kevin looked at her as if she was crazy. "I am not letting you stick those in my ears." Only one woman had cleaned his ears his whole life, and that was his mother.

"Come on," she urged. "I do Kayla's all the time."

"No," Kevin pouted.

She smirked. "Now look at who's being a baby."

Kevin cringed. It was the equivalent of a double-dog dare, and no matter how much he hated it, he had to give in. Reluctantly, he laid his head on her lap.

Nikki's fingers tugged his ear lobe, and the soft tips glided smoothly around in his ear. She motioned for him to turn, and he did obediently, so she could clean the other. For a few seconds, he was in heaven.

"Okay," Nikki said. She wrapped the Q-tips in the tissue and set them aside.

Kevin rose, quickly wiping his mouth before Nikki could see the drool. "You really know how to take care of a brother, don't you?" he smiled, rewarding her with a kiss.

"If you let me," Nikki said.

Kevin liked the sound of that. He took her hand and lifted her up. They needed to talk. He escorted her outside to the deck.

Nikki lay on top of Kevin in a lawn chair. The day had gone so wonderfully. She knew he loved spoiling her, but today had topped everything. She just wished she could afford to do good things for him, too. She flinched as Kevin's tugging and snuffing at her hair tickled her neck. She turned to face him.

"You are so beautiful," he said, twirling his fingers in one of her curls.

"Thank you." Nikki's eyes sparkled.

"Just like a model on the cover of one of those bridal magazines."

Nikki frowned and turned her head.

Several minutes passed in silence, until Kevin couldn't stand it. "What are you thinking about?" Kevin asked.

"Graduation," Nikki said, not addressing his previous comment.

"I can't wait to see that! Veronica Katrina Jones, come on down," he said, imitating the announcer's voice from *The Price Is Right*.

"Thanks," she laughed. "I can't wait, either." She looked at the stars sparkling in the sky. "You know what I really wish?"

"Humph?"

"I wish I could get my master's."

"Why don't you?"

She paused. "When my mother was in school and working, she was never home. I don't want that for Kayla." She grinned. "Really, I would love to pursue a PhD in psychology," she chuckled, "but that would really take forever.

"I used to listen to *The Infinite Mind* on the radio every Friday night. One professor tried to talk me into doing an internship for him this past summer, but with Kayla, I needed to make more money.

"I originally volunteered at the youth center. First, I did it for school, but I really liked it, so I continued going after my hours were met. An opening came up, and they offered me a job—$500 more than the internship that summer, but that was Kayla's bed." Her voice trailed.

Kevin grimaced. She felt she had made the right choice, but it was still a regrettable one. College was hard enough academically; he couldn't image how difficult it would have been without his parent's financial backing. "Who would you counsel?" he asked, trying to get her back into a lighter mood.

"Families — teenage counseling, mostly."

"Humph." Kevin grunted. "Just be prepared for a bunch of Babe's kids coming through your door."

They laughed.

"'Dr., please help me with my bad kids! They don't listen to me. They want to fight all the time. I just don't know what to do!'"

Nikki laughed.

He held her tight. "You'll be Dr. Maddox by then," he whispered and kissed the side of her forehead.

Nikki froze. The conversation needed to head in another direction. "What about you?" she said quickly. "What do you want to do? What's your biggest dream?"

Kevin studied Nikki from behind. She wasn't ready to hear it, but he'd try anyway.

Nikki turned slightly, wondering why he was silent all of a sudden.

"Well," he squeezed her. "When I was a teenager, I wanted to do mission work."

"Mission work?" Nikki repeated, surprised.

"Yeah," he whispered softly. "I donate to an organization called Truth for Today. It's for Church of Christ-sponsored missionary work, but I wanted to experience it myself. My father and I went on a mission trip a couple of years ago. It really opened my eyes.

"I told myself that before I turn thirty-five, I would take a year off to do it. But now," he paused. "I'm starting to think I won't have time. Maybe I'll have a wife and kids by then. I may have to put it off, or not do it all." He touched her hair gently. "That is, unless she was willing to come with me." He studied her hair as his hands glided down the strands. "Someday."

Nikki was speechless. Kevin's allusions to marriage were truly scaring her. She had never wanted to get married. She just wanted to be with him. Why couldn't he get that through his head? She popped up from his lap. "It's getting late. I'm gonna grab Kayla."

Kevin stared at her quietly. He didn't understand why she didn't even want to discuss it. He rose and escorted her back inside.

●●●

Nikki approached the church building with Kayla. Melanie was standing in the doorway, handing out programs. She had met her only a few weeks prior. She frequently called her to check on how she was doing and update her on events at church.

Their eyes met, and Nikki smiled.

"Good morning," Melanie said, handing her a program and giving her a hug. "Where's your boyfriend this morning?"

"He went out of town for a wedding and isn't coming back until later tonight."

"Oh," Melanie grinned. It was the first time she had seen Nikki come to worship without him. "He didn't take you with him?"

Nikki nodded. "He wanted to, but I have too much work to do. Besides, I didn't want to get on another flight, anyway."

Melanie smiled. She squeezed Nikki's hand. "Well, *we're* certainly happy to have you."

"Thank you," Nikki said. She took Kayla's hand, and they walked into the auditorium.

CHAPTER SIXTEEN

"Oh, we rolling big-time, now!" Anesa said as she opened the passenger door to Kevin's BMW.

"Mine's in the shop," Nikki explained as Anesa sat beside her. She had promised to drop her off at the OB/GYN for a check-up.

"I forgot about that. How much is it going to cost?"

Nikki shrugged. "I don't know. Kevin had it towed somewhere, and he won't tell me."

"What's he driving?" Anesa asked, settling into her seat and closing the door.

"He's out of town for a convention. He'll be back tomorrow."

Anesa strapped on her seat belt, looking around the car's interior. "This feels as nice on the inside as it looks on the outside," she said.

"You like it?" Nikki asked nervously. "I had it detailed for his birthday."

Anesa chuckled.

"What?"

"So you finally let him have a sniff, huh?"

"No!" Nikki blushed, shocked her cousin even asked such a question.

"Relax, Nikki. I'm just kidding," Anesa laughed. "He finally trusted you with his wheels?"

"I've driven his car before—plenty of times," Nikki answered. "You've just never seen me."

"Oh! Excuse-a-olay-o-me."

Nikki rolled her eyes playfully and pulled out of the driveway.

"Girl, I can't wait to drop this load," Anesa declared. After seeing the doctor, they had stopped at North Lake Mall for a bite to eat.

Nikki groaned. "I can only imagine."

Anesa watched Nikki tuck a half of a sandwich away in her purse. She cleared her throat. "So, how many kids do you and Kevin want?"

"Me and Kevin?" Nikki mused. "Never thought about it."

"Never thought about it?" Anesa pressed. "Come on, Nikki—you never thought about it?"

Nikki shrugged, stuffing a fry in her mouth. "Why is that so hard to believe? We don't talk about stuff like that."

"What do you mean, 'stuff like that'?"

"You know—having a family, things down the line—we're just happy with the way things are."

"So you all have never talked about a future together?"

Nikki shook her head. "No."

Anesa sighed. "Is it that you haven't talked about it, or that you don't want to talk about it?"

Suddenly, Nikki was annoyed. "What difference does it make? We're happy the way things are. I like to live in the present, okay?"

Anesa picked up her drink and slurped on the straw. "You don't have to get testy."

"I'm not getting testy. I just don't understand why you're pressing the topic."

"Pressing the topic?" Anesa fussed. Suddenly, she burst into laughter.

"What's so funny?"

Anesa set her drink down. "The two of you are hilarious."

"What?"

"Nikki, this weekend, you all are going on vacation—together," she emphasized. "Wake up."

"I am up. What do you mean?"

Anesa sat up in her seat and stared across the table. "Kevin, my dear, is in love with you. You are in love with him. It's obvious."

"He's not in love with me," Nikki corrected her.

"How do you know?"

"He would have told me, 'Nesa." Nikki argued.

Anesa stared at Nikki and shook her head. "Not necessarily."

"What do you mean, 'not necessarily'?"

"Just because he hasn't told you that doesn't mean he doesn't."

"Why hasn't he told me then?" Nikki argued.

"For the same reason you haven't told him," Anesa said, sitting back in her seat easily, sipping again on her drink.

Nikki fell quiet. "Anyway, who said I was in love?"

"Girl, please," Anesa said, throwing her hands up and rolling her eyes. "He's trying to show you he can provide for you. He let you use his ride while he was gone. You have a key to his condo. He lets you answer his phones—both cell and home. He gave you expensive jewelry. He's paying for that broke-down car of yours to be repaired. You see each other every day?"

"Not really. Only about—well, maybe."

"Exactly." Anesa threw up her hands. "Girl, you're practically married." Nikki was suddenly uncomfortable. "What is it about the M word that scares you?"

Nikki let her guard down. "I don't know," she sighed. "Growing up, watching the mess that went on in our house—I don't know. I think you and Malcolm have a good marriage, and my aunt seems to be happy, but—but—I don't know. I mean, I really, really like Kevin—it's not him. I just—I can't explain it, and the more I try the less it makes sense." She paused. "I guess I need to know that he won't run out on me and that our love will last forever," she said, emphasizing the last word, adding a magical twist to it. "But that sounds so Cinderella."

"Nikki, everyone feels that way. But when the time comes, you weigh how you feel, and you just know."

You just know. Anesa's words echoed in Nikki's head. If she wasn't in love, then she didn't know when she would be. She spent most of her days daydreaming, longing for them to be together again, and even when she closed her eyes at night to sleep, she found him there in her dreams. Her mind was flooded with thoughts of him. Her heart jumped every time he touched her, and whenever they kissed.

"You ready?"

Anesa's voice suddenly broke Nikki's thoughts. "Yeah." She answered back nonchalantly gathering her things. She didn't want to let on but the conversation with her cousin definitely had her thinking.

One thing for sure, this was the best relationship she had ever had, and she didn't want it to end.

●●●

Nikki pulled up alongside the Delta terminal curb. She saw the reflection of the white BMW in the glass entranceway. She hoped

Kevin would be pleased with the car. It was one of many surprises she had for his birthday. Suddenly, Kevin emerged, and her heartbeat accelerated.

Kevin smiled brightly and got in the passenger seat. Nikki was wearing his favorite combination—her powder blue, spaghetti-strapped, lace top with form-fitting blue jeans that accentuated her hips and butt. "Hi," he grinned, landing a big kiss on her lips.

"Hi," Nikki returned. "I missed you."

"Likewise," he said as they embraced tightly.

"So," Nikki gestured around the car with her eyes. "What do you think?"

"It looks great, baby." He kissed her again. "And so do you."

Nikki was always happy to see him when he came home from his business trips. But this time was different.

"Reservations for two, under Jones."

Kevin listened as Nikki spoke to the hostess at the podium. He looked around uneasily. The restaurant was dimly lit. A pianist played at the center of the restaurant, and he heard water falling somewhere in the room.

Nikki turned towards him. Her eyes sparkled with excitement. "It's just going to be a moment. We're a few minutes early."

"Humph." Kevin said, wrapping his arms around her as they sat.

Suddenly, Nikki turned towards him. "I'll be back."

He watched as she dashed off, presumably towards the rest-room, disappearing down a corridor. He stood and walked towards the hostess. "Hi. May I get a menu?"

"Sure." The woman bent over and handed him one.

"Thanks," he said, taking it with him. He pulled back one of the flaps and was stunned.

Nikki returned. She saw the menu in his lap. Their eyes met, and she smiled inside.

Kevin rose. "We're leaving."

"What?" Nikki asked, confused. "Did something happen?"

The hostess looked at them. He pulled Nikki back down the hallway. "Nikki, these prices are ridiculous."

"Kevin, it's your birthday. This is a special occasion. It's my treat."

"I don't want you to spend thirty-five dollars on me to eat."

"It's one of my gifts to you."

Kevin grabbed her by the hand. "We're leaving."

"What?"

"We're leaving."

"No, we're not!"

"Fine," Kevin huffed. "I'll pay for dinner, and you can pay the tip."

Ever since he had done her taxes, he had been treating her differently. "Why are you doing this?" Nikki fussed, lowering her voice as she saw a man walking towards them. She was sick of being treated like a charity project. "It's your birthday. Why can't you just let me do something special for you?"

"Because I don't want you to."

"Jones," came the hostess' voice.

"Come on, that's us." Kevin wrapped his arm around her.

But as they walked towards the hostess, Nikki felt sick, and the restaurant lost its appeal. She stopped dead in her tracks. "I want to go home."

"What?"

"I said," she swallowed, "I want to go home!" Though she started the sentence softly, by the end her voice was trembling, and she was on the verge of shouting. "Right now!"

Kevin knew the hostess had heard Nikki. "Baby, calm down."

Kevin just wasn't getting it, so Nikki decided to send a clearer message. She folded her arms and stormed out the door.

"Nikki? Wait!" Kevin tossed the menu to the hostess. "Nikki!" he shouted, running up behind her in the parking lot.

"Take me home!" Nikki fumed, still walking. She stopped at the passenger side of the car and shoved his keys in his hands.

Kevin was baffled. He didn't understand what had upset her. "Baby, what's wrong?"

"What's wrong?" she mocked. "You completely humiliated me back there!"

"Baby?" his heart dropped. He tried to console her, but Nikki opened her door, got in, and slammed it.

Kevin stared for a moment. He would never have done anything to intentionally embarrass her. He had simply tried to do the right thing. Finally, he walked over to his side of the car.

Kevin shut the door. He watched as Nikki tossed her keys on the coffee table and flopped down on the couch. Then she lay down, turning her back towards him. She purposely poked her butt out, just so he couldn't sit next to her.

He had never seen her so pissed off before. Ordinarily, he would know what to do to get her back into a good mood, but by the looks of things, this was going to take extraordinary measures. He walked into the kitchen, deciding that the best thing to do was to let her cool off.

Nikki was a good southern woman; he could always count on her having something tasty socked away in the fridge. He found a few dishes and sorted through them. He took out a set of plates and heated up the leftovers in the microwave.

"Baby." He shook her. "Come on. Let's eat." He swallowed, hoping she would go along with it. To his surprise, she got off the couch and followed him into the kitchen.

When he had almost finished his plate, he gazed across the table at Nikki; she had barely touched her food. Besides his prayer, no words had been spoken since they sat down.

"Finished?" Nikki said, rising and taking his plate. She walked to the kitchen sink and ran some water.

Kevin watched as she scraped her remains into the garbage disposal. "Baby, you're killing me. I can't stand it when you're mad at me."

Nikki turned around. She wanted to snap, but she felt too horrible. The whole occasion had been ruined, and now they were spending Kevin's birthday at her apartment, eating two-day-old leftovers, which had not been her idea of how things would go. "Why can you do things for me, but won't allow me to do them for you?"

"Baby," he whispered. "Look, I know how much you wanted to take me to that restaurant, but it was too expensive. We didn't have to leave; I was willing to pay."

"I have the money."

"No, you don't," he corrected. "Besides, that's money you can spend on yourself and Kayla, not me. Why are you so angry with me? You were the one who wanted to leave. I was willing to pay."

"It's not the same."

"Baby, what difference does it make?"

She pointed to her chest. "Because I wanted to do something nice for you, for your birthday, and now we're stuck here."

Stuck? He arched his eyebrow. "Baby, you know how much I like your cooking, and I don't view spending my birthday cuddled up next to my woman as 'stuck.'"

"Kevin," she huffed, disgusted.

"Look—" He put his arms around her. "I don't want to fight anymore," he whispered. She looked down and away, but Kevin lifted her head. "The whole time I was on that plane, all I could think about was coming here and being with you. That's all. That's the biggest gift you could ever give me—"

"Kevin, I—" Nikki began to protest.

"Shh. Let's not fight anymore. It *is* my birthday," he declared. "I missed you."

She had missed him, too. She finally cracked a restrained smile.

"There she goes," Kevin said, planting a kiss on her lips.

"How 'bout some birthday cake?" Nikki beamed, twirling from his arms and lifting the cake in the cabinet. She got out a knife, cut a piece for both of them, and placed them on saucers. She sat on his lap and sang, "Happy Birthday."

Kevin set his saucer down, and watched Nikki eat the last piece of her cake. She had picked away the icing.

"Oh," Nikki moaned. "That was good." She moved to set her plate down, but ended up smudging her fingers in discarded icing.

Kevin snatched at her hand playfully and licked the icing off her fingers.

The feeling of Kevin's warm mouth made Nikki nervous. "Kevin, you're so greedy," she teased and yanked her hand back. "If you keep it up, you're gonna be fat." She patted his stomach then locked her hands behind his neck. Their foreheads touched gently, and she chuckled softly. "But I'll still love you."

Kevin's heart stopped. Neither of them were the kind of people who tossed the "L" word around loosely. She had never joked with him like that before.

Suddenly, there was a noise, and they both jumped.

Kevin was relieved his phone had rung. He signaled to Nikki that he had to take the call.

Nikki watched him disappear into the hallway. She picked up their glasses and put them in the sink. She felt so vulnerable. Why had she talked herself into going through with this? She had always wanted to be told she was loved first, not the other way around. Now she hoped he thought she was kidding.

Kevin returned to the room.

Nikki looked his way nervously. "Randy?"

"Mmm," Kevin nodded. All this time, he had been in love with her, and he didn't understand why he couldn't tell her. "Ready to watch a movie?"

"Sure." She suddenly felt sad. "I'll be in, in a minute—I need to finish up these dishes." She had practically poured out her heart to Kevin, and he had said and done nothing.

Kevin tilted his head, disappointed.

"It'll only take a second." She pushed him towards the living room.

"Okay." Kevin walked into the living room.

She had thought he loved her, but he'd had the opportunity to tell her, and hadn't. She turned towards the cabinets, feeling tears coming.

Kevin looked at his watch. It was 10:35. He had been waiting for Nikki for over an hour. He didn't know what to do or think. Though her car was gone, he had hoped she was home, but when he knocked on the door, there was no answer. Something had told him to bring her grandmother's number with him, but he had left it at home, thinking he wouldn't need it.

He massaged his head, thinking of the previous night. She had told him she loved him. He hadn't meant to leave her hanging, but the whole thing had taken him by surprise.

He couldn't blame her for rushing him off after dinner. She said she needed time to pack, but he knew the real reason and still couldn't bring himself to say anything. He shook his head, disappointed with himself. He wouldn't be surprised if she had decided to take her sister to the beach without him.

He looked up, and saw Nikki's car pulling into a spot a few cars down from his. His heart relaxed. "Good morning," he said cheerfully, watching Nikki undo Kayla's car seat.

She didn't respond, but Kayla did. "Good morning!" she yelled, flying into his arms.

"How's my sunshine? Good?"

Kayla nodded vigorously.

"Give me some sugar."

Kayla complied with a loud smacking sound.

Nikki was unloading the trunk. He hoisted Kayla in one arm and reached for a piece of luggage. "I got it."

"No, I have it," Nikki said, making no eye contact. She hurled the tote over her shoulder, and then picked up a suitcase and another tote with wheels.

Kevin watched as she started towards his car. She was struggling, but her pride wouldn't allow her to ask for help. He shook his head. *Girl, you're as sweet as sugar, but just as stubborn as a mule.*

Kayla stared, too. "You make her mad?"

Kevin kissed her cheek. "Come on," he said, easing her down. He walked up behind Nikki.

"I got it," Nikki huffed.

"No, I have it," Kevin said firmly, pulling the luggage from her. They made eye contact briefly, and Nikki turned to head back to her car.

"That's it," Kevin said, closing the trunk. Between the three of them, so many bags had been jammed in that he was amazed he was able.

Nikki turned to climb into the car when Kevin caught her arm. "I'm sorry I was late. My grandmother—"

Kevin shushed her. "Look, baby," his voice softened. "I apologize for yesterday. I know what you were trying to do, and I sincerely appreciate it. My mom always told me to take care of my woman. What would I have looked like letting you spend that money on me when I know that you and your sister need it more?" He paused. "Baby, you just don't know how much I care about you." He touched her cheek. "How much I—"

Oh, my God. He's going to say it. Nikki's heart raced.

"I—" Kevin stuttered.

"Nikki!"

Oh, no, not now Kayla! Nikki ran to where her sister had been strapped in the car.

"I gotta go," Kayla whined.

"I thought you went before we left Grandma's."

"I tried, but I couldn't," she moaned, squirming.

"Okay, baby, just wait." She loosened her seatbelt and turned to Kevin. "She's gotta go tinkle," she repeated, as if he hadn't heard.

Kevin watched as they walked towards the apartment. Nikki looked back at him and their eyes met. She turned.

"Let's go. Run, baby."

Kevin looked down at the time. It was 10:59.

CHAPTER SEVENTEEN

"Wanna take me for a ride, cowboy?" Nikki asked sexily. The room was lit softly and smelled of lavender.

Kevin inched up. She stood in the doorway of the bathroom. She wore a rustic cowboy hat and was clad in suede lingerie. Her sarong rode snugly against her hips, and her cleavage bulged brazenly from the strapless bra.

"I—" Kevin started, but he heard a noise—a ringing. He popped up; it was the hotel phone. "Hello?" His voice was groggy. "Thank you," he said, hanging up. He laid his head back against the pillow. He rubbed his head, remembering the dream. This morning, he would need a long, ice-cold shower.

"I'm sorry; I over-slept," Nikki said, sizing up the breakfast selection. They only had thirty minutes before the ferry left for the island, and she needed to grab something quick.

"It's partly my fault. I should've come by when you didn't show. I just assumed you were running late."

"I don't know how I'm gonna get her to eat this so fast, and I don't want to carry food on the boat, but it's gonna be another hour before we get to the other side."

"That's okay. She can eat in my car."

Nikki arched her eyebrow. She envisioned Fruit Loops and milk all over Kevin's backseat. "Kevin, you don't know Kayla."

"It'll be okay," he asserted. "I'll have to clean out my car, anyway—from the sand."

They began to head out the door. "Oh," Nikki grabbed her head, as if remembering something. "I have to go back to the room."

"We're going to miss the tour."

"It'll just be a second. Okay?"

"You want me to pull around and pick you up at the room?"

"No!" Nikki exclaimed, and then realized how loud she sounded. "I mean—don't bother. It'll be easier to just walk back around to meet you."

She walked off hastily, pretending to turn towards the room. Then she stopped and watched Kevin and Kayla exit the breakfast area and go to the parking lot.

She sneaked over to the receptionist desk. "Excuse me," she whispered fiercely. "I'm in room 153. Do you have an envelope?"

The clerk smiled pleasantly. Nikki peeped around the corner and saw Kevin loading Kayla in the car seat. The receptionist handed the envelope to her.

"Thank you," she said, speeding towards their rooms.

She stopped in front of Kevin's door and thought for a moment. She took out a folded sheet of paper, slipped it into the envelope, and slid it under the door.

Suddenly, she heard the sound of a horn. She jumped. She looked and saw Kevin waving from the car.

Had he seen her, she wondered? She walked towards the car cautiously, opened the door, and got in.

"Did you get what you needed?"

"Yeah," she whispered softly.

"You okay?" Kevin asked.

"Yeah. I'm just tired from yesterday. That's all."

"We don't have to go if you—"

"No. I'm fine."

He looked at the clock on the dashboard. "We'll have to boogie, but I think we can still catch it," Kevin said, shifting into first gear.

Nikki gazed in the passenger side mirror as he made a wide U-turn. Kevin would discover her letter, and the issue of love would be forced to the brink—or so she hoped.

The sky was picturesque, a dazzling blue with a dash of cotton balls. From under her sunglasses, Nikki watched Kevin and Kayla splashing in the crystal blue ocean water. She soaked up the sun's rays between catnaps under the shade and comfort of her umbrella.

It was the end of their four-day get-away to the Gulf Coast. Nikki hated the thought of heading back to Atlanta. She leaned back into the seat and closed her eyes.

"Nikki!" Kayla tugged.

She cracked open her eyes; Kayla was on one side and Kevin on the other.

"Come on." Kayla pulled her arm.

"No, baby, you go have fun," Nikki replied.

"Nikki?"

"No."

Kayla folded her arms and pouted.

"Bye-bye," Nikki waved them off. She pulled her straw beach hat down over her eyes and lay back in her seat.

Kevin and Kayla began walking towards the beach. Kevin stopped and smiled at Kayla. She looked at him mischievously.

Nikki felt the air cool around her. She opened her eyes and saw them standing over her, blocking the sun, interrupting her nap again. "What?" she asked with annoyance. As one, they grabbed at and began tugging on her arms. All efforts to fight them failed.

Her hat and sunglasses fell in the sand as she struggled. "Stop! Stop it!"

Other people on the beach looked at them, smiling and pointing.

Kevin picked her up and threw her over his shoulder. He looked around. "Just look at 'em. 'Mommy, mommy, look. The niggras have gone crazy!'" he mocked in a Euro-centric voice.

"Kevin! I'm not playing! Let me go!"

He waded into the water.

She saw Kayla looking up at her, giggling.

"What shall we do, sunshine? What do you say?"

"Do it!" Kayla jumped with glee.

"Kayla?" Nikki pleaded, surprised. "You're going to turn on your big sister?"

Kevin looked at Kayla. She looked back at Nikki and nodded her head.

"Why, you little—" Nikki huffed.

"Okay, on the count of three."

She felt his body repositioning. He was actually going to dump her in the water.

"One—" Kevin and Kayla counted together. Kayla squealed.

"Two! Three!" Kevin blurted, dunking her.

Nikki felt a rush of wind. She screamed. Then she felt the sharp sting of the water. She was suddenly submerged. Her arms flailed helplessly as she tried to get up.

Kayla laughed heartily. She walked over and, adding further injury to insult, splashed water in her face.

Kevin stood back and watched. As she struggled to get out of the water, the back of her swimsuit became caught in one of her cheeks. The water droplets on her body captured the sun's rays, accentuating her chocolaty fineness. The cool water caused her nipples to harden and stand out against her bathing suit and t-shirt.

Kevin felt himself getting aroused. "Okay." He moved quickly to help stabilize her, praying Kayla hadn't noticed. "You okay, baby?" he asked, refraining from laughing aloud. "I'm sorry."

"No, you aren't!" Nikki punched his shoulder with all her might. Then she looked at Kayla. "You little squirt!"

Nikki walked towards her seat under the umbrella, feeling the gritty shells and rocks under her feet.

She heard a burst of laughter. She turned and saw Kevin holding his hand over his mouth, but MiKayla laughed openly. *Teaming up on me.* Nikki was tickled. She gave Kevin a sharp look, but found it difficult not to laugh, too. "Pathetic! Just pathetic."

Kevin pulled up to the hotel. Nikki and Kayla were exhausted, but he could still go a while longer. He moved to elbow Nikki, but her eyes popped open when he pulled in.

"How long have I been asleep?" she asked, stretching.

"Long enough for me to know you better get some rest before we head back tomorrow."

"Mmm," she moaned, laying her head against the window. "I don't want to think about that." She yawned. She looked over her shoulder; Kayla was still asleep. "I guess I better get her into bed."

Nikki undid Kayla's car seat and was about to hurl her over her shoulder when Kevin intervened. "Just get the door," he said, pulling Kayla out of her arms. He followed her into the suite and lowered Kayla on the bed.

Kevin watched Nikki for a moment as she massaged her neck. She flopped down on the recliner beside Kayla's bed, then leaned over and peeled her sandals off. Kayla's head was tilted towards the curtains. Four days away from the rest of the world, and still no time had seemed right.

"I'll see you in the morning," Nikki said, sighing and wiggling her toes.

"Goodnight," he whispered, leaning over and kissing her.

"Goodnight, sweetie." She rose up to walk him out.

"Oh." He turned. "I noticed this place up the road—they had some pretty reasonably priced gas. I think I'm going to fill up for tomorrow."

"Ok." Nikki leaned against the door. "Just be careful."

"I'll come over for breakfast at seven." He grinned. "Or do you need a wake up call?"

"No." She shook her head. "No wake up call. I'll be ready this time. I promise."

"You promise?" He leaned over to kiss her lips.

"Mmm-hmm," she said, kissing him back warmly.

They stared into each other's eyes. "Goodnight."

"Goodnight," Nikki said, folding her arms.

He headed for the car.

She closed the door and latched it. She heard him pull off, sighed, and leaned against the door.

Kevin noticed a soft light glowing in Nikki and Kayla's room as he pulled up. He listened, but didn't hear any noise indicating they were still awake. He desperately needed to speak with Nikki, but remembering how tired she looked earlier, he figured she had drifted off to sleep with the light on.

He pulled his key card out and swiped it, deciding not to bother her. He walked into the room, and knew housekeeping had been there. The bed had been made, fresh towels were in the bathroom, and the curtains were drawn.

He walked to the TV stand and grabbed the remote. The light from the TV blinded him for a moment, and he shrank away. He noticed a white envelope perched against the phone on the nightstand. He walked over and picked it up.

It wasn't heavy at all. He examined the face, but it wasn't addressed to anyone. *Just my luck*, he kidded himself. *Anthrax.* He turned the light on next to his bed, held the envelope up to the light, and made out a sheet inside. He pulled out the single sheet, unfolded it, and scanned it over. He easily recognized the writing.

Kevin,

When I first met you, I thought you were so handsome. Your dark brown eyes and your grand smile — I knew I wouldn't mind getting to know you.

That day, after spending the night at Malcolm and Anesa's, when I passed through downtown to exercise on Ponce De Leon, and I saw you again, my heart fluttered. I looked forward to you jogging up beside me those couple of weeks — too much. The line I gave you about being busy wasn't true at all, unless I was busy avoiding you. I wasn't looking for anything or anyone.

Then I scratched my arm, and you took me in and bandaged me up — seems like you've been doing that ever since.

Every problem I've had, every fear, you've taken me by the hand and cleansed my wounds properly and tenderly.

So many months have passed; I'm grateful you took the time to find me. Not a second goes by that I don't think of you. I never realized how much I wanted to be found.

Nikki

Nikki set up in the bed startled. The light burned her eyes. She looked and saw that Kayla was asleep with her teddy bear, Mr. Huggs.

She reached up to turn the lamp off and heard a soft rap at the door. She climbed out of bed, walked towards the door, and peered through the peephole. Kevin was outside.

"Hey." She opened the door.

"Hi." He examined her face. "I'm sorry. I saw the light, and I thought you —"

"That's okay." Nikki rubbed the back of her neck.

Kevin looked over Nikki's shoulder at Kayla.

Nikki turned and looked, too, wondering if the noise had awakened her, but she was still fast asleep.

"Nikki, I know this is a strange request, but can you meet me at the pool in ten minutes?"

Nikki looked at him, puzzled. She was barely awake. "The pool? Sweetie, I can't do that." She looked back at Kayla. She stepped out of the room and cracked the door. "Kayla's asleep and —"

"I'm not going to let anything happen to her," Kevin said quickly. "Our rooms are right in front of the pool. If you open up the curtains and leave the bathroom light on, we'll be able to see her. Leave the patio unlocked, and we can get to her quickly."

"You've thought this through, huh?"

"Yeah," he said softly, intensely. He grasped her hips. "What do you say?"

She smiled cautiously, remembering what had happened at the beach. "Wait a minute. What makes you think I'm going anywhere near the water with you?"

He grinned. "I won't dump you this time. Come on."

It was too quick. Nikki didn't believe him. "Okay." She leaned against the doorframe. "Promise me something."

He thought of the look on her face when she drove his BMW. "Okay, if I dump you, you can drive my car for two weeks."

"A month!" she bargained.

"Okay." He shrugged.

"What will you drive?"

"I'll rent a car."

"No. Can't do it." She threw up her hands. "Bet's off."

"What?"

Nikki folded her arms and massaged her chin with her hand. "If you dump me, I get to drive your car for a month, and you have to drive mine."

"Nah!" He shook his head.

"I thought you weren't going to dump me?"

He leaned against the wall. Dang, she looked good. "Okay."

Nikki smiled. "Okay. You got yourself a deal." She paused. "I'll meet you in ten minutes."

Kevin nodded, sulking.

Kevin looked up and saw Nikki walking on the bricks that bordered the pool. Her hair was pinned up, and she had a towel wrapped around her body. "What happened to your t-shirt?"

You know what happened to it. She frowned as she stood at the edge.

"So—" he stroked his arms, and the water rippled back. "You going to get in or what?"

"Something tells me I'm going to regret this," Nikki said, removing her towel. She draped it over a chair and turned to face him.

Lord Jesus, Kevin sighed, watching her figure.

She walked a few feet to the bar then climbed in.

Kevin sauntered to her slowly.

"Don't!" she warned.

"I'm not," he assured her. He picked her up in his arms.

Nikki wrapped her arms and legs around him and rested her head against his.

As they bounced in the water, the sound of the waves against the wall was soothing.

Kevin loved the feel of Nikki's body in his arms. "Nikki," he started.

"Hmmm?" She kept her head on his forehead.

He cleared his throat, hearing the nervousness in his own voice. "There's something I need to tell you, baby."

Nikki leaned back in his arms to look at him.

The light bounced off the water and danced in her eyes. "I've been wanting to tell you for a while, but the timing was never right. Being here with you and Kayla has only further confirmed what I already knew." He paused. "I love you."

Nikki's face glowed. She looked in his eyes and kissed him gently. "I love you, too. I don't know what I'd do without you."

His heart flooded with warmth. He felt the same way. "You won't ever have to worry about that." He took his hand. "I promise," he whispered, caressing her. After 7's "Ready or Not" came to his mind, and before he knew it, the song flowed from his lips. When his serenade ended, Nikki reared back, studying his face. Then they kissed.

A short while later, Kevin walked Nikki back to her room. Their declarations of love were fresh in their minds. Neither wanted the night to end.

"Goodnight."

"Goodnight, my love," Nikki whispered. They held each other firmly for several seconds.

"I better go." Nikki turned.

"If you're going to be up, why don't you come over for a few?" He grinned. "I'll rub you down like you like."

"No, that's okay."

He looked at her, puzzled. He had never known her to refuse his massages. "Why not?"

"Because of the way I feel," she whispered.

Her eyelashes seemed thicker than ever. "And how do you *feel?*" he asked softly.

Ever since he had made a pass at her, Nikki's curiosity had been peaked. Initially, she had just wondered about it haphazardly, but over the past few months, her desire for him had grown stronger. No one had ever brought this womanly lust out of her with such intensity and consistency.

Well? his eyes asked, though he knew the answer. Nikki often concealed the lust she felt for him, but seeing it unmasked excited him.

As if reading his mind, a naughty smile crossed Nikki's lips. With the right look, a smile, and a little nibble here and there, she could have him. He might resist at first, but ultimately, he would cave. She kissed him sensually on the cheek. "Goodnight, Kevin." She turned and walked away.

CHAPTER EIGHTEEN

"Still nothing?"

"No," Kevin murmured, looking at his cell phone with annoyance. He flipped it open and attempted to make a call, but once again, the signal wasn't strong enough.

"There's a gas station up ahead. They should have a pay phone."

Kevin pulled into the parking lot and spotted one immediately.

"See?" Nikki smiled.

"I see," he said, leaning over and kissing her. "Be right back."

Kevin dialed Randy's number, returning his call. He couldn't imagine why he needed him; Randy knew he was out of town. A man approached and entered the booth next to him.

"Hey, Jessica. Yeah. Randy tried to call me just now, but I lost the signal."

Kevin heard the rumbling of change, and the man started speaking loudly. He turned his back to hear Jessica more clearly.

"Oh. He's going out of town? I didn't know that. Yeah. Oh, it's no rush. I was coming in tomorrow, anyway. Okay. Okay. See ya." He hung up.

"Hey, your wife's calling you."

Kevin walked towards the store, but the man's voice seemed to follow him. He walked faster to tune it out.

"Hey, buddy."

Kevin turned.

"Your wife." The man gestured.

Kevin finally realized he was pointing at Nikki in the car. He nodded.

"Cute kid."

Kevin gave him a half-smile.

"Yeah, anyway…" The man turned back around.

Kevin approached the passenger side and leaned in the window. "What's up?"

Nikki peered over the rim of her sunglasses. "Could you get us a Sprite, please?"

"Sure, baby." He smiled. "Anything else?"

Nikki shook her head.

He looked at Kayla in the back seat, wondering how the man could have mistaken her for his child. She was much too beautiful to be his daughter. "Be right back," he said, patting the car. He headed into the store. He felt a headache coming on.

Nikki patted Kayla down with a towel. She had just gotten out of the tub; it was her bedtime.

"Can I stay up with you?"

Nikki shook her head, holding Kayla's robe open.

"Please?" Kayla's tone sweetened.

Kayla often used this technique to get her to change her mind. Sometimes it worked, but not this time. "Go get in your pajamas. I'll be in, in a minute."

Kayla sulked then walked to her room.

Nikki began cleaning the bathtub. A while later, Kayla returned, dressed. "Nikki?" Kayla kissed her and wrapped her arms around her neck. "I want to stay up with you."

Nikki squeezed her. "I know, baby, but you have to go to bed. You have a big day tomorrow. Mrs. Starks is going to expect you to be up like the big kids."

"I will." She laid her head on her shoulder.

"Kayla." She looked at her firmly. "I said no. Get in bed. I'll be there in a second."

Kayla pouted, but Nikki pointed sternly in the direction of her room.

Kayla stormed off angrily.

Nikki started the water to rinse the tub once more.

A few minutes elapsed, and Kayla returned. "Where's Mr. Huggs?"

"I don't know." She looked at the tub. "The last time I saw him, he was on the couch."

Kevin looked up from his newspaper when he saw Kayla stump her way into the living room.

Kayla spotted her stuffed animal. It was halfway under Kevin. She went to the couch and tried to yank it from under him.

"Kayla?" Kevin pushed her back gently. "What is wrong with you?"

Kayla stood quietly, staring at the bear.

He picked it up. "Is this what you want?" he asked, holding it in front of her.

Nikki had heard the commotion. She came down the hallway and was about to intervene, but decided against it. Instead, she went into the kitchen.

"What's wrong?"

Kayla ignored him, her arms folded. Finally, she broke her silence. "It's mine!" she said, attempting to snatch it again.

Kevin held the bear securely. "No, no, no!" He pushed her back gently. "You have to ask politely, Kayla."

Kayla looked at the bear then at Kevin. She didn't want to ask nicely. Mr. Huggs belonged to her. She grabbed the bear's limbs and pulled with all her strength.

Kevin caught Nikki's eye. He wondered why she hadn't come over to help.

"Spank her," Nikki mouthed.

Kevin stared at her. Kayla continued to tug viciously. He picked her up and bent her over his knee. He didn't know how much force to use. He didn't want to hurt her. He hit her a couple times.

Nikki stepped back and hid behind the entrance. He looked so disoriented she couldn't help but laugh.

When Kevin finished, Kayla jumped from his lap and looked back at him. Tears streamed down her face. She ran through the apartment looking for her sister. "Nikki, Nikki!" she shouted frantically, spotting her in the kitchen.

Nikki took her by the shoulders and tried to slow her down. She could hardly understand her.

"He hit me," Kayla finally managed to get out, pointing to Kevin.

"I know, but what did he ask you to do?"

Kayla thought to herself. She couldn't get it out of her mind. "He hit me," she repeated.

"Kayla, what did Kevin ask you to do?"

Kayla was silent for a few seconds. She began crying harder, but the tears were different.

"You have been rude and disrespectful. I want you to apologize to Kevin."

Kayla walked towards Kevin.

"And tell him goodnight," Nikki added.

Kayla approached Kevin. She held one arm behind her and hung her head. "I'm sorry."

Kevin lifted her and sat her in his lap. "I know," he said, kissing her and wiping her tears.

Kayla smiled and gave him a hug. "Goodnight." She kissed him on the lips.

"Goodnight."

Kayla was about to climb out of his lap, when she turned back. "I love you."

Kevin was dumbfounded. "I love you, too, precious."

Kevin handed her the teddy bear. She jumped from his lap and sprinted to her room.

Nikki came around the kitchen corner. "You two sure are hitting it off well," she remarked, surprised at Kayla's words. "Not that I had any doubts." She reached for the back of her head and pulled out the clip. Her hair fell to the side of her face and across her shoulders. "I'll be right back."

"I think I should be going." Kevin stood. He didn't like having to discipline Kayla.

"What? I'll just be a few —"

"I gotta go. It's been a long day." He walked towards the door.

"Hey." Nikki wrapped her arms around him. "Don't worry, cowboy. You didn't hurt her." She chuckled. "You barely touched her."

"No, that's not it."

"Then what?"

He had finally met the woman of his dreams — and for what? He had been living in a fantasy world; now they were back in reality. He hugged her quietly then kissed her cheek. "Goodnight."

CHAPTER NINETEEN

"Okay, baby; I'm here," Kevin said, talking into his cell phone. He climbed up the stairs and approached his door. "I'll call you before I go to bed."

"Promise?"

"I promise," Kevin answered sweetly, and then hung up. He was relieved to be home. He was exhausted and just wanted to crawl into bed. He stuck the key in the door and flung it open.

Nikki leaped off the sofa and flung herself into his arms.

He stared at her, confused, and then realized Nikki had called him from her new cell phone. She had finally agreed to get one on the way home from their trip.

Nikki kissed Kevin's face all over. She had been busy with school, and he had been tied up with work; they hadn't seen each other since the trip. "Surprised?"

"Yeah," Kevin mumbled. He thought he had made it perfectly clear that he needed to catch up on some rest. He threw his briefcase down and slid his jacket off.

Nikki shrugged off his grumpiness. She knew he had had a long day and was tired. That was why it was so important that she be there. "I've got shrimp pasta cooking, and it's almost ready," she said, watching him. She imagined he had been eating out all week, and wanted to make sure he had a good meal. He was about to sit, but she stopped him. "Come on. I'll let you sample a little," she said, taking him by the hand playfully.

Kevin let himself be dragged behind her as she danced into the kitchen. She took a large wooden spoon, dipped it into the sauce, and brought it to Kevin's lips. "Good, huh?" She was proud of herself; she thought she had duplicated his mother's recipe to a tee.

It wasn't bad, but he just really wasn't in the mood. "Baby," he called, watching as she opened the cabinets and got plates out.

Nikki smiled excitedly. "You think we should eat on these, or these?" she asked, displaying first a blue set of dishes, and then a silver set.

He felt a headache coming on. "Baby," Kevin called again.

"Never mind," Nikki said, hastily putting the dishes back. "You look tired. We'll just eat on paper plates. You won't even have to load the dish washer."

"Nikki."

But she completely ignored him.

Nikki put the plates back in the cabinet. "You know what? Why don't you just go sit on the couch, and I'll bring dinner out to you."

Kevin's anger soared. It was the tenth time he had tried to tell her he wasn't hungry. Here she was, in his house, telling him what to do, when all he wanted was to come home and go to bed. "Nikki, I can not spend every waking moment of the day with you!"

Nikki froze, speechless. The room was dead silent. "You're right." The hurt in her voice was unmistakable. She charged past him, towards the door.

Kevin cursed in his head, running after her. She grabbed her purse and was almost through the door before he could stop her. "Baby, I'm sorry. I didn't mean that." He pulled her towards him, trying to kiss her, but she pulled away. "I've just been under a lot of stress at work lately. I'm sorry."

Nikki shook her head.

"I'm sor—"

Nikki turned and walked out. She couldn't let him see her cry. Ever since they had been back, he had been acting funny, saying he was busy, and acting as if he didn't have time for her. They hadn't had lunch or dinner together all week because of his schedule, and he had just confirmed that it wasn't her imagination.

"Hello?" Nikki clutched the phone, Kleenex in her palm.

"Nikki, baby." Kevin closed his eyes. "I'm so sorry."

Nikki listened intensely. If he didn't want them to be together anymore, all he needed to do was say so, and she would be out of his life forever.

"What I said back there..." He paused. He held his forehead and massaged it. He never meant to hurt her feelings. "I know there's no way I can take that back. Randy's been on me at work about these reports, and I've been behind on my—" Suddenly, he realized what he was doing. "There's no excuse. I didn't mean to take it out on you. I love you, Nikki. You mean everything to me."

Nikki sniffled and dabbed her face with the Kleenex. It was the first time he had told her he loved her since the evening in the pool.

"Will you ever forgive me?"

There was a long pause, then, "Yeah," she whispered.

"You still love me?" Kevin asked softly.

Nikki paused again. "Yes."

Kevin's heart warmed.

"Goodnight," Nikki said abruptly.

Kevin heard the phone click. He slid the phone down slowly from his ear. There was a much deeper problem, and he couldn't keep telling her he was busy to avoid discussing it. He hung up the phone and lay back against the pillow.

Nikki heard a tap at her door. She threw her robe around her and went to open it. To her surprise, Kevin stood in the doorway.

The morning light broke across his face. "I—um—" Kevin paused, looking into her eyes. "I wanted to see if you'd like to have breakfast with me."

Nikki smiled inside, flattered. He had driven all the way to Cobb County, just to have breakfast with her. He'd have to drive all the way back to DeKalb for work. Since she was still somewhat angry from the previous night, she didn't let it show. "What about your job?"

"For you—" Kevin smiled a little. "I can be a little delayed."

Nikki looked at the time. It was ten minutes to seven. "Can't. I have a test in a couple of hours," she announced firmly.

"Oh," Kevin said, disappointed. He felt like a fool. Normally, he would have kept up with stuff like that, but had been so preoccupied lately that he had forgotten. He turned to leave.

"But—" Nikki said quickly. She took a step down from the doorway. "That doesn't mean you can't cook something for me."

Kevin turned around and smiled. Nikki stepped into the apartment, and he followed her in.

"Knock it out, baby," Kevin said, kissing Nikki.

Nikki's face shone. They had made up, and she felt pretty good about her test.

"I will," she said. She turned to leave, took a few steps, and then turned again. She threw her arms around Kevin, and they kissed. "That was for luck," she said, backing away from him. "I love you."

"I love you too, baby," Kevin declared, watching her step towards the door.

Nikki waved goodbye.

Kevin waved his hand playfully.

"See you tonight," she said, finally closing the door.

Kevin looked at his watch. Though he would have to high tail it back to Decatur before his first client arrived, and Randy was probably going to have a fit because he hadn't finished the report, the morning had been perfect. Being in Nikki's apartment early in the morning, cooking breakfast for her, and watching her head to school made everything seem right.

He loaded up the last few dishes in the dishwasher and wiped the counter down. He grabbed his jacket and headed towards the door.

CHAPTER TWENTY

Nikki looked outside. The slightest noise alerted her. She had been waiting for Kevin for over an hour, and he still wasn't here. He was always punctual. She dialed his cell phone again and wondered why he hadn't called back. She theorized that his batteries had run low or his car had broken down. Either way, she was worried sick.

She heard a noise. She peeped out the window and saw Kevin getting out of his car. Her heart relaxed. He had barely tapped on the door before she flung it open to meet him. She pulled him to her, hugging him. "Kevin, you scared me to death! I was beginning to think something had happened. Where were you?" she started to ask, and then noticed his eyes were dark and distant. "You okay?"

"Yeah," he whispered, pushing past her.

Nikki closed the door. "Are you sure? You don't look so good," she said as she walked with him to the couch.

"Yeah," he said softly.

She knew something was wrong, but didn't want to press. She turned towards the kitchen. "I'll be back." She began to walk away. Then she ran back to him, smiling. She kissed him again on the lips. "'Let him kiss me with the kisses of his mouth: for thy love is better than wine.'" Her eyes glittered. "Guess where I got that?"

"Nikki," Kevin whispered.

"Kevin, relax." She put her hands on his shoulders and pushed him down to sit. "You're not at work anymore." She turned and walked towards the kitchen.

"Nikki," he called after her softly.

Nikki turned to look at him, but he hung his head low. Then he looked up. "Come here, baby. We need to talk," he said, patting the couch beside him.

She walked back and sat. She wrapped her arms around his neck. "What is it, cowboy?"

He leaned his head on her shoulder, took her hand, and kissed it. Then he took her arm from around him, held her hands in his, and rested them in his lap. He looked into her eyes. "Nikki, you are a really good woman," he whispered.

Nikki smiled a little. She didn't understand what this had to do with her.

He looked at their hands. "Baby, I don't think—I think we need to stop seeing each other."

Nikki's heart stopped. "What?" He couldn't mean what she thought she just heard. "Stop seeing each other?" she repeated.

Kevin sat quietly, staring down at their clasped hands.

Nikki pulled away. "What's going on, Kevin?" She paused. "I thought we—I thought we loved each other."

He couldn't bring himself to look at her. "Nikki, I do love you," he emphasized, nodding his head slowly as he said the words.

Nikki rose. She folded her arms, looking down at him. "Then why are you breaking up with me?" Her voice trembled with anger.

"I just—I just—"

"Is it something I did?"

He raised his head enough to look in her eyes. "No, baby. You haven't done anything. It's me."

Nikki knelt again on the couch, propping one leg under the other. She wrapped her arms around his neck. "Kevin, whatever it is, we can work it out—together."

"Nikki." Kevin shook his head slowly. He tried to stand, but Nikki held her arms around his neck firmly, stopping him.

She smiled hopefully in his eyes, but Kevin knew it wasn't enough. He slid his fingers over her arms.

"Kevin?" Nikki caressed his face.

Kevin closed his eyes. He absorbed the feeling of her soft fingers on his face. He wanted to hold on to this moment, to remember her just like this. He opened his eyes and studied her for a long moment, then closed them, leaned over, and kissed her gently.

Nikki kept her eyes open.

He rubbed her arms gently. The hurt he saw in her eyes almost killed him. He could feel the tears coming. He unwrapped her arms, stood up, and headed for the door.

"Kevin?" Nikki's heart bled. "Kevin?" she called again, but she spoke only to his back. She wanted to go somewhere and hide—scream. A new thought popped into her head, and she needed to know. She folded her arms, and with all the strength she could muster, asked, "Is there someone else?"

He stopped. He turned towards her. "No. Of course not."

"Then why are you walking away?"

Kevin looked at her quietly. His face was worn and tired. Without responding, he walked out and closed the door behind him.

Nikki stood for a moment, stunned. She heard his footsteps walking away outside her apartment. She felt like she was dreaming.

She went to the window and watched. He got out his keys and unlocked the car door. Her heart sank. She couldn't breathe. Seconds later, the parking spot stood empty. Kevin was gone.

Nikki sat on the couch. She combed her hands through her hair and rubbed her forehead. Warm tears formed and ran down her cheeks. Abruptly, she stopped crying. She wiped the tears from her eyes with her fingers. "He just needs space," she told herself. "I'll just give him some space."

● ● ●

Several days passed, and Nikki hadn't heard anything from Kevin. She had spoken to Anesa a few times during the week, and whenever she asked about Kevin, Nikki had simply told her he was fine. Besides, the last time she saw him he *was* doing fine, it was she who had been broken up inside.

Her stomach ached for food, but though she was hungry, she couldn't eat. Her overworked body screamed of sleep deprivation, but whenever she got in bed, she tossed and turned.

She picked up the phone, clutching it tightly. They had never gone this long without communicating. She wondered what he was doing. She needed to speak to him. There had been a terrible misunderstanding; she needed to find out what she had done. Finally, she dialed.

"Hello?"

Nikki froze. She hadn't expected to reach him so easily. "Hi." Her voice was soft.

"Hey," Kevin grinned, happy to hear her voice.

She could tell that Kevin was smiling. She heard laughter in the background. "How are you?"

Kevin paused. He wondered if it was a trick question. "I'm okay."

There was silence on the phone.

Kevin looked over his shoulder and saw his co-workers motioning him to the car. "Listen, I'm out of the office right now. Can I call you when I get back?"

Nikki's heart warmed. "Yeah. That's fine."

"Okay?"

"Okay." Nikki heard the phone click, then a dial tone. She hung up. Soon, everything would be okay.

Jessica watched Kevin when he hung up. She leaned into Marla's ear. "Must've been Veronica—he's been a grouch all week."

Nikki sat on her bed, a book propped in her lap. She gazed at the phone at the side of the bed. Hours had passed, and Kevin still hadn't called. She picked up the phone and stared at it, then clicked the receiver to check for a dial tone.

Kevin had always been good about calling her back. She imagined he had gotten busy when he returned to work and hadn't had a chance to call. She wanted to let him know she was still home, that she hadn't gone out or anything. She picked up the phone and dialed the numbers to his cell again.

Kevin looked at his cell phone and saw Nikki's name flash across the screen. It was the one conversation he had been trying to avoid all week. "Don't force it, baby," he whispered. Then to his relief, it went away.

Though he felt guilty for not answering, there was simply no other way. He had known long before Nikki had spoken the words, how much she loved him, but her love alone was no longer enough.

"Knock, knock."

Kevin looked up and saw Marla, a new employee, coming through his door. His anger kindled. This was not the time. "Would you mind *waiting* until I respond next time?" he snapped, his voice harsh.

Marla stepped back. "I'm sorry. Jessica said you needed these right away."

Kevin's irritation faded. Those had been his exact words, and the secretaries moved freely inside their offices all the time. "You're right." He breathed deeply. "I'm sorry."

Marla shrugged. "That's okay." She walked the papers to his desk. "Jessica told me you've had a chip on your shoulder all week, anyway."

He felt bad and watched as she placed the items on his desk. She turned to leave. "Marla, I owe you an apology." He hesitated, but felt he owed her an explanation. "My girlfriend and I broke up last weekend—"

"Really?" she suddenly turned sympathetic. "I'm sorry. What happened?"

Kevin dropped his head. She didn't need more of an explanation than what he had already given. "I'm sorry," he said, ignoring her question. "It won't happen again."

Marla nodded and left the room.

Nikki fell over. She looked around, dazed, and rose from her pillow. She had drifted to sleep waiting for Kevin's call. What if he had called and she had slept through the ring? She picked up the phone and clicked it, but to her disappointment, there were no messages. She hurled the phone on the bed angrily. She had actually believed he was going to call.

Nikki woke at five o'clock in the morning. She had only slept a couple of hours, but she needed to get up and do something. She threw on some clothes, got in her car, and drove.

Though she had no destination, she needed to get out of her apartment. There were too many memories there, and remembering was the last thing she wanted to do. She headed down Thornton Rd and popped onto I-20. She approached downtown, musing as thousands of lights illuminated the night. She merged onto I-75/85 and took the Freedom Parkway exit before realizing where her heart had navigated.

It wanted Kevin. She needed to see him, taste him, and breathe him. Though it had only been eight days, she couldn't stand the isolation any longer. She figured he hadn't called the day before because he had gotten a special assignment and had to leave town immediately, but she wanted to be there when he returned to sort all this out.

She drove into Kevin's neighborhood and pulled onto his street. Her eyes darted around for a parking space, and then she spotted his car. Her heart ached. Whenever he left town, he parked at the airport, but if he was home, why hadn't he called?

All the reasons she had given for his absenteeism were excuses her mind had composed to make herself feel better. The fact of the matter was that Kevin was available—just not to her.

Fury burned inside her. He had told her he loved her, and she really thought he was sincere. Now she realized it had all been a hoax—a final, desperate attempt to get her into his bed. She scolded herself for entertaining the thought that someone actually loved her enough to want to spend the rest of his life with her.

She wanted to take her keys and run them up and down the side of his car or smash out his windows. She still had a key to his apartment; this would be an opportune time to use it—to see for herself the woman he had let come between them.

Tears streamed down her cheeks, uncontrolled. She tried to catch her breath, but she couldn't. She dropped her head into her hands and sobbed. "He doesn't care about me," she murmured. Then she caught a glimpse of herself in the visor. Her eyes were red and her face was pale and puffy where tears had fallen all night. "It's okay," she assured herself. "You don't need him."

She cranked up the car and drove away.

At about seven-fifteen, Nikki found herself in her cousin's neighborhood. She pulled into the driveway and wondered if anyone was awake. She still had the bag Anesa had left behind in Kevin's car. She looked inside and saw the baby outfit. She held it in her hand for a moment, thinking back to the day she had dropped Anesa off to see the OB/GYN. Anesa had told her she was in love.

She got out of the car and walked slowly to the front door. She rang the doorbell, wondering if this was a mistake. She was about to walk away when Anesa answered.

"Nic-Nic? What are you doing on this side of town this early in the morning?"

Nikki looked at her quietly. Then she held out the bag. "I thought you might want this," she said, gesturing with the bag, and then folding her arms.

Anesa took the bag and looked inside. "Don't tell me you came all the way over here for this," she joked, dangling the bag loosely. Then Anesa studied her face and noticed Nikki's sorrow. "Why don't you come in?" she said softly, stepping back to let her in.

The kitchen door swung on its hinge; Malcolm walked through then stopped dead in his tracks. Nikki's back was to him, and she was sobbing in his wife's arms. Anesa caught his eyes, and he knew what had occurred. His anger kindled.

Anesa put a cup of coffee in front of Nikki then sat beside her. They had congregated around the kitchen table.

She rubbed Nikki's back as she drank a few sips. "Don't worry. He'll realize he made a mistake. Then he'll be back."

"And it'll be too late," Malcolm snickered. Anesa stared at him disapprovingly, but Malcolm didn't recant. "I'm glad it's over with, to be honest with you. I wondered how long he would last."

Anesa huffed. "Malcolm, what are you talking about? Kevin is a good man, and he was good to Nikki."

"Good to her? Look at what he's done." He gazed at Nikki. She sniffled and resumed drinking her coffee. He gritted his teeth. "I ought to go over there and—"

"He knows Tae Kwon Do, Malcolm."

"What? That doesn't scare me. I—"

"Malcolm, will you please shut up! This isn't about you." She stopped rubbing Nikki's back. "Don't worry about him. Trust me when I say he'll be back. Then what are you going to do?" The last question was directed at Nikki.

"What do you mean what is she going to do?"

"Malcolm!" Anesa hit the table.

"She's going to not do anything. Two months of working 'in town,' and he can't be faithful?"

Anesa looked at him, confused.

"Oh, yeah, all that talk about 'business trips.' What do you think he's been doing?"

Nikki froze. She had never thought about that. She burst into tears and bolted out of the kitchen.

"Malcolm!" Anesa hit him in the chest. "Now look at what you've done. She came here for support."

"I'm glad everything's out in the open. She needed to hear it. I know cats that get off on doing things like this. It's like a game to them, and she needs to know it."

"Kevin isn't like that! You never even got to know him. He took her to meet his parents and everything—"

Nikki stood in the powder room listening to her cousins arguing. She stared at herself in the mirror. Everything had been a big illusion; she wondered how she had ever let herself fall in love. She splashed cold water on her face, then dabbed it with a hand towel.

Anesa walked into the room. "Girl, don't listen to him," she said, shutting the door behind her. "He's just upset, that's all." She ran her hand up and down Nikki's arm. "You know Kevin is a good man. Do you actually think he was in a relationship with you for that long if nothing he felt for you was genuine?"

"I honestly can't answer that right now," Nikki replied. She wanted to believe, but this time, she thought Malcolm's instincts were right. She left the powder room and picked her purse up off the sofa.

"Hey," Anesa called.

Nikki stopped.

"It's going to be okay."

"I know," Nikki nodded. She opened the door and left.

CHAPTER TWENTY-ONE

Nikki scanned the aisle. From the descriptors, she couldn't figure out which aisle the Shake and Bake was on. She was in a rush and had paced several aisles to no avail before spotting an assistant. She called after him, but he continued walking down the aisle. She got close enough that she thought he would hear her, but then she heard another voice calling her name. She looked around, bewildered, and saw a man approaching.

"Veronica? I can't believe it's you." He was tall, dark-skinned, and handsome. Muscles strained through his clothing.

"Mike?" she said, not believing her eyes. Of all the people she could run into, she would run into him. In high school, she'd had a huge crush on Mike. They had even gone to the prom together his senior year, but it never blossomed into anything because soon after their date, she left town.

"Yeah," he grinned. They embraced. "It's good to see you."

"Yeah. You, too," she said, stepping back to look at him. "What are you doing here?"

"I have family here."

"Oh, that's right. Your parents live here."

"Well, they did."

Nikki looked puzzled. "Oh, did they pass?"

"No. No." His lips curved. "They moved to Kansas. I'm just here getting some things out of storage to ship to them. My sister just had her first baby, and they wanted to be closer to her."

"Oh, how sweet," Nikki nodded. "You don't have any yet?"

"Me?" He pointed to his chest. "Heck no. How about you?"

"No. I don't have any, but I'm taking care of my little sister, MiKayla."

"Really?"

"Yeah." She smiled. "It was good seeing you, Mike. I have to go. They're waiting in the car for me."

"They?" Mike inquired.

"My grandmother and MiKayla. My grandmother lives here. I live in Atlanta now."

"Oh." He nodded. "Let me get your number," he said, reaching into his pocket and pulling out a pad of paper. "We should keep in touch."

"Okay," Nikki said hesitantly. She dug in her purse and found a pen. Her palms felt sweaty, and she struggled to keep her hands from shaking as she wrote. "Okay. I better get going."

"Okay. I'll be talking to ya."

Nikki smiled and took off. She didn't want him to see her blush. She turned down one of the aisles, and her heart pounded. "Dang, he looks good."

Anesa hung up the phone. Malcolm could tell she was bothered by something, but didn't want to ask.

Anesa looked at him, concerned. "Have you spoken to Nikki?" She put her hand on her hip. "I've called her several times this week, and she's yet to return one—"

"You know Nic. I'm sure she's just busy with school." Malcolm spoke with an illusion of confidence. "She probably spent the weekend at her grandma's."

"Nah. She would have told me." Anesa rattled her brain. "I'm getting worried."

"About what?"

"You know how Nikki gets depressed."

"What?" Malcolm snapped. "She was depressed one time, and it wasn't over no nigga. It was because her father passed."

Anesa looked at him, surprised. It wasn't like Malcolm to be so cold and insensitive. She wondered how long his behavior would continue because she couldn't take much more of it.

"She'll get over it," he said nonchalantly, walking out of the kitchen.

Anesa sighed. Judging by Malcolm's reaction, he was worried, too. She would definitely go see her tomorrow.

Nikki awakened from a deep sleep. It had gotten dark. The parking light shone into the window. She moved to close the blinds and began stretching. She looked at her telephone and noticed that the message light was blinking. She picked up the phone and listened. It was Anesa; she had just missed her.

She felt bad for not returning the calls, but Anesa had been calling at the wrong times, though she hadn't felt like talking much, anyway. The telephone rang, and she answered.

"Veronica?"

"Yeah," she yawned.

"Did I catch you at a bad time?"

She stretched. "No. I was just getting up."

"Just getting up?" he mocked, looking out his window at the sunset. "You're not one of those kinds of people are you?"

"No, after the exam—"she paused. "Who is this?" She had thought it was a guy from her study group, but realized the voice was different.

"Mike." He grinned.

"Mike? I can't believe you actually called."

"You got a man or something? I don't want to cause any friction—"

"No, it's not that. You know how you run into some people, and they ask for your number, but never call? I just thought you were being nice."

"Nice? I've been waiting six years to get those digits."

Nikki blushed, flattered. He was the same old Mike.

"I'm going to be in your neck of the woods tomorrow. Mind if I drop by?"

The day was pretty and bright, a perfect day to go see her cousin. Anesa knocked on the door. She was relieved Nikki's car was in the parking lot. She would've called to let her know she was coming, but she was starting to think Nikki was avoiding her.

"Anesa?" Nikki answered the door, surprised. She squeezed through and cracked the door behind her. "What are you doing here?"

"I came to check up on you." She smiled, and then realized Nikki hadn't invited her inside. "Can I come in?"

"This isn't a good time."

Anesa looked over Nikki's shoulder into the apartment. There was a man sitting on the sofa. "Who is he?"

"He's just a friend," Nikki said, looking back at Mike briefly then completely shutting the door.

"A friend?" Anesa searched Nikki's face, but her cousin eluded her gaze.

"Nikki," Anesa began, "I don't think this is smart."

"What?"

"Veronica, you're rebounding."

"Rebounding? Anesa, you're supposed to be on my side. Kevin broke up with me," Nikki huffed. The blind unquestioning faith Anesa held in Kevin sickened her to the core.

"Exactly," Anesa paused. "Nikki, I am on your side. Look, girl, I know you can't see it right now, but this isn't good. You're hurt, and you're trying to get rid of the pain. But getting into another relationship—"

"I'm not getting into another relationship," Nikki corrected. "I told you—he's just a friend."

"A friend?" Anesa repeated, crossing her arms.

"Yes."

"Then why don't you introduce me to him?"

"Because he's just passing through."

"Just passing through? Nikki, you know nothing about this man, and you have him in your house?"

"I never said I knew nothing about him." Nikki paused. "I've known him for a long time."

Anesa looked confused.

"It's Mike," she said, pointing inside.

"Mike? Mike who?"

Nikki's eyes sparkled with excitement. "Mike. You know— prom Mike."

Anesa shook her head. "Nikki, I don't think you should do this."

"Do what?"

"I know you don't see it right now. You're hurt. Okay? Either you're going to get hurt again, or you're going to hurt him."

"Frankly, I don't care what you think, Anesa. Mike likes me for who I am, and so what if I'm interested? I'm tired of you meddling in my business. Your advice is what got me into this predicament in the first place."

Anesa looked at her in disbelief. All she had ever tried to do was be her friend; she couldn't believe Nikki was blaming her for what had transpired with her and Kevin. Anger gripped her, and if she didn't leave soon, she would lose her temper. "Fine, then!" Anesa stomped away. "You don't have to worry about me meddling in yo' business again!" she shouted.

Nikki had seen the pain in her eyes, and she knew she had crossed the line. "Anesa," she called after her, but her cousin stormed away in the direction of her car. "Anesa!" she shouted again, wanting to apologize.

Anesa threw up her hand, and her pace increased.

"Whatever then," Nikki huffed under her breath, and then Mike emerged.

"Is everything all right?"

He was so tall Nikki had to look up at him. "Yeah," she said softly, watching Anesa drive away.

"I've got to go meet up with my boy." He looked her over. "But maybe I could drop back by later?"

Even if Anesa were right, she would still rather have the company. "Okay."

"I'll see you later," he grinned. He took her hand and kissed it. Nikki quivered as his lips touched her hand.

He smiled and walked away.

Malcolm heard keys rattling outside. Then the door flew open, and Anesa marched in. He sat up. "How's she doing?"

"I don't know. I didn't get a chance to ask," Anesa snapped, storming past him. "She was too busy 'entertaining.'" She darted up the stairs.

Malcolm heard their bedroom door slam, and Anesa burst into tears. "Oh, boy," he said, slumping into the couch. From the looks of things, it hadn't gone well.

Nikki heard a faint knock. She looked up from her book. She had papers scattered over the cocktail table and couch. *One last major project*, she thought to herself, *and it'll all be downhill.* She looked at the clock. Eleven-forty-seven. The news had just gone off. She turned the TV down and listened again.

There was another knock. This one was clearer. She pulled herself off the couch.

"Who is it?" she asked, standing some distance from the door.

"It's Mike."

Nikki breathed. She opened the door, and saw him standing there, his arm propped against the wall. His dark face split into a smile as he saw her.

"Is it too late?"

Nikki thought for a moment. She had been planning to go to bed at twelve. "No." She stepped back to let him in. "I figured you were on your way home by now," she said, scurrying to clean off a place for him to sit.

"I decided to stay overnight." He watched her. "My buddy's got a place here."

They sat down. Mike rested his arm on the back of the chair.

"How was the game?"

Mike shrugged. "It was all right."

"All right? You sound disappointed."

He looked at Nikki and smiled. "Couldn't keep my mind off of you."

Their eyes met. Nikki eased away from him and pulled her left leg under her on the couch.

Mike sensed her uneasiness. "You said you have a little sister?"

"Yeah, MiKayla. She lives with my grandmother." Her face brightened. "But she'll be coming to stay with me in a few weeks."

"How old is she?"

"She's four — going on five. She's really sweet."

They began talking, and before Nikki knew it, it was two o'clock. "Well — " Mike stretched. "I guess I better be going."

Nikki looked at him sleepily. She didn't want the conversation to end. She yawned.

"Yep," he said, watching her.

Nikki laughed at herself. "I'm sorry."

"No, no; don't apologize." He rose and stretched again. "It's my fault, since I came over so late."

Nikki smiled at him. "I'm glad you did."

Mike headed for the door and opened it, then closed it and froze in his tracks. "You know something?"

Nikki gazed at him. His smile was nice, and his lips looked luscious, just as she'd remembered.

"I often wonder what — what would have happened after prom night if I had kissed you." He smiled. "I wanted to kiss you so bad," he laughed, "but I was scared of you, girl. I thought you would hit me. You know what they say about second chances. It's rare that you get one, so you better take it if you do."

Nikki looked at him shyly. Her heart ran a thousand beats per minute. Her hands were sweaty and her legs were weak. This was the chance of a lifetime—something she had often wondered about herself.

He lifted her chin and kissed her lips. "Goodnight." He held her face in his hands.

"Goodnight," Nikki repeated faintly. She closed the door, finally catching her breath. The smell of his cologne lingered in the air.

As much as she enjoyed Mike's company, she had made up her mind that this could go nowhere, so she wondered why she had just locked lips with him.

She fell back against the door, confused.

●●●

There was a tap at the door. Anesa struggled to get to her feet.

"Hey," Nikki greeted Anesa warmly, apology in her tone. She and Kayla stood outside her door for another Friday night card game.

"Hi," Anesa said softly.

"You're big," Kayla squealed. She touched Anesa's stomach, curious.

"Hey, baby," Anesa said. She took Kayla's hand, and they walked to the couch.

Nikki was happy Kayla was there to take some of the tension away. "Where is everybody?" she asked, looking around. Usually people were there playing cards way before she arrived.

"Malcolm's in the kitchen," Anesa answered. She picked up the remote control and handed it to Kayla, then flopped onto the sofa.

Kayla already knew what she wanted to see.

Nikki entered the kitchen.

"What's up, baby girl?" Malcolm asked. He stood over the kitchen sink washing dishes. He had a cloth towel over his arm.

"Where is everybody?"

Malcolm rinsed a few dishes and placed them in the dishwasher to dry. He smiled and looked at her. "Anesa doesn't feel well, so we called and cancelled."

"No one told me," Nikki said softly, realizing that 'no one' would have been Anesa. "What are you about to do?"

He turned around briefly and looked at her. "Well, since you're here, I'm going to Joe-Joe's house for a little while. He has a card game going over there."

"I wasn't planning to stay," Nikki blurted. Malcolm's face turned troubled. "Kayla and I have things to do at home. See you later." She turned to walk out the door. "Bye."

"Nic-Nic," Malcolm stopped her. He set the cloth down and leaned back on the sink. He stared out the window. "Look, I don't know what's going on between you two, but ya'll need to straighten this mess out." He picked the cloth up from the sink and draped it over a hanger. "And on that note, I'm out." He threw on a jacket then headed out the door to the garage.

Nikki stood in the kitchen alone for several minutes, pondering whether to leave or stay. She walked into the living room. Kayla was sitting Indian-style in front of the TV, flipping through the channels. "Kayla."

Her sister turned her head.

"Can you give us a few minutes alone?" She gestured towards the kitchen with her head. "I fixed some chocolate milk for you."

Kayla jumped up and dashed into the kitchen.

Nikki walked towards Anesa and saw a tear fall from her eyes. She didn't know what to say, so she decided not to say anything. She walked over, wrapped her arms around her, and hugged her.

More tears flowed.

"Hey, Mommy," Nikki said, embracing her.

Anesa chuckled.

Nikki kissed her on the cheek. "I'm sorry."

"Don't be," Anesa waved.

"No, you were right." Nikki squeezed her. "I was rebounding. I'm not going to see him again."

Anesa clasped Nikki's hand and guided her to the couch to sit beside her. She wiped a tear from her eyes. "I'm sorry. I guess sometimes I do meddle." She shrugged. "When I lost my first baby," she nodded her head, "Malcolm handled it his way, and I handled it mine—you were right there beside me." She took her hands and rubbed them. "I remember one day you came over, and said, 'Let's go out.' You wouldn't take no for an answer." She smiled. "I knew you were broke, but you took me to Spa Sydell's, and we went and got pizza. That was the sweetest thing anybody's ever done for me.

"I never had any brothers or sisters, and when I look at you—"
She paused. "I see my sister, and I want to be there for you, like you
were for me." She shook her head. "I just don't want to see you
hurt, because when you hurt—" She held Nikki's hand to her heart.
"I hurt."

Nikki smiled, and they hugged.

● ● ●

Nikki stared at herself in the mirror as she held up a three-piece
suit. Tomorrow was the big day.

"Will that be all?" the cashier asked at the register.

"Yes," Nikki said, looking at Kayla and handing the attendant
her credit card.

"Miss Jones."

Nikki rose, smiling pleasantly. She shook the HR representa-
tive's hand stiffly, once, just like instructed at the Careers Center at
school.

"You can have a seat in my office. I'll be with you in just a moment."

Nikki clutched her portfolio tightly. She walked in and sat
down. Her heart beat rapidly. This was the first interview of many.
She wanted to make a good impression. She took a deep breath and
began rehearsing her responses.

CHAPTER TWENTY~TWO

T hough her name wasn't on it, Kevin recognized Nikki's hand-writing on the package from Fed-Ex. He opened it promptly, and found, amongst other things, the diamond and aquamarine heart necklace he had given her for Christmas, the key to his apartment, and a couple of pictures he had given her of himself. He sighed.

Nikki heard the phone ring. "Don't play with that there, honey. Move it over here," Nikki said, pointing Kayla away from her plants. Then she picked up the phone. "Hello?"

"Hello? Nikki?"

Nikki's heart froze. It was Kevin.

"You didn't have to send—" Kevin heard a click. "Hello? Nikki?" Then he heard a dial tone. He picked up the phone and di-aled again.

Nikki had been walking away from the phone when it rang. She looked at Kayla, who stared back at her, wondering why she wasn't answering the phone. Nikki sat next to her on the floor, picked up a toy, and began playing.

At least she knew he had received the package. She didn't want a single item he had given her laying around, reminding her of the past. Everything he had given her went into that box, and what didn't fit, that she didn't think he needed, like the clothes he had bought her, went to Goodwill.

Kevin listened until Nikki's voice mail came on. Without leav-ing a message, he hung up the phone. Then he redialed and listened through the rings. His hands were sweaty as he tried to think of the right words to say. Finally, he heard a beep. "Hello, Nikki. I know we haven't talked for a while, and you have every right to be angry with me, and you probably never want to hear my voice again." He paused. "But please, call me, baby. We need to talk. It can be any time you want, day or night. I'll be here. Until then—" He hung up the phone.

Later that evening, as Nikki prepared to go to bed, she decided to listen to her messages. She knew Kevin had tried to call, and more than likely, it was just him. She played the message, and it confirmed her thinking. The very sound of his voice irritated her, and when she heard it, she promptly mashed the delete key. She placed the phone on the receiver, cut the kitchen light off, and re-treated to her bedroom.

●●●

"Are you sure about this?"

Anesa heard a woman's voice. She looked over a rack of shoes. She had found a pair she liked, and knew they would look great on her, but it would take a miracle to shove her swollen feet into them. She sighed and put them back.

"Would I ask you all the way over here if I wasn't?" The man paused. "I've never been more sure about anything in my life."

Anesa froze. She recognized the voice, but couldn't place it. She looked up and saw someone that greatly resembled Kevin. He and a light-skinned woman in her mid-twenties were stepping onto the escalator.

She looked around the department store, wondering if they were with someone else, but didn't see anyone. She debated before she picked her purse up off the bench, swung it over her arm, and stepped onto the escalator herself.

On the upper level, she quickened her pace to catch up to them, but left enough distance that she wouldn't be spotted. The pair conversed as if they had known each other a long time.

Finally, they slipped into a jewelry store. Anesa went to a deco-rating shop across from them. She walked around the store casually, picking up pieces here and there, hoping no one noticed what she was doing.

She stared at the man. They had been on the move, so she hadn't been positive it was Kevin. Now she knew it was he. He ap-peared a bit nervous, but was chuckling and talking with the woman and the attendant.

The girl's face shone brightly as she pointed to something in the jewelry case. Kevin nodded approvingly and motioned to the attendant. Nothing could prepare her for what happened next. The attendant took out a key and opened a latch. She pulled out the ring and handed it to Kevin.

Anesa's heart raced, but she couldn't take her eyes away. She watched as Kevin held the ring, examined it closely, and turned it around. Finally, he turned to face the woman. He seemed anxious. He took her right hand and slid the ring on the woman's finger.

Anesa's heart melted. All she could think about was her cousin. Nikki often went shopping with her, but she was glad she was not here to see this. Anger ensued, and she knew what she had to do.

"May I help you, ma'am?" asked a sales associate.

"No," Anesa snapped back, never looking at the woman. She left and stormed to the other side of the mall. She walked into the jewelry store and headed straight towards them. "Excuse me!" Anesa forced herself between Kevin and the woman.

"Anesa? What are you—?"

"Kevin, I don't believe this!"

"Anesa? What are you—?"

Anesa used her stomach to pin him against the display case. "After all the hype you paraded yo'self to be with my cousin." She looked him up and down. "You're nothing but a sorry, low-life, good-for-nothing snake that—"

"Excuse me," the woman Kevin was with interrupted.

"No, excuse me," Anesa said, turning and rolling her eyes and neck. "My beef is not with you." She waved her finger in the woman's face. "Okay?"

Kevin stepped back just enough to maneuver himself free. He grabbed Anesa by the arm and yanked her out of the store.

"Kevin, if you don't get your hands off—"

"Anesa, what do you think you're doing?" He said, low, but intense. "Why are you making a scene?"

Anesa snatched her arm from his grasp. "What am I doing? No, Kevin. The question is what are *you* doing? My cousin was in love with you." She watched as the woman walked towards them. "When you broke up with my cousin," she said, looking over at her, "when she was ready to blast you and shrug you off, I took up for you."

رد though

"Anesa," Kevin said, low.

"And to think that she's been crying her eyes out for you?"

"Anesa, you don't know—"

"No, Kevin. I'm talking," she fussed. "I can't believe that you're here with—" She looked the woman up and down. "With—" she stuttered. She had to have a good insult if it was going to be worth anything.

"With my sister," Kevin finished.

Anesa froze. "Your sister?" she exclaimed. She gazed at the woman's fingers and noticed a wedding band on her left hand.

Kevin motioned Kacie over. "Nesa, this is my sister, Kacie."

Anesa looked at them. As much as she wanted the woman to be his sister, she also needed her not to be. "You're kidding, right?" she smiled nervously, noting the resemblance.

"No," he answered, in an understanding voice. "Kacie, this is Nikki's cousin, Anesa."

Anesa smiled. She stuck out her hand, embarrassed. "Kacie." She recalled the name; it echoed in her mind. "It's nice to finally meet you."

Kacie smiled back suspiciously. "Likewise," she said, eyeing Kevin.

"Right," Anesa mumbled. She had made a complete fool of herself. She dropped her head in her hand, and then looked up, blushing. "You guys, I am so, so sorry."

"Kacie, can you excuse us?" Kevin asked. He watched as she walked back into the jewelry store.

"Look, Kevin, I'm—"

"It's okay. I'm going to ask Nikki to marry me."

"You what?" Anesa's eyes sparkled. "Oh, my God!" she gasped, wanting to cry.

"But I want it to stay a surprise."

She giggled. "Oh, it'll be a surprise!"

He looked at her. "So, whatever happens, please, just don't say anything." He paused. "That means not to friends or relatives. Not even Malcolm. And especially not Nikki."

"But—" Anesa looked at him.

"Promise me."

"Okay. Okay." She nodded. She mimed zipping her lips.

● ● ●

For several days, Kevin tried contacting Nikki. Each time, she hung up on him or wasn't home; at least, that was the impression she gave him. He knew seeing her wasn't going to be easy, but he had never imagined it would be this difficult. He thought love would have been enough of an incentive for her to see him. Now he realized it had been foolish to assume she would reenter their relationship with no qualms.

It was a Friday afternoon, and he had spent most of the day daydreaming in his office. He looked at the clock on his desk. It was three-thirty. He looked at his phone. More than likely, she was home, but she must have gotten caller ID, because she wouldn't answer his calls.

He needed to speak to Nikki desperately, and he was willing to do anything to make it happen. He knew that once they spoke, she would understand. Then they could have a future together.

He had an idea. He pushed the button on the telephone to page Jessica.

"Hello?"

Kevin smiled. Nikki's sweet voice soothed his heart. He pressed his head further into Jessica's cell phone. "Hey," he started, but could tell she was about to hang up. "Nikki, wait! Don't hang up!"

Nikki listened, annoyed that he had tricked her into answering. She had sent his stuff back so she wouldn't have to deal with him, but every since, he had been blowing up her phone, calling her everyday, and getting on her last nerve. Soon she would have to have her number changed.

"I really need to see you."

"Kevin, I'm not interested."

She was about to hang up again. "Nikki, please!" He threw his free hand up, as if she were standing in the room in front of him. "Baby, please. Just five minutes."

Silence gripped the phone.

"Nikki?" He listened. "Hello?"

"I'm here," her voice broke the silence.

"So, is it okay? If I come over?"

There was a long silence. "When?"

He wanted to smile, but kept his cool. This was no guarantee that they were getting back together. "Whenever you want, but preferably today."

"Today?" Nikki exclaimed. She had no plans for the evening, but he didn't need to know that.

"But it doesn't matter," he quickly added.

There was another silence. "Okay. Six," she finally answered.

"All right. See you then."

He heard a click.

He hung up the phone. "Thank you," he said, closing his eyes and clasping his hands together. He laid his chin in his hands. He had been waiting for this moment forever, and it was finally here. He jumped up from his desk and paged Jessica. He would be leaving early.

Nikki hung up the phone and sighed. She couldn't explain her sudden change of heart, and then she knew. She had spent the last several weeks feeling isolated and betrayed. Towards the end of their relationship, she had been so infatuated with the concept of being in love that she questioned whether she had ever truly loved him or not. Either way, none of it mattered. This was her final chance to get some closure.

CHAPTER TWENTY~THREE

N ikki pulled a corner of the curtain back slyly, hoping to get a peek of Kevin before their meeting. She cringed; her heart literally felt like it was about to beat out of her chest. She paced, fanning herself with her hand, not understanding her sudden anxiety.

She looked in the mirror again. She saw a strand of hair dangling and pulled it back in place. She wanted to look perfect. One look and she knew Kevin would regret breaking up with her. She smoothed some of the wrinkles out of her shirt that had accumulated. She would just stand from here on out. She didn't want to look too rumpled.

She walked back to the living room. She paced a little then she heard a noise outside. Her heart raced. She ran to the couch and peered out the window.

Nikki looked at her watch. It was six-fourteen, and there was no sign of Kevin. She shook her head and began crying. She had tried to convince herself she didn't love him, yet with one call, the feelings came back, full circle. She buried her head in her hands and scolded herself for being so gullible.

Kevin looked into his right mirror. He put his signal on to switch lanes. He was merging into the right lane when he heard the blare of a horn. He looked again and noticed a car approaching at high speeds. He scrambled to get back into his previous lane as the 2003 Chevrolet Corvette Coupe zoomed past. He breathed a sigh of relief. A second later, and the man would have sideswiped him. He stopped at the traffic light, but noticed the sports car turning down the same street he was headed. He felt something wet under his feet. He turned around and looked at the floor of the back seat. The vase of flowers he had gotten for Nikki had tipped over. He gnashed his teeth and hit the steering wheel.

Kevin pulled into the apartment complex. He slowed down as he saw the sports car park in reverse. He rode by and looked it over, but the windows were tinted, and he couldn't make out the driver's face. He fumed. To make matters worse, the man had the audacity to double-park, and he was already running late. Kevin searched, but didn't notice any other parking spaces.

At the knock at the door, Nikki wiped the tears from her eyes. "Just a second," she yelled, pretending confidence. Then she panicked.

She ran into the kitchen and splashed cold water on her face, then ran back to the door. Her hand quivered as she reached for the doorknob. She took a deep breath and opened the door. "Mike?" Her eyes got big. "What are you doing here?" she asked, looking for Kevin.

"I came to see you, beautiful," he grinned, looking her up and down. "You busy tonight?"

Nikki paused. "No."

"You sure?" Mike said to her slow response.

"Yeah. I mean, no! No, I'm not busy." She stepped back from the door. "Come in."

Mike walked in then stopped. "Where's your sister?"

"Oh." Nikki closed the door. "She's with my grandma. I have a project I'm finishing this weekend, and she stayed with her."

"Oh. You sure I'm not imposing? I don't want to—"

"No, Mike. Trust me. It's fine. I was just taking a break." She stared at him; he seemed a little hyped up. "What's up?"

"I was hoping you could join me for a night of food and fun." He shrugged. "Maybe a little dancing."

"Dancing?" Nikki's ears perked. "I haven't gone dancing in a long time." Whatever Kevin wanted to talk to her about must not have been very important, because once again, he had stood her up. This time would be his last. "That would be nice."

"Well, let's do this, then!"

Kevin fanned his car mats. The last thing he wanted was to have standing water smell up his car. He needed everything to be perfect. Getting Nikki to say yes was going to be difficult enough.

His stomach roiled with anxiety. Though the forecasters had predicted rain, he hoped the nice weather would continue. He wanted to take Nikki to Piedmont Botanical Gardens and propose to her there.

The site served two purposes. First, it was a nice, romantic spot. They could stroll amid hundreds of beautiful flowers, and the fragrant smells would relax them both. They could catch up on the time they had been separated, and then confess their continued love. Yet it was also private enough that if she rejected him, it wouldn't cause a scene.

Suddenly, his eyes caught two people coming out of Nikki's apartment. He froze, not believing his eyes. Nikki was walking with a man. Her hand was tucked in his elbow; she appeared to be leaving with him.

Kevin was crushed. The thought of her dating another man deeply troubled him. He wondered if this was what she had planned all along—the old boyfriend shows up, and the new boyfriend waltzes in, introduces himself, and flaunts his relationship with her in his face. This must have been her way of telling him their relationship was over.

Kevin's body trembled. The man escorted her into the parking lot then led her to the double-parked car that had cut him off only minutes before. It was because of him that the light caught him. It was because of him that he had to search and find a free parking space. It was because of him that had to pause briefly to clean up the mess.

His temperature spiked.

A driver blew his horn and eyed Mike and Nikki daringly. Mike flared his arms; obscenities spewed from his mouth. "Did you see that?" He furrowed his eyebrows angrily.

"Yeah," Nikki said, annoyed.

"What's wrong?"

"Was all that necessary?"

"What?" Mike shrugged loosely. "My cursin'? Veronica, the guy was a—oops." He caught himself. "Sorry. I don't usually curse this much." He looked at her. "I guess I'm just excited about being with you."

Nikki felt Mike staring at her, but she looked out the window silently. She was glad her sister was nowhere around.

"What? You 'saved' or something?" Mike looked at her.

Nikki thought hard, but was unable to come up with an answer.

"That's cool," Mike said, putting both hands on the steering wheel. "I'm a believer, too. Just slip up, sometimes."

Nikki peered out the window. She couldn't believe Mike had chosen the one restaurant she and Kevin had frequented.

"You okay?" Mike asked, sensing her uneasiness.

"Yeah, I'm fine," she whispered.

"If you don't think you'll like the place, we can go somewhere else."

"No, no. This is fine. I guess I'm just more tired than I thought."

"We don't have to stay too long," Mike grinned.

As they entered the restaurant, Nikki looked around nervously. A live R&B band was playing, and the place was crowded. Christina, one of the waitresses, had often served her and Kevin in the past. She wondered if she was there tonight.

They were seated, and soon Nikki began remembering. She looked around, bewildered. After all the time she and Kevin had spent together, and the memories they shared, she didn't understand how she was here with Mike.

"Wow! This place is nice."

Nikki snapped out of her trance, suddenly remembering Mike. She took a sip of water.

"You been here before?"

She gulped. She hoped her body language hadn't made it obvious. She set the glass on the table. "Yeah."

Mike looked at her, disappointed. "I'm sorry. I guess I should have asked."

"That's okay. It's a really nice restaurant. It's just that we're so close to the smoking section. The smoke irritates my nose and eyes."

"We can move if you want."

Nikki felt bad. She had been in a sour mode all evening. Mike had only been trying his hardest to please her. "No, Mike." She reached across the table and clasped his hand. "This is fine. Thank you."

Mike smiled warmly.

"Is there something I can help you with?"

The leaves of the fern shivered as Kevin jumped at the waitress' voice. He had been standing behind them watching Nikki. "No," Kevin said, clutching the bouquet. "I was looking for someone." His eyes dimmed. His baby, Nikki, was gone. "But—"

"She's not here yet?" the waitress concluded. "I'd be happy to get your name and go ahead and seat you. Once she comes, I'll—"

"That won't be necessary," Kevin interrupted solemnly. He pushed past her towards the exit.

"You ready to order?"

Nikki and Mike were having a good conversation. She had finally relaxed when she looked up and saw Christina. Their eyes met, and she knew Christina had recognized her.

"Yes, I am. How 'bout you?" she asked Mike.

Mike's phone rang. He gazed at the number. "I'm sorry; I have to take this." He stood abruptly.

"Wha—?" Nikki gasped.

"It'll just be a minute." He turned and left.

Nikki watched Mike, perplexed. She wondered why he had to run off in such a hurry for a phone call.

Christina folded the pad shut and stuffed it in her apron. "How 'bout I check on you guys in a few minutes?"

"Thanks."

Christina nodded and winked, and she walked over to the booth where the hostess stood. "How's it going?"

"Okay," the hostess said. "This guy was just over there," she pointed towards the ferns, "and I could've sworn he was looking at someone, but when I asked if I could help him, he said 'she hasn't arrived yet.'"

"Really?"

"Yeah. It was weird. He had a huge bouquet of flowers in his hands and everything. Poor thing. Guess he got stood up."

"Humph," Christina mumbled.

Kevin stood in the men's bathroom, in front of a sink. He dropped his head into his hand. This was the worst day of his life. He pinched the bridge of his nose; so much tension had accumulated there that he could barely think.

Suddenly, the door swung open. Kevin gazed in the mirror and saw the man Nikki was with walk through. Kevin lowered his head. He cut the faucet on and pretended to wash his hands. He fumed under his breath, blaming himself for letting Nikki get away.

"Yeah, well, Felicia'll be home in a few days."

Felicia? Kevin's ears twitched.

Mike was on the phone. "Her mother's a lot better now." He snickered. "Thank God, when she got sick, she went up there..."

Kevin took some paper towels out and dried his hands.

"No, believe it or not, I get along fine with my mother-in-law. Just not her."

A surge of confidence engulfed him. Kevin tossed his paper towel in the trash. Nikki was his woman, and there was no way he was going to let this sleaze have her. He picked up the bouquet and went out the door.

"Anyway, I gotta go," Mike said, standing in front of a urinal. "Yeah, I'm in Atlanta, taking care of a little business."

Nikki sat at the table, looking at the menu. She had thought she knew what she wanted, but she had changed her mind. Suddenly, a huge bouquet of flowers appeared before her eyes. She smiled, and touched them lightly, then pulled them towards her.

"Thank you." She blushed. Now she knew why Mike had run off. "How sweet of—"

Their eyes met.

"Kevin? What are you doing here?"

"You said we could meet," Kevin said softly.

"Meet?" Nikki said, looking around. "You followed me here? You had no right!"

"I just want to talk to you for a few minutes. You said we could talk."

"Talk? You had your opportunity to talk, and you didn't show," Nikki stated firmly.

"I'm sorry baby, I—"

"I'm with someone, and he'll be back soon, so I suggest you leave."

"Baby, you said we could talk."

He was crazy. Obviously, nothing she had said had sunk in. She cleared her throat.

Christina scanned the restaurant. Though she had gotten there just a short time earlier, it was an exceptionally slow evening, and she knew the slower it was the longer the night seemed. "It's Friday night. Where is everybody?" she asked the greeter.

"Girl, you know black people and rain don't mix."

"It's been overcast all day, but it hasn't done anything yet."

"Just the threat will keep us away," the hostess jeered.

Christina saw Mike exit the restroom. She sighed, relieved. Finally, she could do something. She was preparing to go back to their table when her eyes fell upon Nikki. She didn't look very happy and seemed to be exchanging harsh words with someone.

Then she spotted Kevin, obviously her ex now. She tapped the hostess on the shoulder. "Is that the guy you were talking about earlier?" she asked, pointing at Kevin.

The hostess looked where Christina pointed. "Yeah," she announced, surprised. "I thought he left."

Mike entered the eating area. A man was standing in front of their table and flowers were in front of Nikki. The man and Nikki were talking, but Nikki looked annoyed. He didn't know what was going on, but he didn't like it. He ran over to the table. "Hey, hey, hey! Is there a problem here?"

Kevin ignored him. "Nikki, baby, I just need to talk to you—"

"Baby?" Mike walked over and stood across from Nikki. "She's with me!"

Kevin's eyes never left Nikki. Nikki appeared to be thinking it over.

Mike became enraged. "Let's go, Veronica!" he demanded, yanking her arm.

"Let her go!" Kevin gritted his teeth and slammed his fist on the table. No one treated Nikki as if she was some type of possession. He wanted to smash his fist into Mike's face.

"Wait!" Nikki had never seen Kevin so crazy. She threw her hands up, and Mike's grip loosened. "Why don't we all just calm down?"

Christina rushed over and stood in front of Kevin. "Sir, I'm going to have to ask you to leave." It was awkward, but she had to keep the peace. "Right now!"

"Nikki, please. I'll be outside—in our spot." Then he turned and left.

Mike straightened his jacket. He sat and looked at Nikki. "Who the hell was that?"

Nikki took a deep breath. "Kevin—my ex-boyfriend."

"What? Did you tell him to meet you here or something?"

"No. He followed me here."

"Followed? You seeing him, and me, too?"

Nikki gasped. "You came to my house. I didn't ask you to come over."

"What does that mean? You don't want to see me?"

"And where do you get off thinking we're 'seeing' each other?"

"So it's like that? You're going to sit here and tell me that kiss didn't mean anything to you. Nothing?"

Nikki's thoughts were a jumble. "I need some fresh air." She stood.

"You're going to talk to that fool? After the way he dumped you?"

Dumped. Every ounce of her feelings of worthlessness screamed at the way he exaggerated the word. She shot Mike a sour look, picked up her purse, and headed for the exit.

"Veronica!" he called realizing he had probably blown whatever edge he had. "Wait!" He watched as she headed towards the door. "Veronica!" He looked around and saw a few people staring his way. "She just went to use the restroom." He said loudly. He took a sip of his drink, and then pounded his fist on the table. He sat back in the seat lazily, picked the flowers up, and slammed them to the floor.

Kevin sat outside under the post. The night was clear. Cars zoomed by. Suddenly, he saw Nikki exit into the courtyard. He stood as she approached. "Nikki—"

"I can't believe you followed me like this. Are you crazy?"

"Just about you."

Nikki turned away from him.

Kevin walked up behind her. "Look, I know I messed up, baby, but I needed to clear my head."

Nikki turned to face him, annoyed. "What do you mean, 'clear your head'? Kevin, I haven't seen or spoken to you in almost two months!"

"Nikki, I'm sorry. I know there's no excuse, but you have to believe—"

Mike burst between them. Neither had seen him coming. "Aw-ight, aw-ight. That's enough. Let's go."

She stared at Kevin for another second then turned to walk with Mike.

"Nikki, I'm still in love with you."

Nikki stopped.

"I don't want you to go with him. Come with me."

Nikki turned and looked in his eyes. They were so bright and brown.

"Yo, I said that's enough!" Mike stood between them. "What? You want a piece of me, or something? Is that it?"

Kevin took a few steps back. This time, they weren't inside. He knew once he was angry enough, there was no turning back. He turned and walked away.

Mike picked up his foot and thrust it into his back.

"Kevin!" Nikki gasped.

Kevin threw his arms out to break the fall as he tumbled to the ground. He smirked. His assessment had been right. Mike was a hothead, and no hothead could resist a turned back. The assault was all the excuse he needed. Now it was time to take care of business.

"Come on, Veronica. Let's go!" Mike called.

Nikki was motionless, wondering if she should help.

Kevin lifted himself from the ground.

"I said let's go!" Mike grabbed Nikki's arm. Suddenly, Mike heard footsteps. He turned and saw Kevin speeding towards him. He let go of Nikki's arm and moved to throw his hands up, but Kevin was too fast.

Kevin delivered a roundhouse kick, and Mike plummeted to the pavement.

"Kevin!" Nikki screamed. She shook her head.

Mike popped back up. He grimaced then felt his lip. A small stream of blood ran from the side of his mouth. He balled his fist and took a few steps toward Kevin.

"Mike, stop! This is insane!" Nikki tugged at his arm.

He snatched his arm away from her. "Move out the way, Veronica! So, what's up now?" Mike hollered. "Now that we're facing each other like men?"

Nikki's eyes meet Kevin's. She shook her head, and Kevin backed away.

He bent over and picked up his cap.

"Yeah, that's what I thought. Punk!" Mike put his arm around Nikki and turned her away. "Let's go." They began walking off.

"Nikki, you don't love him." Kevin hollered after her.

She continued walking.

He didn't want to hurt her, but she had to know. "He's married."

"What?" Nikki stopped. She turned to face Kevin then looked at Mike.

"Don't listen to him," Mike chuckled anxiously. "He doesn't know what he's talking about."

"I heard him talking about it before I came to your table."

Mike shrugged his shoulders. "I don't know what he's talking about."

Nikki studied his body language. "No. You're lying," she huffed. "I can't believe it. You're married, and you didn't tell me?" She shook her head, disgusted and embarrassed. She stormed off.

"We're getting a divorce," he shouted after her.

For a moment, the two men stood there, alone. Kevin perked up, realizing that this was his opportunity. "Nikki!" he called, jogging after her, but she was some distance ahead of him. "Nikki!" He caught up to her, but she kept moving. "Baby, slow down."

"Get away from me, Kevin!" She gnashed her teeth.

He touched her arm. "Come with me. I'll take you home."

"I don't need you to take me home. I want you to leave me alone," she said, yanking away. She hailed a cab.

"You don't need to be out here alone. Let me take you home."

"Kevin—" She waved her hand, silencing him.

"Nikki, I'm still in love with you."

Finally, she looked back.

A cab pulled alongside the curb.

"Can we talk?"

Nikki got into the cab.

"Nikki?" Kevin pleaded. He leaned into the window, waiting for a response.

Suddenly, raindrops fell, and the roar of thunder followed.

"Okay," she finally said. "Tuesday. At two."

CHAPTER TWENTY~FOUR

There was a tap at the door. Nikki pulled it open.

"Hey," Kevin whispered, smiling. She didn't say anything. He stepped inside then turned to face her as she closed the door behind him. Her hair dangled gracefully over her shoulders and eyes, partially concealing her face.

Nikki leaned against the door.

The room was dark. The light from outside was dim. They stood for a moment quietly.

"Let's sit." Kevin motioned towards the couch.

Instead, she walked towards the window. She stopped and stood opposite him, across the cocktail table. Kevin leaned against the kitchen wall. He thought hard, searching for the right words.

"I thought you wanted to talk."

Kevin swallowed. "I just want to start off by saying I'm sorry. It's difficult to explain my actions, but—"

"Why don't you try?" Nikki interrupted.

"I'm sorry for what I did, but I want you to know I still love you, and would like us to be together again."

A twinge of anger shot up her spine. "Together?" Her voice began to rise. "Kevin, I haven't seen you in two months! Kayla's asked about you. Until a few days ago, you acted as if I didn't exist. I didn't think you cared about me at all!"

"Nikki, that's not true. You know how much I care about you, baby," he pleaded. "I love you."

She laughed. "Love?" Her face hardened. "If you love me so much, Kevin, why did you call it quits? Why did you tell me it was over?"

"I never said it was 'over'. I said we needed to stop seeing each other."

"What?" Nikki shook her head, confused. In her mind, they were the same. She felt dizzy. She sat down on the couch and wrestled her thumbs against each other aimlessly, until Kevin walked over and sat beside her.

He felt her thigh. "Baby, I love you." He touched a strand of hair and moved it away from her eyes. "You mean more to me than anything in the world." He studied her face. He glided his right hand along the side of it. "I missed you."

Blood shot to her head like a spring. He called it off. He hadn't returned her phone calls. "Just save it, Kevin!" She rose to get away from him. "I'm not interested in any more of your lies," she said, folding her arms.

He rose. "Nikki, I've never lied to you. When have I lied to you? Everything I've done or said has always been honest. Baby, I've never lied to you. You know that."

"No, I don't!" Her eyes locked on his coldly. "People who love each other don't walk away from each other, Kevin." Suddenly she was exhausted. "I trusted you. I told you things I've never told anyone — things I've been ashamed of."

"What? Nikki, you have no reason to be ashamed, and you know — you know I care about you, baby."

Baby? Her stomach cringed. "Stop calling me that! I'm not your 'baby,' anymore. Remember?"

Kevin's heart sank.

"Do you have any idea how I feel? You filled my head with all this stuff. And then, in the end, you walked away." She threw her hands up helplessly. "And there was nothing I could do about it." She turned and moved a few steps closer to the patio.

"Nikki, I never walked away." He saw the pain and disappointment in her eyes. "I just needed time."

"Time for what Kevin? Time to go sow your royal oaks?"

"What?" Kevin exclaimed.

"Oh, yeah. You think I'm stupid? That night, when you supposedly went to get gas — you went to get condoms. Didn't you?"

Kevin remembered that night. He had been standing in line waiting to pay for his gas and spotted a new home magazine. He had felt compelled to pick it up. He thumbed through it casually before the attendant motioned him forward. "No," he answered softly.

"I thought you were different, Kevin." She stood in front of him, by the coffee table, searching for the right words. She wanted to say something to hurt him. She needed to make him feel the same pain she felt. "You're no different than any of the other guys I've met. The only difference is that you hide behind your Christianity. In the end, all you want is the same thing." She thought back to the time he had told her she was a blessing. Now, she could clearly see, "The only thing you ever wanted was for me to bless your dick!"

"What?"

"I guess after I didn't sleep with you on the trip, you just couldn't wait any longer. Could you?"

"What?" he asked, baffled. He had no idea to what she was referring.

"Could you?"

"Baby?" He couldn't believe all her accusations — that she didn't trust him and thought he had only been plotting to sleep with her the whole time. She was acting as if he had gone off to have some big orgy or something. "You really think I broke up with you so I could sleep with other women?" he asked softly, trying to conceal his pain.

Nikki dropped her head. In her heart, she didn't believe it, but what other explanation could there be? "I don't know what to believe anymore, Kevin."

"Nikki, I love you," he muttered, fighting back tears. "I'd never do anything to destroy the trust you have in me. I haven't slept with anyone. I love you!"

"Then why did you break up with me?"

"It had nothing to do with you," he pleaded. "It was me!"

"You keep saying that, but you won't give me a reason."

Kevin wanted to explain, but the words wouldn't come to him. He cleared his throat.

"You know what?" Nikki threw up her hand. "It's okay. I don't want to even hear it!"

For a moment, he didn't recognize her. He wasn't used to seeing her angry and didn't like the way it felt directed towards him. The music blaring from the upstairs apartment had stopped. "Nikki, lower your voice."

"No!" she exclaimed hotly. At that moment, she realized that the one person she loved most she also hated with intensity and passion. He made her sick to her stomach.

Her head was spinning. She took a deep breath. "Do you know how it feels to love someone, trust someone, and have them turn their back on you?"

Kevin listened. He knew the feeling all too well. He lowered his head.

"So, no, Kevin!" Her voice finally cracked. "I will *not* lower my voice!" Tears streamed down her face. She felt so helpless. She turned towards the patio, embarrassed that she had started to cry. "I loved you. And you—you hurt me. I never thought you would," she said, getting a whiff of the spring air.

Kevin's heart melted. He couldn't stand seeing her angry with him and crying. He walked towards her. "Nikki," he whispered, reaching out to touch her. She pulled away.

She inched closer to the patio door, placed her hand on the knob, and gazed outside. She wiped the tears from her eyes, but it was useless, as more kept coming.

"Bab—" He caught himself. "Nikki, I never meant to hurt you." She felt the heat from his body.

He shook his head. "That was never my intention." He imagined how cold he must have seemed the day he broke up with her. He touched her gently on the shoulder. "Nikki, I love you." Kevin thought about Mike, and he wondered if she had dated anyone else. "Do you still love me?"

Nikki stared out the window. Confessing her love to Kevin was all she had wanted to do from the beginning. How had everything become so complicated?

"Nikki?"

Suddenly she realized her vulnerability. As much as she wanted to tell him she loved him, she couldn't. Her strength had been all she ever had. He had stripped that from her and left her feeling weak, and she hated feeling weak.

"Nikki?" Kevin whispered again.

Nikki continued looking out the window. There was a slight breeze; she saw the tree limbs dancing in the air. She felt his breath on her neck.

Her throat was dry, and her mind was cluttered. Tears flowed down her face. "Everything you've told me has been a lie." She closed her eyes. "I don't ever want to see you again." Her head dropped. "I hate you."

Kevin's heart sank. He moved closer to her. She couldn't have said what he thought she said. "Nikki? You can't mean that. With everything we have—turn around and look at me and say that to me."

Nikki stared out the window for a few more seconds. She turned slowly and their eyes met. She swallowed. "I don't ever want to see you again." Then she turned back towards the patio door. "Goodbye, Kevin."

Kevin stood in disbelief. He kept hoping she would turn and smile at him the way she used to. He wanted her to understand how much he loved her.

"Please." Nikki shook her head. "Just go."

Kevin couldn't move. "Nikki?"

Nikki spun around. "Get out!"

Kevin turned quickly and started towards the door.

His chest was tight and his limbs rubbery. He opened the door. He looked at her one last time. "By the way, if I wanted to make love to you, I wouldn't use a condom." He closed the door.

Nikki gasped.

Kevin walked toward his car. Stabbing pain invaded his chest. His experience had taught him not to cry in front of a woman, but out in the fresh air, that was a different story. He let the tears flow. Through the corner of his eye, he saw a blind creeping open from the apartment above Nikki's, but he didn't care.

Mariea approached riding her tricycle. "Hey, Mr. Kevin," she said, smiling up at him.

He couldn't bring himself to speak. He felt her gaze upon him as he moved to his car. His eyes burned as he searched for his keys, sobbing and rubbing his palms against his face.

He lifted his keys and started the ignition. He looked towards Nikki's apartment one last time, hoping she'd have a change of heart, but she never came out.

He pulled away.

"He was here," Nikki said softly. She leaned against the fridge.

Anesa's eyebrows arched. "Who?"

Nikki paused. "Kevin."

Anesa sat up with the phone. She remembered seeing Kevin and Kacie in the mall. "What did he say?"

Nikki couldn't bring herself to tell her. She knew how much Anesa liked him. She shook her head.

"Nikki?"

"He told me he wanted to see me again."

Anesa's shoulders relaxed. "What did you say?"

Nikki paused for a long time. "I told him I didn't want to see him anymore."

Anesa couldn't believe her ears. She knew how much her cousin loved Kevin. She replayed in her mind the promise she had made. She wondered if she should inform her.

Nikki continued. "I—I didn't know what to say." She rested her head against the fridge and stared up at the ceiling. "And when I saw him this afternoon, I just got so—so angry," she recalled, choosing her words carefully, deliberately leaving out the near disaster at the restaurant with Mike and Kevin.

"I'm just not ready for a relationship again. I want to be by myself. You know, Kayla and me."

Anesa could tell Nikki was very upset. She didn't want to make her feel worse by sounding unsupportive. "I understand," she whispered. "Sometimes it's good to spend time alone—to take care of you." She rubbed her stomach. "I'm sure you made the right decision."

Nikki was surprised at her cousin's response. She was so confused. She didn't want her cousin to agree with her. Fresh tears flowed down her cheeks. "Yeah. You're right." She uttered agreeably, though ambiguity echoed in her voice.

● ● ●

Nikki opened the envelope cautiously. Her heart raced as she unfolded the sheet delicately and read:

Miss Jones, thank you so much for taking the time to interview with us. Unfortunately, we are not able to extend you an offer at this time....

Of all the interviews she had gone to, not one had panned out. Though she knew her job at the youth center was always available, it wasn't her dream job; she had always pictured herself doing something different. The only leads she had were with temp agencies, yet with Kayla moving in soon, she needed something permanent. Nikki let the sheet fall, and she broke into tears. Everything was going wrong.

CHAPTER TWENTY-FIVE

"I'm so proud of you." Jackie gave Nikki a big hug then stepped back and examined her. Nikki wore her black cap and gown, accented with a yellow ribbon that showed she was graduating with honors.

"Thank you." Nikki's eyes sparkled. The day had finally come—her graduation. "I'm just glad you could make it."

Jackie's lips curled. She embraced Nikki again. "I wouldn't have missed it for anything in the world," she whispered, rocking her.

Nikki embraced her, Jackie's words echoing in her head. It was the same sentiment Kevin had uttered while they were dating, and despite everything, Nikki still yearned to see Kevin on this very special occasion. Knowing he had done nothing to see it only further validated her belief in his dishonesty and lies. That knowledge had made her sad all morning.

Finally, Jackie pulled back. "I've been dying to meet this boyfriend of yours." She smiled brightly. "Where is he?"

Nikki swallowed. "We broke up."

Jackie gazed at her, perplexed. The last time she had seen her, they seemed so happy. "I'm sorry to hear that."

"It's fine," Nikki said, shrugging it off. "It just wasn't meant to be. Right?"

But Jackie had an unconvinced, if-you-say-so, look on her face.

Someone called Nikki's name.

"Anyway, gotta go," Nikki said cheerfully. She waved then darted towards the gymnasium.

Jackie watched her until she disappeared inside.

"Your cousins are nice people," Jackie said, peering over Nikki's shoulder towards Malcolm and Anesa's house.

"Yeah, they are." Nikki smiled. The day had gone so fast, and once again, she found herself saying goodbye to Jackie.

Jackie thought about Nikki's response to her sympathy about the break-up. Nikki had obviously taken it hard, and she wanted to make herself available, without stating the reason. "You know, Nikki, maybe you should come visit me in Charlotte. It'd be a nice getaway."

"I don't know," Nikki answered nervously. As much as she wanted Jackie back in her life, she needed it to occur gradually.

"Well, if you decide otherwise, I'll be there." She paused.

Nikki heard the disappointment in Jackie's voice, and she didn't want her to feel she was turning her down completely. "Thank you," she answered. "I may take you up on it."

They embraced. Nikki watched Jackie's Toyota Camry pull out of the driveway. She sighed. Finally, the party was over, and she could put this day behind her.

Kayla hummed to herself as she sat on the floor between Nikki's legs having her hair plated. Her sister was putting the last bow on when Kayla remembered seeing Kevin that day.

He had been standing a short distance from them, wearing a light gray suit. He had a fresh haircut. He held a gift in his hand, accented with a fuchsia bow.

When Kayla spotted him, she was so excited that she was going to point him out to her sister. However, when he saw her turning to tell, he gestured for her to stay quiet. The next thing Kayla knew, he was gone. "Nikki?"

"What, baby?" Nikki asked, removing the bow from her mouth and tying it around a lock of hair.

"Is Kevin coming over tomorrow?"

Nikki sighed. She knew Kayla missed Kevin, but her insistent pestering about him was inexcusable. "Kayla, I told you, Kevin and I aren't seeing each other anymore."

"But—"

"MiKayla." Nikki's voice echoed with irritation. "We've talked about this over and over. I am telling you for the last time—don't ask me anymore questions about Kevin!"

Kayla sprung from her lap, turned, and looked at her. Her eyes dropped, and Nikki was suddenly aware of how harsh she had sounded.

Nikki's voice softened. "Kayla, I'm sor—" she tried to apologize, but Kayla darted towards her room.

"Kayla? Sweetheart?" But Kayla slammed her door shut.

Nikki took the remote and turned the TV off. She had been watching it for the last couple of hours, since Kayla had gone to her room, but still didn't know what she was looking at. Her mind was in a daze as she walked into the kitchen. She sighed, wondering how this supposedly momentous day had slipped past so easily.

She picked up a book she had found—a children's book written by Dr. Seuss. It had been propped beside the door when she came home. She had gone to Mrs. Martinez' house to ask if the book belonged to Mariea, because it certainly wasn't Kayla's, but no one was home. She picked the book up and threw it on top of the refrigerator. She would wait until tomorrow and ask then.

She walked down the hallway, stopped at MiKayla's door, opened it, and peered inside, but MiKayla was fast asleep. Her heart ached, thinking of how she had treated her. She closed the door quietly and retreated to her bedroom.

Kayla sat up in bed. She heard a low noise coming from her sister's room. Though she couldn't make out the sound, it sounded distressed.

Cool tears flooded Nikki's warm face. She shook her head in despair and sobbed. No matter what she did or how hard she tried, she could not get him out of her head. This was supposed to be one of the happiest days of her life, but it was flooded with gloom, depression, and anger.

She felt helpless. She wanted to pray to God, to ask him to take the pain away, but felt it was too frivolous a request. Other people had legitimate prayers—people whose children were dying of cancer, people who were praying they could find something to eat for the night, or whose husbands or wives had died. Those were real prayers, for real problems. All she had was a broken heart.

Kayla saw her sister's silhouette shivering in the darkness. "Nikki?" Her voice trembled.

Nikki quickly wiped the tears from her face.

Kayla walked over and stared. "Why are you crying?"

"Come here," Nikki said and picked her up and sat her on her lap.

They embraced then Kayla pulled back. "I'm not mad at you anymore."

Nikki smiled, grateful. "Thank you." At that moment, Nikki realized that she had lost focus. She wanted nothing to do with all this "being in love" business. It was time for the fairy tale to end. She renewed the commitment she had made in her heart to Kayla. "You know what?" Nikki asked, looking down at her sister. "I will be so happy when you come to live with me. When you're away, I miss you so much." She began to cry again.

Kayla's eyes sparkled, and her mouth dropped into a wide smile.

"Soon, you and I are going to be a real family." She squeezed her. "I love you so much, Kayla. Never, ever, forget that. Okay?"

Kayla nodded.

Nikki squeezed and rocked her until they both fell asleep.

"Hello?"

"Hello."

"Nikki?" Jackie exclaimed, surprised to hear her voice.

"I'm sorry to call so early. I just wanted to make sure you got home okay."

"Yeah." Jackie sank back into her pillow. "Got in about ten."

"Good," Nikki said low. She paced around her bedroom. "I don't want to hold you, but I wanted to tell you again how much I appreciated you showing up yesterday."

"No problem—happy to be invited." There was a long pause, and Jackie suspected Nikki hadn't called for mere chitchat.

Nikki had spent the night thinking about the way she had been acting, the crying spells, depression, and anger. "I was thinking. Maybe I will take you up on that offer."

CHAPTER TWENTY-SIX

"Lunch?" Marla stood in the hallway and grinned at Kevin.

"No, not this time," Kevin answered, then without a pause. "Have you had a chance to work on the Anderson account?" He no longer looked forward to Friday lunches.

"Yes. But it's not finished yet."

Kevin looked at the clock. It was almost noon. He knew Randy left for lunch, like clockwork, every Friday at twelve. "Just get it to me sometime after lunch."

"Okay." Marla watched him disappear into his office. She looked at the clock. It seemed no one would be going to lunch today but she and Randy. Jessica had a doctor's appointment, and she had taken the rest of the afternoon off.

She walked over to Randy's office. To her surprise, a client was in the room. "I'm sorry, Mr. Powers. I didn't realize anyone was with you."

Randy looked up. "That's okay, Marla." He looked at the clock. "Give me about thirty minutes."

Marla went back to her desk. Since he wasn't ready yet, she would finish the work for Kevin. She made a few minor adjustments, typed the final paper, and put it in a folder.

Her stomach was growling now. It had been almost forty minutes and there was no sign that Randy was finished. She walked the folder to Kevin's office. His door was ajar, and she didn't hear any voices, so she decided to let herself in. Kevin's chair was turned away from the door. He appeared to be staring out the window, but as she moved closer, she realized he wasn't looking out the window at all.

Kevin's face was reflected in the window glass. His cheeks were wet. His shoulders heaved gently as he cried. She didn't want him to know she was there, but if she didn't leave soon, he was bound to hear her stomach pangs.

She backed up quietly. She made it to the door and looked back. His chair still faced the window. She squeezed through the door and pulled at the knob gently.

The sky was overcast, and it was cool for May in Atlanta. Kevin pulled into the parking lot. Nikki was standing outside the youth center wearing a long sleeved t-shirt. All the little kids were gathered around her. He had intentionally parked far away. He didn't want Nikki to spot him.

The kids ran off in different directions. He rested his head on the seat and watched them play kickball for about fifteen minutes. Finally, Nikki was up. She kicked the ball, and the kids scrambled to catch it. He smiled to himself, watching her sail through the makeshift cardboard bases. The kids chased after her, but their legs were no match for hers.

Then his mind began to wander. What could he say that would make her realize he made a mistake, a terrible mistake — one he had regretted ever since. He stared at her in the distance. She sipped on bottled water and yelled at the kids on the opposing team. He would drop to his knees and beg her to see him again. It seemed an obvious solution, and it was certainly not beneath him after what he had done.

He would tell her how much he missed her and needed her. He would tell her what he had intended to tell her the night he came over and saw her leaving with Mike — that he wanted to marry her and start a new life together.

He studied his hands as he played with them and made up his mind to do it. He got out of the car and walked slowly towards the gate. A rumble sounded in the clouds, and raindrops began falling.

That didn't matter, though. Their relationship had ended so abruptly. He loved Nikki, and she loved him. They were perfect together. She made him complete. He couldn't accept that things were truly over. He needed to talk to her again, to make sure she meant what she said. He had to convince her that he loved her. Even if she never wanted to get married, that was fine with him; he was willing to do anything to put an end to his pain.

The raindrops picked up, and in seconds, the shower became a torrential downpour. The kids screamed hysterically. Nikki blew her whistle. One of the children handed her the ball. She opened the door for them, and they ran inside. After the last kid had entered, she followed behind and slammed the door.

Kevin stopped in the middle of the parking lot. He stared at the door, hoping it would reopen.

"Nasty out there, isn't it?" Jessica peered over her glasses at Kevin.

"Yeah." Kevin wiggled his umbrella a few times and pulled it into the door. "I thought you were out for the rest of the day."

"My appointment didn't last as long as I thought. I didn't want to get too behind before the three-day weekend."

"Oh."

Her eyes watched his. "So how are you?"

"Okay." He answered quickly.

"Coming in from lunch?"

"No." He looked down for a moment. "Had an errand to run."

"Oh." Jessica smiled. Kevin had been short on words lately.

"Got a minute? Come see the new pictures of my baby."

Kevin turned reluctantly.

Jessica reached into the drawer and pulled out a grayish 8" x 11" folder. She spread the pictures out on the desk. They made Kevin feel even more miserable. He missed Kayla—her laughter, her smile, and the sometimes annoying way she used to sing to him. "She's cute," he mumbled. He felt he should be saying more, but he couldn't think what.

"Kevin." Sherrie walked over to them. She was a partner in the company, in her late thirties. "How are you today?"

"Good." He cracked a smile, surprised. She was so involved into her work she hardly ever took the time to speak.

"Good?" She grinned, watching him. The three stood for a few seconds in silence. "Okay, well, see you around."

He drummed his fingers on Jessica's cubicle countertop. "Look, I'll catch you later," he said, backing up and colliding with Scott, another consultant.

"Oops," said Scott. "How's it going, buddy?"

"Fine," Kevin mumbled faintly. It was a little strange; he had already spoken to him earlier. He wondered why everyone was acting so friendly. An eerie feeling came over him, and without another word, he pushed past Scott and into his office.

Kevin rubbed his forehead as he looked over the summary Marla had left him. He couldn't wait to leave work, but didn't have anything to do once he left.

The phone rang. He looked at the lit buttons; it was either Randy or Jessica. He picked up the phone and answered. It was Randy. He wasn't up for much conversation, but he mustered the friendliest voice he could.

"Kevin. Come see me in my office."

Kevin walked into the office. Jessica was bent over Randy, going over a memo he wanted her to send out. Jessica saw Kevin walking in, and she hastened her last thoughts.

"Kevin," Randy grinned. He motioned towards the chair across from him. "Have a seat."

Kevin sat down as Randy picked up a folder in front of him. He put his glasses on and studied the folder for a moment, swiveling in his chair. He put the folder down and removed his glasses. He leaned forward and rested his arms on the desk. "Kevin." He cleared his throat. "You're young, black; of course, you're smart. You got a lot of charisma. Frankly, you've done well here. The clients like you."

Kevin allowed himself a little smile.

Randy continued. "So you can imagine my surprise when Jessica handed me your request for a transfer to the Fort Worth district. You're not getting bored here, are you?"

"No, sir. Just want to move a little closer to home."

"Home?" Randy leaned into his seat. Kevin had been seriously dating someone, and he was surprised by the sudden departure.

"How is everything in Dallas? I've been meaning to call Philip and Priscilla. How are they doing?"

"They're doing well."

"What about the rest of your family?" Randy waved his glasses in his hands as he spoke. He was trying to sift out the source of the sudden onset of grief that suddenly plagued this young man's life.

Kevin felt like he was being interrogated. "Everyone's doing well."

"Really?" Randy asked, unconvinced.

"Yeah."

"Then why the sudden change? Wanting to transfer and all. I thought you were happy here."

Kevin breathed. Randy was one of his father's buddies, but this was getting a little too personal. "I have my reasons."

"I can't grant the transfer. I need you too much here."

Kevin rose. "I put my condo up for sale. As soon as I get an offer, I'm moving."

Randy was disappointed. Kevin was almost like a son to him. "I hope you'll reconsider."

"If there's nothing further?" Kevin ran his hand over his tie to smooth it.

Randy tilted his head.

Kevin turned and walked out the door.

Randy sighed. If he hadn't known something was eating at him, he would have assumed he was just being arrogant. "Kevin."

Kevin turned to face Randy.

"Look, son," Randy started, speaking not as his boss, but a family friend. "If you ever want to talk about anything—I mean anything at all—my door is always open."

"Thanks." Kevin shook his head, but he appreciated the sentiment.

"I'm sure if something happened to his family he would have said something."

A couple of people were standing in front of Jessica's desk. Kevin walked into the break room, poured some water from the water cooler, and took a sip. He studied the notes he'd jotted down from his last client.

"I can't believe it," said a male voice. "I couldn't go out like that. He was just sitting at his desk, crying?"

Kevin froze, suddenly interested. He dared not think about whom they were talking. He moved to the doorway and looked toward the voices.

"Man, I can't believe he punked out like that." Derrick the security officer shook his head.

Jessica didn't like the direction the conversation was heading. She liked Kevin. He didn't speak down to her like many of the other consultants. He often asked her about her daughter, Brittany. On the Fridays Randy wasn't there, he often took them out and paid for their lunch, instead. Sometimes, he even invited her to his church, though she always declined. In her hometown, when a man invited you to church, things were getting pretty serious, and she knew their relationship was strictly platonic. "I think it's sweet. He was in love with her." Jessica leaned back into her chair.

Derrick shook his head again. "Whatever."

"I wonder why he broke up with her." Marla interrupted, resting her elbows on Jessica's countertop.

"We don't know who broke up with whom," Jessica corrected.

"Humph," Marla growled. Her dreads shook as she tossed her head. "She would have to be stupid to break up with him. Kevin's a good man." Her voice dropped. "I bet she was just playing him for his money! Mmm-hmmm. I betcha she was a ho, and he found out about it!"

Kevin couldn't believe his ears. He knew office gossip was big, but he never imagined he would be the center of it, nor could he believe how nasty they were being. Nikki had often joined them for Friday lunches. Everyone had always commented on how nice she was. How had she suddenly become a 'ho'?

Anger filled him. He wanted to speak up and clear Nikki's name. He stared at Marla's reflection. The nerve of her—getting into his business, and discussing it so loosely.

"That, or he finally hit it, and it wasn't good." Marla laughed. "But most men are willing to work with you on that."

"I wouldn't know anything about it," Jessica smiled. Derrick smiled and looked at Marla.

Kevin walked towards them. He wanted to break up the mud slinging and clear his girlfriend's—Veronica's name. He wanted to tell them all off.

His body was shaking. *Wait,* he stopped himself. He was too upset; he needed to calm down. A voice inside reminded him he was a Christian.

"So I heard," Marla declared. "Anyway, you said it yourself. He was in love with her. Why else would they break up so fast? You go on vacation one week, and by the next you done broke up?" She shook her head. "Most men don't care if you're using them a little, as long as they get theirs." She spoke firmly. "She was a ho. Trust me."

"I don't think that was why they broke up." Jessica shook her head, frustrated.

Derrick shrugged; he nodded his head at Marla's previous statement.

"Oh, don't listen to her," Jessica laughed. "She thinks everyone is an undercover ho."

"Mmm-hmmm," Marla laughed, nodding her head in agreement. "If you'd seen some of the stuff I have—you'd think so, too." She glanced at the window and saw Kevin's reflection.

"What?" Jessica's laugh trailed off as she stared at Marla's frozen face.

Marla's eyes led hers over her shoulder.

Jessica stood up a little, caught a peek through a space between Marla and Derrick, and saw Kevin. His face showed a mixture of anger and betrayal.

"'Afternoon, Mr. Maddox," Derrick said quickly. He tilted his hat, but didn't look him in the eyes. He hurried away.

Marla turned around nervously. "I was supposed to be getting that information to you, wasn't I? I'll be right back," she said, darting in the direction of her desk.

Jessica lowered her head. Out of the corner of her eye, she saw Kevin turn and walk away.

Kevin heard a tap at his door. He looked up and saw Jessica.

"Here's the info from Marla," she said, coming forward and laying the information on his desk. She smiled lightly and turned around.

He rested his elbow on the desk and pressed his hand against his head. "Who knows?"

Jessica let out a deep sigh then turned around. "Marla told me and Derrick and apparently some other people. But I told Randy. I was concerned about you, especially after finding your transfer papers on my desk."

Kevin nodded his head reflectively. Everything made sense.

"If you need anything else, I'll be at my desk until six." She headed for the door.

"Oh," Kevin said, changing his posture.

Jessica turned to face him.

"For the record, she's not a whore."

Jessica shook her head. She closed the door behind her.

"Pssssst." Marla hissed as she saw Jessica emerge from Kevin's office. "What did he say?"

Jessica flinched. She couldn't believe Marla had the gall to ask.

"Well?" Marla's eyes were excited. She couldn't wait to be dished some new dirt.

Jessica stared at her. Only because she was her cousin had she agreed to step into Kevin's office and deliver her assignment for her. Now her favors were over. She regretted ever telling her cousin about the position. "Marla, you talk entirely too much!" she said, sharply rolling her eyes. She walked towards her desk without looking back.

●●●

Kevin closed his briefcase. He stepped towards the door, but Natalie crossed his path. They were at a singles retreat hosted by their church, and he had volunteered to teach about financial planning.

"Mr. Maddox, I must say — that was the simplest explanation I've ever heard. You are good at explaining things." She smiled brightly. "Have you ever considered teaching?"

"Thanks," Kevin blushed. "Actually, my father is a minister." He paused, seeing a sudden glitter in her eyes.

"Oh, he is?" She smiled even brighter.

"Not *the* minister," he clarified. "But I've never had the knack for it."

"So it runs in the family?" she teased playfully. "I haven't seen your girlfriend around in a while. Nikki, right?"

"Yeah." Kevin drooped a little. "We're not seeing each other anymore."

"Really?" She looked puzzled. "I couldn't help but notice her picture in your briefcase."

Kevin smiled slightly. "Well, some people need caffeine to jumpstart their day, but all I needed was Nikki," he said, reminiscing. "I guess I'm still addicted."

Natalie smiled. She held her hand to her chest. "I think that's the sweetest thing I've ever heard. Sounds like she was a lucky girl to have you." She looked around. There were only a few people there. "Would you —" she stuttered, "like to grab some lunch?"

"It's funny. There are so many roads, but they all lead to nowhere." Kevin's eyes met Natalie's. "When the woman you love tells you she hates you," he shrugged, running his hand up and down his glass, "it just does something to you." His voice trailed off. He massaged his forehead. "I blew it."

Natalie eyed him sympathetically. He was so lovesick. She thought for a moment then looked at him mischievously. "I bet I know what will make you feel better."

CHAPTER TWENTY~SEVEN

Nikki flung open the door to Kayla's room. Kayla stepped in, and her mouth dropped. Her eyes glazed. Nikki smiled inside. Instead of taking a week off after her graduation as she planned, she had worked. Kayla's reaction made it all worthwhile.

She knew how much her sister loved Hello Kitty, so she had totally remodeled it with accessories and the pink and white theme. There were Hello Kitty pillows and comforters, Hello Kitty curtains, a Hello Kitty chair, and even a Hello Kitty rug. In the end, Nikki had jumped on board herself, and purchased Hello Kitty undies.

Kayla turned and hugged her sister tightly.

Nikki squeezed her back. "Welcome home, baby."

●●●

Nikki and Kayla spent a day shopping at the mall. They went to a booth to get their picture taken. Nikki held onto Kayla tightly as she sat in her lap. Ecstatic, they looked at the camera. A few minutes passed, and the picture was ready to view.

As they gazed at the picture together, each marveled at the image of the other. Each had her own ideas of what life would be like from here on out. Though she missed her grandmother, Kayla knew she could expect fun times ahead. She was often bored with her grandmother, sitting around, listening to her chat with her old friends; Nikki was more inclusive. Even when her friends or Uncle Malcolm and Aunt 'Nesa were around, she always tried to fit her in, and she did fun things with her, like take her roller-skating, or to the park or movies.

Nikki knew that things would change, too. Growing up, she had always wanted a sister. Now she understood why she had never gotten one. Though she'd had a lonely childhood, she was relieved her sister hadn't lived through the same circumstances she had. She would make sure she never did. As a molestation survivor, she knew the damage it had done to her. If anyone ever laid a finger on her sister, she wouldn't freeze again.

Now that they were together, she would protect her and be there for her. She wanted to do so many things together, things she was never able to do when she was her age. She envisioned slumber parties, girls' night outs, and canvassing neighborhoods with Girl Scout cookie sign-up sheets. There would be PTA, spelling bees, and homecoming. She would instill in her sister the belief that she could do and be anything she wanted, and she would be there to love her and support her through it all.

"Over there!" Kayla pointed, dragging her sister along. She stopped in front of a jewelry stand.

Nikki looked at the display. All the necklaces had names engraved in cursive writing. "What are we stopping here for?" Nikki looked at Kayla. "I said no more jewelry."

"Please?" Kayla stared back at her with puppy eyes. "I promise I won't lose this one."

Nikki thought it over. The last piece of jewelry she had gotten her had been a pair of Australian crystal earrings that disappeared mysteriously at the playground. "Okay," she finally said, "but this you will only wear when I say so—on special occasions."

"Okay!" Kayla nodded compliantly. As they waited for the necklace to be made, they walked around to the other side of the booth. There a sign listed every name under the sun and its meaning.

"There's my name." Kayla pointed. She was thrilled to spot it.

Nikki took a step closer to look. "You're right. Guess what it means? Pure."

"Pure?"

"Yep. You know what that means?"

Kayla thought to herself, confused. She had seen several commercials on TV, and the only thing she could remember being described as 'pure' was water. "Does that mean it's without all the icky stuff in it?"

Nikki laughed. She bent over and pecked her on the lips. "That's right, baby. You're free from all the icky stuff. You're just how God wants us all to be."

"Really?" Kayla danced excitedly.

"Okay," the attendant announced.

"How much do I owe you?"

"It'll be $19.99."

"Nineteen ninety-nine!" Nikki exclaimed.

Kayla batted her eyelashes, looking up at her innocently.

"You have expensive tastes, little girl," Nikki said, forking over the money.

While she waited for her receipt to print, she gazed at other names. She saw "Kevin" and blushed. "Handsome, gentle, lovable."

She smirked. They were right about that, though she questioned the gentle and lovable part. Then she froze. She looked again in disbelief. "Jackie: Gracious gift of God;

One who replaces another."

"Here you go, ma'am. Come back and see us."

Nikki took the receipt, shaken. Her heart dared not think the obvious. "Come on, baby, let's go." She took Kayla's hand.

On their way back to Nikki's apartment, Kayla sang and danced in the back seat.

"Kayla, please," Nikki asserted, looking in the mirror, feeling the side of her head. "Do you have to be so loud?" Pressure mounted in her head, unlike that of a headache.

Kayla stopped for a second, but then the chorus came back on, and she began singing again.

Finally, Nikki turned the radio off. Now just wasn't the time. She remembered going to service with Kevin, and a special message she had heard one day. The minister had preached about God's providence. He taught that nothing happened by accident; it was all by divine orchestration.

Kayla stared out the window. It would be a long, boring ride without the radio. She began to sing. "Jesus loves me, this I know, for the Bible tells me so. Little ones to him belong; they are weak, but he is strong. Yes, Jesus loves me." She paused, expecting Nikki to come in with the chorus, but she didn't. Nikki drove on in silence. Nikki always sang her church songs with her; she didn't understand why she wasn't singing now. "Why aren't you singing?" she inquired.

Nikki kept her focus on the road.

Kayla restarted. "Yes, Jesus loves me." She paused.

"Loves me," Nikki sang softly.

"Yes, Jesus loves me."

"Loves me." A tear dropped down Nikki's face.

"Yes, Jesus loves me, 'cause the Bible tells me so."

Feelings of guilt and hurt stained Nikki's heart. She pulled to the side of the road and wept.

"Are you crying again?" Kayla sighed, exhausted. Taking care of her big sister was not going to be as easy as she originally thought.

Later that evening, Nikki couldn't sleep. She thought about things that she had experienced, like being reunited with Malcolm and meeting Kevin and Jackie.

She searched through her filing tray desperately. The concept had amazed her so much that she had jotted down the verse, planning to look it up later, but she never had. She found the program from a certain day in church and flipped to the back, where she'd scribbled Acts 17:26-27.

She reached for her Bible, and read.

And God made from one man every nation of mankind to live on all the face of the earth, having determined their appointed times and boundaries of their habitation, that they would seek God, if perhaps they might grope for Him and find Him, though He is not far from each one of us.

Her heart froze.

Nikki pulled up to the building and saw Melanie standing in the doorway, waiting for her. A silk scarf was tied around her head, and she wore baggy pajama pants. Nikki walked towards her, holding Kayla, who was still in her pajamas. She looked around sleepily. Nikki smiled at Melanie quietly, and Melanie smiled back. She took Kayla from her arms. "I'm sorry; I didn't mean to wake you."

Melanie shushed her. "Don't apologize. When God calls and touches our hearts, we must answer, whatever the time of day." She motioned her towards the auditorium.

Inside, Nikki saw the minister and his wife sitting in the front pew, waiting. As she approached, the minister stood. Kayla's eyes were now open; she stared quietly at Nikki as Melanie pointed to her and whispered in her ear.

The minister hugged Nikki.

"In the name of the Father, Son, and Holy Ghost, I baptize this repented believer for the forgiveness of her sins. Amen."

"Amen," voices echoed.

Nikki's hand braced the minister's on her chest. She closed her eyes as she went under the water, but the shock made her open them again. She could make out Melanie and Kayla standing on top of the baptismal pool. Though blurry and contorted, their eyes were lively, and they clapped their hands. As she rose from the water, "Victory in Jesus" was sung. Her heart warmed.

CHAPTER TWENTY-EIGHT

N ikki sat on the couch with a book nestled in her lap. Though in some ways she missed school, she loved having extra time on her hands to do whatever she wanted. She turned the page.

"Nikki." Kayla walked into the living room. She frowned. "I don't feel good."

"You don't?" Nikki twirled around, dropping her book to the sofa. "What's wrong?"

"My head hurts."

"A headache?" Nikki inquired.

Kayla nodded.

"Okay. Come on," Nikki said, standing. Kayla followed into the kitchen. Nikki opened a cabinet, pulled out a bottle, and gave Kayla a tablet. "Chew this," Nikki said, handing it to her. "It'll make you feel better."

Kayla took the tablet and popped it in her mouth.

"It's getting late, anyway." Nikki hugged her. She folded back her hair and kissed her on the forehead when she noticed her skin was hot. "You are burning up." She said feeling her over, not understanding how she missed it before. "Why don't you go lay down, and I'll bring your pajamas to you when they're dry."

"Okay, munchkin." Nikki opened Kayla's door, holding Kayla's pajamas in her hand, but when her eyes fell upon her, she shrieked in horror.

Kayla lay on top of the bed, jerking violently.

"Malcolm—" Nikki began. Her face was stained with tears.

"Nikki!" He grinned. "That was fast!"

Nikki paused, puzzled.

"I just tried to call you."

"Tried to call?" Nikki was confused. How could he have known?

"We're on our way to the hospital. 'Nesa's in labor." He snickered. "Again."

"In labor?" she repeated.

"Something wrong?"

"No!" She tried to smile, but couldn't. "That's great news." She paused. "I'm at the hospital."

Malcolm's eyebrow arched. Now he was confused.

"Kayla's sick," she explained.

"Sick?"

Nikki shook her head. "I don't know what's wrong with her. They're running tests, but—" She paused, sniffling. "She just started seizing."

"Seizing?"

"I called my grandmother; she said she's never done it before. I want to pick her up, but I don't want to leave Kayla."

Malcolm eyed Anesa. She was toppled over in pain in the passenger seat. Though this was their third trip, he wanted to be sure. "I'll get someone to pick her up for you."

"Thank you," Nikki sniffled again.

"Don't worry. I'll be there as soon as I can."

"Did she say what was wrong?" Anesa asked during a calm period. She and Malcolm sat in a delivery room. Anesa had wires attached to her belly measuring her contractions and the baby's heart beat. Something told them this would be it.

"Uh-uh." He stroked Anesa's stomach. "They're running some test. I'm gonna call Mario and ask him to pick up her grandmother."

"Why?" Anesa looked at him intently.

Malcolm was puzzled. She wasn't herself when her labor pains hit, but he hadn't expected her to be so cold. "Her grandmother would want to be there."

"That's not what I meant. You know how Nikki and her grandmother are." Then Anesa clarified. "Call Kevin."

"Kevin?" Malcolm huffed. As far as he was concerned, he was out of the picture. "What for? Ain't no need calling and getting him mixed up in this."

A labor pain hit. Anesa braced herself and gritted her teeth. "Get on that phone and call!"

Malcolm's tone softened. "Okay, baby. Just calm down. Breathe. Okay? Breathe."

Anesa nodded, but she didn't forget. "Call him. Now!"

Nikki was in the waiting room. She rubbed her legs. She didn't know what was going on with Kayla, and she hadn't been able to get in contact with Malcolm to confirm that Anesa had gone into labor, and her grandmother still hadn't arrived. She walked to the nurse's station and asked about her sister, but there had been no change. She walked back into the waiting room, but couldn't sit.

"Nikki?"

She turned. "Grandma." Her heart relaxed. They embraced for a long time.

Finally, Odessa spoke. "Any word yet?"

Nikki shook her head. "No, grandma. Nothing. When did ya'll get here?" She peered out the door. "Where's Malcolm?"

"Malcolm? Oh, no, honey. Your boyfriend brought me."

"Boyfriend?"

"Yeah, your boyfriend," Odessa reiterated confidently.

Just then, Kevin slid around the corner.

How dare you? Nikki's eyes demanded defiantly. She folded her arms and looked at Odessa. "He's not my boyfriend!" She corrected.

Odessa waved her hand nonchalantly. "You young people break up and get back together so many times, I can't keep up."

Kevin sat down, too, but he didn't look at Nikki.

"I'm going to check on Kayla," Nikki announced, leaving them. "You can find yourself another waiting room!"

"Nikki! Don't be so nasty." Odessa yelled after her.

But she was gone.

Kevin rose. This had been a bad idea from the start. He had even offered to pay Odessa's cab fare, but Anesa had insisted he be here. He should have gone with his gut feeling. "Look, Ms. Odessa, I'm doing more harm than good here. I'm gonna go."

Odessa patted Kevin's hand. "Oh, don't you worry 'bout her." She gestured for him to sit back down. "She could never keep a grudge for too long. She'll cool off."

Nikki marched into the hallway. How did he have the audacity to show up now, when a couple of months ago he hadn't cared about Kayla?

She knew she needed to calm down. She leaned against a railing and took a deep breath. Now was not the time to get worked up about Kevin. Her sister was the most important thing, plain and simple. She took a deep breath, turned around, and walked back.

"Nikki!" Her grandmother motioned to her as she walked into the waiting room. "Kevin went looking for you."

A doctor was standing in front of her grandmother.

"Ms. Jones?" He smiled slightly. "Why don't you all have a seat?"

Already Nikki didn't like the sound of things. She sat between the doctor and her grandmother.

Odessa noted that the doctor appeared particularly young, and concluded that he must have been a resident.

"We've administered a course of antibiotics—Rocephin to be exact." He paused. "We're doing a lumbar puncture on MiKayla."

"Lumbar puncture? Why do you have to do that?"

"We suspect she may have meningitis."

Nikki gasped.

"Though rare, it's notorious for infecting young children. There are two forms—bacterial and viral. Both have similar symptoms—nausea, vomiting, lethargy, fever, headache—seizures. The bacterial infection is very dangerous, and many long-term complications can result. The viral form is less severe, and children often lead normal lives afterwards."

"You said the bacterial form could be dangerous. Exactly what are you saying?" Nikki inquired.

"It could—" the physician stuttered, "could—possibly—"

"Kill her?" Odessa blurted, tired of his fumbling.

"Yes," he confirmed.

Nikki's head fell into her hands. It was surreal. This couldn't be happening.

Odessa patted Nikki on the back.

"If she does survive, there are possible long-term complications, such as paralysis, learning disabilities, hearing problems—" He paused. "When she was admitted, you told the nurse she'd had an earache a few days ago. Is there anything else you can think of that you can tell us?"

Nikki thought hard. "She had some diarrhea and a little vomiting," Nikki said quietly. "But I thought that was a result of the medicine she was taking."

Kevin reentered the waiting room. Seeing the grim look in Nikki's eyes, he knew the story was not good.

The doctor patted Nikki on the leg. "Well, if you can think of anything else."

"When will we get to see her?" Odessa asked.

"The nurse will be out to get you soon. We've had to do a few things, just in case. We started an IV line with fluids and antibiotics and put a catheter in place."

The nurse pulled back the curtain. Nikki and her grandmother walked up to Kayla's bed. Because of the room's tight size, Kevin stood some distance back.

Guilt overwhelmed Nikki as she scanned her sister. Only two weeks after moving in with her, Kayla was very sick. More wires and tubes than she could imagine were hooked up to her.

"Is she conscious?" Odessa finally broke the silence.

"Yes." The nurse smiled. "The medicine we gave her to control her seizures has zonked her out, but other than that, she's very conscious."

Nikki stood behind her grandmother. "When are we going to know something for sure? About what's causing all this?"

"Mmm." The nurse peered out the door. "It should be relatively soon. Let me go check on that for you," she said, excusing herself.

As she stepped out, Kevin moved forward.

Odessa started crying. "I can't stand to see my grandbaby like this." She shook her head in disbelief. She turned abruptly and ran out the door.

Nikki followed.

Kevin walked forward. His heart was heavy as he stared down at Kayla. He lowered his hand over her rail, touched hers, and stroked it gently. A tear trickled down his cheek. Never in a million years had he imagined this young child, so full of life and energy, would wind up in the hospital like this.

He rubbed Kayla's forehead as more tears flowed. He wanted to say something good to her—something on the lines of being strong and brave, but it didn't seem enough or appropriate. How could she be strong or brave when a deadly organism festered in her body, zapping her life from her?

He sniffled, closed his eyes, and said a prayer. He leaned over the bed rail and began singing Elton John's "Blessed." Right as he got to the end, a noise startled him.

"I'm sorry." Lydia, the nurse, had returned. "I didn't realize anyone was here. I thought I saw—"

"It's okay." Kevin wiped the tears from his cheek.

"I'll give you more time," she said, backing out of the room.

Nikki stepped in again. She looked at Kayla and began sobbing.

Kevin wrapped his arms around her. "She's going to be okay," he whispered softly.

Nikki nodded. In the past, his words had comforted her, and she would have believed, whole-heartedly, the things he said, but this time, she just didn't know.

Even if Kayla were to survive, the long-term complications were severe, and possibility debilitating. Her mind couldn't fathom how she would manage with a physically or mentally disabled child. It was overwhelming. "How could this happen?" She cried, collapsing in Kevin's arms.

Kevin was stumped. He didn't know what to say, so he just held her. Kevin's phone rang, but he didn't answer. It rang a few more times, and then stopped.

Nikki pulled back. Here he was, consoling her, but he had business of his own to attend. His phone rang again. "Excuse me," Kevin said, pulling back apologetically. "Hello?" he turned and answered.

Nikki stepped over to her sister's bed.

"I'm sorry, Natalie."

Natalie? Nikki turned towards Kevin and stared for a second before dropping her eyes back to her sister.

"I'm at the hospital—" There was a long pause. "With Nikki," he said in a hushed tone. "Listen, I'll call you back later." His voice dropped lower. "I'll explain later. Bye."

Nikki looked down at her watch. She squirmed in her seat. It was two-thirty. After five hours, the chairs had become quite uncomfortable. Her grandmother was snoozing, and Kevin was bent over, massaging his temples and forehead.

Suddenly, Kayla's doctor walked in. Kevin picked his head up immediately, and Odessa awakened. It was the moment they had been waiting for.

Right there, she decided the verdict didn't matter. Her love for her sister was eternal, and she would always be there for Kayla, just as before.

The doctor sat across from them stoically, but then smiled. "We ran the test, and there are no traces of bacteria."

"Thank God!" Odessa shouted.

"That's great news!" Kevin said, touching Nikki's back.

Nikki touched her chest, exhilarated. She began to choke up with tears.

"We're going to d/c all the medications, but because of the seizures, we'd like to keep her here the rest of the night to monitor her. Okay?"

"Does that mean we can take her home tomorrow?" Nikki mustered.

"Yes," the doctor said adamantly.

Nikki nodded happily. She said a quiet prayer of thanksgiving in her heart.

"We're still going to have to follow her over the next couple of days, but as long as she doesn't worsen, she won't have to be readmitted."

"Can we see her?" Odessa asked.

"Sure." The doctor smiled. "We're going to move her to a regular room where you'll be able to sit with her, but it's limited to two people."

They visited with MiKayla until the orderly came to transport her. Then Nikki turned to her grandmother. "It's been a long night. Why don't you let Kevin take you home? I'll stay with Kayla."

Kevin thought it was Nikki's way of telling him he was dismissed. Though it appeared Kayla was out of the woods, he still wanted to be with her.

Nikki touched Kevin's elbow, but didn't look at him. "Can you bring my blanket when you come back? When the ambulance came, I rode in with Kayla."

"Sure, Nikki." he answered softly, hoping she could sense his sincerity. "Whatever you need." Then he started down the hall with Odessa.

Lydia entered the room right before they transported Kayla. "Your husband is so sweet," she said, peering at Nikki.

Nikki didn't respond, and the nurse didn't know if she had heard her.

"You have a sweet guy," she said, touching her arm. "He really loves that little girl."

"Yes, he does," Nikki finally answered.

Nikki followed closely behind Kevin as he carried Kayla into the house and placed her in her bed. Though Kayla was still asleep, Nikki was relieved to have her back home.

Nikki dressed her in her pajamas then tucked her in. Though the doctor said it had been temperature related, and her fever was under control, ever since her seizure, she had been afraid to take her eyes off her. She sat at her bedside for several minutes, watching as she slept. She heard a tap at the door. She rose and cracked it open. It was Kevin.

"What do you want for breakfast?"

"Breakfast? I'm not hungry."

"Not hungry?" Kevin mocked. She hadn't eaten anything all night. "Come on, Nikki. You gotta eat something. I'll make you some eggs and toast. Is that okay?"

"Sure," Nikki said reluctantly.

"I'm glad she's going to be okay. I was really scared," Odessa said, breaking the silence. She sat at the kitchen table across from Nikki watching as Kevin finished up breakfast. He stood over the stove, scrambling eggs in a skillet. "I don't like my eggs too hard, sugar," She said to Kevin, eyeing Nikki. "It sure was nice of you to make breakfast for us."

"I don't mind. You all have had a long night." He smiled. "Whatever I can do to make it easy on you."

"Well, you had a long night, too," Odessa hinted, eyeing Nikki again.

Nikki picked up her glass of juice and ignored her.

"You must be tired," Odessa added.

"I'm okay," Kevin smiled, spooning the eggs out of the skillet and unto their plates. He placed the skillet on the counter, and then he sat.

"So you like to cook, eh?"

Nikki wished her grandmother would just stop asking Kevin questions.

"From time to time," he answered.

"Ever cook for my grandbaby?"

"Nikki!" came a small voice.

Nikki jumped from the table and ran to Kayla's bedroom.

She was sitting up in her bed.

"You're home, baby," she said, huddling her under her arm. "You remember anything?"

Kayla shrugged and shook her head.

"Good," Nikki said, kissing her forehead. Nikki looked up as Odessa moved to sit on the other side of Kayla on the bed.

Suddenly, Kayla's eyes sparkled. Kevin was standing in the doorway, peering in.

"Hey, sunshine. We were worried about you."

Nikki squirmed. "I'll be right back, baby," she said, rising abruptly. "I'll bring you some juice, okay?"

She stepped into the hallway and turned to Kevin. After all he had done, she felt funny about what she was about to say, but it needed to be said. She cleared her throat. "I know your being here means a lot to Kayla, but I think it's best that she focus on her recovery."

Kevin scratched the back of his head, embarrassed. Once Kayla had stabilized and gotten back to normal, she kicked him out. How could she be so cold? "Okay." He looked around, frustrated. "I guess I'll be going." He turned to walk down the hall.

Nikki folded her arms and followed, watching him pick up his things and walk to the door.

Kevin turned. "If you need me for anything, don't hesitate to call."

After Nikki closed the door, Odessa emerged and stood at the corner where the hallway met the living room.

"Sometimes I wonder if there's any limit to your stubbornness." She paused. "Was that really necessary?"

"I'm only trying to protect Kayla."

Odessa stared solemnly. "Are you?" she shook her head and turned back to Kayla's bedroom.

Nikki hugged herself in contemplation.

CHAPTER TWENTY~NINE

T hings were starting to go right again in her life. Kayla was doing well, though Nikki was playing it safe and quarantining her
from others. Her new position at the youth center as the crafts and
arts/special events coordinator was more intriguing than she had
thought it would be.

She rumbled around in the kitchen. She wanted to redo her pan-
try and make certain things more accessible for Kayla. Plus, after
working and being in school all year there was some much needed
tidying to be done. She took a dishcloth and began wiping things
down.

She reached the refrigerator and looked at it for a moment. A
stool rested in the corner of the kitchen and she reached, dragged it
to her, and placed it in front of the fridge. She stood on the stool,
began wiping the top, and felt something.

She pulled the object down. It was a book. She examined it,
hoping she hadn't forgotten to return one of MiKayla's books to the
library, when she remembered the book she had found propped
against her door the day she graduated. She had no idea who it belonged to, and had planned to ask some of her neighbors, but had
forgotten.

The book hung loosely from her hand, as she stepped down
from the stool. She heard a "swish" noise. Her eyes scanned the soft
white and gray tile floor. She spotted a folded sheet of paper and
picked it up. She figured it had fallen out of the book, so she
opened it, hoping it would give her some clue as to who owned it.

To her surprise, it was addressed to her.

05-17

Nikki,

The day has finally come. You worked so hard to see this happen. I know that God is blessing you for your tenacity, and I know you'll do something truly special with your life someday.

I wanted to tell you how proud I am of you, but you looked so happy, and I didn't want to do anything that would've removed that beautiful smile from your face, or diminished any joys of the day.

Anyway, I'm sorry for the pain I caused you, and I hope that someday we can at least be friends again.

Kevin

PS: Hope you get something out of it. It was written for people like you.
Keep your dreams.

Nikki examined the face of the book. The squiggly lines and funny colors were characteristic of Dr. Seuss. *Oh, the Places You'll Go,* she read, smiling to herself. She had never figured the book was intended for her.

Sadness overcame her. She thought back to her graduation. The smile had been a facade. Inside, she was miserable and depressed. Only Jackie had been able to see through it. *It doesn't matter anyway,* she thought, staring down at the book quietly. *It's over now.*

Nikki opened the book and flipped through a few pages. Then she pulled a chair from the table. She turned back to page one and began reading.

● ● ●

Nikki paused in front of a mirror, catching a glimpse of herself. She ran her fingers through her hair and studied the rest of herself. Kevin had called only moments ago. He said he was coming over to see Kayla, that he had a birthday present for her.

She couldn't understand why she felt so giddy. She hunted through her dresser for a moment, picking out a nice blouse. She found one and held it against her chest as she analyzed how it moved with her. Then she froze. "Look at me," she whispered under her breath, realizing what she was doing. She folded the blouse and placed it back in the drawer.

The doorbell rang. Nikki sat up. She walked out of her bedroom and peered over into Kayla's room. She was sitting in bed sulking. Nikki walked down the alternate hall. With each step, her heart beat three times faster. She approached the front door, took a deep breath, and opened it.

Kevin stood there, smiling.

"Hi." Her voice was low, business-like. "She's in the bedroom," she said quickly. They walked towards her room. "I didn't tell her you were coming. She's much better—back to her old self." She was rambling, not wanting a moment of silence to come between them. "She's sitting in her room depressed because she couldn't have her birthday party." She paused. "I'm just thankful she had another birthday."

They approached the door. "She's a little moody," she warned. "I was hoping that by staying up late last night, watching TV and playing games, that she would be too sleepy today to really miss her party, but—" Nikki shrugged. She tapped on Kayla's door and peeped in. "Guess who's here to see you?"

Kevin stuck his head in the door.

"Kevin!" Kayla exclaimed, tossing Mr. Huggs aside. She jumped off the bed and leaped into Kevin's arms.

Nikki leaned against the door trim, watching.

Kayla gave him a hug and kissed him on the cheek. "Where have you been?" She rested her head on his shoulder. "I missed you."

He squeezed her. "I missed you, too, baby."

Nikki stepped back into her room quietly and shut the door. She stretched across the bed and looked blankly at the NAS bible. She was on the same passage she had been on when Kevin called an hour ago. She picked up a pencil and began jotting notes.

A short time later, she heard Kayla squealing from the living room. Then the familiar tune from *Scooby-Doo* blared, and they were laughing and talking.

"Eat some of my cake!" Kayla looked at Kevin. "Please!"

"Okay."

"Yes!" Kayla jumped off his lap, and tugged at his fingers. She led him into the kitchen, then stopped at the counter in front of it and danced around. "It's chocolate!"

He pulled off the lid. "You haven't eaten any. You sure it's okay?"

"Yeah!" She shrugged. "I want some now," she said, reaching to open the utensil drawer.

"Hey, hey, hey!" He put his hand over hers. "I'll get that." He reached in and grabbed the cake cutter. The cake weighed a ton, so he carried it to the table. He picked Kayla up and placed her in the chair. "I'll let you have the honors, birthday girl."

She picked up the cake knife and began pressing down on the cake with all her might. She couldn't quite get it to go through all the way, so Kevin pressed his hand over hers, and they put the first line through. "How big do you want it?"

Kayla moved the knife to about a 4 x 3-inch line.

"Whoa!" Kevin smiled. "Are you going to eat all of that?"

She nodded her head up and down adamantly.

"Okay," he complied hesitantly. He slid the cutter under the bottom and plopped the slab on a saucer.

"Now it's your turn."

They cut another slice for him then Kayla jumped out of the chair and ran for the door.

"Where you going?"

She danced around excitedly. "I'm going to see if Nikki wants some, too."

Kayla reached for the knob and flung the door open. "Nikki, Nikki!"

Nikki sat up.

"Kevin's cutting a piece of my birthday cake! Want some?"

Nikki smiled. "Maybe later."

Kayla looked at her for a moment. "Why are you sitting in here?" She began tugging at Nikki's fingers, trying to pull her off the bed. "Come out with us."

"No, baby. Kevin didn't come over here to see me. He came over to see you."

Kayla looked up at her, puzzled. "But he always comes over to see us."

Nikki nodded her head. "Not this time." She ran her fingers across her cheek. "Kevin came all the way over here to see you. And you know why?"

Kayla shook her head.

"Because you're a special little girl."

A smile broke through her lips.

"And he wants to spend some time with you for your birthday. So let him. Okay?"

Kayla nodded and ran back into the kitchen.

"What did she say?" Kevin inquired.

"She doesn't want one."

Kevin nodded, not a bit surprised. The timer went off on the microwave.

"What'cha doing?"

"I'm heating mine up. Want me to do yours?"

Kayla shook her head, taking her piece from Kevin. She handled the cake carefully as they walked into the living room.

Kevin picked her up and sat her on his lap. Kayla plowed her fork into the cake and ate a piece then watched Kevin as he ate his.

Kevin noticed her watching. "Want some?"

She looked at the cake. The chocolate oozed down the side, and the smell was intoxicating. She nodded.

Kevin lowered the saucer.

She plowed her fork into his cake and tasted it. "Umm." She rubbed her stomach.

Kevin ate another piece.

Kayla slid her cake to the side and began eating Kevin's.

Kevin set on the sofa quietly, overcome by gloom. Kayla had fallen asleep soon after eating. He had been sitting with Kayla for an hour now, and she still hadn't awakened. He rubbed his fingers over her face and through her hair. He couldn't think of another reasonable excuse that would allow him to come over and see his girls.

He picked Kayla up gently in his arms and placed her back on the couch. Only a couple of weeks ago, she was laying in a hospital bed barely clinging to life. He thanked God for delivering her, and was grateful it hadn't been more serious.

He kissed her gently on the cheek. The thought that he was saying goodbye brought tears to his eyes, but he wiped them away quickly. He had to face Nikki to tell her he was leaving. She hated him so much that she refused to join them for cake. He looked at Kayla one last time. He pressed his lips to her forehead. "Goodbye."

Nikki heard a tap. She rose, confused, and then remembered Kevin. She walked over and opened the door.

Kayla had heard the knocking. She rose and peeled the covers off discreetly.

"I'm sorry." Nikki felt the back of her neck where a crick had formed. "I must have dozed off." She looked towards the living room. "Where's Kayla?"
"Asleep on the sofa."

Kayla heard Nikki and Kevin's voices. She peeped around the corner and saw them talking.

Nikki leaned against the wall and folded her arms. "I guess we were tired," she said, massaging the back of her neck.
"Do you want me to move her to her room?"
"No, that's okay. She'll be fine there."
Kayla breathed a sigh of relief.
"How's your family?"
"They're fine. Anesa decided to extend her pregnancy leave, and Malcolm's doing good." She thought to herself. "And, oh—I have to tell you about my grandmother. According to Kayla, some man started coming to see her a month or so before she moved here! I haven't even met him. Can you believe that? After all she put us through..." Her voice trailed off.
"Really?" Kevin smiled.
"Yeah." Nikki smiled back. "I didn't know anything about him until I pulled up early one day to pick Kayla up, and he was backing up out of the driveway in his shiny black Lincoln."
"Mmmm. Go 'head, Granny."
They gazed into each other's eyes quietly for a moment, but Nikki broke it off and swallowed. "Oh, I've been meaning to tell you—I got baptized."
"You what?" Kevin beamed, grabbing her and embracing her.
Nikki couldn't help but remember how good it felt to be back in his arms, but things weren't the way they had been before, so her hug was loose and ended abruptly. Her excitement was squashed by powerful feelings of betrayal, but she covered it up and smiled.
"When did you get baptized?"
"A few weeks ago. Right before Kayla got sick."

Kayla had to do something. She remembered being on vacation, waking up, looking outside, and seeing Kevin and Nikki in the pool together. She couldn't recall Nikki ever being happier.

Kayla clasped her hands and pointed them towards the sky. She closed her eyes tightly and began praying. "Please, God! Please."

"That's wonderful. I've been praying for you."

Nikki was stunned, wondering if he was for real. After all the awful things that she had said, now she didn't know what to say. Then she wondered if this had been the reason for their meeting in the first place. Her falling in love with him had just been a casualty of circumstance; he had only been placed in her life to save her soul.

His boyish grin extended across his lips. "I'm really happy for you."

"Thank you. The Bible you gave me really helps. It's a lot easier to understand."

"Good."

They stared at each other for a bleak moment.

"Well, I better get going," Kevin finally said.

Kayla tiptoed back to the sofa and covered herself. She heard them walk down the alternate hall.

"Thanks for coming. It really made her day."

Kayla peeped through the covers, watching attentively. *Please God!*

Kevin quickly scanned Nikki. She looked as fine as ever. If only she knew how he felt. "Bye," Kevin whispered. He turned and walked away.

Nikki shut the door behind him.

Kayla's heart sank. *He didn't kiss her.* She closed her eyes as Nikki closed the door.

Nikki walked to the couch and stood over Kayla. The covers completely covered her. She thought about pulling them back, but feared that if she accidentally woke her, Kayla might become more ill than she had already been. Instead, she walked to the patio door and drew the blinds, then went to her bedroom.

● ● ●

"Coming," Nikki yelled as she rushed out of the bathroom. She ran to the front door, wrapping her robe around her waist. She hadn't expected anyone and hoped whoever it was hadn't left by the time she got there. "Hi." She smiled.

A UPS courier stood at the entrance. He looked annoyed, but shoved an 11" x 16" flat package at her and gestured for her to sign. Nikki was confused. She checked the name on the receiver's end then signed it. "Thank you," she said, handing the clipboard back.

"Good day, ma'am," the courier said, turning to leave.

Nikki looked at the package, puzzled, and then closed the door.

Nikki woke abruptly. She looked at the clock across the room. Three-twelve, the clock read. She had had several nightmares since the night she rushed Kayla to the emergency room.

She felt silly, but as she had done many nights before, she rushed out of bed and peeped into Kayla's room. Kayla lay there quietly, fast asleep, her arm wrapped tightly around Mr. Huggs.

Nikki's heart relaxed. She knew she wouldn't be able to get back to sleep right away, so she went to her bedroom and cut the TV on. She turned the volume low, so as not to disturb Kayla. Nothing interesting was on, so she began reading, but her mind couldn't concentrate on the words. She laid the book on the bed, turned towards her nightstand, and grabbed a few sheets off it.

She began to read again. Mike had sent her a copy of his divorce papers. She studied them carefully, then she turned to the last page. He had written a letter to her. In it he was very apologetic about concealing his marriage, but assured her that things were 'officially' over. He invited her to come up for the weekend to experience Juneteenth festivities. He had even included his number and address, something she had never had before.

She placed the letter back on the nightstand, more confused than ever.

CHAPTER THIRTY

"Say, 'I'm doing good now, Auntie Nikki,'" Anesa said in a baby voice, rubbing Elijah's stomach gently. "My mommy's fed and changed me."

Nikki gazed at Elijah, thrilled. It was the first time she had been able to see him since Kayla's illness. "Gosh. I can't believe how much he weighs," she said, watching his eyes close sleepily.

"Yep." Anesa placed him in his crib. "I'm a greedy little rascal."

They giggled, watching as he settled into a spot. "When was the last time you heard from Kevin?"

"He came over to see MiKayla last Saturday for her birthday," Nikki answered reluctantly, wondering why her cousin inquired.

"How's he doing? The day I called from the hospital, I wasn't exactly able to talk much."

Nikki was annoyed. *Why couldn't Anesa just accept that things were over between them?* "He seemed to be fine," she swallowed, trying to conceal her feelings. "We didn't talk long. I was in my room while he was visiting MiKayla."

"Mmm," Anesa said, looking at her. "Did you mention the letter?"

"No." Nikki shrugged. "It didn't cross my mind."

Anesa stared at Nikki. Her body language said something different. Her cousin had a lot of pride. She touched her on the hand. "Why don't you just call him?"

"Why should I?" Nikki asked, riled.

"Because I know he still cares about you, about MiKayla," she said. She kept her voice low, careful not to disturb the baby.

Nikki knew he still cared, too, but that was beside the point. "I can't."

"Why not?"

"Because—" Nikki paused. "The last time we saw each other, I said some pretty ugly things to him; I'm sure he doesn't want to see me anymore, anyway."

Anesa gasped. "Nikki, that's absurd. When Kayla got sick, he came to the hospital to be with you."

"No," she corrected. "He came to the hospital because you asked him to. Kevin," she shook her head, "has this sense of obligation."

"Obligation? Nikki, the boy is in love with you. Maybe there was a sense of obligation, but not because I asked him to."

"I can't have this conversation with you right now. You know how he did me."

"What did he do to you that you didn't want done?"

"What are you talking about?"

"You wanted to break it off with him, but he broke it off with you."

"I didn't want to break up with him then. Things changed."

"What if things changed with him?"

Nikki was confused. She had no idea where this was going.

"He went because he loved you. He still does."

Nikki shook her head. "He can't."

"Why not?"

"Because I said some really mean things to him. Okay? When I saw him last, before Kayla got sick," she closed her eyes and nodded her head, "I called him a hypocrite and a liar, and threw his past in his face."

Anesa thought of the choice words she had had for Kevin when she saw him at the mall. She chuckled and patted Nikki's back. "That doesn't sound so bad, given the circumstances." She didn't know if she was trying to console Nikki or herself.

Nikki remembered the pain in Kevin's eyes—that she had gone there. At the time, she hadn't cared. She wanted to hurt him; she had been willing to say anything to bring it to fruition. She was tired of people hurting her; and Kevin had been the last straw.

"You were hurt, and Kevin had just walked out on you. You had every right to be angry. Who could blame you for that?"

"Anesa?" Malcolm stood in the doorway. "What did you want from the store again?"

"Diapers, Malcolm," she said, with a hint of sarcasm in her voice. "Diapers."

"Oh, that's right," he smiled, remembering. He hesitated, glancing between her and Nikki.

Anesa tilted her head at him.

"Okay." He took a final glance at Nikki. "Be back in a few."

"Okay," Nikki replied cheerfully.

Malcolm tapped the doorframe a couple of times to signal he was leaving.

Anesa listened to the front door close and thought about the mall again, and wondered if she should inform Nikki of Kevin's intentions.

"I know what you're going to say," Nikki mumbled, feeling her draw close.

Perhaps telling her about the mall wasn't such a good idea. She had never actually seen Kevin purchase the ring. When Nikki said he had come to see her, he hadn't mentioned a thing. She put her hands on Nikki's shoulders and leaned her head on her.

She knew they were two people that cared deeply about each other, yet were apart. In her mind, that was the most important thing. "You know, you're never going to know what he thinks or how he feels unless you call."

"It's too late. I blew it. I've made too many mistakes." Nikki's voice trailed away.

"Mistakes? What are you talking about?" Anesa shook her head. "It's not too late. Not when you're still in love."

"None of it matters; he's seeing someone."

"Seeing someone? Since when?" Anesa's eyebrow arched, confused. "You know what? I don't care if he is seeing someone. She ain't you. I can tell you he'll never be satisfied with her because he loves you. You, Nikki. You." Anesa gazed firmly in Nikki's eyes and took her hand in hers, hoping she could get it across to her without saying it.

Nikki laid her head on the headboard. She stared across her room until her eyes fell on her boom box. She walked over and examined the CDs on the shelf. She spotted Sade's, inserted it into the CD player, and listened to "Love is Stronger than Pride" over and over again.

She would give into her wanting. She would call Kevin and listen to his voicemail. She had inadvertently pushed the memory key earlier in the day, called his office, and had listened long enough to know he had been traveling. She dialed the numbers.

"Hey, this is Kevin—"

His voice always excited her. His speech was soft but firm and she could imagine his smile as he left the message.

"I'm not able to take your call right now; but please leave a message, and I'll be in touch. Bye."

She rushed to hang up the phone before the beep. She felt a little better. She slumped into the bed and picked up the remote. Now that school was over, she often felt lonely. She wished she could find something to do to occupy her mind, or at least allow her to go back to sleep. She thought about Kevin again. "Okay," she whispered. She picked up the phone and pressed redial.

"'Hey, this is Kevin. I'm not able to take your call right now, but—' Hello?" A deep, groggy voice answered.

What was he doing home?

"Hello?"

Think, she told herself. A second later, she slammed the phone down.

Kevin set up in bed. He dialed *69 to find out who called. The phone slid from his ear as he froze, astonished that it was Nikki. He retrieved it up and placed it back on the receiver.

Questions ran through his head. Was something wrong? Did she want to talk? Was everything okay with MiKayla? That thought sent him into a panic, and he picked up the phone and dialed.

When the phone rang, Nikki jumped, startled. It rang a couple of times, but she didn't know what to do. If she didn't answer the phone, Kevin would suspect something was wrong and keep calling, but if she answered, she didn't know how she would explain the late night phone call. She rushed to her bedroom door to close it. Across the hall, Kayla stirred under the covers. She ran back and answered. "Umm, hello?"

"Hey." Kevin's voice was clearer now. "You just called?"

Nikki paused. "Yeah."

"Is everything okay?"

She could sense Kevin's concern. "Yeah, I'm sorry for calling so late. I didn't think you would be home." She cringed, fussing at herself. She didn't want him to know she had been calling and listening to his prerecorded messages. She had to fix it. "I called your office earlier today, but got a message that you were out, so I didn't leave a message earlier, and was calling back to." She cracked her door and peeped into Kayla's room. Kayla was settled again. "I wanted to ask if you would like to come to Kayla's performance on Saturday. Since I was up, and I didn't think I would be waking you, I called. I'm sorry."

"You don't have to apologize. You can call me anytime." There was a long pause. "What time is it, anyway?"

"Twelve-fifteen."

Kevin chuckled. "No. I mean her thing—on Saturday."

"Right." Nikki chuckled, too. "It's at one o'clock."

"Mmph! I have to be at the airport no later than 9:30, and fly out at 11:35. I'm sorry."

"No. I'm sorry. I meant to tell you before, but we've been so busy—"

"That's okay. How are things going with her?"

"Good. She's doing good, thank God."

"Good. She's a strong little girl—just like her big sister. She'll be fine."

There was a long pause.

"When did you get in?"

"About three hours ago. I took a late flight in. I didn't want to wait until tomorrow morning to leave. My place is crazy, and I have a few errands to run tomorrow."

"I know you must be tired—"

"I'm okay. Did you see the last episode of *24*?" he asked quickly, trying to keep her talking.

"Yeah. It was good, wasn't it?"

"I didn't see it. What happened?"

Nikki began. It reminded him of old times. He liked hearing her tell the story—the rise and fall of her voice. It soothed him. He wanted things the way they were before—when they could talk without all the tension, anytime, night or day.

"I do think I better let you go." Nikki paused. "I'm sorry I woke you."

"Nikki, it's okay, really."

"No, it's late. I'm sure you have to be up early in the morning. I won't hold you."

Silence gripped the phone.

Finally, Kevin spoke. "Okay. Can you do me a favor?"

"Yeah," Nikki said softly. "What?"

"Tell Kayla I'm sorry I couldn't make it."

"Okay. Sure. Goodnight."

"Goodnight," Kevin whispered, waiting until she hung up. Then he heard the click.

He didn't want the conversation to end, but Nikki didn't want to talk anymore. He leaned back in bed. He lifted his remote control and began playing Maxwell's "Whenever, Wherever, Whatever." As the song played, he reached into his nightstand and pulled out a picture Nikki had given him long ago when they first started dating. He missed her so much.

It was amazing how the small things, even now, caused him to think of her. When they went out, she always put a straw in his drink for him. She always laughed when he cracked jokes, no matter how corny, and sincerely seemed tickled. He couldn't have asked for a better woman, and he marveled at how easily he had let her slip through his fingers. Impulsiveness had ruled him, and after the trip, he had become afraid that they didn't want the same thing out of life. Despite their declarations of love, the only thing he could think of was to ditch her before she ditched him. It had been imminent, right? He knew how difficult it was for him to detach himself from those he loved, regardless of how much they hurt him. It had taken him years to get over Toni, and he knew if Nikki broke up with him, it would take a lifetime.

Finally, the Maxwell song ended. He picked up the remote and turned the DVD/CD player off. "Forever and a day," he murmured reminiscing one of the verses. He cut the light out and rolled back under the covers.

●●●

"Is this seat taken?"

Nikki looked towards the voice; to her surprise, it was Kevin.

He held a small bouquet of fresh wild flowers and wore Dockers and a polo shirt.

"No," she said, moving a program off the seat next to her. She looked at his profile slyly, marveling at his new goatee. He looked irresistible. "I thought you were flying out at—what was it—eleven-something?" she asked, pretending not to remember.

"Yeah." He settled into the seat beside her. "I was, but I thought this was more important. So I postponed it a few hours."

He handed the bouquet to Nikki. "For Kayla."

Nikki took them from him. "I'm sure she'll love them. They're pretty."

"Not as pretty as you," he said softly.

Nikki turned away abruptly, feeling herself blush.

When Nikki turned her back to him, Kevin thought it meant she wasn't up for compliments. She still had harsh feelings towards him, and he only hoped she would stay civil. "I won't be around too long. I think it'll be better if I leave before she sees me."

She turned back around. "Why do you say that?"

"You said it yourself. She asked for me, and I wasn't around. I don't want to get her hopes up."

"Oh, you don't have to worry about that," Nikki said quickly. "She understands that our relationship has changed."

Ouch! Kevin thought to himself, but he wasn't as much worried about Kayla as he was himself. Seeing them again, though it comforted his heart, also tortured him. "I still think it'll be better if I disappear."

Nikki twirled the flowers in her hand, inspecting them. Kayla would be ecstatic to receive them directly from Kevin. "You can give them to her yourself," she said, shoving them into his chest. The firmness in her voice surprised her, but she couldn't let on how giddy he made her feel.

Kevin glanced over his shoulder briefly as he took the flowers back. His face was flushed with embarrassment. He hoped the people sitting near them hadn't heard the exchange.

His hand brushed against hers, and Nikki yanked her hand back quickly, hoping Kevin hadn't noticed her trembling. A shot ran down her spine. She felt hot. If she didn't do something soon, he would see her anxiety, and she would look ridiculous. "Excuse me." Nikki popped up.

Kevin noticed a teacher coming onstage. The show was about to begin. He stood, blocking Nikki's way. "Don't worry. I'll move."

Nikki's heart sank as Kevin turned away. She must have looked aloof and short-tempered. She sat back down, watching as he walked away and settled in another seat across the way. She took a deep breath, picked up a program, and began fanning fiercely. Though Atlanta was known for its hot and humid summers, nothing but Kevin could give her fever like this.

The show ended, and Kevin hid the flowers under one of the booths in front of the seating. Nikki raced to the stage to meet Kayla, whose face lit up when she saw Nikki approaching.

Kayla was so precious. She was dressed in a purple leotard with wings attached to her back. The wings were radiant with color and splashed with silver.

Nikki's eyes caught his. She bent and whispered something in Kayla's ear. Immediately, Kayla's eyes scanned the crowd until her eyes fell upon him. His heart warmed as a big smile crossed her face.

Kayla took off for him. His heart beat wildly; he wanted to meet her halfway, but restrained himself. Then, as she drew closer, he couldn't withhold his excitement any longer. She leaped, and he happily accepted her into his arms. She laid her head on his shoulder and clutched his neck tightly.

"Hey, baby." He looked at her and kissed her gently on the forehead. "You were wonderful."

Kayla never looked at him, and she completely ignored his greeting. She held him tightly.

"You're not going to say anything to me?" he asked, whispering softly in her ear. She shook her head, and he figured she was mad at him for leaving without saying goodbye on her birthday.

"He's really good with her."

Nikki's concentration broke. She had been staring at Kayla and Kevin. She turned to face Ms. Martinez. "Yes," she said tearing her gaze away. "Yes, he is." Then she dug into her purse. "I found them," she said, pulling out some coupons. "I was rushing so much earlier that I thought I left them at home, but they were in my car." She paused. "I'm ready whenever you are."

Ms. Martinez's eyes looked over Nikki's shoulder. Kayla and Kevin hugged in the distance. She snatched the coupons out of Nikki's hand. "I'll have her back by 3:30," she said, walking off and waving them in the air.

"Wait," Nikki said, following her. "I haven't given you any money!"

Ms. Martinez smiled back slyly. "I know where you live."

Kayla spotted Ms. Martinez marching towards them and her sister trailing behind.

She lifted her head and motioned Kevin to bend to her level.

He leaned over, tilting his ear towards her. She cupped her hand over his ear. "You wanna know a secret?"

Kevin didn't say anything, but he continued to listen.

"My sister misses you," Kayla announced matter-of-factly. At least, that had been the explanation offered by her grandmother after she had confided in her about Nikki's gloomy disposition.

Nikki saw Kayla whispering in Kevin's ear, and her heart stopped. She was sure her sister had ratted her out and told Kevin she had never invited him to come because Nikki had forbidden her to speak of him.

Kevin was flabbergasted. Nikki and Ms. Martinez were approaching. His mind fogged, and his hands became sweaty.

"Kevin," Ms Martinez smiled. "How are you?"

"I'm fine," he said, trying to make himself sound cool and collected. "How are you?" He saw Nikki out of the corner of his eyes, but she turned away. She seemed fascinated by something she had found to read at the booth.

"Oh, I'm fine. Just about to take these kids to Chucky Cheese. They've looked so forward to this day."

"Mmm." Kevin squeezed Kayla a little tighter. "And how's Mariea?" he asked, looking over his shoulder at Nikki.

He never knew Kayla to fib, but with all that had happened, Kayla's assessment of her sister was totally off. The whole day, Nikki had been curt and made little to no eye contact.

Suddenly, he was laughing. He looked at Ms. Martinez; she was laughing, too. She must have said something funny, and he had laughed because she had, but he couldn't recall a single word she had said. Then he remembered—something about kids and pizza.

"Anyway," she smiled pleasantly, "it was good to see you again, Kevin."

"Likewise." He smiled warmly, relieved she hadn't noticed that his mind had wandered.

"Come, Kayla," Ms. Martinez said, touching Kayla's back.

"No," Kayla whined.

Kevin saw Nikki's head lift, and she walked towards them, standing opposite Ms. Martinez.

"Kayla," Nikki said in a firm voice.

"No," Kayla whined, but this time it was more an admission of defeat.

Kevin felt Kayla's grip tighten around his neck. "I wanna stay with Kevin." She pleaded.

Kevin felt bad. He had wanted to prevent this from occurring, but Nikki had insisted he stay.

"Kayla, Kevin can't stay with you. He has a flight to catch."

"No," Kayla groaned.

"Kayla," Kevin whispered in her ear, "you have to go. You have to celebrate all the hard work you put into this play." She was listening, but he knew she wasn't going to give up without a fight.

Nikki's heart bled for Kayla. She had been too hard on her — not even letting her speak of him — it must have been hard on her not to see him anymore. "I'll tell you what." Nikki's face brightened. Kayla's head was pressed against Kevin's chest. "If you go with your friends today, and if it's okay with Kevin, and if he doesn't have anything to do, he can come over next weekend and spend the whole day Saturday with you." She looked at Kevin briefly, and he nodded his head. "Okay?"

Kayla finally lifted her head and looked at Kevin.

"See there?" He smiled. "It's all settled."

Kayla needed to be sure. "Promise?"

Kevin nodded his head. "I promise, sunshine."

Her mood lifted, and her face shone brightly.

Kevin felt her trying to wiggle out of his arms. "Wait. You got to seal the promise."

Kayla looked at him, confused.

"Give me a kiss."

Kayla smiled. Kevin puckered his lips, and Kayla happily reciprocated. As he was about to let her down, she threw a mischievous wink at him. His eyebrows shrugged, and he turned to see if Nikki or Ms. Martinez had noticed, but they were talking. "See you next week," she whispered slyly.

Kevin stared as Kayla and Ms. Martinez walked away.

"What happened to the flowers?"

Kevin turned and saw Nikki standing in front of the booth with her arms folded.

"Oh." Kevin had forgotten them. "I hid them under the table." He reached down and pulled them up. "I can't believe I forgot to give them to her."

"That's okay."

He noticed a smile on Nikki's face.

"I think she was happier to see you than flowers any day."

"Yeah?" Kevin said, looking down at them.

"What time is your flight?"

"Six-thirty."

He was still upset he hadn't given the flowers to her.

"Ms. Martinez is bringing her back at 3:30. You can still give them to her if you want."

Kevin knew it took a lot for Nikki to suggest such a thing.

"No." He shrugged. "I wouldn't want to —"

"Come on." Nikki grabbed him by the arm. "I'm starving. I'll fix us some grilled ham and cheese sandwiches." Then she stopped. "That is, if Natalie doesn't mind."

Kevin chuckled to himself. If Nikki didn't hate his guts so much, he would almost think she was jealous. "Oh, I'm quite sure she won't," he asserted. "She's been my prayer partner for the last month." He paused. "We did hang out a few times at the arcade, but she's out of town visiting her fiancée this weekend."

"Fiancée?" Nikki gasped. "That was fast!"

"Well, I guess when you know —" he paused. "You know."

CHAPTER THIRTY~ONE

K evin followed Nikki back to her apartment. The sky was overcast so he reached back in the car, grabbed his umbrella, and
followed her inside.

"I can take that for you," Nikki smiled, grabbing the umbrella.

Kevin stood against the kitchen wall and waited for her as she
placed it in the porcelain umbrella holder by the patio. Her sudden
kindness surprised him.

Kevin sat at the table and watched as Nikki prepared the meal.
After eating, they set at the table chatting. He knew he was still on
thin ice with Nikki, and didn't want to risk saying anything that
would potentially upset her, so he primarily listened while she did
most of the talking. But it was still a nice moment. Perhaps the road
to friendship wasn't as far off as he'd thought.

"You want some more?" Nikki stood and nodded at Kevin's
half-full glass of tea.

"No. No thanks."

Nikki went to the refrigerator, got out the pitcher, and poured
herself some more tea.

When Nikki turned, Kevin glanced down at his watch.

She looked at the time on the stove. It was three-fifty. "You have
to go, don't you?"

As much as he had enjoyed his time with her, he had to leave.
"Yeah," he answered reluctantly.

Nikki couldn't believe how quickly time had passed. "I'm sorry.
I thought for sure she would have been back by now." She looked
at the flowers stretched across the kitchen table. "I'll make sure she
gets them."

Kevin smiled back warmly. Their fingers were only inches from
each other. Kevin wanted to reach over, take Nikki's hand, and pull
her body to his. "I better get going."

Nikki couldn't place the look in Kevin's face. She followed him
out of the kitchen, folded her arms, and leaned against the wall. "I

thought the reason you picked this job was so that you wouldn't have to do so much traveling."

He turned to face her. "Since I lost you, it doesn't matter," he said.

Nikki's throat went dry. She didn't know how to respond. "Well, I'm glad your schedule allowed you to be here a few weeks ago." She paused. "I've been meaning to thank you for being there for Kayla."

Kevin nodded. "You're welcome." He turned and headed for the door.

"And me," Nikki whispered softly.

He turned, and they gazed into each other's eyes. Her gaze fell to his lips.

Suddenly, the phone rang. Nikki hesitated for a moment. She held up her hand to signal that she would be back and ran into the kitchen. "Hello? Anesa? What?"

Kevin listened in the other room. He was sure Nikki didn't want him to leave.

"Nesa, I can barely hear you. Hang up and call me right back. I can't hear you well on this phone. I can't—Call back!"

Kevin heard the phone click, and his heart sank.

Nikki emerged from the kitchen, and the phone began ringing again. "It's Anesa." She smiled at Kevin.

Kevin nodded his head. "Bye."

"Bye."

She watched as Kevin walked out the door, then turned and ran to her bedroom.

Kevin had almost closed the door behind him when he remembered his umbrella. He heard Nikki's footsteps running down the hall as he reentered.

Nikki caught the call just before it went to voice mail.

"Were you talking to someone else on the phone?" Anesa asked. "I can call back."

"No." Nikki paused. "Kevin was just here."

"Kevin?" Anesa repeated.

Kevin heard Nikki's voice from the living room, but couldn't make out what she was saying. He lifted the umbrella out, and his eyes wandered to the side table, where he saw the book *Guess How*

Much I Love You; under it, he noticed a spread of brochures for apartment homes. Then he saw a sheet of paper for Crossroads Apartments and a receipt. His heart turned to mush.

He couldn't believe his eyes. He backed away in horror. He couldn't believe she would move away without informing him. He bumped his shin against a sharp corner of the coffee table.

Nikki heard a noise from the living room. "Look, Anesa, I'll call you back," she whispered. She hung up and listened. She didn't hear anything, and though it was probably nothing, she wanted to be sure.

Kevin massaged his knee. The throbbing pain that had gripped him left just as quickly. His legs felt weak beneath him. He didn't know if it was due to the pain of the cocktail table, or the truth he had just uncovered. She had moved on.

He heard her bedroom door crack and hoisted himself up as he heard her footsteps move down the hall.

Nikki walked down the alternate hallway, towards the front door. The door was locked. She stood on her toes and looked out the peephole. Then she felt a weird sensation, as if someone was in the room with her.

She turned and saw Kevin. The shock startled her, and she fell backwards.

Kevin reached out to catch her.

"Kevin!" she breathed, holding her chest. "You scared me to death."

He backed up and stood close to the wall.

"Did you forget something?"

"Yeah," Kevin whispered, holding up the umbrella. He scratched his head as if he had an itch. "I couldn't help but notice," he said, gesturing at the pamphlets. "You're moving?"

Nikki had been in such a hurry earlier, trying to get Kayla ready, that she had forgotten she left them there. "Yeah," she said softly.

"Just like that?" Kevin whispered. Though he had planned to move himself, it was different. He was moving because she didn't want him around. She was moving, he figured, to get away from him.

"I guess so," Nikki finally answered. She looked at her hands and began playing with them. "I put down a deposit today." She shrugged. "It's smaller, and it's about $200 more a month, but I'll be closer to Malcolm, Anesa, and the baby. And at least I'll still be going against traffic." She smiled faintly, but Kevin was not amused. "I've been on the waiting list for a couple of months, and she finally called today and told me something fell through, and if I still wanted it, I could have it."

Kevin nodded his head, but he barely heard her. He just saw her lips moving. *What if?* he thought. He wrestled with the idea in his head, wondering what he had to lose.

Nikki couldn't figure out the expression on Kevin's face. He hadn't said anything, and his quietness unsettled her. "Kayla doesn't want to move, though," she babbled. "She thinks she's never going to see Mariea."

Kevin walked towards her.

"But—" Nikki paused. Her throat went dry. She felt the warm air from his nostrils as he bent his face towards her.

Nikki dropped her head. What did he think he was he doing? He couldn't kiss her. He wasn't her boyfriend anymore, and they had broken up. She breathed deep. "Don't."

Kevin moved closer and pressed his lips to hers. He kissed her softly and tenderly then lifted her chin. He looked into her eyes as he drew close, and their lips touched again. He felt her lips tremble under his. His right hand cupped her face.

Nikki had tried to forget how juicy his lips were. They were thick and soft. She felt his lips part; she craved to taste the warmth of his mouth.

Kevin wrapped his arms around her waist. His warm tongue entered her mouth. Nikki wrapped her arms around his neck and kissed him back. Their tongues danced in joyous harmony. Nikki felt Kevin's hand gently press on the back of her head. Their tongues rejoiced even more passionately. His hands glided up Nikki's back. Nikki felt her knees buckling, but Kevin held her firmly. Finally, the interlude ended, and Kevin kissed her softly one last time.

She was dazed. She had been captured, and she could no longer hide her true feelings. She had missed his embrace. She closed her eyes and laid her head against his collarbone. Her wish had come true.

Kevin was shocked when Nikki laid her head on him. It had seemed seconds before that the very sight of him sickened her to the core. How often he had longed to feel her in his arms. The pleasure of her soft, warm body coincided with the scent of her hair and skin. The intensity of the moment overcame him. He sank his chin into her shoulder and cried.

Kevin's embrace tightened so hard that Nikki thought she would pop. She gave him a soft squeeze and noticed wetness against her face. His body shivered in her arms. "It's okay," she whispered reassuringly, but she felt him shake his head.

She pulled away and saw a stream of tears running down his cheeks. She took him by the hand and led him to the couch. She sat beside him and took him into her arms. She comforted him as he cried, ignoring her own silent tears that flowed down her cheeks.

A few minutes passed, and she went into the kitchen. She pulled the knob to the water filtration and looked to the living room, where he sat. His head was in his hands.

She knew he felt bad for what he had done. Only a few weeks earlier, she would have wanted him to. Justin Timberlake's "Cry Me a River" was more her theme then. He had hurt her, and he needed to pay. Nothing would have brought her more pleasure than to see him crumble to his feet.

She no longer felt that way. She was still in love, and her resentment and anger had subsided.

She walked back to him and tapped the side of his hand with the glass of water.

He raised his head. "Thank you," he said softly. He took a long sip.

Nikki slid back near the arm of the couch. She twiddled her thumbs nervously. "What are we going to do now?" She felt awkward and vulnerable asking, but she could no longer lie to herself anymore, either.

Kevin sat quietly for a moment. He took her hand from her lap. He kissed it and rubbed it against his face. Then he got up from the couch and knelt in front of her. He took her other hand and held both of hers in his. "It's funny. After I told you that I loved you, I remember thinking I didn't want to tell you too many times because I thought it might get old. So many days have passed." He gulped. "That I wished I could tell you I loved you, and you would hear me. I mean really hear me." He paused. "I love you, Nikki. Do you still love me?"

Nikki's gaze flickered across his face. "I never stopped loving you," she sniffled, and then chuckled. "I actually think I love you more."

Those words were music to his ears. He gripped her waist and hugged her. "I'll kiss the ground you walk on, baby," he whispered in her ear, then he began to cry again.

Tears ran down Nikki's face, too, and she held him and ran her fingers across his shoulders. They rocked in silence.

Kevin shook his head. "I never meant to hurt you."

"I know —" Nikki started.

But Kevin waved his hand to stop her. He pulled away and held her face. He moved his thumb to wipe a tear from her eyes.

"I'm sorry I let you down, baby."

Nikki shook her head. "I'm sorry, too. I never meant to say those things —"

"Shh. Shh." His forehead wrinkled as put his finger over her lips. "You were right. Christmas, at my parents' house, you didn't say anything, but I saw it in your eyes. I had to forgive Toni and let go before I could fully love you. Trust you." He paused. "I had to overcome my fear of losing you, of you never loving me the way I wanted you — needed you — to. Living without you — it's like an out-of-body experience. I mean, I'm there. My body's there. My mind's there. But my heart and soul were with you."

"Nikki, you're smart and beautiful." He sucked his lower lip. "Any guy would be lucky to have you." He looked around for a moment, searching for the right words. He was nervous but tried to curtail it. "I want you to be happy. You and Kayla mean the world to me." He took her hands and looked down. "I just want to make you happy," he said, looking into her eyes. Nikki's expression told him that she wasn't following.

"You're strong; you're smart, beautiful, and sexy." He was starting to repeat himself. "And you're caring," he added. "I know I'm not making much sense."

Nikki felt Kevin's hands trembling.

It was a little silly, but he couldn't let another opportunity pass. "Close your eyes," he said, reaching up and closing her eyes with his hand.

"I know this is cheesy, but —"

Nikki felt her left hand being straightened, and then something slid over her ring finger. Her heart raced. She opened her eyes and looked down. It was Kevin's college ring.

"Imagine a diamond ring there."

"What are you trying to tell me, Kevin?" She held her hand over her heart and began crying. Deep inside, she knew it would come to this. She would have to make a decision.

Kevin swallowed. "I know I won't be perfect, but I promise I will do everything in my power to make you happy, and most importantly, love you." He looked in her eyes. "And MiKayla." He looked down. "Not that I have anything against them, but I don't want you moving to be with Malcolm and Anesa. I need you with me, baby—a part of *my* family. I love you, baby."

Nikki studied his face. He really meant it.

"Veronica?" He looked at her. "Will you marry me?" He dropped his head. Without a beat, he continued. "I know you have some reservations about it—"

His hands trembled on Nikki's leg. Beads of perspiration had formed on his brow. She covered her mouth to keep from laughing, but seeing Kevin get worked up over her was a sight. It was sweet. She let out a kiddish giggle.

Kevin stopped and looked at her. He didn't understand what was so funny. "What?"

Nikki lifted his chin. She pressed her lips against his. She pulled away and looked deep into his eyes. "Yes," she said adamantly, nodding her head.

Really? Kevin's face lit up. A boyish smile moved across his face.

"Yes, really," Nikki said, as if reading his mind.

He rushed to hug and kiss her.

"I love you so much," Nikki said, between Kevin's kisses.

"I love you, too!" Neither could breathe from the excitement.

"When do you want to get married?" Kevin asked as he took a deep breath, still not believing she said yes.

"I don't know. When do you want to get married?" Nikki inquired, though she already had an idea.

"Kayla will be out of school in December; we could get married over Christmas break."

Nikki thought to herself as he played with her hair. "How about August?"

"In a month?"

"I was thinking before Kayla started school," Nikki clarified. "We've been separated long enough, and I don't want to be separated from you any longer."

Kevin grinned. "Whatever you want, baby," he said, pulling her on top of him. He wanted to celebrate.

Suddenly there was a tap at the door.

Nikki gave Kevin an excited glance, lifted herself up, and answered the door.

Nikki greeted Mrs. Martinez, but before she could take Kayla's hand to pull her into the apartment, Kayla's eyes spotted Kevin.

Kayla sped towards him and plunged on top of him on the couch.

"Hey, sunshine," he said, squeezing her.

"Thank you." Nikki closed the door. She folded her arms and walked towards them.

Kayla rested her head on Kevin's shoulder and closed her eyes. He rocked her in his arms. Nikki liked watching them together. She sat on the couch, facing them.

"My little angel," Kevin whispered softly.

Kayla lifted her head. "Wait. What are you doing here?"

Kevin looked at Nikki and smiled.

Nikki's heart pounded. "Kayla," she said softly.

Kayla looked at Nikki.

"Kevin and I," she started, "we want you to know we love you more than anything in this world."

Kevin saw the nervousness in her eyes. He held her hand.

"And we," she paused, unable to contain her excitement, "are getting married!"

"Aaaahhhh!" Kayla screamed, bouncing on the sofa and clapping her hands.

"We're going to be a family now," Nikki whispered.

Kayla held Kevin tightly and extended her arm to Nikki. As Nikki scooted closer, Kayla leaned over and kissed her. Then she kissed Kevin. She stared at them quietly for a second, her eyes darting between them. Kevin, hoping he understood, leaned over and kissed Nikki squarely on the lips.

"Yes!" Kayla exclaimed with glee.

Then he kissed Nikki on the nose, cheeks, chin, and then her lips again, her ear... "Mmmm," each time his lips landed.

Nikki happened to glance at the clock. It was four-fifty-eight. "Honey, you're going to miss your flight!"

CHAPTER THIRTY-TWO

"Hello?" he answered calmly.

"Philip, Katie said you wanted me to call you right away. Do you feel all right? Why did you go home?"

"Kevin's here."

"What? He didn't tell me he was coming home."

"Yeah."

Priscilla noticed a change in his voice. "Philip, what's wrong?"

"He wants to talk to us." He paused. "In person."

"In person?" Priscilla's heart dropped. "Philip, you're scaring me. I don't understand. Why would he travel all the way here to speak to us?"

"Look, 'Cilla, he said he'd explain everything once you get here. Can you come at lunch?"

Priscilla looked at the clock; it was eleven-fifteen. "I'm coming *now*," she said, slamming the phone on the receiver.

Priscilla pulled into the driveway. Seeing the Decatur license plate parked in the driveway made her heart flutter. Kevin always flew and got a rental. What could have been so important that he had to rush home without booking a flight or giving her notice?

She knew he had been hiding something, but didn't know what. Lately, she felt lucky if she got a ten-minute conversation out of him, and though she wanted to ask why he and his girlfriend had broken up, she didn't, because she didn't want him to think she was meddling. With Toni, he had told her everything. With Veronica, the details of their relationship were so secretive.

If it hadn't been for Kacie, she would have had no idea he had been seeing somebody, and if she hadn't suggested, she doubted she would have met Veronica at Christmas.

She jumped out of her car, thinking the worse. Then it dawned on her what Kevin had to tell them. At only twenty-eight years old, her son had been diagnosed with HIV. During her nursing career, she had treated many young black men, and each of them had said the same thing—they never thought it would happen to them. Why hadn't he listened?

She rushed past his car, scrambling to get her keys out. She walked through the front door, stood in the foyer, and scanned the den, but saw no one. Her mind was a jumble. She breathed deep. She had to look calm.

Suddenly she heard what sounded like laughter coming from outside. She walked through the living room and down the hallway, towards the deck, her eyes immediately falling on Kevin. He was leaning against the deck overlooking the yard.

"Kevin," she called hesitantly.

He turned, smiling. "Mom."

Priscilla was taken aback. She had thought the worse, but he seemed so happy.

He walked over and gave her a big hug.

"Kevin, your father called me at work. He said there was something you needed to tell us." She looked around the deck. "Where is he?"

"He's down there." Kevin pointed towards the yard. "With Mi-Kayla."

"MiKayla?" Priscilla frowned. She walked to the edge of the deck and looked over.

"Hi, dear," Philip smiled and waved. MiKayla looked up and waved, too.

She arched her brow, confused. Why was Phillip grilling in the middle of the day, in the middle of the week, and why was this child traveling with Kevin? She waved back and turned to Kevin. "Son, what's going on?"

"Hi, Priscilla," said a familiar voice. She spun around.

Nikki stood in the doorway.

Suddenly, she understood. Her gaze dropped to Nikki's hand, where she noticed a ring on her left finger, and her jaw dropped. She covered her mouth, startled.

"It's good to see you again," Nikki smiled.

Priscilla was overcome with joy. She reached her arms out to Nikki, gesturing her to come. "Welcome to the family, baby," she squealed as they embraced. She freed one of her arms, gesturing Kevin to come, too.

"When are you getting married?"

Kevin looked at his watch. "Forty-three days, and counting."

"Kevin," Nikki blushed, hitting him in the chest.

"Well," Priscilla blushed a bit, too. "Come," she said, grabbing Nikki's hand. "We have so much to talk about."

Kevin watched as Priscilla whisked Nikki away.

It was a great day.

●●●

Nikki was engrossed as she and Kevin drove down the road. She had spent the whole day sampling wedding cakes and finding a bridesmaid dress for Anesa; right before Kevin picked her up, she had dropped off their invitations at the post office. Though so much was done, the trip to Texas had thrown her way behind.

To make matters worse, because of the short notice, in order to acquire certain vendors, they were forced to have a Friday wedding, instead of the traditional Saturday, which meant guests would actually begin arriving on Thursday, which meant requesting time off, and with such short notice, in Nikki's mind, that equated to people not showing.

As if reading her mind, Kevin squeezed Nikki's leg. "Don't worry, baby. It's all going to work out."

Nikki breathed, frustrated.

"My family knows I'm only getting married once. Tell them when to come, and they'll be there."

"I know," she whispered softly. "I just wish—" she started, but stopped abruptly. Despite all that had gone wrong, in less than a month, she would be married to Kevin.

She stared out the window, admiring the neighborhood. The drive was exactly what she needed to decompress. The streets were tree-lined; the homes set away from the road. Teens walked on the sidewalk, people worked in their yards, and she spotted a few neighbors at the edges of their driveways, conversing casually. "This seems like a nice neighborhood," she remarked, taking note of the predominately black middle-class surroundings. "It's always good to see *us* progressing."

"Yeah," Kevin responded.

Finally, they pulled into a driveway. A two-story, olive-colored home accented with pale brown brick and cedar shakes loomed before them. A 2003 Maxima was in the driveway. "Who did you say we were meeting again?" Nikki asked, unbuckling her seatbelt.

"You'll see," Kevin answered, helping her out of the seat. He took her by the hand, and they walked towards the door.

Kevin rang the doorbell. As they waited for someone to come to the door, Nikki admired the nice flowerbed in the front yard, full of day lilies and an assortment of wild flowers, all with bright, vibrant colors.

"Hey!" A woman in her mid-forties greeted them at the door. She wore a two-piece business suite and half-inch heels. "Mr. Maddox," she said, smiling, and shook Kevin's hand.

Nikki frowned for a second. She wondered why Kevin hadn't warned her that this was a formal business transaction. She would have worn something nicer than her Georgia State t-shirt and blue jeans.

Kevin turned towards Nikki. "This is my fiancée, Veronica." He grinned, patting her hand.

The woman shook Nikki's hand once, firmly, and smiled. "Nice to meet you."

They stood quietly for a moment.

"I'm sorry; I didn't catch your name," Nikki said.

The woman looked at Kevin, then back at Nikki. "Karena Brooks. You can just call me Karena." She shrugged then looked at Kevin. "Well, you know my cell number," she said, stepping through the doorway and down the steps.

Nikki looked at Kevin puzzled. *Where's she going?* she wondered.

Kevin had a serious expression on his face. "Come on," he said, opening the door.

Nikki stepped into the foyer, where a shiny hardwood floor welcomed her. A flight of stairs about seven feet from the door led upwards, and as she looked down the hallway, she saw a kitchen. "No one's here." She looked at him, perplexed. "Kevin, what's going on?"

Kevin motioned her to look to the right side of the hall. She looked over her shoulder at what appeared to be a living room—but there was no furniture. Now it made sense. "Kevin." She squeezed his hand. "What have you done?"

"Nothing—officially." He smiled at her. "I wouldn't make a decision like this without you."

Nikki gasped, excited. She stepped forward to take in the home. Kevin watched as she stepped into the living room. Her gaze fell on the huge red brick fireplace.

"Come on; let's go upstairs," he said, beckoning with his head to follow him. He took her upstairs, showed her the secondary and the master bedrooms, then led her back downstairs. "What do you think so far?"

Nikki shrugged, speechless.

"It's close to the Silver Comet Trail. We can get some bikes and all go riding," he added as a sales pitch. "Once Kayla gets old enough, we can go jogging by ourselves."

They walked under the stairwell diagonal from the kitchen into another empty room.

"And this is the office."

Nikki held her chest. It was all so much. The house had high smooth ceilings. The master bedroom had a double tray ceiling and crown molding, and the master bath featured a garden tub with jet sprays. The kitchen had a backsplash and Corian countertops. The house was unbelievable, like something she'd seen in magazines, more than anything she could have imagined.

He pulled at her hand.

"Wait a minute," Nikki said, stopping in the doorway. "What's that?" She broke Kevin's grip and walked toward the opposite wall, where a small, shiny object rested on the sill of the double window. She bent over and picked it up. Kevin walked up behind her.

It was an 8" x 2" gold nameplate attached to a wooden mount.

Veronica K. Maddox, Doctor of Psychology

"Kevin?" she smiled, turning towards him. "What's this?"

"Well," he said, wrapping his arms around her, "I figure since you'll be spending so much of your time studying when you go back to school this fall, whenever you get burned out, you can look at this and remember what you're doing it for."

"I told you before; I can't go back to school—MiKayla?"

"Shh." He shook his head. "I'll watch MiKayla. She's just as much my responsibility as she is yours. We're a family now. Remember? I love you, Nikki, and I want you to be happy. You can't be happy until you do what you think God has set in your heart to do."

She nodded. An opportunity to return to school, a new house—her heart wouldn't allow her to accept such grand gifts. "I thought we were going to live in your condo."

"My condo is under contract."

Nikki looked at him confused. "Under contract? Since when?"

"Since we got back together," he explained. "Some new Emory professor and his wife wanted it, and have to relocate here before the school year starts. They gave me an offer I—we—couldn't refuse. Plus, it gives us the opportunity for this."

"But—" Nikki resisted, but Kevin cut her off.

"Come here. There's one last thing I need to show you," he said, grabbing her hand. He walked her through the kitchen. As they approached the back door, he stopped her and covered her eyes. Then he opened the door, and they stepped into the yard. He dropped his hands.

Nikki's jaw dropped. She bounced happily, turning towards him. They ran a few yards then stepped up into the gazebo. It was an old oak structure, tucked away under a grand maple tree.

Kevin watched her look up at the ceiling of the dome. Suddenly, her mood changed. She began to cry.

"Baby, what's wrong?"

Nikki looked around the yard. Then she looked at the ring on her finger. It was surreal. She felt so unworthy.

She took a deep breath. "There's something I—" Then she looked into Kevin's eyes and saw fear, as if he were about to lose the one thing that he loved more than anything on earth. She knew that feeling all too well.

Her heart broke. She loved him so much. The last thing she wanted to do was hurt him, and she knew this last secret would. "Never mind." She leaned her head onto his chest. "It's perfect."

"There goes the happy couple!" Anesa beamed, opening the door. Nikki, Kevin, and Kayla walked through. "Have a seat right over here," she said, motioning them towards the couch. "I'll get Malcolm."

"Oh, I want to see the baby," Kayla exclaimed.

"You want to see the baby? Well, come on." Anesa grabbed her by the hand and escorted her away.

Nikki snuggled into Kevin's chest.

Anesa and Kayla reached the top of the stairwell. "I need to talk to Malcolm for just a second. You wait in there. He'll bring him over in a minute," she said, letting go of her hand and watching her go into the nursery.

She opened her bedroom door. Malcolm was perched on the bed, Elijah asleep, stretched out on top of him, watching the Atlanta Braves baseball game. "They're here," she announced, though she knew he had to have heard the doorbell.

"Okay," he answered.

Anesa's stomach tightened as she walked down the stairs. She approached the couch slowly. Nikki and Kevin were snuggled up and making out. "Ahem," she said, clearing her throat.

They giggled and whispered, but then stopped and looked up at her, smiling.

"Can't leave you two alone for a minute." Nikki and Anesa locked eyes. "Come on, girl," Anesa said, waving her away. "I need to talk to you about this wedding."

"Be right back," Nikki said, rising.

"Okay," Kevin said, wondering why they were acting so strangely. They went down the hallway and vanished around the corner.

Anesa grabbed Nikki's hand. "Girl, this thing is a weapon. How many carats is it, again?"

"Two." Nikki grinned.

Anesa squeezed her hand, genuinely thrilled. "I'm so happy for you."

They walked into the laundry room.

"Sit down over there." Anesa pointed to two chairs against the wall.

Nikki sat down.

Anesa reached into the dryer and began taking out clothes. She placed them on a small table and began folding them.

"Let me help you with that." Nikki rose.

"You don't need to be dealing with our funky clothes."

"I used to live here with you, remember?" she said, picking up some pants and folding them.

"I know it's going to be weird for you." Anesa laid some clothes on the table. "The fall coming, and not being in school anymore."

"Actually—" Nikki paused, folding a towel in half. "I'm returning to school in the fall."

"Really?"

Nikki nodded. "Just a couple of evening classes—and I'll still work, but only about twenty hours a week. Kevin wants me to 'fulfill' my dream."

"Your dream?" Anesa questioned. "What's that?"

"To become a psychologist."

"Really?"

The surprise in Anesa's voice and slight disappointment in her face made Nikki realize that she had never told her. "Yeah," she answered apologetically.

"That's great, girl. Kevin's a good man."

Nikki explained. "One of the things that almost broke his parents up was that when his mom went back to school, his dad wasn't very supportive. With three kids and working full-time... Anyway, I'll be able to apply for next fall's graduate program once I get the prerequisites behind me. Kevin's going to watch Kayla while I'm in school." She chuckled. "I warned him she's a handful, but he said he could handle her."

Anesa walked around the table, facing the washer and dryer. Her back was towards the door, as she moved some clothes from the washer into the dryer. "Are you going to hyphenate your last name?"

Nikki shook her head no, as if she hadn't ever given it a thought. Then, out the corner of her eye, she noticed Kevin passing in the hall, walking towards the bathroom.

"Quick! Ask me that again," she whispered.

Anesa smiled mischievously. "Are you going to hyphenate your name?"

"I don't know. I'm thinking about it."

Kevin arched his eyebrow.

They chuckled softly.

Then Anesa thought about Malcolm and became annoyed. Kevin would not have been wandering the hall in the first place if Malcolm had been with him. "I'll be right back, girl."

"Okay." Nikki continued folding the clothes. She heard Anesa run up the stairwell. Then she felt Kevin's warm embrace.

"'And they both were called Adam,'" he whispered in her ear.

"What?" she pretended. "What are you talking about?" She twirled in his arms to face him.

"I overheard you talking to Anesa," he said, looking into her eyes. "You're mine. You'll carry my name."

Nikki giggled. "I knew you were listening," she said, falling into his arms. "I just said that to mess with you."

"Oh. You thought that was funny, huh?"

Nikki nodded her head and sucked on her lower lip.

Anesa peeked in the nursery. Kayla sat idly fiddling with Elijah's toys. She opened the door to their bedroom. Malcolm was in the same position on the bed. She fumed.

She marched to the TV and turned it off.

"What?" he gasped.

She gently took Elijah out of his arms. "I told you fifteen minutes ago that Kevin was downstairs."

"He had just fallen asleep, and I didn't want to move him —"

"Malcolm LaDarius Walker, if you don't get yo' butt down there, right this instant, and apologize —"

"Okay! Okay!" he said, finally rising.

Malcolm walked down the stairs and entered the living room. The TV was on, but no one was there. Then he heard giggling. He followed the sound down the hallway and peered into the laundry room. Nikki was perched on top of the washing machine, and Kevin was standing curiously close. He thought he heard Kevin mumble something about Hello Kitty, and then Nikki laughed playfully. Seductively?

He cleared his throat. "So that's where you went off to?"

Nikki pulled back, staring at him with innocent eyes.

"Can I talk to you for a second, man?"

They walked into the kitchen.

Malcolm opened the refrigerator and got out two beers. He handed one to Kevin.

Kevin looked at it blankly. Even though Nikki didn't mind him drinking when they were with Malcolm, he couldn't remember the last time he'd had one. "That's okay," he said, handing it back.

"I know — Nic-Nic," Malcolm said, understanding. "So, ya'll decide where you're going for your honeymoon?" He snapped the cap off his beer.

"I wanted to take Nikki to Hawaii, but she swears she's never getting on another plane. Especially since 9-11."

"September 11ᵗʰ? That was two years ago," Malcolm mocked. "Didn't she get on a plane to go to your parent's?"

"I know." Kevin shrugged and nodded. "But since Kayla was sick and all — we both didn't want to travel too far. My parents have some friends that have a time-share on the beach in Savannah. We're going there. It's supposed to be nice. Plus, it's free."

"I heard that, man," Malcolm said, taking a swig. "Ya'll going to drive up there right after the wedding?"

"Nikki's never been on a train, so she wants to ride the train up. Thinks we'll be too tired to drive. But we'll rent a car there and to come back." He chuckled to himself. "I told her we were going to look pretty odd, getting out of a limo and into a train, but whatever she wants."

Malcolm looked at him and smiled. "All right, all right." He nodded in approval and took another swig. "She's a good woman."

Kevin nodded in agreement.

Malcolm clutched the beer tightly. "Look, I know that in the past we've had our issues, and we've harbored some bad feelings toward one another, but—"

Kevin arched his eyebrow. "I've never harbored any bad feelings towards you. I know she's like a sister to you, and I respect that."

Malcolm nodded, listening. "So I've been the only fool?"

They chuckled.

"Seriously, though," Malcolm reflected, "take care of my—" He paused, looking into Kevin's eyes. "Take care of each other, man," he said, extending his arms.

Kevin hugged him. Finally, they were brothers.

Anesa and Nikki walked in.

Nikki was shocked. She couldn't believe they were hugging.

Anesa cleared her throat. "Hope we're not interrupting anything, boys."

Kevin and Malcolm pulled away, sticking their chests out, macho-like.

"We're going for a little spin," she announced.

Nikki walked over to Kevin and looked at him in disbelief, smiling. She looked at Malcolm. Then she slid the keys from his back pocket.

"Guess we'll see you boys in a few."

"Wait!" Nikki remembered suddenly. "You haven't seen the baby, have you?"

"No." Kevin shook his head, realizing that he hadn't.

Nikki grabbed his hand. They walked upstairs towards Elijah's room.

Kayla stood beside the crib, peering through the bars. She sang the same tune Kevin had sung to her while she was in the hospital.

Nikki heard Kayla's voice as she approached the door.

When Kayla saw Nikki and Kevin approaching, she ran up to them. "I was really quiet, Nikki. I didn't wake him!"

"I know, Kayla," she said, rubbing her hand over her head. "Kevin wants to see the baby."

They walked over to the crib. Kevin picked Kayla up and held her in his arms, and they all watched Elijah as he slept.

Kevin grabbed Nikki around her shoulder. His arms slid slowly down her side, and then rested over her stomach.

CHAPTER THIRTY-THREE

" And with that," the minister smiled at Kevin and Nikki pleasantly, "our sessions are over."

Kevin rose and shook the tall, stocky man's hand. "Thanks so much for doing our premarital counseling."

"It was a pleasure," he smiled, now shaking Nikki's hand.

"We're sorry to rush off like this, but—"

The minister motioned with his hand. "I understand. Though it sounds like a magnificent house, I can't say I envy your having to move at all."

"Thanks. Do you have a bathroom I may use?"

"Sure, sure. Straight down the hallway and to the right."

Kevin sped off.

Nikki sat back down in her seat and smiled kindly to the minister. She realized that she had never been alone with him; at each of their interactions, Kevin had always been present.

She peered down the hall, wondering when Kevin would return.

"Do you mind if I eat this?"

Nikki looked across the desk; a sandwich had suddenly appeared in front of the minister.

Nikki smiled. "No, not at all," she said, pretending something had caught her attention across the room.

"You know, that's a mighty fine young man you have," he said, wiping the corners of his mouth. "I remember the first time he brought you to church, seeing this glow about him. He's kept it ever since."

Nikki's lips curled slightly. She knew exactly what he was talking about it. She had seen it, too.

Her throat went dry. She sat up in her seat a little. "Do you think it's important that couples know *everything* about one another before they get married?"

The minister set his sandwich down and chuckled. "Well, I don't think Mrs. Roberts cares to know whether I ate all my spinach when I was a little boy or not."

Nikki smirked.

"The key is intimacy and trust. Whether real or imagined, distrust will quickly erode any relationship. Usually, as soon as a person begins to feel they can't trust someone, that person will, in turn, become less intimate and less trustful. If each person strives to create an environment where the other feels they can share information openly, without judgment, usually the other partner reciprocates, intimacy occurs, trust is affirmed, and the relationship grows."

Nikki stared at him. The specifics were on her lips, but her jaws were tight. He was a minister after all.

Kevin emerged from the hallway. "Ready, baby?"

"Yeah." She smiled. Kevin planted a kiss on her cheek.

"Thanks again, Br. Roberts."

"Thank you," Nikki added.

Kevin opened the door for Nikki, and she stepped into the sunshine.

The minister sat back at his desk, perplexed. Finally, he picked up his sandwich and took another bite.

Kevin swallowed hard.

Nikki sat quietly across from him. They had stopped at a diner for lunch after the counseling session. She stared at him as he put his sandwich down. She saw the hesitancy in his eyes. Though they had discussed many things, from birth control to positions and the fact that he kept his virginity until meeting Toni again his senior year in college, when it came to disclosing how many women he slept with, he was always evasive.

"I don't understand why this is so important," he said.

"Important? Kevin, we're about to get married. You don't think it's important that we know each other's sexual histories?"

Kevin cleared his throat.

Nikki flinched and looked over her shoulder, but no one had picked up on the topic of the conversation.

Kevin breathed deep and cleared the remnants of the sandwich from his throat. "Nine, ten, maybe even eleven." He shrugged. "I don't know. I didn't keep count." He said sincerely, though even to him, his voice sounded shrewd.

Nikki fell silent. In a way, she had always thought there were more. She dropped her head. She couldn't believe he had actually told her. She never thought he would.

"I'm sorry, baby. I know you probably didn't think there were that many, but I was young and stupid at the time. I swear, none of them meant anything." He reached across the table and lifted her head. "I'm not proud of my past; it is what it is—nothing can change that." He caressed her cheek. "I love you. The women I've been with in my past have no bearing on the feelings I have for you. You are my wife, my eternal soul mate."

Nikki smiled lightly. She ran her fingers alongside his hand. She opened his palm and kissed it, and then laid her head against it.

Now she had a decision of her own to make.

Kevin sighed. "Thank God, that's the last one," he said, placing a plate in a box and folding the lid over. Nikki came along with the tape and sealed the flaps.

"That's teamwork," Nikki said, smiling and looking around his condo. Everything had been packed away neatly. All the movers had to do the next day was take it over to their new home.

"Come here." Kevin grabbed Nikki by the waist and eased her to the couch.

They had had a long laborious day, and Kevin was ready to be rewarded.

"Kevin," Nikki whispered, pushing back on his shoulders gently as he teased her neck with his lips. "There's something we need to talk about."

"Not now, baby," he murmured, kissing her clavicle bone. Only a few days, and he would be able to delve fully into all her luscious layers of chocolate.

Nikki flinched. "Kevin, I'm serious," she said, pushing away from him.

"Okay." Kevin sat up sternly on the cushion. "I'm sorry. What is it you want to talk about?"

Nikki lowered her head. "Kevin, you know how much I love you, and you know I would never do anything to intentionally hurt you, but with the wedding coming up and all," she smiled, "and our marriage, I think it best you know the truth." She had his full attention now. She lowered her head. "I slept with Mike."

Kevin frowned. She couldn't have said what he thought he heard. "What?" He shook his head in disbelief. "What do you mean 'slept with'?" Kevin questioned. "You fell asleep at his house, in his bed, or what?"

"Don't make me say it." Nikki pleaded.

Kevin stood abruptly.

"It was a week before we got back together—before we got engaged." She began to cry as Kevin walked into the kitchen. " I'm sorry," she whispered after him. She rose and followed him into the kitchen. "He sent me a letter that showed everything with his divorce had been finalized." She shook her head, not wanting to believe her own words.

She had dropped her sister off at her grandmother's for the weekend, then she drove up to see him. Though every fiber of her body was screaming for her to stop and turn around, she had ignored it. She needed to feel special and loved again, something she hadn't felt since breaking up with Kevin. Yet after the night had ended, she felt worse. Letting Mike love her had been no consolation to her wounded heart. His love, no matter how pure, was not the love she sought.

After leaving his place in the middle of the night and returning to her hotel, she wondered how she had allowed herself to get into such a situation. Remnants of cabin fever, mixed with insanity, were her only explanations.

She moved closer to Kevin, who stood bent over the countertop now. "It was just that once, I swear, and when he asked to see me again, I told him I couldn't see him anymore, that I had made a mistake—that I was still in love with you."

Mike had gotten so angry when she said those words. He had demanded she give him a timeframe when she would be over Kevin. She had felt bad enough, and hadn't expected him to react as he had, and after telling him she didn't know, and that he wasn't 'making it easy,' he really blew it. He swore at her, telling her to lose his number, and stormed out of the hotel room. Seconds later, she heard the screech of tires.

Kevin's mind was scrambled. He couldn't believe the blow Nikki had just landed on him. He couldn't believe she had given herself to Mike. It had been easy for her to tell him 'no,' so he could not comprehend why Mike hadn't been told the same. He shook his head and began to cry.

Nikki laid her hand on his shoulder. "I'm sorry. I'm so sorry," she whispered as tears streamed down her face. "I never meant to hurt you." Then she stopped as he walked a short distance from her again.

Kevin shook his head. He knew Nikki was saying something, but he found it increasingly difficult to listen. He needed a moment of reflection, and the only way he could do that was to shut her out.

"When you asked me to marry you, I was so happy. I wanted you back in my life so badly I wasn't willing to look at the past. But going into marriage, I didn't want to start off in lies and deceit." She paused staring at Kevin. "Will you forgive me?"

Kevin fussed at himself. If only he hadn't been so cruel, she would have never agreed to see Mike, yet alone sleep with him. His own insecurities and indecisiveness had driven the woman he would have given his life for to seek refuge in another man's bed.

"Kevin?" she whispered softly, wishing he would say something. Finally, she dropped her head. She knew what he was thinking, and she couldn't blame him. He had always admired her for her chastity and virtue. Seeing the disapproval in his eyes, she felt like nothing more than a mere slut, certainly no longer fit to be his bride.

Now she realized that being open had its limits. "My only prayer is that you, and God, may forgive me someday." She paused. "I'll call the movers tomorrow."

She pulled the engagement ring off her finger, and placed it on the counter. She grabbed her purse and closed the door behind her.

Kevin remembered the night he had seen Nikki and Mike together—the way he had grabbed her wrist, demanding she go with him. He balled his fist and gritted his teeth angrily. *I knew I should have socked him.* Then he heard a noise. He turned around, but didn't see Nikki.

Though she knew the path all too well, Nikki stumbled clumsily to her car. Her eyes were stained with tears. So many times now, she wished she could take that day back. She fumbled through her purse, searching for her keys. Her hands trembled as she lifted them to the keyhole. Then, just as she pulled her car door open, she felt a push.

Kevin was behind her. Shamed, she turned slowly to face him.

"Come here," Kevin said, taking her into his arms. He held her tight. He wanted to erase Nikki's notion that she had to be a perfect person to be with him.

He lifted her chin and looked into her eyes. "God's already forgiven you." He wiped a tear from her eye. "And as for me—" He removed her ring from his pocket. "My ego may be bruised," he paused, lifting her hand and sliding the ring back onto her finger, "but my heart hasn't changed."

A smile crossed Nikki's lips.

"I love you, baby."

"I love you, too!" Nikki gasped. She felt her feet lifting off the ground.

Kevin spun her in his arms. "We're getting married!" he shouted.

CHAPTER THIRTY-FOUR

The sweet sound of instruments filled the summer air. Nikki took a deep breath and stepped into their backyard, which had been transformed into a gardener's paradise, to Kenny G's' "The Wedding Song." The fresh scent from her bouquet was intoxicating. The moment was surreal; she floated more than walked.

Kevin stood in front of the gazebo nervously. When Nikki emerged, his heart beat rapidly. She looked beautiful. Her already lovely face was accented with just the right amount of make-up. Her hair was held up in the back with flowers, and a few soft curls adorning her cheeks. Then there was the dress.

The cream Medieval-style dress moved gracefully with each step she took. It was made of silk with a chiffon overlay and silk chiffon half-sleeves. It teasingly sloped down her chest, exposing part of her cleavage. Under her bosom, there was a satin ribbon that separated her bust from the remainder of the dress. The smooth fabric accentuated Nikki's thick hips and fluttered playfully in the breeze as she moved towards the archway, barely kissing the ground.

He took a quick breath and exhaled. She looked like a princess.

As Nikki approached the archway, she was done over by the decorations. Sage and plum ribbons were neatly woven between the lattices of the archway, interspersed with white lilies and vines of ivy. Three white lily flowers were tied together, accented with greenery, and adorned each outside chair.

Malcolm stood at the head of the white carpet in front of the archway. He extended his elbow to her, and she took a deep breath, preparing to travel the short path to the gazebo, where her groom awaited her.

The audience of fifty or so sat watching. Their smiling faces and excited eyes stared on approvingly as she traveled down the aisle.

Then her eyes meet Kevin's. He was immaculate, decked out in a white tux. He had a fresh haircut, and his goatee was neatly trimmed. He smiled warmly, staring delightedly as she approached.

Anesa and Kayla watched as Nikki drew closer, on standby to fluff out her train.

Finally, Nikki arrived at the threshold. Malcolm departed, and Kevin stepped down and braced her hand. *I got you,* his eyes told her as he pulled her to himself, handling her delicately.

They greeted each other happily with their eyes, and they turned to face the minister.

The minister cleared his throat. "Dearly beloved, we are gathered here today to witness the union of this fine couple—Veronica Katrina Jones and Philip Kevin Maddox. If anyone has any just cause why these two people should not be united, speak so now, or forever hold your peace." The minister paused.

There was dead silence. For a moment, Nikki's heartbeat accelerated. She had heard of brides left standing at the altar by their grooms, who chose the worse recourse to get back at them for some misdeed.

"Let us continue."

Nikki breathed a sigh of relief. *He really loves me,* she thought to herself. A tear formed in her eyes.

Kevin listened closely while the minister said a few more words. Then his time arrived.

"The couple has prepared their own vows, which they will now speak."

Kevin reached into his breast pocket and pulled out a small sheet. He cleared his throat. "Nikki, the first time I saw you, I knew that there was something different about you. You have proven yourself more than I could ever imagine. You looked beyond my faults, forgiven my shortcomings, and loved me even when I didn't deserve your love. I love you, and I want to spend the rest of my life with you. Without you, I'm nothing."

Nikki began to cry.

TJ handed Kevin Nikki's ring.

Kevin grasped the ring tightly. "This ring symbolizes the love I have for you. Its shape is the circle, a full three hundred and sixty degrees; the diamond is you—the point I find myself if ever I try to escape your love—because its radiance and inner beauty, just like your radiance and inner beauty, draws my attention, and makes it impossible to ignore or escape. The band is platinum, a precious metal, that represents how much I treasure you; it's solid, the way my feelings are and shall ever remain." He slid the ring on her finger. "From this day forth, I promise to love and cherish you, as Christ gives due honor to his bride, forever hoping for and seeing the best in you, forever nurturing and protecting you; forever praying for you and doing good to you; and as your husband, forever being the anchor you can lean on and draw comfort and support from. This is my pledge to you, through sickness and health, richer or poor, from this day forth."

Nikki's heart was overjoyed. She wiped her tears away, and said her vows. "Kevin, from the first day I met you, you've been chasing me."

The crowd chuckled. Priscilla and Philip gazed into each other's eyes. Philip squeezed her hand softly.

She looked into his eyes. "I'm not running anymore. You've been the answer to all of my dreams and more. Only through God could I have met someone as sincere and loving as you. On this day, I vow to love and respect you. When the pressures of life overcome you, I will be your cushion to lean on, and when the time is right, I'll be your cheerleader. I believe in you, and trust you. And on this day, I pledge my love to you."

Anesa handed her Kevin's ring, and Nikki gave her the bouquet.

"This ring is a symbol of my love for you. Though it is small, its circular shape represents the continuity of love I have for you. Unlike my ring, which was costly and scattered with jewels, your love is incalculable; you are the precious jewel. I hope you'll accept this as a humble token of my love, and a pledge to be your helpmate forevermore—through sickness and in health, richer or poor, till death itself shall separate us." She slipped the ring on his finger.

Kevin bit his lower lip and hugged her.

The minister smiled. "Through the power vested in me. I now pronounce you husband and wife." He turned to Kevin. "Sir, you may kiss your bride."

They drew close and kissed, long and deep.

"Oh!" A hush went over the audience.

MiKayla, Mariea, and Pete giggled, covering their mouths and whispering to one another.

Kevin and Nikki pulled back with love sparkling in their eyes.

The minister cleared his throat. "There is another union that will take place here today."

Priscilla looked on, perplexed. Then she looked at TJ, who smiled back at her slyly.

"A different type of commitment—" Br. Roberts continued. He looked around soberly then his eyes landed on Kayla. "MiKayla Jones, will you please step up?"

Kayla, who had been sitting in Jackie's lap, climbed down. She moved to stand in front of Kevin and Nikki.

TJ handed Kevin a white rose.

Kevin took it from him, and, holding it firmly, he gestured towards her. "MiKayla, this rose symbolizes the love I have for you. The white symbolizes the purity of your youth and the purity of my love. Unlike the rose, which will wither and die, my love for you never will. I am not your father, but I love you no less. You've loved me unconditionally, and that is the greatest gift any person could ever ask.

"My pledge today extends beyond being a husband to your sister. I pledge to look out for your best interests—spiritually, and mentally— to raise you in a God-fearing and God-loving home, and to nurture and protect you. I pledge this to you from this day forth, as God is my witness." He handed her the rose.

"Aw," the audience sighed.

"Oh, my baby, my baby," Priscilla cried, looking at Kevin proudly.

MiKayla took the rose. Kevin squatted down to hug her, and she kissed him on the lips. "I love you."

"I love you too, sunshine."

"May I present to you Mr. and Mrs. Philip Kevin Maddox—" He peered at Kayla. "And MiKayla Jones-Maddox."

The guests stood and clapped as Kevin and Nikki jumped the broom, then both held Kayla's hand and hoisted her over it, too.

After going down the aisle, they were shuffled to the entrance of the yard, where they began receiving and greeting their guests. After most people had come through the line, Nikki suddenly remembered something. She excused herself and ran into the house, into the office, to get something. Though boxes were all over the room, she quickly found the one she needed and started digging through it.

After a while, Kevin missed her, and he went looking for her. He found her in the office, absorbed in her search and moved to stand behind her. Startled, Nikki jumped as Kevin wrapped his arms around her. Finally, Kevin brushed away a strand of Nikki's hair and planted a warm, soft kiss on her neck. Her body relaxed against his. He gave her another quick squeeze, and though no words were exchanged, much communication flowed between them. Each imagined the joy yet to be experienced, and contemplated the fantasies due to be fulfilled come nightfall. They sighed simultaneously, and then burst into mischievous chuckles, each knowing the sensual nature of their thoughts. Kevin smiled to himself. He loved the way they could communicate with one another without uttering a single word. "One hour to go," he whispered, rocking her. "It's our wedding day, and I haven't spent any time with you. I'll be glad to finally get away from all these people."

"All 'these people' are our family."

"Yes." He grabbed her by the waist, and breathed seductively in her ear. "And I can't wait to make you a part of mine." He ran his hands alongside hers. He breathed heavily in her ear. "Be assured, my dear—there'll be no apologizes for the way I touch you tonight."

Nikki's heart raced. She felt her head spinning dizzily as Kevin's words reverberated in her ear. His voice, and the soft wind from his breath, sent tickling sensations that excited every nerve in her body. Nikki breathed deeply; if his words had such an effect, what would it be like when he made love to her?

"Hope I'm not interrupting anything."

Nikki and Kevin jumped.

Anesa was standing in the doorway. "Perhaps we need to come back later," she grinned, gesturing someone to step forward.

"Of course not," Kevin said. "We were just—"

"Looking for something," Nikki interrupted, adjusting one of her curls. "Honey, I think it's in one of the boxes upstairs," Nikki said, playing it off.

"Oh, yeah. Right," Kevin said, smiling; he was about to leave when a woman in her early forties entered the room and grabbed his arm.

"Now don't you go nowhere. I wanted to speak to you, too."

"Aunt Barbara!" Nikki exclaimed. She began to cry. "I didn't think you were coming."

They embraced.

Though she grew up with Malcolm and Aunt Becca, age-wise Aunt Barbara had been the closest to her mother. Nikki's mother had talked so much about her, and how close they were when they were growing up. But Nikki never really got a chance to know her since her aunt moved to Illinois shortly after she was born.

"Girl, you disappeared before I got a chance to greet you and your husband," she said, smiling at the two of them.

"I'm sorry. I didn't see you. I ran in here to find something for Kayla."

She waved her hand. "Oh, that's all right." She turned toward Kevin. "It's so good to finally meet you. I've heard so many good things about you. I was beginning to think Niecy had made you up," she said, hugging and kissing him on the cheek.

"Thank you," Kevin blushed.

"Veronica, you looked gorgeous up there." She looked at Nikki's ring. "I could see this thing from my seat." She looked at her with adoration, wrapping her fingers around her face. "You're looking more and more like my baby sister, everyday." She hugged and kissed her cheek.

"Thank you." Nikki hugged her.

"Went and found yourself a man with a little change." She turned to Kevin. "I don't care how much money you make. This here," she held Nikki, "belongs to us. You better treat her well. All right? 'Cause I don't want to have to make any special trips."

"Yes, ma'am." Kevin grinned at Nikki.

Then she turned towards Nikki. "And as for you—always make his dinner, and never skimp him on his dessert. You know what I'm saying?"

"Yes, ma'am," Nikki blushed, eyeing Kevin.

"And ya'll will be alright."

They returned to the reception area, and things got back on track, but the naughty thoughts Nikki had previously had of Kevin only deepened. She said a silent prayer to God that he would keep her from throwing herself at him, and hoped that, despite the length of the remaining activities and the train trip to Savannah, Kevin would still be up for the feat later that evening. After the wedding party was introduced, they were whisked to their table, the prayer was said, and dinner was served. They enjoyed their conversation only briefly, before well-wishers arrived to greet them.

Before they knew it, they were being toasted and applauded as they rose to take their first dance.

Gee, great, Nikki thought to herself. Just when she had finally gotten control of her hormones, she was being forced together with Kevin. "You again," she said, teasingly draping her arms over his shoulders and around his neck.

"You can't get rid of me now," Kevin whispered in her ear, resting his hands on her waist. Stevie Wonder's "Ribbon in the Sky" began to play. Throughout the song, they held each other's gaze, remembering the brief moment they shared in the office, wishing they were back there, sealed off from the onlookers, wrapped in each other's arms.

The song finally ended. It had truly been magical. The words were just what Nikki needed to hear to reassure her of Kevin's love and commitment. The thought of being shuffled off again saddened her, and she wished she could rest her head on her husband's chest for the remainder of the day. Just then, the wedding director approached, and as if he had read her mind, Kevin touched Nikki's hand lightly. When she looked into his eyes, they undeniably confirmed that despite the hustle of the preliminaries, no plans had been changed. Tonight was it.

The rest of the reception went quickly, and before Nikki knew it, Anesa was informing her that the limo would be pulling up shortly to take them to the station. After wrapping up her conversation with the guests, Nikki pulled aside her grandmother to remind her when they would be returning and go over the final arrangements for Kayla. Moments later, Kevin alerted her that the limousine had arrived. The wedding was finally over, and it was time for their lives to begin.

Nikki stood at the entrance of their home as Kevin and the driver placed their luggage in the trunk. She gave Anesa a heartfelt embrace. "Thanks, Anesa, for believing in us."

"You're welcome," Anesa whispered almost inaudibly. Then their embrace broke. "Oh, go on, before you make me cry." Anesa flagged her away, wiping at the corner of her eyes.

"I love you," Nikki waved, walking towards the limo.

"I love you, too, girl."

Kevin hugged her and kissed her on the cheek. "Thanks, 'Nesa, for everything."

"You're welcome." She looked towards the car. "Just take care of my girl."

"I will." Kevin smiled mischievously and waved.

Anesa watched Kevin step into the limo. She waved goodbye as they pulled off, and kept watching until the limo disappeared from view. She stood on the front porch of their home musing. Finally, she turned and walked back inside.

●●●

Nikki opened her eyes. She felt Kevin's warm embrace around her as they lay in bed, fully clothed, on top of the comforter. The last thing she remembered was Kevin carrying her inside the time-share and laying her down on the couch while he unloaded the rental. She chuckled to herself. Planning a wedding and moving in the mist of it had taken a toll on both of their bodies.

Suddenly, Nikki felt his body move, and she peered over at him. He opened his eyes. They stared at each other quietly. Kevin took his hand and caressed her cheek. Then, without a word, he took her into his arms, and they kissed.

Nikki sat at a table alone. They were planning to have brunch at a restaurant on the boardwalk, when Kevin disappeared. He had told her he was going to find a restroom and would be right back, but fifteen minutes had elapsed, and Nikki was beginning to get worried, but not so much so that the details of the past evening had escaped her.

Getting from under the covers and resuming normalcy had been a major feat after the night they shared. Making love with Kevin had been exactly what she expected—very tender, passionate, and immensely pleasurable. Though they had greeted each other warmly upon waking, they hadn't spoken much of anything since.

Nikki's mind began to wander. She shifted her legs, suddenly self-conscious. She knew Kevin had many sex partners, and that she was something of a novice, but she still hoped she wasn't a disappointment.

Kevin hurried his pace as he headed for where he had left Nikki. If he didn't return soon, it would only be a matter of time before she left and came searching. The love they shared the evening before flooded his thoughts. To commemorate it, he had purchased twelve dozen red roses, collectively representing the months they had known each other, and the months he'd had to wait for her to be his. He smiled, wishing he had thought of it sooner, but how could he have known the emotion and ecstasy he'd feel being with her.

Strangely, it had taken waking up next to Nikki, for him to realize that he hadn't been dreaming, and to know that, yes, she was really his wife. As their bodies had sweetly intertwined the evening before, so had their souls. As he watched her sleep peacefully in his arms that morning, he realized that a lifetime wasn't long enough. His only prayer was that she would give him every day to prove his undying love and commitment.

Suddenly the sun emerged from behind a cloud, and just as she was about to put her hand over her eyes, she felt a presence.

"For you." Kevin smiled, handing her the roses.

She blushed. "Thank you," she said, taking them.

Kevin sat across the table now, smiling. "There's more," he said, shoving the box she had seen him approaching with towards her. He'd had it special delivered that morning, and thought of the flowers as he went to pick it up.

Nikki looked at the simple, white, square box, puzzled. She pierced the tape and popped the lid, and then sifted through the tissue paper. She looked at him, perplexed, as she removed a brown, rustic cowboy hat. "What's this?"

Kevin didn't answer. Instead, he snatched the hat from her hand and set it on her head, then combed a few strands of hair through his fingers, fluffing them forward and gently draping them over her shoulders. "Perfect," he said, musing.

"Your husband has returned. You ready to order?"

Nikki looked at the waitress, then at Kevin. Suddenly, she understood the meaning of the hat. "There's been a change of plans," she said, handing the menu back. "We'll order a pizza." She jumped up and lifted Kevin's hand. Kevin swung out of his seat, following her cue. They darted back towards the time-share, giggling and flirting under the sizzling summer sun.

Printed in the United States
68919LVS00008B/97

9 781595 266057